Acclaim for Vanessa

What We Found in Hallelujah

"Two sisters reunite with their mother in Hallelujah, S.C., in the satisfying latest from Miller (*Something Good*) . . . A dramatic plot and uplifting resolution . . . The result is a potent testament to the power of faith and family in the face of tragedy."

—PUBLISHERS WEEKLY

"Three strong women, family drama, secrets, and a setting that works masterfully with the plot—Vanessa Miller is at her best in this book! The complex, nuanced relationships between mothers and daughters captured my attention and drew me in from the very first chapters. This book is a heartwarming treat that will leave readers hopeful and singing their own Hallelujah praise!"

—MICHELLE STIMPSON, BESTSELLING AUTHOR

"In *What We Found in Hallelujah*, Vanessa Miller so brilliantly tells a heartwarming, page-turning, beautiful story about family secrets, mother-daughter relationships, forgiveness, and restored faith, and I thoroughly enjoyed this saga from beginning to end! So well done, Vanessa!"

—KIMBERLA LAWSON ROBY, *NEW YORK TIMES* BESTSELLING AUTHOR

"Vanessa Miller has created a soul-searching story in *What We Found in Hallelujah*. Her ability to weed through the hard topics with grace, humor, and family makes her stories like no other. I was invested in the characters and felt like praising with them in the end."

—TONI SHILOH, AUTHOR OF *IN SEARCH OF A PRINCE*

"Vanessa lays a solid foundation for the fictional town of Hallelujah. Her characters are rich in diverse personalities. She layers the plot with an artistic flair that readers race to the finish line for the big 'reveal.' Redemption and reconciliation are sweet in Hallelujah."

—PAT SIMMONS, AWARD-WINNING AND NATIONAL BESTSELLING CHRISTIAN AUTHOR OF THE JAMIESON LEGACY SERIES

Something Good

"A prayer for 'something good' brings together the three women in an unlikely friendship, changing hearts and restoring marriages . . . The triumph of faith over tragedy will resonate with inspirational fans."

—PUBLISHERS WEEKLY

"With bright threads of faith, resilience, and finding a way forward where there seems to be no way, Vanessa Miller weaves together the lives of three women in a beautiful tapestry of redemption and hope, friendship and found family. A story that shows, even when we think we've bolted all the doors, something good can find a way in."

—LISA WINGATE, #1 NEW YORK TIMES BESTSELLING AUTHOR OF BEFORE WE WERE YOURS

"Vanessa Miller's Something Good warms the heart with a vivacious tale of faith, redemption, and renewal. She masterly creates a sisterhood of unlikely friends who realize that there is something good, absolutely wonderful, in accepting people as they are and believing they can be better."

—VANESSA RILEY, BESTSELLING AUTHOR OF ISLAND QUEEN

"Something Good, by Vanessa Miller, is a literary treat that captivated me from the first page. This story of three women drawn together by the unlikeliest of circumstances had me sitting back and realizing that no matter our backgrounds, no matter our struggles, when it's for God's purpose, we can come together. With characters that I could relate to and women who I wanted to win, I enjoyed *Something Good* from the beginning to the end."

—VICTORIA CHRISTOPHER MURRAY, NEW YORK TIMES
BESTSELLING AUTHOR OF THE PERSONAL LIBRARIAN

"Vanessa Miller's thoughtful and anointed approach to crafting *Something Good* made for a beautiful page-turner full of depth and hope."

—RHONDA MCKNIGHT, AWARD-WINNING
AUTHOR OF UNBREAK MY HEART

"Vanessa Miller's latest novel is a relevant and heartwarming reminder that beauty for ashes is possible. This page-turning read inspires understanding, connection, and hope."

—STACY HAWKINS ADAMS, BESTSELLING AUTHOR

"This real-to-life story doesn't shy away from some hard issues of the modern world, but Miller is a master storyteller, who brings healing and redemption to her characters, and thus the reader, through the power of love and faith. I thoroughly enjoyed this book."

—RACHEL HAUCK, NEW YORK TIMES BESTSELLING AUTHOR

"*Something Good* is much better than good. It's great! Vanessa Miller always delivers, and you know you will get unforgettable characters and a redemptive, heartwarming story that readers will find unputdownable. Get ready to laugh and to feel all the feels."

—MICHELLE LINDO-RICE, HARLEQUIN SPECIAL EDITION AUTHOR

"Vanesa Miller's *Something Good* unveils the reality of living with guilt, shame, and the weight of unforgiveness through the lives of three women. This story will offer readers a beautiful perspective of redemptive healing and the measure of peace that comes with a forgiving heart."

—JACQUELIN THOMAS, NATIONAL BESTSELLING
AUTHOR OF THE JEZEBEL SERIES AND PHOENIX

Other Books by Vanessa Miller

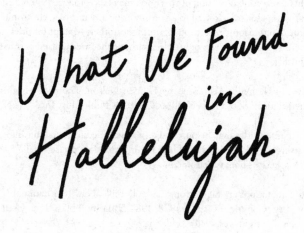

What We Found in Hallelujah

A Novel

VANESSA MILLER

THOMAS NELSON
Since 1798

Published in Nashville, Tennessee, by Thomas Nelson. Thomas Nelson is a registered trademark of HarperCollins Christian Publishing, Inc.

Thomas Nelson titles may be purchased in bulk for educational, business, fund-raising, or sales promotional use. For information, please email SpecialMarkets@ThomasNelson.com.

Scripture quotations are taken from the Holy Bible, New International Version®, NIV® Copyright ©1973, 1978, 1984, 2011 by Biblica, Inc.® Used by permission. All rights reserved worldwide.

Library of Congress Cataloging-in-Publication Data

Names: Miller, Vanessa, author.
Title: What we found in hallelujah: a novel / Vanessa Miller.
Description: Nashville, Tennessee: Thomas Nelson, [2022] | Summary: "Sometimes going home means facing the storms and finding hope amid the pain"—Provided by publisher.
Identifiers: LCCN 2022023768 (print) | LCCN 2022023769 (ebook) | ISBN 9780785256830 (paperback) | ISBN 9780785257073 (epub) | ISBN 9780785257479
Subjects: LCGFT: Novels.
Classification: LCC PS3613.I5623 W47 2022 (print) | LCC PS3613.I5623 (ebook) | DDC 813/.6—dc23/eng/20220519
LC record available at https://lccn.loc.gov/2022023768
LC ebook record available at https://lccn.loc.gov/2022023769

Printed in the United States of America

22 23 24 25 26   LSC   10 9 8 7 6 5 4 3 2 1

To my beautiful daughter, Erin. I love you more than you know. Daughter, when the storms of life rage in your life, my prayer is that you find your hallelujah and never let it go.

Prologue

HOPE REYNOLDS WAS ON HER MARK, FEET ON THE BLOCKS, knees on the ground with arms outstretched. Her long black hair was pulled back into a ponytail. She was running the 200-meter dash against six other girls. College scouts were in the bleachers, and her mother was filming this race because she was just a few seconds away from winning the state title.

Hope had won the state title during her sophomore year in high school, but last year, she went against a top-notch competitor and came in second. That same competitor was running this race with her again, but Hope wasn't taking another loss. Her track scholarship was riding on this.

"Get ready."

Hope lifted her stance, hips in the air.

"Set."

Head lifted, she prayed that she wouldn't let that curve slow her down today. God was with her. Pastor O'Dell had said so.

The gun popped. "Focus . . . You got this." Hope sprinted out of the block, took the curve, which slowed her down, but once the track straightened out, she was like smoke. Her knees lifted high on each stride, arms pumping back and forth The finish line was mere steps away. Out of her peripheral vision, she could see her competition. They were neck and neck. She lost the race last year because she was too busy watching her competition ease up and then pass her.

But her coach told her that she needed to stay focused and lean forward, allowing her torso to cross the finish line first. Hope passed the finish line and kept running a few extra steps as she tried to steady herself. The race was clocked at 22.05, her fastest time yet.

"Yes!"

Hope bent over, hands on knees as she tried to steady her heart rate. She took a few deep breaths, then lifted up straight and pumped her fist in the air.

"Oh my goodness, you did it! You won the race!" Her daddy, Henry Reynolds, ran over to her and swung her around.

He kissed her on her sweaty forehead. He was such a proud papa, and she loved him for his support and encouragement through the years. People in the stands stood and cheered for her as an official handed Hope a dozen roses and congratulated her.

"I did it, Daddy. You told me I could do it, and I did it!"

"Of course you did. You were born for this, baby girl. The sky is the limit for you."

Hope's eyes glistened from the high praise she received from her daddy. This was her day. She was the state champion, and her family was here to see it.

Hope's mother, Ruby Reynolds, lowered the camera and walked over to them. "I got it all on film. Them college recruits are going to be knocking down the door to get you to their schools."

Donna James walked over to Hope and said, "I'm so proud of you. Seems like you get faster and faster with each track meet."

"Thank you, Mrs. James." Hope pointed to the track. "CJ is up next. He's only in the ninth grade, but he's outrunning everybody."

Donna smiled as she looked ahead. CJ was Donna's son, and he was about to get on his mark for the 100-meter dash. "That may be, but I'm proud of you both. You and CJ are the two darkest kids in Hallelujah, but you're stirring up the most noise."

Hope's eyes widened as a gasp made its way up her throat and escaped through tight lips.

Ruby's hands went to her hips. "What does her complexion have to do with anything? You people are something else."

Her mother and her sisters were fair skinned while Hope was a few shades lighter than her daddy, who was dark as night. Ruby didn't like it when people referenced Hope's complexion. Hope didn't like it either; it tore at her heart, making her feel like she didn't belong . . . like she was the other.

"I didn't mean to offend you." Donna turned away from them with sorrowful eyes, like she wanted to take back her hurtful words.

Hope walked with her father and mother to the sideline where her sisters, Faith and Trinity, waited to congratulate her. She tried to let Donna's words slide like peas off of a plate. But looking at the fair skin of her sisters caused her to wonder for the hundredth time why she took her father's coloring rather than her mother's.

"My big sis is the state champ," Faith gloated.

Trinity said, "I knew you would win."

The three of them hugged and jumped around. The joy of winning the state championship was filling Hope's heart and mind again and shoving all thoughts of her complexion from her mind.

The 100-meter dash began, and Hope turned her focus back to the track. There were six guys on the track, but within 10.8 seconds, CJ had smoked them all. Their little town, Hallelujah, South Carolina, now had two state champions.

"Yay!" Hope and her sisters cheered for CJ.

But Ruby rolled her eyes. "Let's get out of here," she said. "Y'all standing there cheering for that boy when I told you that whole James family ain't worth a quarter put together."

Hope just shook her head. Her mother was a handful, but she

loved her dearly. She turned to her sisters. "Let's go to the Ice House. I feel like celebrating with a triple scoop of Cherries Jubilee."

After the meet, her parents drove them home, then Hope, Faith and Trinity walked a couple blocks down the road.

Trinity said, "I'll race you," then took off running.

Hope screamed after her youngest sister, "You little sneak," but she took off after her, with Faith joining in for the race as well.

This was Hope's happy place. She loved living on the beach with her family. After college, Hope planned to come back home and work on turning their beach house into the best bed-and-breakfast this town had ever seen. Her father had been searching for a new home for the family to live in so they could begin building their empire one bed-and-breakfast at a time.

Hope was excited about the future. Life was good in Hallelujah, and it was only going to get better for them.

Chapter 1

Twenty-two years later
Los Angeles, California

EXPECT SOMETHING GOOD. YOU GOT THIS," HOPE REYNOLDS told herself as she stepped out of her office and headed down the long hallway toward the executive suites.

It was her time. Her turn. After the upcoming board meeting, Hope was sure the promotion would be hers, and she would have an office in the executive suites. She just needed to clear up a few things with Spencer Drake before she could finalize her annual report, because from what she was seeing, they had lost money on two events he brought in this year. But the spreadsheet he gave her didn't indicate the losses. Even though she had asked him to correct this information last month.

Hope was not about to turn in her report with incorrect numbers, not when her next promotion was riding on everything she did in the next few weeks. And not even Spencer, her b/b—boyfriend and boss—was going to mess that up for her.

Stopping in front of the full-length mirror that was next to the employees' bathroom, she checked her appearance. Her Afro was lopsided. Hope patted her hair, trying to get it just right. She had left her hair pick in her office, and it wouldn't do to be walking around with a crazy-looking Afro.

Hope was serious about her hair game. She'd stopped relaxing it about twelve years ago. Cutting her long hair to go natural had been a struggle. Hope had cried many nights because she hadn't known what to do with her TWA—teeny-weeny Afro.

It had taken five years of braids and Afro puff ponytails until her hair was finally at the point where she could sport a big Angela Davis, back-in-the-seventies kind of Afro.

Hope even preferred the bell-bottom pants that were popular in the seventies. She had on a gray pair today. This was her style, and she didn't care who didn't like it. She had tried to conform to what others expected of her, but all of that changed after she graduated from Howard University.

Hope had majored in business with a minor in hotel management because it had once been her dream to help her father turn their beach house into a money-making bed-and-breakfast. Then they would open another one and another one until the Reynolds name meant something in the hotel industry. But that was before Henry Reynolds unexpectedly died after a hurricane rolled through her hometown one chilly November day.

Consequently, Hope no longer dreamed about a bed-and-breakfast empire. She was now a thirty-nine-year-old woman and about to be named general manager of Hillsboro Hotel in Los Angeles, California. Spencer Drake, her boyfriend, was the current general manager, but he was being promoted to senior vice president and general manager for all ten of the Hillsboro Hotels.

Hope continued down the hall, thinking about how she and Spencer had gone from a professional relationship to a personal/professional one. Spencer was the owner's grandson and heir apparent to the Hillsboro Hotel chain. Hope had already been promoted three times when Spencer had been assigned to her hotel.

After working with Spencer a few years, Hope discovered that she not only liked him, she respected his work ethic. One night when they were working late, he told her, "I want to ask you out, but I don't want you to feel obligated just because my grandfather owns the company."

Hope had bit down on her bottom lip. Spencer had that rugged kind of handsome face that got a woman's attention. That almond skin tone and his symmetrical mustache, which grew down his lower jawline and looked like an upside down horseshoe, accentuated his square jaw. All the women on the job were after him, so Hope asked, "Why me?"

Spencer leaned back in his seat, loosening his tie. "You really don't know how beautiful you are, do you?"

She had a mirror; she knew she was pretty. But too many people had added the asterisk of "pretty for a dark-skinned woman" for her to ever consider herself beautiful. But the fact that Spencer did gave her pause.

"Yes, okay. I'll go out with you."

They had been dating for a year now. Things were getting serious, and Hope didn't know how she felt about that. She had only been serious about one other man, and he still had a piece of her heart. Spencer was patient with her, and she adored him for that.

Now standing in front of Spencer's door, she knocked, then opened it. "Hey, do you have a minute?"

Spencer was seated behind his desk while Erica Kelly, the catering manager, was leaning in to kiss him. Shocked, Hope's breath caught in her throat.

Spencer jumped out of his seat, straightening his shirt. "Hope, hey. I didn't know you were there."

"Obviously." Hope's eyes darted from Spencer to Erica, then back to Spencer. She stepped into his office. "Is there something I need to know?"

Hope should have known better than to date her boss. But Spencer kept coming at her, kept telling her how special she was. She'd been on a serious dating drought for the past five years. To be honest, she hadn't been booed up with anybody since Nic. But Nic had been all wrong for her, and apparently, Spencer wasn't meant-to-be either.

Spencer nudged his head toward Erica, then lifted the carrot cake from his desk. "Erica baked a cake. I was just getting ready to call to see if you'd like a slice."

Erica didn't bake cakes. She bought them from the bakery two blocks down the street, took them out of the box, plastic wrapped them, then told everyone that she baked it herself. She'd been doing that for the seven years Hope had known her. As their friendship had grown to more of a sisterhood—or so Hope had thought—Erica had let Hope in on a few of her tricks.

Erica walked around the desk, stood next to Spencer's Businessman of the Year award that was hanging on the wall above his file cabinet. "I have a meeting scheduled with a client, so I probably should get back to my office."

But Hope shook her head, eyes burning a hole through Erica. "I wouldn't have done this to you."

Erica averted her light-green contact lens eyes, then ran her hand through her fourteen-inch sew-in. Ol' fake-and-bake with the creamy-tan skin had just been pretending to be her friend.

"I-I'm sorry." Erica lowered her head and rushed past Hope.

Hope turned back to Spencer, hand on hip. "Exactly how many women are you dating at this company?"

He lifted an outspread hand. "Now hold on, Hope. I'm not chasing after women like that. There's just," his hand dropped, "something about Erica. I'm sorry."

Hope knew exactly what the something was. Erica was the kind of beauty who didn't need an asterisk. Hope thought complexion didn't matter to Spencer, but now she knew better. Tears formed in her eyes. She turned away, not wanting Spencer to see that this was so completely destroying her. "Let me get back to my office."

Spencer reached out and grabbed her arm. "You have to believe me, Hope. I didn't mean for this to happen."

She recoiled as if she'd been bitten. "Don't touch me. Stay away from me."

"That's going to be hard to do since we work together. We have to find a way to be civil, don't you think?"

"Civil?" Did he really just say that to her? She rubbed her arms as she walked toward the door, suddenly feeling a chill in the air.

For the first time in the fifteen years she had been employed at Hillsboro Hotel, Hope wondered if it was time to dust off her résumé and find a new job. The year had been going so well, but it was November, and bad things always seemed to happen to her in November.

Hope rubbed her temple as she walked back to her office. It felt like an elephant was stomping on her brain. Sitting down at her desk was something she did every day, but it just didn't feel normal after what she'd just walked into.

Hope opened the bottom drawer of her desk and took out one of the adult coloring books and colored pencils that she used as a stress reliever on her lunch break or when she had downtime at home. Decisions about whether she was going to stay at Hillsboro and watch Spencer carry on with Erica or whether she would start shopping her résumé needed to be made. Right now, Hope didn't know how she felt about working with Spencer and Erica.

She was more hurt than angry about the situation. Erica had pretended to be her friend, and Spencer had pretended that she was enough for him, when she obviously wasn't.

Her cell phone rang. It was her mother. Hope contemplated not answering because she wasn't in the mood for whatever Ruby Reynolds had going on . . . not today. But she knew her mother. Ruby would just keep calling until Hope answered.

"Hey, Mom. I've got a lot going on. Can I call you back?" She rushed the words out, hoping that her mother would just say okay.

But Ruby was hysterical. "You really need to call me back this time because if you don't, I just might go buy a gun and end up with a cellmate that'll stab me to death or worse."

What was worse than death? "Mama, what is going on down there? Who do you want to shoot?"

"The good Lord knows that I'm a peaceful woman, but that Rick Thornton done got my back up. That man ain't right."

She massaged her temples. "Mama, can you just please spell it out for me? What happened?"

"He stole my money, and now I'm about to lose this house to the bank. That's what happened."

Hope opened her purse and took out a bottle of Advil. She popped two in her mouth and downed a half bottle of water. "Mom, is this true . . . or another one of your make-believe stories?"

Hope had caught her mother telling a few whoppers, so she couldn't readily take anything Ruby said at face value.

"Why do you always think the worst of me? If you aren't concerned for me, then what about the house? Do you want me to lose it?"

How was the beach house where she grew up—the beach house that her father spent years building—about to be lost to the bank when there was no mortgage on it? She posed that question to her mother.

"That's what I'm trying to tell you," Ruby said. "Slick Rick had me take out one of them . . . whatchamacallit?"

Hope heard her mother snapping her fingers as she tried to come up with the word she was looking for.

"Home equity loan?"

"Yeah, that's what it was." Ruby took a breath, then continued, "The bank gave me sixty thousand for the repairs I need to turn this house into a bed-and-breakfast. Slick Rick told me he needed thirty thousand up front so he could order all the supplies and whatnot. And now he's in the wind. I haven't seen hide nor hair of that man in a month."

"You just gave this man your money?" That didn't sound like the Ruby Reynolds she knew, but her mother was getting older. Was dementia setting in?

"I messed up, I know that, but now I need you and your sister to get down here and help me turn this house into a bed-and-breakfast so I can start earning money to pay back that loan or the New Year will ring in with a new owner of our beach house. The bank will take the house if I don't start making payments within the next forty-five days."

Whoa . . . Hope hadn't been in Hallelujah in about eighteen years. She was no longer that same small-town South Carolina girl. She was a grown woman who made her own decisions and lived by her own rules. And now her mother was asking her to come back—in November. Uh-uh, she couldn't do it.

"You know I don't like being there, Mama."

"This is no time to be thinking about the past. I need you to come home," Ruby yelled into the phone.

"What do you need me to do that I can't do from right here?"

"I told you . . . I'm finally going to turn this house into a bed-and-breakfast so I can make back the money Slick Rick stole, and I need you to help me get this house in order so I can hang my shingle out front."

"Oh, Mama." She and her father had stayed up late many nights talking about things they could do to the beach house in order to turn it into a bed-and-breakfast once she graduated college, but her father died during her first year of college, and everything changed after that.

"Your daddy would turn over in his grave if I lost this house."

And there it was. Hope could not, would not let the house her daddy built with his calloused hands end up in the smooth, unblemished hands of a banker. This week was the worst time for vacation because they were preparing for the board meeting next week, but Hope didn't care anymore. She had over a month of vacation saved up, and she was headed back to Hallelujah.

She was going back to the place where her heart had been snatched out of her chest, thrown into the ocean, then dragged out of the water as a stampede of thoughtlessness ground it into that sandy beach of a place she'd once called home.

Chapter 2

Faith Phillips was over it and wanted a divorce. If looking at the Facebook post of her husband standing way too close to some random woman who was making kissy faces into the camera wasn't enough, then the fact that Chris hadn't made payments on the home equity loan he took out on their house was definitely strike two.

Standing in front of the bank teller as the stranger broke the news that her business account was now twenty thousand dollars lighter, Faith crooked her neck, staring at the woman like something was wrong with her.

"You're lying."

The clerk shook her head. "No, ma'am. The money was taken out last week. I can give you a printout of your transactions if you'd like."

"Please do."

Faith took the printout from the clerk, looked at it, then took her cell phone out of her purse. Like her mother says, three strikes is out no matter who is doing the counting.

Nostrils flaring like a bull seeing red, Faith didn't make it out of the bank before calling Chris. He answered on the first ring, like he was waiting for her to call and check him for his trifling behavior.

"I'm at the bank," she exploded. "Where's my money?"

A few customers turned to stare as she pushed open the door and headed to her car.

"Now, baby, calm down."

"Don't call me baby. Where is my money?" She pulled out her key fob, unlocked the door to her three-year-old white-on-white BMW and got in.

"I got behind on the flip project I'm working on, but we just sold the house, so I'll be putting the money back this week. Just trust me, okay? I did it for us," he told her.

She poked her forehead with her index finger once, twice, thrice. How could she have been so stupid as to put his name on her bank account? In hindsight, she felt like a fool, allowing her husband access like that, but when she started her interior design business, no bank would give her the loan she needed, so Chris gave her ten thousand dollars. It just seemed right to attach his name to her bank account. But she was over being grateful now.

"There is no *us*, Chris. I want you to pack your stuff and get out."

"Waaaaait a minute, babe. We promised we would never threaten each other with those *get out* words. I know things haven't been great between us lately, but maybe we need to talk to Pastor Green about counseling."

"Maybe you need counseling to learn how to keep your hands off things that don't belong to you, but you can leave me out of that because I'm done."

"What about Crystal? You can't just make rash decisions like this without thinking about our daughter. She needs both of us, Faith."

"Were you thinking about Crystal when you were taking selfies with some woman and posting them on Facebook?" Faith didn't wait for his response. She hung up the phone and threw it in the passenger seat. Her hands covered her face, and she cried angry tears. She wanted out of this marriage, but their daughter was very much a daddy's girl.

The sad truth of the matter was that Crystal just might want to live with her father. Faith didn't know what that said about her as a mother. But in these last few years, she and Crystal had not seen eye to eye about anything. Not the clothes she wore, not the grades she brought home, not the text messages Faith read on her daughter's phone.

A text message popped up on her phone from Chris: Baby, please don't do this. I messed up, but I know we can work this out.

Rolling her eyes heavenward, Faith started the car and drove away from the bank where her account now had just seven hundred fifty-two dollars and thirteen cents.

She and Chris met during her sophomore year in college. His wavy black hair, honey skin tone and light-brown eyes trapped her in a vortex of what she thought was love. When he looked at her with those sexy eyes, she felt all the love he promised to give. Thought he would be the one to unbreak her heart, so she married him. Only to discover that she was still broken.

She dropped out of college and moved to Atlanta with her new husband and all his pipe dreams. She had truly thought he loved her, but how could love hurt this much?

Faith's phone rang again. The number on the display unit in her dashboard was unfamiliar. She had been waiting for a call from a potential client, so she tapped the Accept button on her phone as fast as her finger could reach it.

"Designs by Faith, can I help you?"

"Ah, hello. This is Gladys Milner. You met with me and my husband about redesigning our kitchen."

"Yes, of course, Gladys. I remember you."

Faith silently prayed that Gladys was ready to begin the project. She had been referred to her by one of her celebrity clients. A celebrity client who still hadn't paid her bill, but that was the entrepreneur lifestyle, constantly working to get clients and constantly chasing coins.

"My husband and I were discussing your designs, and we love

everything you're proposing. I can't wait to get my double oven, get rid of that awful countertop and move the island where it should be, but I must be honest with you," Gladys said. "That sixty-thousand-dollar price tag is a bit steep."

Faith did not like to haggle over money. Her prices were what they were. *I mean, come on, I have to eat too.* "There is quite a bit of construction to lay out your kitchen the way you want it. I have to bring in contractors, and they will have to tear out a wall, add a beam to hold up the ceiling, and then we will need to reconfigure the placement of your cabinets and many other little details that aren't noticed but must happen to complete the project in the manner you've requested."

Faith had another call coming in. She glanced at the dashboard, saw that it was her mother and ignored it.

"It's just that . . . things always come up during construction, and then more money is needed, so my husband and I feel more comfortable at a fifty thousand spend."

The phone beeped again. Her mother was going to keep calling; Faith knew how Ruby Reynolds rolled, but she was on a business call. She couldn't just hang up. Her mother would have to wait.

"I really want to do your kitchen for you, Gladys. It will be the kitchen that you deserve and where you'll want to cook those fabulous family meals you told me about, but I don't pad my estimates. There are set fees that I earn and that I must pay out to others, plus the cost of material, so I can't lower my estimate at this time. However, we could try to sell all of the old appliances and cabinets from your kitchen to get some of your money back that way."

Faith held her breath . . . waited . . . waited.

"Well, let me talk this over with the hubby, and I'll get back with you."

"Great. Just let me know when you're ready to begin that beautiful design." Faith tried to sound upbeat and hopeful, but her tone fell flat as she ended the call.

Coming to a red light, she stopped the car and closed her eyes. "Lord, just throw me a bone, a crumb . . . something." Her life was falling apart. Or maybe it had never been put together in the first place, and she had just been playing mind tricks on herself.

Her phone rang. Faith's eyes popped open. It was her mother again. With everything else she was dealing with, she really didn't want to talk to her mother right now, but she hit the button on her steering wheel to accept the call just as the light turned green. "Hey, Mama. What's up?"

"I'm about to lose the house that your daddy wanted to keep in the family, that's what's up. Meanwhile, you act like you don't know how to answer your phone."

"I wasn't trying to ignore you, Mama. I was on a business call." Wait. Had she heard her mother right? Did she say she was about to lose the beach house? "Mama, what's going on down there?"

"I need you to come home. Can you do that for me?" Ruby asked, and then she filled Faith in on the sleazy contractor who ran off with some of her money.

Faith missed the turn for the Lowe's she had planned to stop at. "Mama, you didn't. Haven't I told you about working with contractors before checking references?" Faith wanted to ignore this whole situation and let her mom deal with it the best she could, because she had her own problems, not to mention that the last place she wanted to be this time of year was Hallelujah, South Carolina.

Ruby started crying. "He conned me. Whispering all those sweet nothings in my ear. Rick even promised to marry me."

"Mama! Are you telling the truth?" Faith couldn't count the number of times her mother had lied or stretched the truth. She wasn't in the mood to deal with any of her mother's fantasies.

"Why do you always doubt me? I'm your mother, Faith, or does that count for anything?"

"Why didn't you call me before throwing your money away

like that? I'm an interior designer. I could have recommended some contractors."

"He tricked me, Faith," Ruby bellowed into the phone like her heart had been broken.

Faith's heart went out to her mom, because she knew all too well how men could trick unsuspecting women. She hadn't thought Chris was that kind of man. But in the last year or so, he'd been a little too shady for her. "Did you file a police report?"

"I figured I'd go buy a gun and shoot him myself."

Shaking her head, Faith tried her best not to laugh. Her mother was a character and had no filter. "I thought you were against Black-on-Black crime. Isn't that what you told me?"

"I'm telling you I need help!" Ruby's voice elevated, sounding like a high-pitched soprano.

Faith had just finished her last home designing project for the year. It was the week of Thanksgiving, and she rarely had a job to do in December, because few people wanted their home in a state of disarray while putting up Christmas decorations . . . and her marriage was falling apart. So she really had no reason to hang around Atlanta.

Crystal's last cheerleading competition for the year was coming up, but Chris could take her to that. He took Crystal to most of her events anyway.

"What's the weather like down there?"

"Fair to middlin'."

"I'm serious, Mama. You know I don't like being at the beach in November."

"The sun is out," Ruby told her. "There's not a cloud in the sky. You can check the weather report yourself. You'll see what I'm telling you is true."

Faith took a deep breath, rolled her neck. The one thing she hated about living in a beach town was hurricane season. When she was a teen, Faith had experienced a storm in late November that had been worse than any in her lifetime because of the destruction it left behind. Faith still had deep wounds because of that storm.

Her mother was crying again. Faith hadn't been home in the past three years. Maybe if she had gone home more, her mother wouldn't have fallen prey to this Rick guy. "Okay. Don't do anything crazy, Mama. If you want me to come down there, then you need to go report this guy to the police."

"Why do I have to do that?" Ruby asked as if people didn't normally report robberies.

"If it's no big deal, then I'll just stay in Atlanta and take care of the hundred and one problems that I have." Faith wasn't doing this with her mother. Her mom was going to handle this the right way or forget about receiving help from Faith.

"All right, all right. I'll file the report."

"Great! I'll see you in a few hours." She hung up with her mother and then made a U-turn. Instead of going to the office, she was going home to pack.

Pulling up to her thirty-two-hundred-square-foot home, Faith noticed that the lights were on in the kitchen and family room. She could have sworn that she turned those lights off, and she had been the last one to leave the house that morning.

Faith was about to open the garage and pull her car inside, but then she remembered something Pastor Green said about not letting the left hand know what the right hand was doing. Faith had a suspicion that her wonderful husband had come back home once he thought she was out of the way for the rest of the day. Had he brought some woman to their house? Was he entertaining his side chick, fixing her breakfast and going on and on about how he knocked down the walls that separated the kitchen from the family room so they could have the open floor plan they wanted?

She turned off her car, stepped out and made her way to the back of the house, using her key to enter by way of the mudroom. She would only have a few seconds worth of surprise on her side because she had set the chime on the alarm system to go off whenever a door opened. Chris hated that chime. But Faith told him that as long as they had a teenager in the house, she was going to let their alarm system *chime chime chime.*

Moving from the mudroom into the kitchen, she called out, "Chris . . . Chris. Why aren't you at work?" *Earning back the money you stole from me.* Her eyes shifted this way and that.

Chris wasn't in the kitchen, but the sixty-inch television in the family room was on. And it wasn't on the sports channel where her husband would've had it. Some foul-mouth reality show was blaring through the house as her fourteen-year-old daughter sat on the sofa with the boy from down the street. Their heads swiveled in her direction, eyes huge with alarm.

Faith picked up the remote and turned off the television. "Kenneth Jones, what are you doing in my house in the middle of a school day? I just know y'all aren't skipping school."

The boy stood and started stuttering. "M-m-my m-mom said I could s-stay home today."

"But this mom—" she pointed at herself—"didn't say you could hang out at my house." Faith turned her attention to her daughter, who was sitting on the sofa with her eyes bugging out like she couldn't believe she had been caught. "Is your dad here?"

Crystal shook her head, then rolled her eyes. She shifted so she was facing the wall instead of looking at her mother.

Smoke blew out of Faith's nostrils. "Girl, don't you know I will snap your neck, then the only person you'll be rolling them eyes at is the undertaker." Her mother used to say that to her when she was younger. Faith swore she would never say anything like that to her future children. But life had a way of making a liar out of you.

She turned to Kenneth, the little boy who used to do relay races in the community pool with her daughter and hang out in the backyard. Now they were snuggled up on the sofa with no adult supervision. "You know you're not allowed in my house unless I'm here or her daddy." She jutted her thumb toward the front door.

"I'm sorry, Mrs. Phillips." He rushed past her and headed to the door.

Her daughter jumped off the sofa, like she was about to follow Kenneth to the door. One day, Crystal was a baby in her arms, then as she got older, she started looking more and more like Faith's sister, Trinity. Now Crystal was chasing after a boy . . . just like Faith's sister.

"Get back here this instant, Crystal."

Crystal swung around. Eyes showing all the animosity she felt for her mother. "Why do I have to stay in here with you? You don't want me around any other time."

"Are your eyes red?" She put her hands on Crystal's face and swiveled the girl's head from right to left. "Have you been smoking weed in my house?"

Scrunching her nose, Crystal backed away from her mother. "I don't do drugs. You would know that if you were ever around."

Now it was her turn to roll her eyes. "I work, Crystal. I can't sit under you and your father all day long, or no bills would get paid around here." And they would be standing in the dark having this discussion because the lights would be off.

Every time she thought about what the man who promised to love and cherish her had done to her, she wanted to break down and cry, but there was no time for crying now. She had to get to Hallelujah and stop her mom from crying.

Her arm did a sweeping motion toward the spiral staircase that she loved so much and imagined her daughter walking down for her prom. *Don't cry. Don't cry.* "Go pack your suitcase. I have to go help Grammy, and you're coming with me."

Crystal lifted an eyebrow. "What? I can't go anywhere. I have two more days of school before the Thanksgiving break and a cheer competition."

"I will contact the school and let them know you're going virtual for the next few weeks." The one thing Faith loved about Crystal's school was that they provided the options of in-person learning and virtual. "And you can forget about that cheer competition. Think about it as punishment for disobeying your parents."

"What?" Crystal crossed her arms and stomped her foot. "I'm not going. I'm calling Daddy. You can't do this to me just because I was watching TV with Kenny."

It sounded so innocent, the way Crystal explained away her little excursion, but Faith wasn't buying it. She put a hand on her hip. "For somebody so worried about missing school, you sure had no problem skipping today. How many other days have you done this?" She took her cell phone out of her purse and scrolled through the missed calls. "And why didn't the school notify me?"

Crystal's eyes darted this way and that. "Daddy called and told them I wasn't feeling well so I would be staying home today."

Narrowing her eyes at Crystal, Faith said, "You look like you're feeling pretty good to me." She then pointed toward the stairs again. "Go pack. I don't have time for this." Faith hollered after her, "And if you're thinking about calling your father, don't. I will let him know what we're doing myself."

Crystal stomped up the stairs. Sighing deeply, Faith wished she could leave her here with her father, but she wasn't about to come back to Atlanta to discover her teenage child was pregnant. Not about to happen. Glancing around her kitchen, she saw Crystal's cell phone on the island. She picked it up and entered her daughter's code.

As the phone opened, Faith went to the text messages to see who Crystal had been talking to this morning. The only text she saw came from Kenneth.

You home?

Yeah.

Can I come through?

For a little while.

Sighing, Faith put the phone down, climbed the stairs and went to her master suite. Her daughter was growing up too fast. Telling boys they could come over when her parents weren't home was not cool.

She entered her spacious walk-in closet, opened her suitcase and started packing. She walked from one side of the closet to the other, taking pants and shirts off hangers. She stopped for a minute, hands on hips, a shirt dangling from her right hand as she looked around.

Most women would be over the moon to have the type of space Faith had in her closet. When she designed it, Faith thought this room would be her happy place, but the house seemed more like a war zone than a sweet retreat. Maybe she had been wrong to demand that they buy this house when Chris wanted a smaller home in an up-and-coming neighborhood.

But Faith hadn't wanted to wait for her dream home. She had wanted it all—the husband, the child, the showpiece home—and now she just wanted to get away.

Chapter 3

RUBY TOOK OFF THE HOSPITAL GOWN, PUT IT IN THE RECEP-
tacle her doctor's office used for discarded gowns and then put
her shirt back on. She'd been on the phone with Hope and Faith
while waiting in room number three for Dr. Stein to tell her why
she had been summoned back to his office after her last visit just
two weeks ago.

And she didn't like one word that came out of her doctor's mouth
when he finally stepped into the room. That man had given her more
bad news over the years than she cared to catalog. She should have
traded him in for that younger doctor who set up an office in town
a few years back, but Dr. Stein knew too much of her business.

She opened the door and followed the exit sign to the checkout
counter where Marline, the checkout clerk, asked, "How are you
doing this morning, Ms. Ruby?"

"I've been better, that's for sure," she told the woman as she set
her purse on the counter. "How much do I owe for a visit I didn't
ask for in the first place?"

Marline shook her head. "Your insurance is covering this visit
in full since this is a follow-up."

"Great." Ruby started to turn and walk out the door, but
Marline stopped her.

"Dr. Stein needs to schedule your surgery."

No! No! No! Ruby shook her head. "I've got to check my schedule. I'll get back with you." She left the doctor's office and headed to the police station, another place she didn't want to go. But since Faith said she wouldn't come if she didn't report the theft, she drove down the main strip, enjoying the palm tree–lined street and looking at all of the eateries that had been added to the strip in the past few years.

Hallelujah hadn't always been a tourist destination. It had been a place where families who wanted a quieter way of life settled down. Her husband had been one of those people. Henry Reynolds had come to the island to build houses for the rich folks and ended up marrying her. Then they got a piece of land for themselves. They lived just steps from the beach.

Henry had been so happy when she told him that she'd received a plot of land right on the beach from an unnamed benefactor. Actually, she knew who her benefactor was, but she would not allow that man's name to cross her lips. He had caused her too much harm.

But the land was a beautiful thing. Henry built a home on that land, and they raised their family there. And if it was the last thing she did, Ruby was going to make sure that a member of the Reynolds family stayed in the house that her husband built from the ground up.

She pulled into the police station parking lot. A deep, heavy I-don't-want-to-do-this sigh escaped her lips as she got out of her car and walked toward the Judah Watch Police Station. The minute she swung open the door, the smell of sweat, gun oil and shoe polish assaulted her nostrils. Her stomach lurched. She hated this place.

Ruby made her way to the front desk, trying her best not to think about the last time she was in this old rickety building and was told that she wasn't going to get any help from them. She doubted anything would come of this, but she told the front desk clerk that she needed to report a crime, just as Faith asked her to do. Even though she knew good and doggone well that these Keystone Cops couldn't find the prize in a Cracker Jack box. They hadn't helped her when she needed them most, so . . .

She was seated at a police officer's desk. The officer had red hair. He was skinny, bumbling and Forrest Gump–goofy. She told him her story, and all he said was, "I don't think we'll be able to help much with this, Ms. Ruby."

"But I can still file a report, right? You can handle paperwork, can't you?"

"Ms. Ruby, I'm not trying to upset you, but you don't have a contract or anything to prove Rick Thornton took your money in exchange for the work he was supposed to do on the house."

"Well, what you think he took it for? 'Cause the sky was blue . . . 'cause the tide was coming in? Or maybe you think I just go around handing out money to men like I'm at a strip club, making it rain or something."

"I don't think you just gave him the money, Ms. Ruby, but what I'm trying to tell you is we can't find his name in our database. He must have given you a false name."

Ruby shook her head. "You mean to tell me I been . . ." She snapped her fingers one, two, three times as she tried to come up with the word her seventy-year-old mind was looking for, "Cat-licked?"

"Catfished," he corrected.

In a huff, she stood. "Cat-licked, catfished. Slick Rick has got my money, and I need to file a report." Faith wasn't coming if she didn't file a report, and knowing her daughter, she would ask to see proof.

"Okay, Ms. Ruby, let's write this up." The officer turned to his computer and began typing the information Ruby gave him.

Ruby became animated as she described the man who she claimed took her money. Her voice elevated as she tried to cover up for all the inconsistencies in the report. One minute she said the man was short, then she said he was almost six feet tall. She told the officer that Rick had brown hair at the beginning of the report, and by the end she was talking about a man with black hair.

The police officer stopped typing. "Now, Ms. Ruby, you know it's a crime to file a false report, right?"

Another police officer at the desk across from Forrest Gump *tsk-tsk*ed at her.

Ruby turned toward the officer. "Gracey, if you don't mind your own business, I'll tell your mama that she needs to take that switch to you like she did when you got sassy with me at your eighth grade graduation party."

"Ms. Ruby, I'm a pay-my-own-bills full-grown woman. My mama is not bringing no switch in here."

Ruby harrumphed. "We'll see about that. Just sass off at me if you want to. I'll call Lynn right now." She opened her purse and pulled out her cell phone. Kept staring at Gracey like "don't make me get your behind tore up."

"I'm going for coffee." Gracey rose from her desk. "You have a good day, Ms. Ruby."

Ruby smiled at her as if she hadn't just threatened to have the girl beat in front of all her coworkers. "You have a good day, too, Gracey, and don't forget to swing by the house to pick up that blueberry crumb cake I made for your mama."

"Will do." Gracey waved goodbye as she headed to the breakroom.

Ruby turned back to the goofy officer she had been talking to. "Well, I guess I'll mosey on home . . . for the time that I still have a home since you are absolutely no help." She shook her head, looking perplexed as she scanned the length of him.

The officer lowered his head.

Conviction sprung up in her over her harsh words. After all, she was in here telling a bunch of bald-faced lies. She patted the officer on the shoulder. "I'm sure you're doing a good enough job, so pay me no mind."

He looked up at her with kind eyes. "I'm going to do you a favor and not file this report, Ms. Ruby," he said quietly.

Ruby looked away and shrugged. She'd done what Faith asked. She'd come down to the police station to report what Slick Rick or whatever his name had done to her. It was a big lie, but she didn't feel bad about it at all. Ruby was good at lying. She had been taught to lie as a young child when her mother made her lie about who her father was.

Ruby consoled herself with the knowledge that a contractor had in fact given her an estimate for work on the house. He had told her his name was Rick. Was it her fault that he had lied to her? It was a good thing that she hadn't really given that man her money.

Ruby walked to the door, wanting nothing more than to get out of this place before memories of the last visit filled her mind and tore at her heart. Ruby's hand was on the doorknob, and she was almost on her way when a voice she recognized called out to her.

"Ms. Ruby, wait. Don't leave."

Nicolas Evans came up behind her and tapped on her shoulder. It felt like a thousand prickly ants had come out of the sand from the beach behind her house and were now marching up her back, finding a home in her once long and brown, but now short and silvery-gray hair. She scratched her scalp before turning to face him.

The young man was as handsome as the devil himself. His white skin was always tanned as if he stayed in the sun. Nicolas was the lead detective at the Judah Watch Police Station. He'd come back home after working for the FBI in DC for fourteen years.

Ruby had always liked the name Judah for the police station because it was a play on the town's name, Hallelujah, since *Judah* meant praise. They added *Watch* at the end of the name to remind the townspeople that they shouldn't just praise but also keep a watchful eye out for mischief.

She wished she had taken that "watch" part more seriously a few times in her life. "What can I do for you, Detective Evans?"

Stepping closer to her, smiling, he said, "Why so formal? I've always just been Nickel Knucklehead to you."

She laughed the first good laugh she'd had in weeks. "I haven't called you that since you and Hope were teenagers, out there running around on the beach."

A flicker of sadness danced in his eyes. "How is Hope these days?"

"She's doing fine. Lives too far away. But her career is taking off, so I fly those California skies to see her when I can."

"Tell her I said hello the next time you talk to her, okay?"

"Of course, Nicolas. I'll let her know I saw you down here at the do-nothing police station."

Truth be told, she wished Hope and Nic were still running around on the beach. Wished she could go back in time and get those days back. Because then Nic wouldn't be standing in front of her about to ask her about things she couldn't bring herself to think about—not now, not without her girls.

"*Ummm*, have you thought any more about giving me that DNA sample?"

She put her hand back on the doorknob, getting ready to escape. She knew it, just knew that she wouldn't get out of this station without Nicolas Evans getting in her business—without him staring at her with those confusing eyes of his. One minute they were green, the next they were gray.

"No," she said flatly, "and I don't have time to talk to you about no DNA when I can't get nobody in here to do nothing about the money that's been stolen from me." She made that statement as if it was as true as the sun rising in the morning. She then swung open the door and got out of that station like somebody had just called in a bomb threat and she needed to be on the other side of town before it detonated.

She didn't turn back, didn't want to see Nicolas staring at her. Didn't want to see the pity on his face. No, she wasn't giving him her DNA. She just couldn't. Because then she might find an answer that would be too much to handle at this point in time, along with everything else she was dealing with.

She got in her car and drove home to wait for her girls. Hope and Faith were coming home. Ruby exhaled at that thought. Finally, something to look forward to. Her family would be back in that big old beach house that Henry built. That was at least something to praise God about. When she saw them, she might shout to the heavens with all the joy she had been missing from not having her girls on the land that was meant for them.

Her land was the legacy she planned to pass down to her girls. The beach house would stay in the Reynolds family. Scooter Evans, the town banker and real estate developer, would not get his hands on it just so he could build some grand resort.

When she arrived home, Ruby suddenly felt sick to her stomach at the thought of going inside that empty house. She didn't want to look at what twenty years of neglect had done to her once beautiful home, so she walked to the back of the house and sat in one of her lounge chairs on the wooden deck that overlooked the water.

A cool breeze drifted by. Ruby wrapped her arms around her shoulders as she shivered. Her eyes then darted toward the water. She stood and walked to the edge of the deck. The tide was rising. She could feel it in her bones. A storm was coming.

Chapter 4

FAITH HAD BEEN DRIVING FOR THREE HOURS BEFORE CRYSTAL decided to say one word to her. Actually, she pointed at the exit sign and said, "Bathroom."

"So that's what we're doing now, huh? You point, and I'm just supposed to jump to it."

Faith was outdone with her daughter's behavior. The whole trip, Crystal had been staring out the window or had her nose in a book, pretending to be so interested that she couldn't talk.

Wiggling in her seat, Crystal whined, "Got to go."

Faith took the exit and pulled into the first gas station they came to. She pulled up to the pump. Crystal jumped out of the car and ran inside.

"Don't sit on that toilet and make sure you wash your hands," Faith yelled to her.

"Okaaay, Mom. Dag." Crystal glanced around, then ducked her head like she wanted to be invisible.

Faith pumped the premium gas into her tank. The next time she filled up, she might have to go with mid-grade to ensure she had enough cash while she was visiting with her mom and for the trip home. Although, in truth, she was not looking forward to the journey back home.

She would have to deal with all that came with moving on, like becoming a single parent. And although Chris wasn't the best husband lately, he was a superstar when it came to Crystal. Faith would never be able to compete with him for Crystal's affection.

It hurt recognizing that her daughter wasn't that into her, but she couldn't blame Crystal for that. Faith had chosen career over family and had let Chris take care of Crystal's wants and needs for the past three years. It had just been easier that way.

She put the nozzle back on the gas pump and went into the gas station to wash her hands. Crystal was standing at the sink rinsing the soap off her hands when she walked in.

"You good? We've got about an hour and a half to go. Do you want to grab a snack?"

Crystal turned her back to Faith as she used the paper towels on the counter to dry her hands. "I'll see." She walked out of the bathroom.

"Good talk," Faith said as she stood in the bathroom by herself, looking into the mirror and seeing sad eyes staring back at her. Life certainly hadn't turned out the way she planned it, and now she was headed back home to the place where she first discovered things like pain and longing.

Turning off the water, she dried her hands as she received a text message from Chris.

Where are you?
I'll be gone for a few days.
This isn't funny, Faith. Where is Crystal?
She's with me.

She wanted to tell him about catching the neighbor's son in their house, but she was giving him the same treatment Crystal was giving her.

She put her cell phone back in her purse and released a heavy sigh, feeling a little more of the pain that had lodged itself in the pit of her stomach and sat there like an ulcer that was ready to explode.

She stepped out of the bathroom. When she didn't immediately see Crystal, sweat beaded its way across her forehead like she was having a hot flash.

"Crystal! Crystal," she yelled.

Crystal leaned her head to the left from an aisle up front, looking at Faith like she had lost all her cool points. "I'm over here." Then she rolled her eyes.

Putting a hand to her chest and taking a deep breath, Faith walked over to her. Crystal was putting mustard on a hot dog. "Do you know how long that thing has been sitting out?"

Crystal shrugged. "You told me to get a snack."

Seven words. The most her daughter had spoken to her since they left home. "Okay, get something to drink and let's go."

Faith grabbed a bag of Lay's chips and a Mountain Dew. Crystal put her items on the counter. Faith paid the clerk, and then they got back on the road with minimal conversation the rest of the way until they pulled up to the beach house.

Parking in front of the brick-paved walkway, Faith's eyes misted. So many long-gone memories flooded her mind. Some she would cherish for a lifetime, some she wanted to drown in that deep, dark water behind the house and never let them resurface again.

She took in the grand old house that her father, Henry Reynolds, built with no one but his daddy, a few friends and his wife to help him. A sense of pride bubbled within. Her daddy had been a master builder, an architect who hadn't been taken seriously in the South.

They hadn't wanted to give him his due. Her father spent most of his life working in construction, building houses rather than designing them. But he not only built their beach house, he designed every aspect of it, and the townspeople envied the masterpiece he created. The Reynolds beach house was the best piece of property in Hallelujah.

That's why some of the jealous white folks in town kept trying to take it from him.

But Daddy never worried about any of those vultures. He had outsmarted them all. He once told her, "A man's word is his bond, but sometimes you got to get it in writing so that bond will stick." How she wished she could tell him that she followed that rule as she ran her own business. Every client had to sign a contract. That way, the bond would stick.

Faith reached in the back seat of the car and grabbed her sketchbook. Her daughter looked out the window with her arms folded across her chest.

"Go on in the house. I'm sure your grammy will be excited to see you." Crystal never called her grandmother Granny or Grandma. When she was a little girl, she had dubbed her "Grammy," and it had stuck.

Crystal doubled over. "My stomach hurts."

"I tried to warn you about that hot dog at the gas station." Opening the door, Faith got out of the car. She tilted her head back as she took in her childhood home. The brick layer on the bottom had four archways cut into it on all four sides of the house. The archways were big enough for a car to drive through, but it had not been built to house cars. It had been built to weather the storms. When Daddy first built the house, the first level had been made of wood stilts, but he didn't like how much the house swayed during terrible storms, so brick by brick, he added this eye-catching foundation.

The aged house had twin staircases. Both led from the brick-paved walkway, then passed the arched brickwork that held up the lower level. The stairs ended directly centered on the front door and were attached to the massive wraparound porch where you could see spectacular views of the beach on whichever side you stood.

The wind blew. Faith inhaled. Her lungs filled with sea air, and suddenly she felt right at home. Just as she had felt when she was a kid. But she wasn't a kid anymore. And this place had caused her too much pain to ever be called home again. She closed her eyes as she drowned, drowned, drowned those memories, then she exhaled.

Glancing around, she noticed that Crystal was still in the car, leaning forward, holding on to her stomach. "Girl, if you don't get yourself out of that car and go use the bathroom—"

"You should have stopped so I could use the bathroom an hour ago."

Why did everything have to be a battle with this child? "Crystal, we're here now. Just get out of the car." Faith tapped her foot, getting ready to count to three like she used to when Crystal was younger.

But just as Faith reminded herself that she had a stubborn teenager on her hands and no amount of counting would change that, Crystal must have realized that she wasn't going to win the battle, so she opened the passenger side door and got out of the car. "All right, I'm going," she huffed, then mumbled, "Still don't know why I couldn't stay home with Daddy."

Amazingly enough, Crystal straightened up as she got out of the car and didn't seem to be in any discomfort whatsoever.

"I don't have time for your mess today. Not today, Crystal. I promise, you don't want to try me." Faith flicked her wrist and pointed toward the trunk of the car. "Get our bags, and come on here." She was way out of patience with this child who acted like she was grown but would starve to death if left to feed herself.

Faith used her key fob to pop the trunk. Crystal's eyes bugged out. "That's a lot of bags. What do you want me to do?"

Very slowly and deliberately, Faith said, "Take. The. Bags. Out. Of. The. Car." She pointed toward the house. "Walk. Up. The. Stairs."

"But that's not fair. You're not carrying any bags."

"You tried it." Faith's lips pursed as she pointed from the trunk to the house, like no more words needed to be said. That was the way she was raised. Matter of fact, Ruby Reynolds would have already given her a fat lip for even questioning what she had been asked to do. This child wasn't going to worry her.

Crystal took two bags out of the trunk and started her trek up the stairs.

Faith took a pencil out of her purse and opened her sketchbook. She noted that the house's white siding was now gray from years of caked-on dirt. The paint was chipping off of the stairs. The roof hadn't been replaced since Daddy built the place about thirty years ago.

"Whoa," Crystal yelled as she wobbled with the suitcase.

Faith lowered her sketchbook. "What's wrong?"

"This step feels loose."

The front door opened, and Ruby came out onto the porch, hands perched on her hips, her eyes filled with joy. "Is that my Crystal? Chile, get over here and give me a hug."

"I need help, Grammy. These bags are heavy."

"Don't you dare help her with those bags, Mama," Faith yelled from below. "My mother is seventy years old. Your fourteen-year-old, half-grown self better get them bags up those stairs."

"But, Mom, the stairs are loose," Crystal whined.

"Don't come up the right side. Those steps are loose, and Grammy hasn't gotten them fixed yet." Ruby pointed to the stairs on the left. "I always use the left side."

Crystal had only gone up three steps on the right side. She backtracked, then went up the stairs on the left, finally managing to get the bags up the stairs. She hugged her grandmother.

Ruby leaned back to look at her granddaughter. She blinked twice, rubbed her eyes, then her eyes grew bigger as her hand flew to her mouth. "Oh my dear Lord, you look . . ." Ruby shook her head. She kissed her grandchild. "The older you get the more you—"

"Mama," Faith yelled from below, "can you let Crystal inside so she can use the bathroom?" Then Faith walked to the back and stood on the wooden deck. She took note of the rotting wood and the loose boards on the deck. Home sweet home.

Chapter 5

IT FELT LIKE SHE WAS BORN TO SUFFER—LIKE GOD THOUGHT Ruby's shoulders were broad enough to carry all the misery dumped on her doorstep. And more misery was piling on by the day with what her doctor told her and that Nic Evans sniffing around. Ruby couldn't bear the storm on the way . . . not without her girls here to hold her up.

Ruby hugged Faith as they came inside the house and stood in the living room. "I'm so glad you're here, daughter. When your sister gets here, we can sit out back and discuss what you've been drawing in that sketchbook of yours."

Faith stepped back. "Hope hasn't been home since she left almost twenty years ago. What makes you think she's going to show up now?"

"You're talking out the side of your neck 'cause your sister should be here any minute."

"I'll believe it when I see it," Faith said as she glanced around the living room.

Ruby didn't like the way Faith was always downing her sister when she didn't know the full story. Granted, Faith didn't know the story because Ruby couldn't fix her mouth with the words to tell it, but still, Faith needed to let up on her sister.

"How am I talking out the side of my neck? Has Hope been here and I didn't know about it, or have I been the one who has come down here whenever you needed help?"

Faith walked over to a small decorative vase that had willow twigs in it. She picked it up from its spot against the wall and placed it on the sofa table. "There, now it's perfect."

"Will you stop moving my stuff around every time you come to visit?"

"That vase is too small to be on the floor, but placing it on the sofa table makes it more of a statement piece." Faith scrunched her nose. "But it really can't make much of a statement surrounded by all of this old furniture. We'll need to get some new pieces in the living room."

Ruby wasn't ready to talk about furniture. "And you can't judge Hope because I haven't seen you in over two years, and you know it." Her daughter didn't just design homes, she tried to design everybody's life, and Ruby wasn't having it.

"I've been building my business, Mama."

Ruby flung her hand in Crystal's direction. "I barely even recognized my granddaughter. She looks so much like Trinity, I had to adjust my eyes."

Faith raised an eyebrow. She turned toward her daughter. She tilted her head as she kept looking at Crystal. "I mean . . . maybe when she wears her hair down."

"You never let me wear my hair down," Crystal said. "You're always making me put my hair in a ponytail like I'm a little kid or something."

The doorbell rang. Faith said, "I'll get it." She rushed to open the door.

"Hey, my peoples." Hope stepped into the house, struggling to pull her two African-print suitcases behind her. "I can't believe I'm actually back on the beach."

Faith's jaw dropped. "I can't believe you're here either. Oh my goodness, it's been so long since I've seen you."

"Way too long," Hope said, hugging Faith. "I've missed you, sis."

Ruby smiled as she watched Hope and Faith hug. Hope had come into the house wearing a beautiful African-patterned jumpsuit. She even had on green, black and red earrings that were shaped like Africa.

Faith reached out and touched one of Hope's earrings. "What are you supposed to be, Mother Africa?" Eyes bulging with amazement, Faith gawked at her sister. "I just don't remember you being so . . . Afrocentric."

"A lot can change in ten years," Hope told her.

"Wow! Has it really been that long? Seems like yesterday when you told us that you were going to stay in Hallelujah and build the empire you and Daddy talked about." Faith lifted her hands, let them flap to her side. "Then you left."

Ruby rushed over to Hope and wrapped her arms around her. She felt that old familiar tinge of pain that came on at the first sight of her oldest, like regret clings to a death row inmate as he takes that long last walk. So many things she wished she could change. She stepped out of their embrace and wiped her eyes. "If you ain't a sight for these old eyes."

"Mom, stop." Hope reached up and wiped the tears that fell from her mother's eyes. "You just saw me last year at Christmas."

"I know." Ruby took some tissue off the corner table and blew her nose. "It's just that you haven't been in this house in so long. I've missed seeing you here . . . on the beach, where you belong."

"Mama, you already know why I don't like coming home." Hope clasped her hands together. "But I'm here, and I'm so happy to see all of you." A smile etched across Hope's face as she walked toward Crystal. "You standing over here quiet, but I would recognize you from anywhere." Hope pulled Crystal into her arms.

"Hi, Auntie Hope," Crystal said as the two embraced.

When they pulled apart, Hope asked, "Do you remember me?"

Crystal looked thoughtful for a minute. "I know you send me Christmas presents every year."

Hope turned to her mother. "Now I feel like crying." She turned back to Crystal. "I haven't seen you since I came to Atlanta for your fourth birthday party, but I have loved you since the moment you were born. I'm just happy I get to spend some time with you while I'm here."

"I want to spend time with you too. I always ask Mommy and Grammy about you."

Ruby watched as Hope did a double take, put a hand to her mouth and stepped back. Her head swiveled from left to right as she eyed Crystal. Hope glanced back at Ruby. "Do you see what I see?"

Ruby nodded. "Just as you were knocking on the door, I was telling Faith how much this child looks like Trinity."

Hope shook her head in wonderment as she continued to stare at Crystal. "She has Chris' caramel coloring, but everything else is Trinity."

A look of confusion crossed Crystal's face. "I don't remember what she looks like. I haven't been to visit Grammy since I was ten, so I don't remember seeing any pictures of her."

Ruby turned to Faith. "Don't you have pictures of Trinity?"

Faith shook her head. "Not at home."

Shock registered in Hope's eyes as she looked at her sister like she was an alien from outer space.

Faith crossed her arms and smirked at Hope. "Don't look at me like that. She doesn't remember you either."

"Whose fault is that?" Hope asked her sister with a lifted brow.

"It's yours." Faith pointed an accusatory finger in Hope's direction. "You're the one who left us to fend for ourselves. All of it is your fault, and you know it." Faith's chest heaved as she spat out her condemnation.

Ruby watched anger build in her daughter. She wondered if she had made a mistake by demanding that they come to the beach house at the same time. They had once been the best of friends. Faith followed Hope around, wanting to go everywhere, be everywhere Hope was, but life had dealt them a low-down and dirty blow, and now all that was left was shame and blame.

As calmly as she could, Ruby said, "I asked the two of you here to help me save this house that your daddy built with his own two hands, but if y'all would rather help that ol' rotten Scooter Evans finally lay claim on this place, even though your daddy fought all his life to keep it out of that man's hands, just keep arguing."

Faith picked up her sketchbook. "Well, I for one came to work."

Hope pointed at her sister's sketchbook. Looked like a distant memory danced across her eyes. "You paint now?"

Faith shook her head. "What I do could in no way be considered painting. I leave that to Mama, but I have my own design business now." She lifted the sketchbook. "I use this to sketch out my thoughts for my designs."

Crystal chimed in, "I like to draw."

"You know that gift came from your grandmother," Hope told her. "When I was a kid, I would sit outside with her for hours just watching her paint. That's probably why I enjoy adult coloring books so much."

Crystal's eyes got big as she turned to Ruby. "Can I see you paint? I'd love to watch you."

Ruby rubbed her hands. "This arthritis has been messing with me so bad that I haven't done much painting lately."

"Let me put my bags in my old room." Hope started rolling her suitcases to the room that had once been hers.

Ruby held out a hand. She knew she forgot to do something. "Wait . . . wait . . . wait." But Hope was already walking down the hallway toward her old room.

"I'll be right back, Mom. Just let me put these bags in my—" She placed a hand on the doorknob and opened the door to the room. Hope did a double take, head bobbing from one direction to the other. "What the devil?" Leaving her bags against the wall outside of the room, Hope trotted back to the living room. Pointing toward her room, she said, "So are you becoming a hoarder or what?"

＿＿＿

Hope's eyes bulged as she took in painting after painting, all strewn around the room. She stepped inside and picked up one of the paintings; Ruby and Faith were standing in the doorway. "I love your paintings, Mama, but where am I supposed to sleep?"

"Looks like you're sleeping on the couch tonight." Faith laughed at her.

"Nobody needs to sleep on the couch. I forgot to move this stuff, but you girls can help me get these things to the attic," Ruby told them.

"Mom, look at your room," Crystal called from down the hall.

"Why, what's going on?" Faith eyed Ruby like "what did you do" as she headed down the hall. "Are you kidding me?"

Hope rushed out of her room, down the hall and then burst out laughing as she saw mounds and mounds of dolls and doll clothes atop Faith's bed. "I guess you're going to be on the couch with me."

"Oh no, I'm not." Putting a hand on her hip, Faith turned to Ruby. "Mama, what were you thinking?"

Ruby stood, running her hand through her short, layered, gray hair with her lips pursed and twisted to the left side of her mouth like it always did when she didn't want to 'fess up.

"Uh-uh, Mama, you don't get to clam up now." Hope flailed her arms. "You asked us to come down here and help you turn this house into a bed-and-breakfast so you won't lose it to the bank, and you're hoarding in these rooms. Daddy would be rolling over in his grave if he saw this."

Wagging a finger at Hope, Ruby said, "Now that's a bald-face lie. I haven't trashed your daddy's house, and you're not going to fix your mouth to lie on me like that."

"Well, then what would you call it, Mama, because the house is in disrepair, and what you're doing in these rooms isn't helping," Faith said.

"I call it 'none-of-my-daughters-showed-up-to-help-me.' That's what I call it."

"Just shaking my head. Just shaking my head." Hope had no other words.

"We can stand here all night, or we can move some of this stuff up to the attic." Ruby's head cocked to the side. One leg was in front of the other, knees slightly bent. "Now, what y'all wanna do?"

Hope recognized her mother's I-will-fight-you stance. When she was a kid, Ruby had gotten so riled up because the boys next door kept picking on Hope that she went outside and threw rocks at their house, yelling at them to come outside. She threatened to jump on the mama, daddy and their two boys if they didn't get ahold of their kids and stop them from harassing Hope.

Her mother had been standing just like she was now, and the neighbors had recognized that she wasn't playing. Hope never had another problem with those two snot-nosed brats next door. Never a dull moment with Ruby Reynolds.

"Calm it down a bit, Mama. I don't mind moving some of these things to the attic, but can we eat first? I'm starving." Hope sniffed the air. "And I'm smelling shrimp. Let's get this party started."

———

And just like the days had not turned into so many nights that Ruby had lost count of the last time her children were in the same house together, they moved toward the kitchen, talking about all the seafood they'd be eating in this house. But Ruby only half smiled as she listened to Hope and Faith. Her mind drifted to another place and time, because one of her heartbeats still wasn't here . . . hadn't been for a long time.

Chapter 6

Standing in the kitchen, Faith rubbed her stomach. "You can't get shrimp in Atlanta like the shrimp we have in Hallelujah. It's like God Himself blessed the shrimp that comes out of the water down here."

"California can't compete with the shrimp we get here either." Hope turned to Ruby with a lifted eyebrow. "Please tell me you didn't go shrimping by yourself."

Ruby waved off that notion. "Chile, I done got too old to be out there wading around in that water. I hung my net up years ago. I picked this shrimp up at the fish market in town."

"Luke's Fish Market?" Faith had fond memories of going to that fish market with her dad when she was a kid. Luke was a part of the Gullah community in town. The Gullahs were descendants of West Africans who were enslaved near the South Carolina coast. They always had the best seafood.

"The one and the same," Ruby answered.

"Oh, they definitely went shrimping. They were always casting a net and bringing whatever they found into that stinky fish market." Hope lifted the lid off one of the pots on the stove and breathed in the aroma.

Grabbing a plate and heading over to the stove, Faith said,

"Hey, remember that catfish Daddy used to bring home from Luke's?"

"Do I." Hope smacked her lips. "That net of theirs lures in the best shrimp and fish I have ever wrapped these lips around."

The four of them filled their plates with shrimp, corn on the cob and roasted garlic fingerling potatoes. Ruby had placed newspapers on the kitchen table so they could throw the shells from the shrimp there. They sat at the table and ate until their bellies were so full that they had to rest on the sofa in the family room and take a nap. Ruby let Crystal lay down and rest in her room.

After the nap, they pulled the attic ladder down and got to work taking the items in Hope's and Faith's old rooms to the attic. They were halfway finished putting the paintings and dolls in the attic when Crystal brought a painting to her mother and asked, "Is this Auntie Hope?"

Faith took the painting. She stared at it. Memories cascaded through her mind. A smile crept across Faith's face. Hope's hair was straight and flowed just past her shoulders. She remembered how Hope would pull her hair into a messy bun at the top of her head on hot summer days. "Yep, that's your auntie. Before she went all Mother Africa on us." Faith admired the portrait once more. "Wasn't she beautiful?"

Hope walked over to them and glanced at the painting.

Crystal's eyes darted from the painting to Hope. "I think she's beautiful with straight hair or natural."

Hope hugged her niece, giving her sister the side-eye. "Aww. Thank you, sweetie. I'm thankful you can see that true beauty doesn't come from a box of chemicals."

"She's only saying that to be disagreeable. If I say up, Crystal is going to say down, so don't read too much into that one."

"Haters gonna hate," Crystal said, taking the cell phone out of Faith's back pocket.

"Give that back." Faith reached for the phone.

"You're holding my phone hostage. All I want to do is check my Instagram account, and I'll give it right back." Crystal kept walking toward the living room.

Hope brought more paintings out of her old room and took them up to the attic.

———

Faith didn't have time to argue with her child. "Don't call your daddy," was her only command as she went into her old room. Standing there with hands on hips, she looked at all the dolls her mother had collected throughout the years. Some were purchased as collectibles, and the others were purchased for her children's enjoyment. Most of the dolls were in pristine condition.

She and her sisters might not have appreciated that they were playing with Baby Alive, American Girl dolls, Cabbage Patch Kids and Barbie dolls, but there were kids who would love to have them.

When Faith's mother was fifteen, Mattel introduced the first Black doll. She wasn't dubbed an actual Barbie, but it was good enough for Black folks to have a doll that resembled them. So, in 1967, her grandmother bought her mother a Black Francie. The doll had the same face mold as the Caucasian Francie. Then in 1968, her mother also received the Black Christie, who premiered as one of Barbie's friends, sporting an Afro. Ruby had been too old to play with dolls by this time, so the dolls had been left in the box as treasured gifts.

Her mother had told them that in 1980 when the first Black Barbie—actually branded as a Barbie—came on the scene, Ruby was twenty-eight years old with no children, but she marched her happy self right into that toy store and bought Black Barbie anyway.

Barbie had recently come out with an Inspiring Women series. And of course, her mother had the Ida B. Wells, the Rosa Parks and the Maya Angelou dolls. Faith wondered how much all these dolls might go for on eBay or another online auction site.

She grabbed an armful of the dolls from her bed and took them to the attic. On her way back down, Crystal was yelling for her.

"Mom, Mom . . . Daddy wants to talk to you."

Walking down from the attic to the first floor, she scowled at her daughter. "Didn't I tell you not to call your daddy?"

Crystal handed her the phone. "He wants to know when we're coming home. You can't keep me here forever. I have things to do, too, you know."

Putting the phone on mute, Faith reminded Crystal, "You brought your laptop, so you can do your schoolwork anytime you please."

"You can't keep me out of school for a whole week. That's truancy."

Jabbing a finger toward the front of the house, Faith told Crystal, "Stop being a drama queen. You only have two more days of school this week, and you're doing those virtually."

"Arrgghh." Crystal stomped her foot and then headed to the living room.

Watching her child retreat, she took the phone off mute and said, "Hold on." Faith walked outside, not wanting anyone to hear what she had to say to her husband. When her feet were firmly planted on the beach, she said, "What do you want, Chris?"

"I want you to come home. This is crazy. I don't want a divorce."

"That simply doesn't make sense, Chris, because any man who runs around on his wife the way you do has got to want a divorce."

"I'm not running around on you."

"Facebook and your girlfriend say different."

"What girlfriend? What are you talking about? And why did you go to your mother's without talking to me first? Crystal has two more days of school this week."

"Crystal was in the house with the neighbor's son when I came home this morning. Did you tell her she could have company?"

"Crystal knows better than that. I would never let her have company if one of us wasn't at the house."

"Well, that's why I brought her with me. I need to be here with Mama, and I wasn't going to let her stay there by herself while you were at work."

"Good thinking," he said, then asked, "When do you think you'll be back home?"

No, she wasn't doing this. She wasn't going to have a normal conversation with Chris, like everything was okay, because it wasn't. "I can't stand here talking to you all day. I need to get back in the house." She hung up the phone and then turned toward the sea. The water was calm. It was cloudy out, but the wind wasn't blowing.

Living on this beach had been the best kind of life. It was a slow, sleepy town where nothing much happened outside of swimming in the ocean, lounging on the beach and taking in the beach air. Life had been good here . . . until it wasn't.

A ping from her phone alerted her to a text message. She glanced at the screen.

Why are you so coldhearted? was the text that Chris sent to her.

She wanted to invite him to live in her body and feel the things she felt for just twenty-four hours and then let him come back and tell her how chilly he felt. But instead she texted back, I need my money. As far as Faith was concerned, Christopher Dwayne Phillips was the lying, cheating, stealing kind that she wanted nothing to do with.

She slipped the phone in her pants pocket and sloshed her way back through the sand until she reached the beach house. Chris hadn't responded to her text. She knew he wouldn't. He thought he was so slick. Thought he was going to bleed her drier than the Sahara Desert and she was just going to keep taking it and then beg for more.

She was sick of people laughing behind her back and whispering about this can't-get-right man that she married who jumped from one big idea to the next just like he changed the television channel. As far as Faith was concerned, it was time to throw out the trash and smell some fresh air.

She climbed the stairs and opened the front door, ready to get back to work and take her mind off the big mistake she made when she fell into stupid but mistook it for falling in love.

Faith entered the house. Hope had just taken the last of the paintings to the attic. Her room was also clear of dolls. She took a moment to look around the house. The baseboards and the walls screamed for attention. She clasped her hands together as she said, "Mama has a little more than a month to get this place together so she can start renting out rooms, so I say we wash down these baseboards and the walls tonight."

"Tonight?" Crystal complained, "but we just finished moving all that stuff to the attic."

"Your mom's right. This house needs a good washing, inside and out." Ruby held up her curving fingers. "But with the arthritis, I haven't been able to clean like I used to."

"Okay, Grammy, I'll help."

They took several buckets out of the pantry, put a cleaning rag in each bucket, then filled them with soap and water. Hope, Faith and Crystal each took a wall. Ruby began sweeping the floors.

It took an hour and a half to clean the living room, kitchen and hallway walls and baseboards. Everyone was exhausted when they finished. But Faith had one more task before she could call it a night. She opened her Home Depot app and snapped a picture of the living room.

"What are you doing now?" Hope asked.

"I'm going to find the best paint color for the walls, and then I'll go pick it up at the hardware store tomorrow."

Hope smiled at that. "Good idea. Gray is hot these days."

"Yeah, but what shade of gray?" Faith asked.

While Hope and Faith were talking about paint colors, Crystal walked over to the door that was just behind the living room area.

"Grammy, is this a bedroom? Mama snores so loud, I can barely get any rest."

Faith dropped her phone. Crystal was about to open the door to a room that Faith had not entered in eighteen years. It was too much. Too painful. She didn't want to see the inside of that room. How could this wound still be so fresh after all these years? Faith didn't have the answer to that, but she knew that the scab would be ripped off if her daughter opened that door.

"Nooo!" Faith rushed over to Crystal and moved her away from the door.

"What's wrong with you?" Crystal looked around the living room, looking from her grandmother to her aunt. "What did I do?"

"Nothing." Hope walked behind Faith and put her hand on the doorknob. "Your mother is just tripping."

"Don't, Hope." Faith could feel her body shaking as if the house was being torn apart by an earthquake. When the tearing finished, Faith wanted to be on the side of the house that didn't have access to that room.

"Faith, quit tripping. Mama has filled both our rooms. We've been working hard all evening moving this stuff to the attic. If this room is full of stuff, too, we need to get it moved." Hope swung the door open.

Faith's heart beat so fast, she thought it would burst out of her chest and run out of the house. She looked into the room and saw the canopy bed with the ruffled pink comforter and the furry pink rug. The white desk with that big clunky computer on it was still there. The room looked just as it had almost twenty years ago.

Crystal turned to her grandmother. "Why haven't you filled this room with junk like you did Mama's and Auntie Hope's rooms?"

"Chile, when your mama and auntie Hope left, I figured they weren't coming back, so I put things in their rooms that they loved. That way it didn't hurt so much when I went into their rooms. But

Trinity will be back someday, so I just left the room like it is. She can make changes however she pleases when she gets here."

Faith and Hope exchanged glances but didn't say anything, then Faith noticed the stack of "Have You Seen This Girl?" flyers on the desk. "Mama, you're still passing these out?"

"Of course I am. They found that Carlina Renae White after she was missing for twenty-three years. Who's to say the same can't happen for Trinity?"

Faith hoped her mother was right. Trinity had been lost to them for eighteen years this month. The odds weren't in their favor.

"But I can have the room for now, right, Grammy?" Crystal's eyes gleamed as she walked into the bedroom. "I love it. Look at that bed."

Ruby rubbed the back of her knuckle against Crystal's nose. "Since you look so much like Trinity, I think it's fitting that you hang out in her room. I just washed the sheets about a month ago when I was in here wiping down her desk and things, so the room is ready for you."

Crystal climbed on the bed and got under the covers like she was getting ready for a nap. "Yes! I'm taking this room."

Hope pulled the covers off. "Oh no, you don't. We still have more work to do, and you're helping."

"But I'm so tired from all the helping I already did."

"Out of that bed," Hope warned.

Crystal got up, walked over to the desk, and ran her hand along its desk. "Does this computer work?"

Faith held out a hand. "Don't touch it!" The last time Faith turned that computer on the screensaver read something like, *Live until the living is done.* She didn't want to see those words again.

"Okay. Dang." Crystal rolled her eyes, then she picked up a flyer. "Wow! I really do look like her."

Faith exploded, "Stop playing around, and get out of Trinity's room!"

Crystal threw the flyer back down on the desk. "What do you

care what room I sleep in? It's not like you want to spend any time with me."

"Don't talk back to me, Crystal. Just do what I said."

Crystal looked so dejected. She rolled her eyes as she walked past Faith and didn't say another word to her for the rest of the day.

Faith wanted to apologize. She wanted to explain, but she couldn't tell her that she had been so spooked by how much Crystal truly resembled Trinity. Because if she said those words, it would make it real. And Faith had been trying to ignore how much her daughter resembled her sister for the past three years.

She only prayed that, one day, she would be able to make up for all of the harsh words, all of the neglect, but she just didn't have the strength to try right now.

Chapter 7

It was 6:45 in the morning. Hope rolled over in bed and picked up the remote. Her mattress was lumpy and uncomfortable. She stirred several times during the night. They certainly wouldn't be able to open a bed-and-breakfast with beds like this. She would have Faith add new mattresses to the list of must-haves.

Giving up all thoughts of sleep, she turned on the television. Spectrum News 1 was on. The meteorologist predicted a thunderstorm later in the evening. Hope rolled over, almost closed her eyes, then she heard the word *hurricane*.

Turning back toward the television, rubbing her eyes, Hope listened as the weatherman warned of a hurricane over by the Caribbean Islands. Hurricane Lola was just sitting in the warm water, with no clear path. But the prediction was that it would either hit Charleston or Hallelujah depending on the direction it took. They had four, maybe five days to prepare, but there were no mandatory evacuations in place because they couldn't be sure which direction Lola would travel once she got going.

"Arrgghh!" Hope threw the cover off. Ruby would never agree to leave town without a mandatory evacuation. She put on her cheetah-print robe and slid into her matching house shoes.

Coffee. She needed coffee and an airline ticket on the first plane heading back to California, where hurricanes didn't roll in and turn her whole life upside down. She was about to pass the bathroom in the back of the house on her way to the kitchen when she heard a god-awful retching. It sounded like chunks of food being dumped into the toilet.

"Who's in there? Are you okay?" Hope put her hand on the doorknob and twisted it, but it was locked.

"I'm okay," the voice mumbled. *Plunk . . . plunk.*

"Crystal? Is that you?"

The door opened. Crystal pulled some tissue off the toilet paper roll and wiped her mouth. She flushed the toilet.

Putting an arm around Crystal's shaking shoulders, Hope asked, "Are you okay? Do you need me to wake your mother?"

Crystal vehemently shook her head. "No. No. I'm okay. My stomach was just upset, that's all, but I feel better now."

"You sure?" Hope didn't know if she should let this go, but she didn't know her niece well enough to make a judgment. If the child said she was okay, then maybe she was.

"I promise, Auntie Hope." Crystal pointed toward her bedroom. "My first class is about to start, and I need to get ready."

"Okay, if you're sure."

Crystal walked away. Hope went into the kitchen, her mind turning back to the coming storm. She tried to think of a way to tell her mother they needed to get out of Hallelujah ASAP.

She put water in the coffeepot and searched for the package of ground coffee. The brand was too strong for Hope, but since it was the only one available, she scooped the coffee out of the bag and put it into the filter.

Leaning against the counter, she closed her eyes. Her lungs filled with the smell of her morning good-good that would wake her brain and get her body moving. She heard a noise. Her eyes popped open as Ruby entered the kitchen.

"I knew you were in here when I smelled that chocolate crack."

Hope smiled at that. Most of the people she knew referred to coffee as a cup of Joe, but her mother lovingly referred to it as chocolate crack. Hence the reason Hope would forever think of coffee as crack. Maybe she needed to seek therapy for her coffee obsession.

"Good morning, Mother."

"Good morning to you as well." Ruby opened the fridge, pulled out a carton of eggs, sausage links and butter. "What's got you up so early?"

"Watched the news this morning. Weatherman said a hurricane is in the Atlantic Ocean. Lola will either be here or in Charleston in the next few days, so we need to make some decisions." ·

Putting a skillet on the stove, Ruby waved her hand. "They're not calling for evacuations."

Oh great, her mother must have been up watching the news also.

Glancing out the kitchen window, noticing the clouds in the sky, Hope said, "We need to get out of here, Mama. She took her cell phone out of the side pocket in her robe and started searching the web. "I don't even know if we can get a flight today or not."

"What's going on?" Faith asked as she entered the kitchen.

"Lola the hurricane is on its way," Hope said.

Faith's hand went to her heart as fear etched across her face. "Not another November storm." She lifted her hands in the air. "Why, Jesus?"

Hope scrolled down her phone looking for flights. She then turned to Ruby. "Okay, I found a flight. Make up your mind, Mama. Are you coming with me or not?"

"A flight?" Faith questioned with an I-can't-believe-you stare, a hand on her hip and lips pursed.

"Yes, Faith, a flight. I didn't come down here to deal with a hurricane. I'm going back to California."

"That's right," Faith said, sneering, "run away, like you always do."

Hope flailed her hands. "What do you want me to do, Faith? Stay here and stop the hurricane? Being Mother Africa doesn't give me super hurricane-fighting powers, you know."

"No, I don't want you to stop a hurricane," Faith mimicked, "but it would be nice if for once in your life you pitched in to help your family. There's a lot to do to prepare this house for a hurricane, and you know that Mama is not going to leave before this house is secured."

Hope doubted if Ruby would voluntarily leave even if the house was secured, but she put her phone back in her pocket and nodded her understanding. They were in this together.

Ruby put the sausage links in the skillet. She then grabbed a pot, went to the pantry and came out with a box of grits. "The roads might be shut down for days after the storm. What if I can't get home to check on this house?" Ruby stubbornly shook her head. "I promised Henry that I would take care of this house until the day I die, so I can pass it to you and your sisters."

"Then why'd you give all that money to that contractor and put the house in jeopardy?" Faith asked.

"Because the house has some wear and tear and I need to get it fixed." Ruby waved a defiant hand in the air. "Never you mind who I gave money to. I'm still not going to leave my home."

"But, Mama—" Hope wanted to scream. Her mother could be so obnoxious.

"No 'buts' to it. I ain't dead yet, so I'm going to keep my promise." She poured water into the pot and lit the fire beneath it. "Least that's one promise I can keep."

Hope hadn't known of one soul on God's green earth who had ever won an argument with Ruby Reynolds once she had made her mind up about a thing. Her daddy used to say, *Your mom is right. How do I know? Because she told me so.* Glancing around the kitchen, Hope's eyebrow arched. "Where's your radio?"

"What radio?"

"You used to keep it in the kitchen and play gospel music while you cooked. I can't count how many mornings we woke up to Yolanda Adams, Mary Mary or Donnie McClurkin."

"Chile, that old thing broke years ago. You know that."

How could she have forgotten? She had been the one to break it. But Hope had tried to forget everything about the awful day that broke her heart into so many pieces that she still had not recovered.

Hope shuddered, wrapping her arms around her chest as her mind tried to take her someplace she didn't want to be. Not now, not today; she still wasn't ready. "What about an Alexa?"

"Who is Alexa? And what does she have to do with what I listen to on my radio?" Ruby asked as she put butter in the skillet to fry her eggs.

"I'll get you an Alexa. This kitchen needs music," Faith agreed.

"It just doesn't feel right being in here watching you cook without some kind of music playing." Hope went to her room and grabbed her cell phone. She went to YouTube and found a gospel mix, then blasted the music from her phone.

Hope reached into the cabinet, took down three coffee mugs, filling them with coffee while she danced to "We Livin" by Tina Campbell. "That's what I'm talking about. Living that blessed life."

"Grab the cheese out of the refrigerator for me," Ruby told Faith.

"Sure." Faith pulled the bag of extra-sharp cheddar cheese out of the refrigerator, handed it to Ruby, then danced around the kitchen with Hope.

Hope started doing the bump.

Faith laughed. "Girl, you've been in Cali too long. Coming in here with them *Soul Train* moves. Ain't nobody still doing the bump."

"Oh, okay." Hope pointed at a spot on the floor. "Then show me some new dances."

Faith waved a hand in the air. "You got to ask your niece for that."

Ruby turned the sausage in the skillet as she asked Hope, "So how's that job of yours going?"

Hope stopped dancing and picked her mug back up. "It's fine. We're busy as usual." Hope lifted the mug to her lips and took a long sip, hoping her mother wouldn't ask another question about her job.

Glancing out of the kitchen window, Ruby waved. "Javon is here."

"Who's Javon?" Hope looked out the window to see a young man. She'd put him at about fifteen or sixteen. He had a pretty brown complexion and a handsome face that looked a lot like a guy she went to high school with.

"That's Luella Mitchell's grandson."

While wondering how time moved so fast, Hope's head whiplashed in her mother's direction. "Don't tell me that's Jay Mitchell's son."

Ruby nodded. "Yes, ma'am, that's who he is. I called Luella when I saw the weather report this morning. She sent Javon over to help. Now let's go get some things done on the outside of this house."

Faith got on Hope's case about checking for flights out of town before helping her family prepare the house for a hurricane, but in truth, the last place she wanted to be was in Hallelujah right now.

Chris had been texting her all night long. She had ignored his messages, even as he pleaded for her to bring Crystal back home. Then she woke up this morning to the news of a hurricane. How was she going to justify putting Crystal in harm's way by bringing her to Hallelujah rather than leaving her with Chris? Faith let those thoughts ricochet around her brain as she knocked on Trinity's bedroom door.

Closing her eyes, Faith reminded herself that this week, the bedroom belonged to Crystal.

"No locked doors, Crystal. It's daylight, there's no need to lock your door." Faith didn't allow Crystal to lock her door during daylight hours, because if she needed to get in her room to see what was going on, she didn't want a lock to slow her down. Like Reagan said, trust but verify.

Actually, if Faith was being honest with herself, she didn't trust even after she verified. Never knew what these kids were up to. She held up the plate in her hand and knocked again. "I have your breakfast."

"Okay, okay, I'm coming."

Crystal sounded agitated, like Faith was bothering her. Faith knocked again, because it took Crystal longer than she thought it should to unlock the door. A door that shouldn't be locked.

The door swung open. Crystal rolled her eyes. "Yes?"

"Good morning to you too." Faith was determined not to lose her cool as she handed Crystal her plate, but she glanced up, looked directly at Crystal and then froze.

"Mom, I'm in class. Can you just tell me what you want?"

Crystal had taken her hair out of the ponytail and was letting it hang down. Faith blinked, then rubbed her eyes. For one split second, she thought she'd gone back in time and Trinity was standing in front of her with a bad attitude, acting as if she was bugging her.

She turned away from her daughter, just as she had turned away from Trinity's rude behavior. "Go on and do your schoolwork. When you get a break, please put your hair in a ponytail and come outside to help us get ready for this storm."

"Storm? What storm?"

"There are reports of a hurricane." Faith's cell phone rang. She looked at the caller ID. "Let me take this. Just come outside on your break."

Before Crystal closed the door, Faith said, "Don't lock it." There was more she wanted to say to her daughter this morning, but the words had gotten lost.

She hated that she was rushing away from her daughter because she couldn't stand to see her look so much like Trinity. But life wasn't kind to her . . . hadn't been for a long time. She put the cell phone to her ear. "Designs by Faith. Can I help you?"

"Hi, Faith. This is Gladys. How are you doing today?"

"I'm doing good," she lied. "How about you?"

"I'm doing my meal prep. I have tons of family coming in for Thanksgiving, but I'm in my kitchen wishing I had those double ovens we talked about."

"Those double ovens are perfect for Thanksgiving dinners." Faith held her breath, didn't say another word for several beats.

"I talked to my husband," Gladys continued. "He's on board, so I'd like you to start the job right after Christmas if that time works for you."

Faith looked to heaven, said a silent *thank You*. "That sounds great. Let me check my schedule, and I'll get back to you with the exact date that I can start."

Faith did a dance that she'd seen on TikTok and then headed outside.

Chapter 8

By late morning, Javon had cleaned out the gutters while Faith, Crystal, Ruby and Hope worked on filling sandbags that they would place around the house. After only filling one bag, Crystal headed inside.

"If that child ain't lazy," Ruby said as she nudged Faith. "Reminds me of someone else I know."

Faith shook her head. "You can't put that kind of lazy on me, Mama, because we had chores and responsibilities. Crystal won't even keep her room clean."

"Maybe she really likes her next class and couldn't wait to get to it," Hope said with a smirk.

"Yeah, right." Faith twisted her lips. "The girl skipped school yesterday. That's why I brought her here with me."

Hope heard a car pull up in the front of the house. She turned to her mother. "You expecting someone?"

Ruby shook her head.

"I am," Faith told them as she and Ruby brought some plywood from the side of the house and set it on the back patio. "I figured we could get some estimates on all the things that need fixing around the house before we head out of here."

"Good thinking." Hope stood. "I'll get the door." Hope entered the house through the back patio. She heard the toilet flush and then the water in the sink came on, but it didn't sound like Crystal was washing her hands, more like she was gargling and spitting the water out of her mouth.

The bathroom door opened, and her niece came out of the bathroom wiping her mouth. The doorbell rang.

"You okay?" Hope asked.

Crystal jumped backward. Held on to the wall. Took a deep breath. "Auntie, you can't sneak up on people like that."

"Wasn't trying to sneak." The doorbell rang again. "I'll talk to you in a minute. Let me get this door."

"Okay." Crystal headed back outside.

Hope continued to the front door. Her heart was heavy as she wondered what was going on with her niece. Though Crystal was only fourteen, she wondered if the child could be pregnant. Her niece was too young for that kind of trouble, but these kids grew up too fast these days.

However, the minute she opened the door, all thoughts of the kind of trouble Crystal might be in left her mind because she would now have to deal with her own kind of trouble—the kind with greenish gray eyes and sun-kissed skin. Nicolas Evans, the white boy her mama warned her to stay away from, was at her front door again, after all these years.

Back then, Nic kept his sandy-blond hair long. Now he had a buzz cut. Probably got that at Quantico. Nic had been gung ho about joining the FBI. She wondered what made him come back to Hallelujah when all he wanted to do when they were younger was get away.

She still remembered hot summer nights when the two of them lay out on the beach while she ran her hands through his hair. Remembered how he had said I love you first and how she kissed him until their lips burned from the friction.

He had been her everything, taking her breath away to the point that she almost died from not being able to breathe when their love had fizzled out. She swore she would never, ever love another man so deeply, especially one she shouldn't have been with in the first place.

"Nic, what brings you to this side of town?" Her palms were sweaty, but she hoped that she looked cool, unbothered.

"I–I, wow . . . Hope." He rubbed his forehead. "I didn't expect to see you here."

With a lifted brow, she said, "I'm not sure how to take that. Is it a good thing or a bad thing to see me here?" So much for unbothered.

Nic shifted from left to right. "O-o-of course it's a good thing. Of course, I'm happy to see you, Hope. It's been a long time."

She didn't see a ring on his ring finger, but that didn't mean he wasn't taken. Men as sinfully gorgeous as Nic Evans didn't stay single for eighteen years, three months and seven days. She was still holding onto the door, barring entrance into the house. "So I guess I'm going to have to ask again. What brings you this way?"

"I'm looking for your mom."

Her mother told her that Nic had moved back to town about a year ago and was working at the Judah Watch Police Station as the lead detective. She leaned against the door. Interest piqued. Gave him a tell-me-more look. "What did she do? Do we need bail money?"

He smiled at her. That smile of his used to spark a fire in her heart. Cause her knees to buckle and her mind to dream of a future that wasn't meant to be.

"I'm actually here about Trinity. I think we've found her."

A sharp intake of breath. Hope's hand went to her chest. "Trinity . . . is alive?"

Nic's eyes shadowed over. He rubbed his face. Rocked backward on his heels. "I don't know if you are aware, but I moved back to town a year ago when there was an opening in the cold case unit."

"Cold case unit." Hope repeated those words before it hit her. Nic's visit was not a good thing.

"I'm sorry, Hope, but we think we've found Trinity's remains. I've been trying to talk to your mother about this . . ."

Hope interrupted him. "My mother already knows?"

"I've been trying to get DNA from her, but I think she's avoiding me." He put a hand on Hope's shoulder. "I know I'm not bringing the news you all hoped for, but this might at least bring closure."

Her mother was good at avoiding situations that she didn't want to deal with. Good at putting bandages on wounds and hoping that it would heal. Well, Hope was about to pull the bandage off the worst trauma her family had ever experienced. Maybe it would actually mend after all these years. "She's in the back. We're getting sandbags ready and trying to convince Mama to leave the island for a few days."

She signaled for him to follow her as they walked through the house toward the back.

"I hope you can convince her to leave. These storms are unpredictable."

"Don't I know it." More than any other family on this island, the Reynolds family knew all too well how much could be lost in a storm, which was the reason Hope didn't understand why her mother refused to leave the island.

They stepped onto the back patio. The first thing Hope noticed was that Javon had finished with the gutters and was now watching Crystal like he was being paid to do it. Her niece was only fourteen years old. Hope still wasn't sure what all that throwing up was about, but if she wasn't pregnant, Hope wasn't going to let the Mitchell boy do the deed. She would keep an eye on him and tell Faith to keep an eye on him as well.

"Bring that contractor over here, Hope. I need to look him in the eye and make sure he's not up to no good," Ruby said as she sat down in one of the lawn chairs.

Nic was standing behind her, just out of view. "It wasn't the contractor, Mama."

"Then who is it? Don't these people know that a storm is coming, and we don't have time for visiting?" Pulling a handkerchief out of her pocket, Ruby wiped the sweat from her forehead.

Nic stepped around Hope. He waved. "It's me, Ms. Ruby."

Faith was on her knees wiping down plywood. She swung around and just shook her head. "Hope hasn't been back home for two full days, and you already sniffing around."

"It's nice to see you, too, Faith." Nic waved in her direction. "But I'm not here to see Hope. I came to speak with your mother about Trinity."

Faith stood. Her eyes filled with longing. "What about Trinity?"

"Never you mind," Ruby said as she came and stood by Nic. "Nickel Knucklehead don't know what he's talking about, and we don't have time to entertain him." She shooed him away with her hands.

But Hope wasn't having it. "Oh no, Mama, you don't get to sweep this under the rug like you do with everything else. Nic needs something from you so he can determine if they have found Trinity or not."

Still clutching at her chest, Faith bent over. "Oh God . . . no."

Hope was surprised that Faith immediately assumed "found" meant dead. Because Faith had gotten in Hope's face during Crystal's fourth birthday party, ready to fight when Hope said that if Trinity was alive, she would have come back home by then. Her sister had even blamed her for Trinity's disappearance and had barely spoken to her after she couldn't stay past a week to help with the search party.

Hope had desperately wanted to stay, but after a week with no sight of her younger sister, Hope had to get away because each day she stayed only reminded her of how badly her heart had been broken just a few months before Trinity's disappearance. Faith didn't understand why Hope had to leave, but there were two people standing in this backyard who had been responsible for her broken heart, and as she looked from her mother to Nic, she prayed she could stay strong and not run away again.

Chapter 9

June 25, 2004

Hope was having the time of her life at the church picnic. God's Holy Word Church had the best picnics in town. But today's was special because they were celebrating her college graduation. She had been attending God's Holy Word Church since birth. This was her family church, but even if it wasn't, she would still be a member because Pastor Rufus O'Dell was the coolest pastor on the planet.

Another reason she loved her church was because the church mothers threw down in that kitchen. Hope couldn't wait to wrap her lips around that low country boil. Her mother was in the kitchen with Mrs. Luella and Donna today. Those women didn't play 'bout their food. Every bite had been delicious.

The nice breeze coming off the water made the ninety-five-degree temperature bearable. Mary Mary's new song "Heaven" was being blasted through the airwaves while she and Nic jumped and jumped in their potato sacks all the way to the finish line. Jay Mitchell and CJ James were teamed up next to them. But Hope was going for the win.

Yes, the food was good and the games were fun, but the

most beautiful thing about today was that she and Nic were home together.

Nic had been her love since tenth grade. His father wanted him to attend Duke, his alma mater, but Hope had her heart set on attending Howard University. Even though they had attended different colleges, they talked on the phone late into the night several times a week. They would see each other one weekend a month and during school breaks.

But this break was different because they were finally done with school, and she could stand next to Nic and hold his hand while they walked down the beach without thinking about how soon they had to leave each other. It felt to her like that Bible verse in the Song of Solomon. She was his and he was hers.

Hope pumped her arms in the air, gloating, letting everyone see the trophy that she and Nic had won.

"Let me see that. You did have a partner in that potato sack, you know." Nic held out his hand.

Hope gave him the trophy. She ran her hand through her long black hair. "You didn't even want to race. This trophy is going to my mama's house."

"You can have the trophy. I just want us to relax, spend the summer laying on the beach and make plans for the day you become Mrs. Hope Evans. Then the trophy will be in our house."

Hope's eyes lit up like Fourth of July fireworks. "You serious? At twenty-one, you're ready to talk about marriage?"

They arrived at the boardwalk and leaned against the railing. As they faced each other, Nic told her, "The way I see it, when you've found the one you want to spend forever with, it doesn't matter how young you are."

"Forever is a long time, Nic. You might get sick of me." Hope's hair blew in the wind. She smoothed her long strands back in place so that they cascaded down her left shoulder.

Nic ran his fingers from the back of her neck, through her hair. He leaned in and pressed their lips together. "I could never get tired of you, Hope Reynolds. I love every single thing about you."

"Do you really mean that, Nic?" His mom wasn't so keen about her gorgeous white son hanging around the "darkest girl" in town. Those were the actual words his mother let slide out of her mouth when Nic and Hope first started dating.

"Mean it?" He looked befuddled by the question. "Do I have to get down on one knee on this bridge to prove it? If that's what it takes to prove my love, I'll do it." He started bending down.

Hope pulled him back up. "No, you don't have to do that. You have on swim trunks, and this bridge is full of sand pebbles that will grind into your knee." Swim trunks with no shirt, showing off all of his glorious biceps, triceps and those six-pack abs.

She wanted to run her hands down his stomach so she could feel his ab muscles, but Pastor O'Dell had admonished the girls and the guys to keep their hands to themselves. He'd said, *"Overheated teenagers never make good decisions."* But they weren't teens anymore, were they? They were full-fledged, time-to-get-out-of-your-mama's-house grown-ups.

"I'll do it, Hope. I'll scratch my knees all to pieces and then every perp will be able to outrun the cop with bad knees, just to show my love."

There were only two things Hope didn't like about Nic: his mother and that he wanted a career in law enforcement. Why'd he have to pick such a dangerous profession? But that conversation went nowhere with him, so she decided to ask about the first thing she didn't like. "What about your mother?"

"What about her?"

Shoving Nic's shoulder, Hope narrowed her eyes at him. "You know that woman doesn't like me, and don't stand there pretending otherwise, or I'm going to throw you in the ocean, trophy and all."

Nic was quiet for a minute. He ran his hand down Hope's arm. "I'm here with you, Hope. This is where I want to be. I've never wanted anything as much as I want you, so I'm not letting my mother pull my heart out of my chest simply because she can't understand that I truly love you."

He was looking at her so intensely, so lovingly that she felt bad for bringing his mother into a conversation about their love. She was getting ready to apologize, but then he asked her a question that caused her to stumble backward.

"What about your father?"

Holding on to the railing, Hope said, "What does my father have to do with this conversation? He died four years ago."

Nic nodded. "And you've been obsessed with filling his shoes ever since. You attended Howard because that's the school he wanted you to go to, and now that you've finished school, you want to come back here, for what?"

"My family is here, Nic. Daddy's house is here."

His index finger went to her face and traced the lines of her jaw. "Your eyes light up when you talk about that beach house."

"I can't help it, Nic. Daddy had big plans for building another house for the family so we could turn ours into a bed-and-breakfast. With my degree in hotel management, I can do that now."

"But I don't want to live here now that I'm done with school."

Hope picked up a rock from the ground next to her feet and tossed it into the water. "How could you not want to live here, Nic? This is our home. Everything and everyone we love is here."

"I do love my family," Nic agreed, "but I'm not like them."

"Then why did you attend Duke, when you could have gone to any other school you wanted?"

He slammed his fist against the wooden railing. "Because my father wouldn't pay for any other school. I had no choice, Hope, and you know it."

Scooter Evans was the owner of the Bank of Heaven, which was a corny play on the town's name, but everybody was doing it. There was the Hallelujah Gas Station, the Ticket to Heaven amusement park, the mall was on Hallelujah Strip and was aptly named Hallelujah Mall. There was also the Heavenly Bakeshop, and to be honest those cookies did taste like they had been blessed by Jesus and all His disciples.

Most of the people in Hallelujah were as good as gold. But that Scooter Evans was unscrupulous with the way he was foreclosing on properties on the north side of town when everyone knew he was just making way to build some big fancy hotel. It was all about money to Scooter—well, money and hate.

And Scooter Evans hated the fact that her family had the best piece of land on the island. He also hated that when Henry Reynolds was finally able to build his dream home that he built the biggest, most fabulous structure on the island.

"Well, then you better think long and hard about that marriage proposal," Hope told him, "because I want to stay right here and work to make some of my parents' dreams come true."

"Then we have a problem. Because I am scheduled to be at Quantico to begin my FBI training in three weeks."

"Oh my God!" Hope was filled with excitement for him. She didn't want Nic taking such a dangerous job, but this had been his dream since they were kids. She jumped up and down. "You got in! I can't believe this. I'm so happy for you." Wrapping her arms around him, she hugged him and inhaled the scent of his cologne that smelled like lavender and cedarwood mixed with the sweat from the potato sack race.

No, Nic was nothing like his daddy, but the problem they had was that Hope was so much like her daddy that she even took her coloring after him. Henry had been dark as night while Ruby was so light that folks speculated that Ruby's daddy had been a white man.

Folks speculated a lot of stuff that didn't amount to anything on this island.

Hope wasn't as dark as her father, but she was several shades darker than her two sisters, who had taken their coloring after their mother. After being relentlessly teased by mean-spirited kids about how dark she was, Hope would cry out to God and ask Him why she had to look so much like her father and nothing at all like her mother. But now that her father was gone, she was thankful that she could look in the mirror and still see Henry Reynolds.

She just wished she could hear his laugh one more time. Wished she could tell him how much she admired the architect who had to take construction jobs so he could feed his family. Always saving, always dreaming of the day he could build the beautiful beach house for his family. He had only lived ten years after the house was built. The heart attack happened as he tried to protect his family from a November storm.

Hand in hand, they walked along the beach. Nic sounded serious when he said, "I'm not coming back when I leave, Hope, so I need you to make a decision."

Hands swinging back and forth as sand danced between their open-toe sandals, Hope found herself wondering why life forced so many choices. Couldn't life just be filled with easy days and cool-breeze nights? Couldn't it just be filled with love, laughs and a beach full of sand? "I'll think about it."

Before Nic could put more pressure on her, Hope spotted Gullah women at the street market near the beach. She ran over to them because they were selling sweetgrass baskets. Hope took one of their baskets off to college with her. But she had loaded it down with too many books and other knickknack's and the straps broke.

It wasn't like she could go to the store and get another basket. Authentic Gullah sweetgrass baskets could only be purchased from the Gullah people. They were an art form brought from West Africa for cleaning rice and toting fruits and vegetables. Nowadays people bought them for decorations. Hope loved the baskets and picked up a double-handled basket. "How much?" she asked.

"Thirty dolla fo' the pretty lady," the woman said in her strong Gullah accent.

Nic pulled his wallet out of his back pocket and paid for the basket. "Thank you, babe." Hope kissed him. They held hands again as they continued their walk down the beach.

They were about a mile from Hope's house when she saw Faith and Trinity stretch out on blankets on the beach catching some sun. She pointed toward them. "Let me go see what they are about to get into."

Hope tried to untangle her hand from his, but Nic pulled her back and kissed her neck. "Go hang out with your sisters, but don't forget that we are going out tonight."

"Already got my dress picked out, so you better be taking me someplace fancy, or else I'm going to be way overdressed." Backing away from him, she blew him a kiss. He was hers, and she was his, and she loved being with him. Just didn't know how she could ever leave Hallelujah and move someplace else like he wanted.

She was now an adult, just didn't know if she was ready for adult decisions like leaving her hometown for good with Nic. Right now she wanted to hang out with her sisters.

"You two out here sunbathing again?"

"Join us." Faith pointed to an extra blanket.

Putting a hand on her hip, Hope gave her sister a you-know-better-than-that look. "I am not getting ready to lay out in this sun and get any darker than I already am."

Trinity got up and lifted the big umbrella next to the blanket. "We brought this for you. We know how you feel about laying out here."

Putting her hands to her mouth, Hope said, "Aww." She was

touched that her sisters thought about her enough to lug that big umbrella down to the beach. "How did y'all know I would even see y'all laying over here?"

"We didn't know for sure," Faith told her, "but we haven't been able to spend much time with you since you came home."

"Because you stay hugged up with that Nic Evans," Trinity added.

Hope stuck her tongue out at her sisters. "Just wait till y'all find the man you want to spend your life with and then we'll see what you have to say about being hugged up."

Lying back on her blanket sporting an ocean-blue two-piece suit, Trinity said, "I don't care what man comes along. Nobody is going to get in between me and my sisters."

"Spoken like a fourteen-year-old." Faith laughed at her.

"Shut up, Faith. You're only seventeen, so you're not that much older than me."

"Older and wiser," Faith corrected.

"Okay, you two, let's not get it started. Y'all want to spend time with your big sis, then let's keep it mellow out here." Hope looked directly at Faith. "And let's always remember that I'm the oldest and wisest of the three of us."

"Aha, she told you." Trinity high-fived Hope.

Hope spread the blanket on the ground and then pushed the umbrella into the sand at the top of her blanket. She got comfortable, perched on one elbow. "So what's on the agenda for the rest of the summer?"

Trinity sucked her teeth. "Mama thinks I'm going to summer school, but I'm just going to lay right here and collect some sun as many days as I can."

"Didn't you get straight As this year?" Hope asked.

Popping up, Trinity slapped her leg. "Exactly. Can you please talk to your mother and explain to her why I don't need summer school?"

"Oh, so now she's just 'my mother' and not all of our mother, huh?"

"To be exact," said Faith, the one who was always keeping correct records on everything, "it was As and one B."

"That's still really good. I remember struggling my heart out my freshman year of high school, and I still ended up with a C in science and math."

"Tell Mama that. She'll listen to you. She just thinks I'm trying to get out of something."

Hope felt bad for her baby sister. After all, you only live once. Why couldn't Trinity just lie around and enjoy her summer after working so hard to get good grades all year long? "I'll talk to her."

"So you're just going to help the girl be a beach bum?" Faith shook her head.

"Well, what do you have planned for the summer?" Hope asked Faith.

"That's what I wanted to talk to you about." Faith turned sideways on her blanket, facing Hope. She rubbed her hands together. "I'm thinking about majoring in interior design when I go off to school next year, so I was wondering if you would let me shadow you as you work out your plans for the beach house this summer. I've been working on some sketches."

"You've got sketches, huh? When did you get so interested in interior design?"

"I took an art class last semester, and it mostly dealt with interior kind of stuff. I really liked it." Faith sat up. "I could show you some of my designs if you'd like to look at them."

"Are you kidding? I'd love to see them." Hope laughed, then said, "I guess you're going to be artsy like Mama, huh?"

Shaking her head, Faith told her, "I'm not an artist. I don't paint. I sketch."

"I paint," Trinity said. "I started last summer. I'm still trying to figure out if I like it or not."

"Look at the two of you." Hope shook her head. "I just don't get why I'm not artsy at all. I mean, I watch Mama paint all the time. You'd think I would have picked up some of her gift by now."

A harsh wind blew. The sweetgrass basket Nic had just purchased for Hope flew down the beach. Hope jumped up and chased after it. There was a woman in front of her. She was styling a short Afro and a pair of hoop earrings. She grabbed the basket, holding on to it until the wind subsided.

"Whew," Hope said as she reached the woman. "I don't know where that wind came from, but thanks for catching my basket."

"You're welcome," the woman said, but she didn't let go of the basket.

Hope put a hand on the double braided handle, then looked up at the woman to question her about why she was still holding it. Was she going to make her pay to get her basket back? But the eyes that looked back at her, they were like the eyes she saw in the mirror every morning. Round and brown with short eyelashes.

"Do I know you?" Hope asked.

The woman let go of the basket and ran. That was odd, Hope thought as she walked back to her sisters and rolled up the blanket. "Who wants ice cream?"

"I'm in." Faith stood and rolled up her blanket.

Trinity rolled her blanket up. "Oh, me too."

The Reynolds sisters walked a half mile down the beach to the Ice House where thirty different flavors of ice cream awaited them.

The James brothers were standing outside of the Ice House eating ice cream cones. Colton had his basketball in one hand while he ate his ice cream from the other hand. CJ used his free hand to put two fingers in his mouth and whistle as they approached. "What do we have here? The most beautiful girls in town are coming our way."

"Stop all your catcalling, CJ. We are ladies. You don't have to whistle at us. This is not a construction site," Hope told him.

"Well, excuse me, Miss College Graduate."

Colton, CJ's younger brother, shoved him. "You're leaving for college next month while you're messing with Hope about being a graduate."

"And we saw you speeding down the strip in that car your daddy bought you for graduating high school. So excuse us, Mr. High School Graduate," Faith said.

As they walked past the James boys and headed into the Ice House, CJ whistled again. "Dang, Trinity, you gettin' thick."

"Am not." Trinity punched CJ in the arm.

Faith grabbed Trinity and turned to Colton. "Do something with your brother."

They went inside, but Hope noticed the way Faith looked back at Colton. Her sister had written to her while she was away at school about the crush she had on Colton, but Faith hadn't found the courage to make her move. And Hope wasn't trying to give her little sister any pointers because she didn't want them growing up too fast. Didn't want them to change too much from the sweet girls they had been when she left for college.

However, Hope had to admit that things were not the same. Her sisters were growing up on her. But even as things changed with the Reynolds sisters, the Ice House stayed the same with *Happy Days* posters and the big jukebox in the back of the store that played fifties and sixties music.

Hope ordered Cherries Jubilee in a cup, Trinity ordered a chocolate-and-vanilla swirl on a cone, and Faith ordered strawberry ice cream in a cup. CJ was on his cell phone when they stepped out of the Ice House, so they didn't have to deal with his whistles and crude conversation.

They strolled back down the beach, eating their ice cream and enjoying their time together. It was good being with her sisters. Hope had missed them dearly.

As they neared the beach house, Hope said, "I'm going in. I need to get dressed for dinner with Nic."

Faith said, "I need to get going too. You're not the only one who has a date."

"Who are you going out with?" Hope wanted to know.

Faith shrugged. "Some guy named Tommy. He was in my science class last year."

Hope's lip twisted. "Why not Colton? You know you like him."

"He didn't ask me out."

"So what am I supposed to do," Trinity interrupted, "just hang around the house by myself while the two of you go out on dates?"

"Yes, child, at your age I was just hanging around the house."

"Faith, stop messing with her, and you're not even telling the truth because you were following me everywhere I went before I left for college. Nic and I could barely get a moment to ourselves."

"What did y'all need to be alone for?"

"For the same reason you want to be alone with your date tonight," Hope said.

"Then you should thank me for being a pest and following you around. Remember what Pastor O'Dell said about overheated teenagers," Faith reminded her.

Hope playfully popped Faith in the back of the head as they made their way up the steps that led to the beach house. "I should tell Mama to make you take Trinity on your date, the same way she used to make me take you."

"Don't you dare. That would be awful." Faith scrunched her nose.

Hope stopped, put hands on her hips. "Oh, so you knew you were being a pest . . . What goes around comes around, sis."

Chapter 10

June 26, 2004

The next morning, when Hope got out of bed, she glanced out of her window and saw her mother in the backyard with her easel set up getting ready to start painting. She threw on her house-coat; brushed her long, silky hair; then put it in a messy bun on top of her head.

She went into the kitchen, made herself a cup of coffee and then went out back.

"I've missed watching you paint. What's it going to be this morning?"

Ruby was facing the beach, paintbrush in hand, canvas in front of her. "A seagull flew by my window this morning. It inspired me, so I think this one is going to be for the birds."

"I can't wait to see what you come up with." Hope sat on the lawn chair next to the easel and sipped her coffee while she watched her mother fill the canvas with the bluish morning sky. She wanted to talk to her about Nic moving to Virginia and wanting her to go with him.

But Hope knew that her mother didn't deal well with change. Her father's sudden death, almost four years ago, had shaken the whole family, but Ruby withdrew within, like she needed to be somewhere else in order to deal with the pain of losing a man she had loved for almost thirty years.

After her father's death, Hope contemplated leaving college for a few years, but Ruby wouldn't hear of it. *"Girl, if you don't get your behind on that bus and head back to school, I'm going to drive you back there myself."*

Hope had wanted to argue, but she knew that her mother wanted her to succeed in life. *"You're still getting that degree in hotel management, right?"* Ruby had asked.

"Yes," she had answered.

"Good. You're going to come back here and help me turn this place into a real moneymaker so that old Scooter Evans can't take what belongs to us."

So Hope went back to college, and now she was home with plans for this beach house. But for the plans to work, the family would have to move out, just as Daddy had originally envisioned . . . and she would have to stay around long enough to get this bed-and-breakfast off the ground. But what would Nic say if she stayed?

"Mom, I can imagine how delighted our guests at the bed-and-breakfast will be to wake up and come out to the back patio and watch you paint." Hope clasped her hands together as another idea struck her. "You could give painting lessons to our guests."

"Lessons?" Ruby turned around in her seat. "I don't know about that, Hope. I've never taught anybody to paint. Just pretty much learned on my own and been doing what I know to do"—she touched the paintbrush end to her head—"from up here."

"And I was not blessed with one ounce of your"—Hope poked a finger to her head—"painting knowledge."

"But we both have a love for the arts. That's what's important, isn't it?"

A look crossed her mother's face as she adjusted herself in her seat. Her mother almost looked uncomfortable, but that was her favorite stool to sit on while she painted, so Hope didn't understand why she would be uncomfortable. "Want me to get you another chair?"

"Naw, chile, I'm fine." Ruby put more paint on the canvas. "But you know what I could use?"

"What's that?"

"Some good ol' gospel music. Go to the kitchen and bring me that radio. I think that might help me concentrate on this here painting."

Hope put her coffee cup on the end table next to her chair and went back into the house by way of the kitchen. Trinity sleepwalked herself to the fridge, put her cup against the ice maker and let the crushed ice fall into her cup. She then grabbed a spoon and started eating the ice.

Hope had never known anyone who loved crushed ice the way Trinity did. No water, no soda, just ice. "I guess that's your breakfast, huh?"

"I'm not hungry. I just wanted some ice." Trinity dug in with her spoon again. "Did you talk to Mama about summer school yet?"

"I'm sorry, Trinity. I've had my mind on something else, but I'll talk to her. Just let me grab her radio. Gospel music mellows her out."

"Don't put on Kirk Franklin because she'll be up dancing around. That ain't mellow," Trinity said as she walked back to her room.

Her little sister was right. She had to wait until the right song was playing before she challenged Ruby Reynolds about summer school for a kid who didn't need it. She grabbed the radio and then headed back to the patio.

But she didn't open the back door to go outside because she heard voices, and then she saw the same lady who had stopped her sweetgrass basket from blowing away on the beach the other day. What was she doing on the back patio talking with her mother?

Her mother looked nervous, so nervous that Hope put her hand on the screen door to go out there and help her fend off this crazy lady.

But then the lady said, "It's not right, Ruby. You can't keep her from me forever."

Keep who? What was the woman talking about? Maybe this was a private conversation and she needed to let her mother handle it. Hope backed away from the screen door, but she watched them, just in case her mother needed her.

Ruby said, "You gave her to me and Henry, and that's the end of that."

"Not true," the woman yelled. "I never gave my baby to you. You and Henry stole her from me!"

Ruby's tone held sympathy for the woman standing in front of her. "You are not well, Brenda, and you haven't been well for a very long time. I'm sorry that Henry took advantage of you, but do you really think you would have been able to raise Hope and give her all the advantages in life that she deserves?"

"Don't you tell me what I wouldn't have been able to do."

It looked like the woman was revving her arm up for a swing. Hope dropped the radio by the door and rushed out to the patio. "Don't hit my mother."

The woman turned around and looked at Hope with those eyes that looked like her own. "I'm your mother," she said.

I'm. Your. Mother. Hope closed her eyes. *Breathe. Breathe.* The earth seemed to tilt. She felt like she was spinning. *I'm. Your. Mother.* The weight of what this woman had just said to her was too much.

It didn't make sense, didn't line up with everything she knew about her life . . . but then again, it sort of did. All of her life, Hope had wondered why her sisters looked so much like their mother, but she looked nothing like Ruby. She'd thought that she took her coloring from her father.

But this woman standing in front of her had the same eyes and the same milk-chocolate skin tone. Hope's eyes darted from her mother to the woman claiming to be her mother, but she couldn't move, couldn't even make her mouth say the words she wanted it to say.

Ruby threw her paintbrush down on the table and got in the woman's face. One foot in front of the other, knees slightly bent. Her fists ready for action. "Now do you see what you've done? You get out of here, and don't ever step your crusty feet on my property again, or I will kill you. Do you hear me? I. Will. Kill. You."

The woman backed off the porch, hand barely hanging onto the railing for support as she made her way down the stairs and started running down the beach.

Hope's chest heaved in and out . . . in and out. What was happening? What was going on here? Putting her hand to her chest, Hope turned to the only mother she had ever known. "I look like that woman."

Ruby shook her head like she was trying to get some forbidden knowledge to fly, fly away. "That's foolish talk. You look like your daddy, and that's the end of that."

"But I heard you. You said, 'you gave her to me and Henry.' Why would you say that if she was lying?"

Tears streamed down Ruby's face. She tapped her chest with her hand as she said, "I'm your mother, Hope. Whether I birthed you or not, I've loved you just the same."

Exhaling to steady the fast beat of her heart, Hope's legs gave way, and she fell onto the lounge chair, which immediately collapsed in on her.

Frazzled and sickened by the lie she had been living, Hope just wanted to get away. She called Nic to tell him that she wouldn't be able to meet him for lunch.

"What? Why?"

"I've got to get away, Nic. I can't stay here anymore." Holding a mound of clothes in her arms, she shoved them in her duffel bag.

"Hope, are you crying?"

The dam broke then. Her face flooded with tears. She was barely able to speak as she said, "I-it's a-all been a l-lie. A-all a lie."

"I'm on my way to get you. Don't leave before I get there."

"Hurry. I don't think I can stay in this house much longer. I'm packing my clothes now."

As she hung up with Nic, Faith and Trinity ran into her room.

"What's wrong, Hope? Why are you crying like this?" Faith asked.

"Ask your mother," was all Hope said as she kept packing. Kept crying.

Faith stepped out of the room and ran down the hall.

"Where are you going? Why are you packing? You said you were home for good now that you're finished with school." Trinity tried to grab the duffel bag from Hope.

But Hope pulled it back. "I'm sorry, Trinity, but I can't stay here anymore."

Faith came back into the room with a wad of tissue. She handed them to Hope. "Here, wipe your face."

Hope took the tissue and did as requested. As the tears cleared from her eyes, she looked at her sisters. They were light-skinned, and she was dark . . . dark like that woman who stood on the patio with her Afro and hoop earrings. Hope didn't belong here with them. But she didn't know where she belonged because she couldn't get Ruby to give her any information about that woman who claimed to be her birth mother.

Hope hugged both her sisters, and the tears started all over again. She would miss them so dearly, but she couldn't stay, no matter how hard it would be to leave them. Not with her mother clamming up and refusing to tell her anything.

Hope had never seen the woman on the island before. Where had she come from? What was her name? And why had her parents deceived Hope for so many years? Since she was old enough to know anything, Hope knew that she was Henry and Ruby Reynolds' oldest daughter. But if she really wasn't, then she was utterly lost and confused and didn't know where or to whom she belonged.

By the time Nic pulled up, Hope was standing on the front porch with a suitcase and a duffel bag full of clothes, shoes and toiletries, with tears streaming down her face.

He took the bags out of her hands. "What happened? Why are you crying like this?"

"Just get me out of here. I can't be here anymore." Hope sped to his car, opened the passenger door and got in.

Nic put her bags in the trunk and got inside the vehicle. He sat there for a minute, staring at her, then he leaned forward and pulled her into his arms. "Baby, don't do this to yourself. Tell me what's wrong."

Her tears dripped onto his shoulder. "I-I can't talk about it. I just want to leave."

Pulling back, his eyes questioned her. "Leave? Where do you want to go?"

"What about Quantico?"

"But I thought you didn't want to leave the beach?"

"Things change." She looked back at the house. Her sisters were standing on the porch looking as distraught as she felt. After what she found out today, she didn't even know if she was related to them. What if Henry wasn't her father either? That doubt hurt worse than anything. Leaning her head against the headrest, she said, "Just drive. I don't ever want to come back to this town again."

"I'm not leaving for Quantico until next month, but let me take you to my house. We can stay there until we figure something out."

They arrived at the Evanses' house, and Nic took her bags into the guest room and told her to lie down while he talked to his parents.

Ruby started calling Hope's phone. Hope tried to ignore her mother. As her head hit the pillow, the phone rang again. The pain of longing shot through her body. She turned the ringer off before she gave in and answered the call. Her mother admitted that the woman who'd stood on their back patio claiming to be her birth mother was telling the truth. How could Hope ever go back to that house?

Just as she was getting comfortable on the bed, Hope heard Melinda Evans' screeching voice say, "Oh no, you don't."

"Be reasonable, Mom. Hope doesn't have anywhere else to go."

"You are not laying up with that Black girl in this house. I forbid it."

"Calm down, Melinda, and for goodness' sake, lower your voice." That was Scooter Evans. He was Nic's dad, so Hope was always polite when she was in the man's presence, but she didn't like him. Actually, she didn't like him because her mother told her not to like him. Maybe Scooter wasn't as bad as Hope had thought. She'd just learned that she couldn't believe everything that came out of her mother's mouth.

"Don't tell me to calm down!" Melinda yelled. Obviously not caring if Hope heard her. "Your son refuses to date any of the women I have tried to set him up with, then he falls for Hope Reynolds of all people."

"What's wrong with Hope?" Nic asked.

"I'm not a racist," Melinda declared. "I wouldn't have cared if you had fallen for Faith Reynolds, but Hope is too dark. Do you have any idea what your kids will look like?"

Hope's hand went to her heart. Why? Why? Why was her skin color always an issue? And why wasn't her mother her mother? Tears. She didn't want to cry, but the tears came anyway as Melinda's words replayed in her head: *You are not laying up with that Black girl . . .*

She crumbled within herself, as echoes of *"I'm your mother"* also played in her head. What was she to do? Where did she belong? Who did she belong to?

Hope couldn't go back to the beach house, but she couldn't stay here either. Not under the same roof with Melinda Evans. She grabbed her bags and made her way to the living room where the family stood discussing her Blackness.

"Nic, I'm ready to go. Please take me to the airport." Hope still had six weeks left on the apartment she rented in Washington, DC. She would go there until she figured out her next move.

"Wait . . . no. I don't want you to leave." Nic rushed over to her. Put a hand on her arm. He squeezed his eyes shut. "Don't go."

The look of hurt and pain on Nic's face almost changed her mind. She loved this man so much. Had wanted to marry him. Spend her life with him and have as many babies as he wanted.

"Let her go," Melinda said, sneering. "She doesn't belong here anyway. None of the Reynolds belong on this island."

Hope wanted to defend her family. Because nobody belonged on this island more than the Reynoldses. But with the way her heart was breaking, she didn't have it in her to fight.

But then Scooter said, "The Reynolds family has been in this town just as long as the Evans family, so there is no disputing that they belong here." He walked over to Hope, put a hand on her shoulder. "I'm sorry for whatever happened that's caused you to leave home like this. You are more than welcome to stay in our guest room."

"Over my dead body." Melinda wrapped her arms around her chest and patted her small feet on the hardwood floor.

Every word Melinda said was like a knife thrown at Hope's heart. She could never be a part of this family, would never be a part of anything with Melinda Evans. Hope wiped a tear from her face. "I've never done anything to you. All I ever did was love your son. B-but you d-don't have to worry about me anymore." Hope could barely get the words out through the tears that scorched her face and caused her chin to tremble.

Nic held on to Hope's hand as he confronted his mother. His eyes were full of fury. "You are the reason I don't want to be in this town anymore. Rest assured that the children Hope and I have will not be around you. You will not contaminate them with your hate."

Melinda put her hand to her heart. "Nic! How can you talk to me like that?"

Hope turned away from them. Her shoulders slumped with the weight of rejection as she made her way to the front door. She promised herself that she would never enter this house again. Nic might one day forgive his mother for what she'd done, but Hope never would. In the space of a couple of hours, she had lost a mother who loved her, as wrong as her love might be, and a future mother-in-law who despised her for the color of her skin, and Hope couldn't forgive that.

Nic took her bags and helped her to the car. His phone rang. He answered it, then handed the phone to Hope. "It's your mother."

Which one, Hope wanted to ask, but she knew. She shook her head. "I can't talk to her right now."

Nic put the phone to his ear. "Can I have her call you later? . . . I understand, but she doesn't want to talk." Nic hung up the phone, started the car, and within minutes, they were back on the road and headed to the airport, when suddenly he pulled the car over to the shoulder. "What's going on?"

Hope put her hand on her head. She was so confused. Ruby Reynolds was the only mother she had ever known. How could it be possible that Ruby was not who she believed her to be for all of her life?

Tears trickled down her face, her chest caved inward. "I just found out Ruby is not my birth mother, and I don't know what to do with that. I'm completely destroyed."

"Oh my goodness, Hope. I'm so sorry. I didn't know." He pulled her into his arms.

His hug warmed her, but it didn't take away the pain. Pain was all around, eating at her very soul.

When she was a child, Hope had accidentally closed her fingers in the car door. Her mother opened the door and rescued her fingers. The pain had been instant, but she didn't scream. It was like her body went into delay mode, feeling the pain but not knowing how to respond. That was how she felt at this very instant. She couldn't share this pain. And no one was coming to pull her heart out of the vise grip it was now in. She was motherless, hopeless and dark. Too dark.

She pulled away from his embrace and leaned back against her seat. "Everything is all messed up." She wanted to be with Nic, but she didn't want to hurt anymore. Didn't want to think about how different they were. Didn't want to have others point those facts out the way Melinda had so cruelly done.

"Stay."

"Do you have any idea what your kids will look like?"

"I can't" was her simple answer.

He took her hand in his. Lifted her head with a finger so that she was looking into his eyes. "We can get married. Let's just go to the courthouse, get married and then I'll move to Washington with you."

His words sounded so good, like a sweet melody. They belonged together. Were right for each other. But not right now. Hope didn't know who she was or where she belonged for that matter. And Nic's mother would never be happy for them. Melinda would always make her feel like the "other."

Hope never wanted to be anywhere Melinda was again, but she couldn't ask Nic to abandon his mother, and she loved him too much to make him choose sides. Her heart was hurting so much from what she discovered about her mother, she couldn't bear for Nic to be without his mother also, no matter how hateful she was.

No matter where they went, people would look at them and question if they truly belonged together. She never cared about that stuff before, but today, she cared.

Hope started crying all over again. This was supposed to be the summer that she worked the plans she had for turning the beach house into a real, bona fide bed-and-breakfast. She sighed. This was supposed to be the summer that she and Nic made plans for the rest of their lives.

Instead, this was the summer she discovered why her skin tone didn't match the rest of the Reynolds women's. Hope put a hand over her heart. Closed her eyes tight, trying desperately to shut out the pain. "Just take me to the airport."

Chapter 11

Present Day

MAMA THREW NIC OFF HER PROPERTY AND REFUSED TO TALK about his visit with anyone. Faith wasn't sure if she was ready to talk about it either, so she just kept working. Kept her mind occupied with the impending storm. Prayed that somehow, someway, this storm might just bring Trinity back to them. After all, the last time she had seen her sister had been right before that awful storm tore up their small town in the fall of 2004.

The year everything changed.

But Nic thought they'd found Trinity's remains. Maybe that meant it was time to face reality. Time to stop avoiding the truth. And the truth was that this family lost itself even before that storm. Nothing had been right for them since Hope fled the house like it was about to collapse and bury them under the rubble.

Faith remembered how her mother stayed in her room for days on end, refusing to talk to them about Hope or the reason for the big blow-up between the two of them. That was when Trinity met that guy on Myspace. Faith tried to warn her about predators on the Internet, but Trinity never listened to her like she did when Hope gave advice.

To this day, Faith didn't know if the storm or the Myspace predator had taken Trinity away from them. She just knew her little sister was gone, and it hurt. Hurt so bad that when Crystal turned eleven and Faith began to notice how much she looked like Trinity, she pulled back and let Chris step up. He drove Crystal to school, cheered for her at her volleyball games, helped with homework. All while Faith stayed on the grind, building her interior design business.

Being back at the beach and seeing Crystal in Trinity's bedroom helped Faith to finally acknowledge to herself the reason for the distance between her and Crystal. Standing over the kitchen sink, holding on to her second cup of coffee, Faith watched as Crystal and Javon filled the sandbags.

Javon must have said something funny, because Crystal's head tilted backward, and she laughed and laughed until she started coughing. She then held her stomach with one hand and her mouth with the other as if she was trying to stop the home fries and fried chicken Mama had cooked for lunch from coming back up.

"Oh no, please don't tell me she's about to throw up again," Hope said, standing directly behind Faith.

Faith swung around as she directed questioning eyes at her sister. "What do you mean . . . 'again'?"

Hope pointed in the direction of the bathroom that was behind the kitchen. "She threw up twice in there. I was going to ask you if she was pregnant, but then I thought, nah, she's too young."

"Pregnant!" Faith looked like she was about to be sick. Her mind traveled back to the day she caught Kenneth cozied up on the sofa with Crystal with no parental supervision. She swung the screen door open and yelled, "Crystal! Get in here."

Crystal scooped two more mounds of sand into the bag she had open, handed it to Javon and then slowly walked into the house with her arms crossed around her chest. "You didn't have to yell like that," she said as she inched closer to the kitchen door.

"You don't tell me how to conduct myself." Faith grabbed hold of Crystal's shirt sleeve and snatched her into the kitchen.

Crystal leaned back and twisted around, trying to pull her shirt out of her mother's grasp. "What's wrong with you? I was outside helping like you asked."

Faith's eyes blazed with fire. "Are you pregnant?" Faith didn't have time for games. She wasn't beating around the bush with this because she knew for a fact that a fourteen-year-old could get pregnant.

"What? No." Crystal scrunched her nose like she was trying to stop a foul odor from penetrating her nostrils. "Why would you ask me something like that?"

Pointing at Hope, Faith said, "She says you keep throwing up. What's that about if you're not pregnant?"

"You told her that, Auntie Hope?" Crystal had this expression on her face like she had been betrayed.

"I'm sorry, hon. I wasn't trying to get you in trouble. It just looked like you were about to throw up again when you were outside, so I thought your mom should know that you've been throwing up this week."

Faith narrowed her eyes on Crystal. "You and Kenneth were probably doing more than sitting on the sofa before I came in and caught you."

Crystal's eyes grew wide at the accusation. She swung her arms downward as if striking at the air. "I didn't do anything with Kenneth. We were just watching TV." Crystal swung and turned to Hope. "Why did you tell her? She doesn't care about me. She only wants to accuse me of stuff I'm not doing." Crystal took off to her room and slammed the door.

"You get back here. I'm not through with you." Faith moved forward, heading to Trinity's old room, just as she had done almost twenty years ago after catching her sister in the bathroom throwing up.

Hope held up a hand. "Let me go talk to her."

"I think I can handle my own kid, Hope." Shaking her head at her sister, she tried to walk around her, but Hope got in her way.

"Sis, I don't know if you've noticed, but Crystal isn't feeling you. Maybe she's not pregnant, but I doubt she's going to tell you what the issue is."

Faith shouted in Hope's face. "You don't have any kids! How are you going to tell me about my kid?"

"I'm just trying to help." Hope shoved Faith backward until she plopped down in the chair next to the kitchen table. "Can you just for once sit down and shut up so somebody can help you?"

Faith tried to stand, but Hope pushed her back down in the chair. "I'm. Not. Your. Enemy."

Faith heard what her sister said, and she truly did believe that Hope wanted to help, but she had thought of Hope as the enemy for so long, it was hard to think of her as anything else. "Now you want to help? But where were you when Trinity went missing?"

"That's not fair, Faith. I was dealing with my own issues back then. I had no idea Trinity was going to come up missing."

"What issues did you have? You had just graduated college. We were all happy for you. Nic wanted to marry you. He told us all that you were going to be his wife, but you abandoned him just like you abandoned me and Trinity."

Hope leaned down and tried to wrap her arms around Faith. "I love you. I didn't abandon you, and I didn't abandon Trinity."

Faith felt the tears as they bubbled in her eyes. No, she wasn't going to cry about this. Hope didn't care anything about them, and she wasn't going to let her forget that it was her fault Trinity wasn't here with them. If Hope had been there, maybe Faith wouldn't have messed everything all up . . . and maybe Trinity would still be with them.

Pulling out of Hope's embrace, she stood and wiped her eyes. "If you didn't abandon us, then why weren't you here? Trinity would have listened to you. She wouldn't have gone off on her own if you had told her to stay home."

"You blame me for what happened? You think I didn't care, but I tried calling when I found out about that hurricane. I couldn't get anyone on the phone because the lines had gone down. And I tried to get back home, but they wouldn't let me in until the roads cleared."

Faith jabbed an angry finger at Hope's chest. She was yelling at Hope and didn't care who heard her. "Save that song for somebody who might believe it! Bottom line, you didn't try hard enough."

"I tried, Faith, but Trinity was already gone by the time I made it back here."

"You should have never left. You promised me and Trinity that once you finished with college you were coming back here to make something special out of this beach house." Faith began pushing her sister backward, anger spilling over. "So what happened to that promise, huh? What happened?"

Hope's eyebrows pointed downward. Her chest heaved like she was carrying a weight too heavy to hold. "I couldn't stay here, Faith. I just couldn't."

"Why? Why? Why?" Faith screamed at her while flailing her arms in the air. "What is the big secret?"

"Stop yelling at your sister, Faith." Ruby was standing in the doorway with the broom that she used to sweep around the outside of the house. "It's my fault, not hers, so just leave her alone."

Faith felt like her neck was on a string as it swung back and forth from her mother to her sister. "I'm not taking no for an answer today, Mama. If it was your fault, then tell me why she left."

Ruby's mouth opened as if she was about to reveal some truth, but then it clamped shut again, just as it always did when Faith broached this subject. But Faith was tired of all the secrets. She turned to Hope, stretched out her hands to her sister, voice pleading with her. "I can't take this anymore. Please, Hope. Why did you leave?"

Hope closed her eyes for just a moment, but when she reopened them, her eyelashes were wet from the tears that now trickled down her face. "I had to leave."

"Why?" Faith yelled, hands raised as if she was willing to pull down heaven to get the answer she sought.

Hope yelled back. "Because I found out that your mother is not my mother. Are you happy to know the reason I'm darker than you and Trinity is because Ruby is not my real mother?"

Hope turned on her heels and headed toward the front of the house. She called back over her shoulder, "I'm taking the car into town. I'll bring back any supplies I see."

Had she heard Hope correctly? Had Hope just said what she thought she said? Faith shifted her eyes in her mother's direction. She held up her hands, like she was trying to stop the world from turning. "What is she talking about?"

"Why couldn't you just leave it alone?" Ruby went back out into the yard and slammed the screen door shut.

Faith heard Crystal open the bedroom door and run out the front door behind Hope. She sat back down at the kitchen table alone with her thoughts. Alone with her sorrow.

Her sister said, *"Are you happy to know the reason I'm darker than you and Trinity is because Ruby is not my real mother?"*

All the times that she had picked on Hope for being the darkest woman in the Reynolds family, she'd never in her life thought that Ruby had not given birth to Hope. How she must have hurt her sister with all of her stinging insults. She lifted her head heavenward and asked, "Lord, what have I done?"

Chapter 12

HOPE PUT THE KEY IN THE IGNITION, PREPARING TO TAKE HER mother's Jeep for a ride into town, when she saw Crystal run down the stairs toward the car. She unlocked the door and let her in.

"You okay?"

Crystal took a moment to catch her breath, then said, "You can't leave me in there with her. I want to go with you."

"Are you sure your mom will be okay with you riding with me?"

Rolling her eyes, Crystal told her, "She doesn't care where I go or what I do, just as long as I'm not getting myself knocked up."

Hope glanced toward Crystal's belly. "And you're not pregnant?"

"No, Auntie Hope. I'm only fourteen for goodness' sake. What would I do with a baby?"

"Same thing I was thinking. Not the best move for a teenager." She paused a moment, then added, "Although, we would help you and love that child because he or she would be family." Hope handed Crystal her cell phone. "Here, text your mom and tell her that you're with me."

Crystal handed the phone back as she pulled her cell phone out of her pocket. "I took my cell out of my mom's purse last night." She texted her mom, then put the phone back in her pocket.

"Girl, you are a trip. Mama would have beat our behinds if we took something back before she gave it to us."

Crystal scrunched her tiny nose. "Auntie Hope, that's abuse."

Hope's head fell back as she burst out laughing. "When I was a kid, they called it parenting. Even the Bible says, 'spare the rod, spoil the child.'"

Crystal didn't look like she had ever heard such a thing. Nor did she look like she understood it. But this was the generation of whup your child and get locked up.

Hope pulled out of the driveway and headed down the main strip.

"We really shouldn't be going anywhere until we have the whole house secured, but I can't breathe in that house right now."

They passed several seafood restaurants and a few pizza spots. Some of the eateries were new to Hallelujah, but Hope smiled as she drove by Captain Eddie's. She and Nic had their first date at that seafood restaurant. They grabbed all the crab legs they could get off the buffet before the waiter ran them away. She'd never heard the word *teenagers* sneered quite like that before.

"Why are you smiling like that?"

Hope came to a red light, turned to look at Crystal. "Was I smiling?"

"Cheesing big time."

"Just remembered something. That's all." The light turned green, and Hope started driving again. It was quiet in the car . . . too quiet for Hope. She needed her mind to go in the same direction as the car . . . away from the beach house. She was about to turn on the radio when Crystal got her attention.

"Are you sure that Grammy isn't your mother?"

Glancing over at her. "You heard all of that, huh?"

"I wasn't trying to listen, but y'all were really loud, especially my mother." Crystal rolled her eyes, puffed out some air. "So what about it? Are you still my aunt or what?"

"Of course I'm your aunt. Ruby isn't my biological mother, but

she's the only mother I know, and Henry Reynolds is my father."
Allegedly. "So yes, I'm still your aunt."

"Good, because I need somebody I can talk to sometimes because I can't talk to my mother."

"What's the deal with you and Faith? Are you just being a bratty teenager, or is there something you want to talk about?" *Like why you keep throwing up,* Hope wanted to add, but she was going to wait a bit on that.

Plopping her hands against the passenger seat while letting out an exasperated breath, Crystal declared, "She's just such a phony."

"Phony? Your mom?" Hope didn't see it. Faith was a lot of things, but phony was not one of them.

"Yeah. She brings me down here trying to make y'all think she's all motherly and whatnot, but she's rarely even home. My dad is the one who takes care of me."

Hope pulled into the parking lot of the Any Day Mini Market. "Have you talked to your mom? Maybe if you tell her you want to spend more time with her, she'll cut some of her work hours."

Crystal's lip twisted as she gave Hope a go-'head-on-with-that look. "She don't care about me. She barely even looks my way. That's why I called my daddy. He's coming to pick me up."

Hope didn't know what to say to that, but she hoped that Faith and Chris would be able to talk and decide what was best for Crystal. They got out of the car and headed into the store. "I need chocolate," Hope told her as they went down the candy aisle.

"*Oooo,* can I get some too?"

"Of course." Hope pointed toward the carts. "Go grab a cart. I also need to pick up some bottled water if they have it."

Crystal grabbed the cart, then she and Hope stood in the candy aisle and began throwing bags of Snickers, Reese's miniature peanut butter cups and plain M&M'S in the cart.

Hope needed every bit of the chocolate in that cart if she was going to go back to that beach house and deal with her so-called family.

Her phone beeped, indicating that she had a text. She pulled the phone from the side pocket of her purse and glanced at the screen.

We need to talk.

The text was from Spencer. She had nothing to say to him if it wasn't about business. Can't, I'm busy with my family.

I miss you. I broke it off with Erica. I can't stand being here without you.

She almost laughed out loud but held herself in check so she didn't draw attention in the grocery store. You need to get your girlfriend back because I'm done with you, was her text response. She was about to put the phone back in her purse when he texted again.

What about the annual report? I need that for the board meeting.

That was all he wanted anyway. He could have led with that instead of his I-want-you-back lies. I'll email it to you. She put the phone back in her purse and then pushed the cart over to the water aisle, which was almost completely empty except for one thirty-six-bottle case of spring water.

As Hope reached for it, she heard someone say, "Let me get that for you."

She knew that voice. Looking back, she caught a side view of Nic as he picked up the case of water and put it in her cart. Hope got a fluttering in her stomach. She hadn't been around this man in almost twenty years. Why on earth was just the sight of him sending shockwaves through her body?

Slow your roll. He's just a man. A man who is all wrong for you. "Hey, Nic. Thanks for that."

"It's the least I can do."

His voice was silky smooth. Hope wished she could stand there and listen to him talk all day, but she wasn't going to get lost in memories about Nic, not when those memories hurt like a hammer to the head.

Hope paid for their items, then she and Crystal headed back to the Jeep. She was going to try for a quick escape, but Nic was right on their heels, helping to load the items into the back of the SUV.

Hope grabbed her bag of M&M'S and opened them as Nic closed the trunk. "You didn't have to come out here, Nic, but thanks again."

"You didn't think I was going to let you throw out your back picking up that big case of water. They'd take my southerner's card for that," Nic joked.

"Who is 'they'?" Despite herself, Hope grinned at his corny joke.

Crystal got in the car. Nic leaned closer to Hope. At first, she thought he was leaning in for a kiss, and the thought unnerved her. Here it was 2022, and she glanced around, wondering what people would think of this gorgeous white man getting all in her personal space.

But Nic wasn't coming in for a kiss. He said, "Your mom tossed me out of her house, but I still want to help you get answers about Trinity."

Hope reached in her bag of M&M'S and handed Nic one of the brown-coated ones. "I'm sorry my mom threw you off her property."

He popped the candy in his mouth. Then Hope gave him three more. "Sorry she called you Nickel Knucklehead again."

Nic's head flew backward. He gave a good belly laugh. "Your mom has been calling me Nickel Knucklehead ever since our first date.

Do you remember that waiter who called your mom and told her that you and I were trying to eat all the crab legs and leave none for other customers?"

Hope's eyes rolled heavenward. "I remember him." But she was no way, no how about to 'fess up to the fact that she had just been reminiscing about their first date less than an hour ago.

"That waiter had no respect for the fact that I was trying to show off by dating the most beautiful girl in town, and I was using all of my allowance to do it. I wanted to get my money's worth."

Hope laughed at him. "I was right there with you. That place has the best crab legs in town. I don't know what they put in that garlic sauce, but it should be bottled and sold at grocery stores."

"And thus I've been Nickel Knucklehead ever since."

"To be fair, she didn't actually call you Nickel Knucklehead that night." They both said the words in unison, "Don't be a Nickel Knucklehead."

Nic acquiesced with a nod. "Okay, you're right, but after that night, she must have decided that I was in fact a knucklehead because she's been calling me that ever since."

Hope handed him another M&M, and the two of them laughed like they'd never stopped laughing together.

Then Nic got serious. "If you all want to stop wondering about Trinity, I need DNA from one of the Reynolds women. Your mother won't do it, so I thought I'd ask you to do the DNA to see if we get a sibling match."

The word *DNA* caught Hope off guard. She wanted to know more than anything if Trinity's remains had been recovered or if Trinity was still out there, refusing to come back home, but what if Nic did in fact have Trinity's remains and Hope took the test, and it came back with no match?

Her family would then think that meant Trinity might still be alive, when in fact it might mean that Henry Reynolds wasn't her father. That thought about her father had swum around in her brain since she'd discovered that Ruby wasn't her biological mother. She would calm herself with the fact that Ruby had assured her that Henry was her father. But what else would she say?

The strain of his request must have shown on her face because Nic put a hand on her arm. "I'm sorry, Hope. I know this is difficult."

"Why do you think you have Trinity?"

"We found remnants of the yellow sweater she had on the day she went missing."

That punched Hope in the gut. She put her hand to her heart. Took a deep breath. "Did you tell my mother that?"

He shook his head. "She hasn't given me a chance to tell her much of anything."

Hope snapped her finger as a thought came to mind. "What about dental records?"

Nic pressed his lips together, then he said, "No can do. The dentist retired after his office was destroyed during a hurricane a few years back."

"We've suffered a long time wondering what happened to Trinity." Hope was about to ask where this girl had been found when a strong wind blew and she fell into Nic. She breathed in that scent of sandalwood, cedarwood and ginger. He smelled like yesterday. Like the I-love-you, you-love-me days. "You still wearing Prada?"

"You know it," he answered, then his brows furrowed as he stepped back, looked heavenward. "The wind is picking up. Meteorologist said we're in for a thunderstorm tonight. You better get back to the beach house and hunker down for a bit."

Hurricane Lola was still just sitting in the Caribbean getting stronger but not moving. However, the clouds were getting full and dark—a storm was surely coming. "I've got to go." She hopped in the car and told Crystal to put on her seat belt. They sped out of the parking lot and made their way back to the house.

Chapter 13

I can't come to your office right now. I've got too much going on. And if you hadn't noticed, Thanksgiving is in two days." Ruby stood in the kitchen holding the landline and looked at the receiver. She couldn't believe what she was hearing.

"We do understand that the holidays are upon us, but Dr. Stein wants to get you scheduled for surgery as soon as possible. This shouldn't be put off."

Putting a hand to her head, Ruby rubbed her temple. "I've got too much on my mind. I can't think about this right now."

The woman spoke in a calm voice. "Is there someone else I can speak to who might be able to help make arrangements for you?"

"I'm not incapacitated. I can handle my own affairs. I don't need you spilling the beans to my family." Ruby hung up the phone and went back to stirring her pot of collard greens.

"Who was that?" Faith asked as she entered the house holding a piece of paper.

"Just never you mind who I talk to on the phone I pay the bill for." Ruby reached out for the paper. "What's the damage? How much does this swindler want?" The contractor Faith called had finally arrived to give them an estimate.

"I think this contractor knows what he's talking about, Mama.

But even so, it's going to cost about seventy-five thousand to fix this place up."

"Slick Rick said it would only cost sixty thousand. How'd we get all the way up to seventy-five?" Ruby put her spoon down and closed the lid on her greens. Rick might not have stolen her money as she told her girls, but he had given her a better estimate than this swindler.

Faith pointed upward. "The roof needs to be replaced."

"What?" Ruby snatched the estimate out of Faith's hand and looked it over. "I don't have that kind of money."

The front door opened. Hope and Crystal came in the house. Hope carried a case of water while Crystal carried a small bag. Crystal was eating a Snickers bar while talking on her cell phone. Hope put the water down in the kitchen, then popped some M&M'S in her mouth. "I know y'all not eating all that candy when I'm fixing dinner."

With a mouthful of M&M'S, Hope said, "I'm not full. I'm ready to eat right now. What you cooking up in here?"

Crystal followed Hope into the kitchen.

Faith took the estimate away from Ruby and handed it to Hope. "This is how much the contractor wants in order to make all the repairs and updates on the house."

Hope's eyes bulged. She brought the paper closer to her face. "We don't have seventy-five thousand dollars."

"Mama only gave that contractor half of the money, so she still should have thirty thousand." Faith turned to Ruby. "Right, Mama?"

Ruby averted her eyes. "Right."

Faith placed the paper on the table. "But we need to figure out how we're going to come up with the rest of this money. Because if we want to get this work done on the house, the contractor will have to be paid."

"Oh, Mama. What are we going to do?" Hope flopped into a chair at the kitchen table.

Faith glanced over at Crystal. "Who are you on the phone with, and who told you to take that phone out of my purse?" Faith held her hand out for the phone.

"No, Mom. I'm on the phone with Daddy." Crystal turned away from Faith and left the room.

"You heard me, Crystal. I want that phone back."

"Oh, leave the child alone. Just because you don't want to talk to your husband doesn't mean she doesn't want to talk to him," Ruby said.

Faith huffed at that, crossed her arms over her chest. "What makes you think I don't want to talk to Chris?"

"Chile, I'm old, but I'm not stupid." Ruby shook her pork chops in a brown paper bag that had flour and her seasonings in it. She then started placing the chops in the frying pan. "You haven't called that man once since you've been here, and the one time you did answer his call, you took the phone outside so you could yell at him."

"You want to talk about it, sis?" Hope asked.

But Faith snapped, "No, I don't want to talk about it. Just like you and Mama didn't feel the need to tell me what was going on with y'all, I feel like keeping my business to myself too."

Ruby waved a hand at Faith. "Have it your way, but when that man gets here, your business is going to be on full display."

Faith swung around to her mother. "What do you mean? Chris isn't coming here."

Ruby harrumphed. "You might want to ask Crystal about that because she told me he was on his way here to get her."

"Crystal . . . Crystal," Faith yelled for her daughter as she rushed out of the kitchen, heading toward Trinity's room.

Ruby laughed as she winked at Hope. "That girl thinks she knows so much, but it looks like Crystal done pulled one over on her."

"Stop laughing, Mama. Faith is not happy about this."

With a dismissive wave, Ruby said, "I'm not thinking 'bout Faith.

She's too uptight. Maybe Chris coming here is the thing she needs to loosen her up."

"Do you really think she and Chris are having problems?"

"Like I know my name." Ruby turned and looked pointedly at Hope. "Just like I know something is going on with you. But I figure you girls will talk to me when you're ready."

After Hope stormed out of the house that awful summer day, she had only come back once, and that was when Trinity went missing. She stayed a few days to help with the search, then she was out of here. Ruby knew that Hope wasn't ready to talk to her at that time, and with Trinity missing, she hadn't been ready either, so she let it go.

But finally, after about two years of calling and checking on her, Hope had been ready to talk and to forgive her. Hope had told her that as far as she was concerned, Ruby was still her mother, but Ruby knew the matter wasn't fixed because Hope had refused to come back home after the incident with her birth mother.

"Maybe the thing I have on my mind is the fact that you called us out here, and Hurricane Lola is about to roll up in here," Hope said.

Her family was good about keeping secrets. Ruby wasn't proud of it, but she was the one who taught her children how to keep secrets—just like her mother taught her.

She still hadn't told Hope the whole truth about her birth mother. She'd have to do it soon, whether she wanted to or not. "You're worried about something, Hope, and it sure ain't no category 3 hurricane that from the last reports is turning back toward Charleston."

"If you think it's going to turn, then why did we do all of this work around the house?"

"Better safe than sorry." Ruby flipped the pork chops.

"You used to say better prayed up than stirred up. What happened to that?"

Ruby leaned against the wall next to the stove. With a sigh and a twist of her lip, she said, "Got burned too many times, I guess."

—

"Why are you here, Chris?" Faith stood on the front porch, arms crossed, tapping her foot, waiting for an answer. The sky was full of dark clouds. Fat drops of rain were pelting the house and the ground.

"My family is here. Bad weather is on the way. Since it didn't seem like you were coming home, I figured I'd come down here and make sure y'all were safe."

Chris' low-cut wavy black hair blended well with that honey skin tone and those beautiful light-brown eyes. He had his hands in the pockets of his stonewashed jeans, which he had paired with a white long sleeve shirt. Chris had left three buttons of his shirt open, revealing the cut of his pecs. Faith had once been dazzled by every splendid inch of him. But no more.

"We're safe, so you can go back home and tend to your girlfriend."

"What girlfriend are you talking about?" Chris' eyebrows furrowed as his eyes filled with hurt. "I've never cheated on you, and you know it."

"Ha!" Faith laughed. "You should tell Facebook that because your girlfriend sent me a picture of you and her all hugged up."

Chris pulled his hands out of his pockets and flailed them. "What picture? What woman? Show it to me because I don't know what you're talking about."

"A half-truth is a whole lie, Chris. You can't tell me you don't know who this woman is. I don't believe it."

He reached for her. "Look, Faith—"

The wind kicked up. And Faith looked out at the sea. They couldn't stay out here. Lightning would be striking in the sky soon. But she didn't want Chris coming in the house pretending that he was some good guy here to see about his family when he couldn't care less about her.

The front door swung open, and Ruby stood there with her lips tight, glaring at her. "Girl, if you don't let this man in the house, I'm gon' take a branch off that there tree"—she pointed at the tree in the front yard—"and give you the whupping you should have gotten years ago."

Faith looked at the Sabal Palmetto tree her mom pointed at and wondered how her mother thought she was going to climb all the way up that tree to get one of the palm leaves off. But knowing Ruby Reynolds, she would try.

Begrudgingly, she said, "Come on. I'm sure your daughter can't wait to see you."

"I wish her mother felt the same way," he whispered against the back of her ear as they stepped inside the house.

Faith wasn't in the mood to be played for a fool. She swung around, resting a hand on her hip. "I don't have any more to give to you, Chris. You've taken everything, and now I just want out."

"Ah, there you go with that again. What's mine is yours, but what's yours is just yours. Is that the way it works?"

Faith's head bounced up and down, up and down, like a basketball. "If I worked for it, then it's mine, point-blank and period."

"How about when I cashed in my 401(k) to help you start your design business? You didn't seem to mind sharing money then."

Okay, he did help her out when she started her business, but that didn't give him automatic access to her earnings. Eye roll. "Oh, please tell me about how you helped me with my business again."

"Stop it! Stop it!" Crystal bounded out of her room, yelling at her parents. "Can't y'all do anything besides argue all the time?"

"Crystal, honey, I'm sorry." Chris reached for his daughter.

But Crystal backed away. "You were supposed to come here and fix things, not keep arguing with her." Crystal ran toward the back door. "I'm getting out of here."

"No, wait, Crystal. You can't go out there. It's starting to rain."

Faith took off after her child, but Crystal was already down the back stairs and running toward the beach.

Faith tried to catch her, but the girl was fast. She felt rain droplets. This couldn't be happening. What had she done? Dear God, why did she keep messing things up?

"It's raining, Trinity. Come back," Faith yelled and then realized that she wasn't watching Trinity run down the beach. She was watching her daughter—her only child.

"Nooo," Faith screamed and screamed and screamed as she went into full-blown panic mode. Chris wrapped his arms around her.

"It's okay, Faith. Calm down." Chris tightened his hold on her.

"I have to get her and bring her back." Faith reached out as if she could grab Crystal and pull her back so she would be safe.

"I got her, sis." Hope ran past them as she took off after Crystal.

From the back porch, her mother yelled down to them, "Y'all get back in here. You don't want to get struck by lightning."

Chris yelled, "Crystal, quit playing! It's not safe out here."

It was always like this, Faith thought as she watched Hope round the corner, chasing after Crystal. First the wind came, then the rain, then the fear. Fear was everywhere, especially when little girls left home and never returned.

Chapter 14

November 2004

"Come out of that bathroom, Trinity. I know you're in there throwing up again," Faith said, banging on the bathroom door.

The toilet flushed, then Trinity opened the bathroom door while wiping her mouth. "Leave me alone, Faith. I'm not feeling good."

"You weren't feeling good last week or the week before that. Do you expect me to believe you've had the flu for three weeks straight?"

"I never said I had the flu. I said I don't feel well." Trinity headed to her bedroom, holding her stomach.

Faith stood in her way. "I'm telling Mama that you're pregnant. I knew you were up to no good with that guy you keep talking to on Myspace."

Trinity laughed. "I'm not pregnant, and you're not my mother, so back off."

"I may not be your mother, but since your mother is always at work, somebody has to look after you."

"Mama is working hard because you're going off to that fancy New York college soon. She's trying to make money to help you, but you keep ragging on her about how much she works."

"Only because somebody needs to be looking after you. What are you going to do when I leave for school?"

"I'm sure I'll be just fine, Faith. I'll have to be since you don't care." Trinity went into her room, shut the door and turned on her radio. "Pretty Young Thing" by Michael Jackson was playing.

Faith could hear Trinity dancing to Michael Jackson's oldie but goodie like it meant something to her. Was someone whispering in her ear, telling her she was a pretty young thing?

Trinity was always in her room. Always locking the door and getting on that computer. Faith had chased one predator away from her sister who had asked if he could come to the house to meet her. She threatened him with the police, and that was the end of him. But only God knew who else Trinity found on that computer to talk to. Faith decided that she was telling their mother about Trinity and all her trips to the bathroom after meals as soon as she got home.

But when Mama came home that night, she was all frantic. "Girl, why haven't you answered the phone? I've been calling all afternoon."

"I didn't hear the phone ring." But then Faith remembered that Trinity had one of the house phones in her room. "Trinity has been in her room. She's probably been on the phone."

Ruby banged on Trinity's door. "Get out here this instant."

Trinity opened her door. "Mama, Faith is lying on me. I didn't do anything."

"I don't know what you're talking about." Ruby shook her head. "A hurricane is coming. We have to prepare the house, so come outside and help me get these sandbags ready and put these boards on the windows."

"But I had plans for this weekend," Trinity said, sulking.

"Well, I guess a little hurricane done changed your plans." Ruby motioned for the girls to follow her.

Trinity stuck her tongue out at Faith as she walked past.

Faith shoved her in the back. "Who were you on the phone with all afternoon?"

"None of your business, that's who."

"Mom," Faith called out to her mother. Somebody needed to get Trinity straight because she wasn't listening anymore.

"Faith, I don't have time for none of your tattletaling right now. A storm is coming." Ruby headed out the back door.

Faith followed, mumbling, "If you didn't work so much, I wouldn't have so much to tell."

"I heard your little sassy mouth, Faith. Just get out here and help me get these boards on these windows."

Faith rolled her eyes.

Ruby leaned to the side, hands on hips. "Girl, don't you know I will snap your neck, then the only person you'll be rolling your eyes at is the undertaker."

Kicking at the rocks on the ground as she made her way to the pile of plywood in the back, Faith said, "I wasn't trying to be sassy, but you do work too much."

"And you eat too much," Ruby told her while handing sandbags to Trinity.

Faith understood that her mother was trying to say that she had to work to provide for them. She hated that her mother worked so hard, but after her dad's death, things changed—and not for the better. Hope was gone and refusing to talk to Mama or come back to the house, and now Trinity was being secretive about everything.

"Get your mind in the game." Ruby snapped her fingers in front of Faith's face.

Faith blinked. She pulled the tarp off the plywood, and she and Ruby started screwing the boards over the outside windows just as Hope and her dad used to do.

Two days later, the hurricane still had not roared into town. The wind, however, had picked up, and Faith felt the drizzle of rain. Her mother had gone to help board up the insurance company where she was a manager, leaving Faith at home to deal with Trinity's antics.

Faith heard her sister on the phone, making plans to meet up with someone. "You know you can't go anywhere."

Trinity rolled her eyes as she went to the bathroom. Faith heard her in there throwing up again. She had forgotten to tell her mom about that, but she was going to make sure she spilled those beans the minute her mother got back home. "I hear you in there."

"Mind your own business," Trinity yelled back at her.

Then Faith heard the shower turn on. When Trinity came out of the bathroom, she had changed her clothes. Trinity was wearing her favorite sweater with a pair of skinny jeans. "I hope you don't think you're about to go anywhere with this storm brewing out there."

Trinity gave Faith the hand as she walked past Faith and went into her room.

Before Trinity could close the door, Faith stepped inside.

Trinity sat down on her canopy bed. Her Air Force 1s were on her pink fuzzy rug. She moved the shoes by her feet and started putting them on.

"Something is going on with you, Trinity. You and I used to be so close, but now you act like I'm your enemy or something."

While pushing her foot in her gym shoe, Trinity glanced up at her sister. "You're just too nosy, and you still think I'm a kid, but I'm not."

Leaning against the doorjamb, Faith nodded. "I know you're growing up, but you're still thinking like a stupid little kid."

"See?" Trinity pointed at her. "That's what I mean. You still think I'm a kid."

"I don't understand what's going on with you."

"That's because you never bother to listen. You just tell me what I should think about this or that. Nobody bothered to ask what

I thought about Hope leaving. Nobody asked what I thought about you making all these plans to go off to college next year."

"You never said you had a problem with me going away to school."

Lacing up her shoes, Trinity said, "I didn't until you picked New York. Why you got to go so far away? Just like how Hope went to Howard University and then decided she no longer wanted to be in our small town anymore. She barely even has time to talk to us."

"New York School of Interior Design is a really good school for my career choice, Trinity. But just because I'm going to New York doesn't mean that I'm never coming back home."

"It's whatever." Trinity stood and attempted to walk out of her room, but Faith grabbed hold of her shoulders.

There was a howling sound, then the house shook.

"Did you hear that wind? You have no business being outside."

Trinity pushed Faith's hands from her shoulders. "Stop being so overprotective. We have at least another day before that storm rolls in."

"Mama is going to skin you alive if you walk out that door."

Rolling her eyes, Trinity said, "I'll be back before Mama gets home, so she won't know a thing unless you go running your mouth like you always do, Miss Design School Girl."

Faith was not going to argue with Trinity about the college she chose. Hope had been allowed to go to the college of her choice, and Faith was going to do likewise. They all had to grow up and make the right decisions if they wanted something out of life. "You are a talented artist, just like Mama. One day, you'll leave for college or move somewhere that your art can get noticed."

Trinity shook her head. "I'm not like you and Hope. I'm never leaving Mama alone to take care of this big old beach house by herself. You and Hope are selfish. Y'all don't care about anyone but yourselves."

For months, she had tried to get Trinity to snap out of whatever teenage-drama thing she was dealing with, but all she kept getting was hate and accusations from her sister. Faith was tired of the struggle, so if Trinity wanted to run the streets during a hurricane, then she was just going to stand back and let her. With a wave of her hand toward the door, Faith said, "Have at it, boo."

Rushing to the back door, Trinity opened it, then hesitated a moment, looking back at Faith. "I'm sorry I've been so grouchy lately, sis. When I get back, maybe we can play a board game or something."

Sighing, Faith said, "Okay, Trinity. Just be safe, and hurry back."

"Don't worry. I'll be right back." Trinity blew a kiss at her, then closed the back door as she stepped out.

Another howling wind blew, and Faith's eyes darted this way and that as the house swayed a bit. What was she thinking? There is no way to be safe out on the beach during a hurricane. She ran to the door, opened it and stood out on the back patio yelling, "Trinity, wait! No. Come back."

Trinity waved to her, but kept running down the beach.

Faith didn't know who Trinity had gotten herself involved with that would cause her to make such a dumb decision, but she got a sinking feeling in her gut that this wouldn't end well.

Chapter 15

Present Day

Breathing hard, Hope started panting. The rain was spitting in her face. Her knees buckled as she caught up to Crystal. She had run the 200-meter in a little over twenty seconds and received a partial track scholarship, placing all four years that she was on her track team in college. But she hadn't run a race since the summer of 2004.

"Let me go." Crystal squirmed beneath her as Hope fell on top of her, and they both went tumbling into the sand.

Hope took a long, hard breath, then another one and another one. "I can't let you go." She breathed in the sea air mixed with wind and rain again. "It's dangerous for you to be out here."

"I don't want to be around them." Crystal started crying. "All they do is fight. I don't even know why they brought me into this world if they don't like each other."

Hope slid off Crystal's back. They sat on the sand next to each other. "Oh, hon. Sometimes the things grown-ups do don't make a lot of sense. But I can promise you that they will never regret having you."

Crystal was sitting next to her looking lost. Hope couldn't turn away . . . She couldn't unsee the blinking red light in front of her. Something was going on with her niece. Crystal needed help before things got worse, and if her parents didn't stop arguing with each other and pay attention, then this family could possibly suffer another loss.

Crystal wrapped her arms around her legs and rested her chin on her knees. "They act like they regret it, like if it weren't for me, they'd already be divorced."

"Have you talked to them about how you feel?"

Crystal twisted her lips. "My mom gives orders—she doesn't listen—and she's always at work. So when would I talk to her?"

Looking out at the sea, Hope remembered how Faith had lost her focus for a while after Trinity went missing. "I think your mom regrets dropping out of college. She probably works so hard because she's trying to prove that she's just as good as the interior designers who stayed in school and got their degrees."

Crystal's lip quivered as tears ran down her face. "Doesn't that prove my point? Because she quit design school after she met my dad, s-so, she regrets having me."

Lightning cracked the sky. Hope reached over and pulled Crystal into her arms. The child cried so hard, it felt like the storm making its way to the shore would be nothing compared to the storm that was raging inside of her niece. "Let it out, hon. Just let it out."

"W-why doesn't my mom want me, Auntie Hope? W-why?"

As the rain beat down on their heads, Hope was concerned about this little girl who was asking the same question Hope had asked herself ever since she discovered that Ruby was not her biological mother. Why hadn't the woman who had given birth to her wanted her as much as Ruby had?

Hope stood and then pulled Crystal up. She wiped the tears from her niece's face. "The one thing I'm not going to do is let you torture yourself wondering things that no child should have to wonder about."

"But—"

Hope lifted a hand. "No buts. We're going back to the beach house to get the answers you need. My sister is going to make time for you today. I can promise you that."

They rushed back to the house. The rain was pelting them, and as the sun went down, darkness was descending on the beach. But Hope would take a thunderstorm over a hurricane any day of her life. "Ah, man. We really need to get in the house. We're getting drenched."

Crystal lowered her head and rubbed her eyes. Hope put a firm grip onto Crystal's arm as the wind moved them backward a few steps.

"I'm scared," Crystal admitted as she clung to Hope.

"I got you, girl. Remember, I grew up on this beach, so I know a thing or two about stormy weather."

"Look at the water." Crystal pointed toward the sea.

The water was a little choppy, but nothing that gave Hope any cause for alarm. Just another stormy day. "I've seen worse," Hope told her as they made their way through the wet sand. They rounded the corner, placing them back on the side of the beach where her mom's house was. "Just remember that storms don't last. They make a big fuss, but they blow over, then when the sun comes back out, every-thing is peaceful again. If it doesn't leave too much damage, you'll forget all about it."

"What if it causes damage?" Crystal asked as they saw Faith and Chris running toward them.

"Go to your parents." Hope nudged her forward.

Crystal took off running toward her parents, leaving Hope to think about all the storms in her life that had caused damage. The unforgettable ones—the ones that stick and stay no matter how she tried to shake them. She used to pray about it because at one time in her life, Hope believed that God was on her side and that He would never leave or forsake her.

Pastor O'Dell used to preach about a God who could do any-thing. A God who could calm the waves. Hope wasn't so sure anymore.

Crystal reunited with her parents. They hugged her. Hope saw Faith kiss Crystal on the forehead and whisper something in her ear. That was a good start, but Faith would need to do much more.

As Hope got closer to the house, thunder cracked the sky as more rain burst through the clouds and drenched her Afro so bad that it swept across her face. But as she went back inside the house and watched Crystal retreat to her room, she was more concerned about the storm brewing inside the house than anything that was happening outside.

"Faith and Chris, can I speak with y'all in the kitchen, please?" Hope grabbed a towel and wrapped it around her hair as she waited for them to join her.

Faith's head hung low, and she had her arms crossed as she entered the kitchen. Chris put a hand at the small of her back, and Faith stepped away from him.

Sighing, Hope whispered, "I don't know what's going on between the two of you, but Crystal thinks that y'all don't want her."

"What?" Chris' eyes widened like what Hope said was news to him. "Crystal knows how much I love her. I'd give my life for my child."

Hope nodded. "I misspoke. Crystal thinks Faith doesn't want her." Hope looked at her sister and raised her hands, backed up a bit. "And before you tell me that I need to mind my own business—"

Faith shook her head. "I wasn't going to say that." Faith hugged Hope. "I've been terrible to you since you arrived. I panicked out there, but you took control and brought my daughter back. I just want to say thank you. I was terrified for her being out there in the storm."

A lump caught in Hope's throat at her sister's appreciation. Things had once been so good between them. So many things had gotten in the way of their sisterhood. Hope's mind traveled back in time to a Sunday morning when Pastor O'Dell was preaching like his message had been sent down from heaven and he had to tell everyone that "love heals all wounds."

It seemed to Hope that the more she stayed away from the church, the harder it became for her to mend the relationship with her sister. She wanted their sisterhood back, and she wanted Faith to repair her relationship with Crystal, but Hope was starting to believe that it would take an act of God to get them where they belonged.

"Let me ask you something: Do you both still attend that church in Georgia?"

Faith and Chris both nodded.

"Do you still believe that God can do anything?"

"I do," Chris said.

"I want to believe it. It's what we were taught." Faith shrugged.

Chris side-eyed his wife, looking like he couldn't understand why she struggled to believe. But Chris hadn't weathered the storms that had left Hope and Faith questioning everything they knew about a loving God. If God truly cared about the things that concerned them, then why so much pain?

Hope doubted she would receive answers to any of her questions tonight. But she wasn't concerned about herself right now, she was concerned for Crystal. She turned to Chris. "We need to lean on your faith tonight. Can you pray for Crystal? Her poor little heart is breaking. I don't know what she's dealing with, but she needs both of you."

Chris put an arm around Faith. "Of course we will." He turned to his wife. "Would you join hands with me so we can pray right now?"

They all joined hands, then bowed their heads. Chris prayed.

After the prayer, Hope felt like Faith needed some private time with her family, so she went into her room and changed out of her wet clothes. After that, she checked her cell phone. She had two missed calls. The first was from Nic. She knew what he wanted but didn't have the guts to tell him that taking that test might confirm all of her fears about Henry Reynolds not being her biological dad. How could she cope with knowing that she was not a true member of the Reynolds family after all?

The second call was from Spencer. Hope had no desire to hear his voice. She knew what he wanted, so she opened her laptop and emailed him the report she had been working on before she caught him with his new girlfriend.

In her email she noted: *Spencer, there are a few inconsistencies in this report. I still need the numbers from the last two events you hosted to complete the report. If you'd like to send them to me, I can input the numbers into the report, or you can just add the information into the report yourself.*

She hit Send and closed her computer. She was determined not to give Spencer another thought. He was her past. He was a mistake. There was nothing between them but business and that's the way it would remain. She leaned back in her chair and listened to the rain beat down on the house. She was thankful that it was just a thunderstorm. Because she had experienced much worse.

Chapter 16

Ruby hissed through her teeth as a sharp pain shot through her like a bullet ricocheting from her back to her ribs and then landing in the middle of her chest. She wrapped her arms around her chest as if shielding herself from the pain within. Then another pain attacked her body. This one made her get up and search out the Tylenol.

Bent over from the pain still wreaking havoc in her body, she made her way to the kitchen, grabbed a cup out of the cabinet and filled it with tap water, then she went into the bathroom, closed the door and locked it. Ruby opened the medicine cabinet above her sink and clutched the Tylenol as if it was a life preserver.

Opening the container, she popped two of the pills in her mouth, but then she thought about the last time she had a pain like this and took two pills. It took forever for the pain to go away. So she popped a third pill and then drank some water.

Ruby stared at her reflection in the mirror. She had weathered many storms, but she didn't know how much more her seventy-year-old bones could take.

Taking her shirt off, Ruby raised her right arm and felt around the armpit and at the top of her breast. The lump had gotten bigger. She would have to check herself into the hospital as her doctor requested.

Ruby shook her fist to the heavens as she exhaled her disgust. "Always something."

She couldn't just lie up here and die without setting things right with Hope. She definitely couldn't leave Faith stuck with all those feelings of guilt about her baby sister. And it seemed to Ruby that Crystal was dealing with something as well. No, Ruby wasn't ready for them to shovel dirt on her casket and wax poetic about the life she had lived . . . No, not just yet.

Ruby used to believe that the God of Isaac, Jacob and Joseph could do anything but fail, but that was before He failed to come through for her over and over. She had served God for many years . . . had thought she'd made Him her everything, but now as she stood in need of God and she couldn't muster up enough faith to pray about her situation, she looked in the mirror and told herself the truth.

"You don't believe anymore." The cruelest thing this world had ever done was to steal away her ability to believe . . . to trust.

Honestly, if she did pray, she'd probably lift her hands and say, "God, I really need You to show up and take care of business in this here life of mine."

Instead of following through on her thoughts and actually taking her problems to the Lord, Ruby put her arm back in her sleeve, opened the bathroom door and then lay back down in her bed to wait for morning when the rain would stop.

It was still raining outside. Faith started thinking about the past. She realized that some of the things she noticed about Trinity back in the day, she now saw in Crystal. Like those red eyes . . .

Both Trinity and Crystal had lost weight after putting on a few pounds during the summer. Faith picked up her cell phone and googled reasons for throwing up other than being pregnant.

She was shocked at what she read and didn't know why she hadn't put it together sooner. After doing her research, Faith decided it was time to talk to Crystal.

She had tired of the fight and let Trinity go. She'd have to live with what she did that day. But if nothing else, she had learned that no matter how hard the fight is, never give up, so she was strapping on her boxing gloves and getting ready to go as many rounds as it would take to figure out what was going on with her daughter.

Faith, Chris and Crystal were sitting in the living room. Crystal was on the floor next to the fireplace reading a book. Faith was about to tell Chris that it was time to talk to Crystal, but his phone rang.

Chris was seated in the reclining chair, but after answering the phone, he got up and headed toward the kitchen with the phone against his ear. Smile on his face.

Faith took notice. Wondering why he needed privacy for a phone call. And why was he grinning like that? She didn't want to care, but it hurt to think that she had invested fifteen years in a man who was running around on her. She closed her eyes to blot out the pain of feeling like yet another thing had gone wrong in her life.

"Do you want to come in my room so we can talk?" Faith asked as she stood next to Crystal.

Crystal lowered the book she was reading and looked up at her mother. "Are we going to talk, or are you going to yell at me?"

"I want to talk, but if you get disrespectful, I can't promise that I won't yell." She reached out her hand to help Crystal off the floor. "So why don't we both try to control ourselves?"

"I'll try if you'll try," Crystal said.

Chris came back into the living room. Crystal turned to her father. "Are you coming with us?"

"Where are you going?" he asked, forehead wrinkled as he turned to Faith.

"Mom wants to talk in her room."

"That's up to your mom." He kept staring at Faith.

He put the ball in her court, effectively making her Penny's mom on *Good Times* if she said no. It wasn't like Chris had ever been helpful when it came to disciplining Crystal. He was the yes-yes-yes dad who gave Crystal everything she wanted and left Faith looking like Nancy Reagan putting together a Just Say No campaign. "Sure, he can come."

Chris followed them to Faith's room. Faith and Crystal sat on her bed while Chris put his hands in his pants pockets and leaned against the wall.

Taking a deep breath, Faith prayed that she wouldn't mess this up. Crystal wasn't happy . . . she was acting out and, according to Hope, throwing up. And the fact that Faith had only noticed that Crystal had a bad attitude made her feel like turning herself into children's services and requesting parenting classes.

"First, I want you to know that I'm so glad you came to the beach house with me because I had no idea that you were struggling, but I think I know what's going on, and I want to help you."

"Struggling? What is she struggling with?" Chris' eyes darted from Faith to Crystal.

Chris spent more time with Crystal, so she was surprised that he hadn't noticed what Crystal had been up to. "She's been making herself throw up."

Crystal crisscrossed her arms around her chest. Defiant.

Chris' head whiplashed in Crystal's direction. "You've been throwing up again?"

"So you did notice?" Sad to say, but Faith liked it better when she thought Chris was as unobservant as she.

"I walked in on her throwing up last week. She told me that the school was serving old food." Chris narrowed his eyes as he continued to stare at Crystal. "So what's going on, hon? Are you still throwing up?"

Crystal's eyes fluttered in annoyance. "It's not my fault if I haven't been feeling well."

"If you're constantly throwing up and you don't feel well, then we need to make you a doctor's appointment," Chris told her.

Back when Faith had caught Trinity going to the bathroom after meals and throwing up, she had accused her sister of being pregnant. The way Trinity had laughed in her face made Faith wonder if she had been way off base. She had also accused Crystal of being pregnant, but she no longer thought that was the case.

"I thought we came in here so we could talk about you and Daddy. Not about whether I'm sick or not . . . because I'm not." She rolled her eyes as if she was fed up with having to explain that to people.

"Your mom and I will discuss with you what's going on with us after she and I sit down and talk," Chris said.

"What do you need to discuss?" Crystal got off the bed and rushed over to her dad. "You're getting a divorce, aren't you?"

Faith scooted to the edge of the bed. Her feet touched the floor as her hands flopped in her lap. "This is not about me and your daddy. Crystal, you have a problem. I know I haven't been there for you lately, but I'm here now, and I want to help you, baby."

Swinging back around, throwing daggers of hate in her mother's direction, Crystal said, "You don't care about me. All you care about is your job and being angry at Daddy all the time."

Faith lifted her eyes heavenward. She, Chris and Crystal were faithful churchgoers, but somewhere along the line, Faith had stopped spending personal time with God. Stopped allowing Him to make her better, even as she recognized the growing animosity within her.

Things began to change for Faith right around the time Crystal turned eleven and started looking so much like Trinity that Crystal became a daily reminder of how Faith had allowed her sister to go out and battle a storm.

Lightning flashed and thunder roared like God Himself was

calling her out for all the treacherous things she'd done in her life. Faith jumped.

Taking deep breaths, Faith tried to steady her heart, but then she realized that her heart wasn't ready to be calmed because it still hurt for Crystal and for Trinity. Tears rolled down her face. "I'm sorry, baby. I'm so sorry. I'm probably the reason you have an eating disorder."

Crystal stomped her foot. "I don't have an eating disorder." She ran out of the room.

"An eating disorder?" Chris questioned Faith.

She nodded. She wanted to get up and go after Crystal, but her body felt drained, like she had taken sleeping pills and was about to be out for the count. "I think she has some type of purging disorder, just like Trinity."

"Your sister purged? You never told me that."

"Honestly, I didn't realize it myself until this week." She pointed toward the living room. "Can you go talk to her? She listens to you. I think I need to spend some time in prayer because I honestly don't know what to do for her."

"We'll do it together, Faith." When she didn't respond, he said, "I want to do this together. Please don't shut me out." Chris walked out of the room.

Faith got on her knees. Things in her life were like ocean waves crashing into each other. Moving this way and that, unsure of what to do. Just making moves . . . destructive moves. "Lord, I don't know what to do anymore. I've been trying to ignore that my daughter looks so much like Trinity. But history is trying to repeat itself, and I can't lose Crystal the way I lost Trinity. Please lead me and guide me. Show me how to help my child."

Faith leaned her forehead against the mattress and cried. She prayed that God was listening because she didn't have strength to fight anymore. This wasn't just her life that was falling apart; it was her daughter's as well.

The similarities between Crystal and Trinity were so stark and devastating that it threw Faith off her game. She hadn't recognized that the redness in Crystal's eyes was just like the redness she had witnessed all those years ago in her sister's eyes. The sudden weight loss between the summer and fall that occurred for both Crystal and Trinity at the age of fourteen. It was like her sister was sending her subliminal messages from the great beyond, trying to warn her of even greater trouble that Crystal would soon get herself into if she didn't receive help soon.

"God, I need You!" was her earnest plea.

The door inched open. Faith heard the *creak-creak* of the door, which in a way sounded like the cracking of her heart. She turned and saw Hope standing in the doorway.

"Can I come in, sis?"

Hope's face was filled with so much pain, like she hurt just because Faith was hurting. She got off the floor and went to her sister. The two hugged, and it felt to Faith like coming home. Like when she was a little girl and had been out riding on her scooter and skinned her knee. Faith boo-hooed like the world was coming to an end, but Hope had picked her up and made her feel like everything would soon be okay. "I don't know how to fix this, Hope. I just don't."

The two sat down on the bed. Faith leaned her head on Hope's shoulder. "Well, I heard you in here praying, so we're going to trust God to fix the problem. Whatever it is. Isn't that what Mama used to tell us?"

"I-I kn-know. I've b-been praying." Faith wiped her dripping nose with her hand and then looked at it with disgust.

"You need some tissue. I'll be right back." Hope left the room but came back quickly with a box of tissue.

Faith wiped her face with the tissue and then wiped off her hand. "Thank you."

"What good is having a sister if I can't get you some tissue to wipe the snot from your hands?"

In spite of the turmoil that was raging inside of her, Faith laughed. Lifting the balled-up tissue, she said, "It's good to have a sister again."

Hope's face lit up like a sudden warmth had come over her. "You've always had me as a sister. I've never stopped loving you, so don't think like that."

At that moment sitting next to Hope in her darkest hour, Faith felt like telling her sister the truth. "I've had you, but you haven't had me as a sister for many years, and I'm sorry about that. I can be so stubborn at times."

Hope lifted a hand, halting her sister's apology. "We can talk about your bullheadedness another time. Right now, I want to know why you're in here crying like this. What's wrong?"

"What's right?" Faith wanted to know. She took a deep breath. "I was so mean to you when you told me about Crystal throwing up. Truth is, I hadn't been paying attention."

"Crystal mentioned that you've been working a lot."

"I've been running a lot, that's what I've been doing." Faith leaned her head against the palm of her forehead and exhaled. "Do you want to hear my truth, big sis?"

"Of course I do. If you're ready to tell it, I'm here for it." Hope adjusted herself on the bed until her back was against the wall.

"Mama hasn't seen Crystal in the last three years because I noticed the same thing you noticed the minute you laid eyes on her."

"That she looks so much like Trinity." Hope then asked, "You didn't think Mama could handle seeing her?"

Faith pulled a few tissues out of the box and dotted at her eyes. "At first, I told myself that I was trying to spare Mama from having to relive all of that trauma we dealt with when Trinity went missing, but I started avoiding my own daughter because I haven't processed my own trauma."

"Losing Trinity was hard for all of us, Faith. You saw those flyers

Mama has in Trinity's bedroom. She's still passing those things out even to this very day."

"I know, but I have neglected my own child because I can't deal with the painful memories." Agony pressed down on her like a vise grip to her heart. How had she let this happen? "And now Crystal is dealing with the same thing Trinity was before that awful storm."

Hope's eyes shifted up, down, to the side. "What was Trinity dealing with? You never told me about anything."

"That's because just like you assumed Crystal was pregnant, I thought the same thing about Trinity back then. But once she went missing, I didn't want to put that burden on Mama."

"So for once in your life you kept your mouth shut." Hope nudged her sister with her elbow.

"I guess I did." Faith kinda-sorta acknowledged a character flaw.

Hope snapped her finger as if a thought had just come to mind. "But wait a minute, sis. If Trinity was pregnant, maybe Mama is right to keep looking for her. Maybe she did run off with some guy to start a new life."

Faith shook her head. "I think I was wrong about that. None of us were really using Google for anything back then, so I didn't do the Google research we all do these days. Before talking to Crystal, I looked up reasons for throwing up and realized that both Trinity and Crystal fit in a type of purging disorder."

A beat passed and then Hope nodded. "I did wonder if Crystal was throwing up on purpose the first time I heard her doing it. It just didn't sound like an easy flow, if that makes sense."

"It makes perfect sense. I remember thinking the same thing about Trinity. It was like she went into the bathroom, and it took a minute before I would hear her throwing up. And you and I both know, if your stomach is upset, sometimes you can't even get to the bathroom before that stuff starts spilling over."

"I know, right?" Hope agreed. "But are you sure it's purging?"

"I'm not a doctor, so I can't be sure until I get her checked out."

Hope nodded. "Okay. So what are we going to do until then?"

"Honestly, sis, I don't know. All I can do is pray and let God lead me on this one."

"Keep praying." Hope stood and adjusted her shirt, then held out her hand to Faith. "The way I see it, we might not have been able to help Trinity, but we haven't lost Crystal yet, so we don't have time for guilt. Just love."

A tear trickled down Faith's face. She stood with her sister. She was ready to do battle with the demon that was trying to destroy her child, but was she ready to do battle with the one that put a wedge between her and Crystal?

Chapter 17

It was Wednesday, the day before Thanksgiving. The rain had stopped, and Faith was planning to head back to Atlanta so she could get Crystal an appointment with her doctor. Hope suggested that they take a look around the outside of the house to decide on the repairs that absolutely must be done in order to open the B&B, like Ruby wanted. They needed to start bringing in money to pay that loan down.

Chris and Crystal were sitting at the kitchen table playing a game of checkers while Ruby started pulling out all the ingredients needed for her Thanksgiving meal.

"You sure you don't want to stay for Thanksgiving?" Hope asked Faith as they stood on the back deck.

"I wish I could stay, but I talked to Crystal's doctor this morning. He might be able to fit her in on Friday morning, and I don't want to be on the road on Thanksgiving, so it's best to get going today."

Hope would love to spend more time with them, but Crystal's needs came first. "I understand."

Faith pointed toward the floor of the wood deck and then started writing in her notebook. "If we can do this deck ourselves, we could save about ten thousand off that estimate."

"Guests will love lounging out here and being able to see the ocean," Hope said.

"They won't love the condition of the deck. Broken-down lounge chairs and rotting wood." Faith kept writing in her notebook.

Hope looked down at the weathered deck that had once been the gathering spot for her and her sisters. The deck had been gray, but the paint was now only seen in a few spots. Boards were loose, and the wood on the railing was crumbling in certain areas. "Chris, can you come here?"

Faith stopped writing in her notebook. Lifted her head. "What are you calling Chris for?"

Hope looked at her like, *Duh*. "I know we need to save some money, because we'll probably have to make a few payments on the loan as we work on getting customers for the B&B, but I don't know the first thing about restoring a deck. Chris is a contractor."

"He might be a contractor, but he is headed back to Atlanta with his daughter."

"And you," Hope reminded her.

"I'm going for my daughter also." Faith rolled her eyes heavenward as Chris opened the back door and stepped onto the deck.

"What's up, sis?"

Hope directed his attention to the deck. "We're trying to save some money on all the renovations needed to turn this house into a bed-and-breakfast. This deck needs attention, and Faith thinks we can do it ourselves, but I want to know what you think."

Chris wiped his hands on his pants. Touched the cap of the railing, came away with a few splinters of wood. He then looked at the floor of the deck, lightly bounced. "It can be done, but it'll be a lot of work."

"Like what kind of work?" Hope seriously doubted that she was up for the job.

"Stop being a baby about it, Hope. Something has to come off that list." Faith shook her head.

But Hope wasn't feeling it. "I was talking to Chris." She turned back to him. "Go on. What do we need to do to restore this deck?"

Chris walked the length of the deck while ticking off a list of things to do. "The first thing it needs is a good cleaning. We could tighten some screws and replace some of the boards that have rotted out, then paint or stain it, then it will be like new."

"That sounds like a lot." Hope looked doubtful. "I'm thinking we need to leave the deck on the list and find something else we can do, like turning the attic into a bedroom for guests."

Faith threw up her hands. "Now you're trying to add more to the list?"

"We need extra rooms if we are going to make a serious go at creating a successful B&B."

Faith looked down the beach, an expression of longing on her face.

Hope turned to see what she was looking at. A family was playing volleyball. She, Faith and Trinity used to go out to the beach and play volleyball when they were younger. "You okay, sis?"

Faith shook her head. "Not really. Being at this beach house brings back so many memories." Faith bit her lip. Her voice broke. "I just wish things were different. That's all."

"Ditto, sis. Ditto."

Hope heard a car pulling up in the driveway. She went to the edge of the deck and leaned forward so she could see who had arrived. Nic turned off his car and got out. Hope held up a finger to Faith. "Hold that thought." She stepped off the deck and walked toward the front of the house.

Hope tried to wipe the grin from her face, which appeared whenever she was in close proximity to Nic Evans. "Hey. What brings you by?"

"A pretty lady I know hasn't returned my call, so I had to come over here and check on her."

Ahhh. He was concerned about her. That knowledge made her

wish she had called him back. "Sorry. I didn't want to be on the phone with the lightning."

"That's funny. You and I used to talk all night during storms when we were younger," Nic challenged.

"That's because neither of us had good enough sense to realize that we couldn't be on the phone."

"True." Nic nodded. "But seriously, I was concerned about you." Glancing out at the calm waters, Nic said, "I know it was just a thunderstorm, but I wanted to make sure you were okay."

"Thanks for checking on me." Hope began walking toward the beach. Nic followed her.

"So what are your plans, Hope? How long will you be in town?"

Shoving her hands in the front pockets of her jeans, she kicked at the wet sand. "I'm not sure. I need to check to see how things are going at work." She also needed to listen to Spencer's voice mail. That might give her a clue about how long she could stay.

"Will you be in town long enough to go out to dinner with me?"

Hope stopped walking, turned to Nic. Those gorgeous eyes of his and that sun-kissed skin didn't fight fair. She was always down for the count just by looking at him. She was going to try her best to keep her heart out of his grasp. "Are you sure you want to do that?"

"Why wouldn't I? Two old friends getting together for dinner . . . maybe take in a movie. What could be wrong with that?"

"Well, for one, we're not just old friends. You once asked me to marry you, and I thought you were serious about it back then."

Nic nodded. His face contorted a bit as if something about that memory caused him pain. "I was very serious."

"So I'll ask again. Are you sure you want to go back down that road, because it didn't end well for us? And let's be honest, I'm sure your mother is still a racist. And I'm not willing to deal with someone like that."

"So you're not even willing to try, even after all we meant to each other? We were supposed to build a life together, Hope. Then one day you suddenly wanted off the island and never wanted to return."

"And you always wanted to get away from here. I'm still surprised you returned."

Turning his face toward the water, Nic lifted his head heavenward. "I had my reasons."

Hope didn't get it. Nic could have gone anywhere, done anything, but he came back here without a wife or children. "Why didn't you ever get married?"

His shoulders fell forward. Heaving a sigh, he turned back to face her. "You know why."

She did. It was the same reason she wasn't married. They had experienced a once-in-a-lifetime love. Space and time had done nothing to diminish it. Hope had never found anyone to rub out the stain of heartache that leaving Nic had caused.

But she'd always thought that he had moved on—that he was off somewhere living his FBI dreams with a wife whose complexion matched his own, two kids and a dog. She thought he had forgotten all about her and the love they had. Because they were too different for their love to last—too round when the rest of the world was square.

"You were supposed to forget about me," she whispered, hoping that the slight breeze of the wind would carry those words away. Because the truth was, she could never—would never—forget about him. So her heart was glad to know that he hadn't forgotten about her.

His hands lifted and then fell to his sides. "Well, I haven't. So where do we go from here? Are you going to keep telling yourself that we were never meant to be, or will you give us one more chance?"

She heard the plea in his voice, and she would sooner jump in that ocean with her legs and arms tied than to reject him. "There aren't any movies out that I want to see right now, but I'm always hungry."

He smiled, walked over to her, and put an arm around her

shoulders. They headed back toward the house. "I think I'll hang out over here with you for a little while if that's okay."

"You might want to ask my mother about that. I'd hate for her to throw you out again." Hope laughed. Then she laughed some more just for the heck of it. Nothing much had been funny these last few days. Maybe being around Nic again was bringing her a little bit of joy.

Faith was standing on the back deck by herself as Hope and Nic walked up. She seemed lost in thought, like maybe she needed a little bit of the laughing joy that Hope had just experienced. She wished she could help her sister.

"Don't tell me you're still thinking about a DIY project for this deck," Hope said as she and Nic entered the backyard.

"No. You and Chris have convinced me that we need to hire out for the deck. I'm just standing out here because Mama is being insufferable, and I need a minute."

Hope furrowed her brows. "What did she do?"

Before Faith could answer, the back door swung open, and Ruby came out with fire in her eyes. "No sense telling your sister about your harebrained idea. I'm not selling off my memories to the highest bidder, and I don't care what you say."

Hope looked to Faith for answers. "What's she all worked up about?"

Rolling her eyes, Faith lifted her phone. "I just watched an auction online where they sell all of the old junk that's been laying around in people's homes."

"I don't have no old junk. I have memories," Ruby said, then she pointed at Nic, who was standing behind Hope. "What's he doing here?"

"I came to check on y'all."

Ruby pursed her lips, gave him a look that said, I doubt that. "You haven't come to check on 'us'"—Ruby did air quotes as she said the word *us*—"since Hope left."

"Okay, Mama, you win. He came to check on Hope. Now can we get back to this auction?" Faith rubbed her forehead like she was trying to stop it from throbbing as she turned back to Hope. "I suggested to Mama that we sell the paintings and all those dolls that nobody plays with anymore so we can come up with the money to pay on her loan and fix the house."

Ruby turned toward Faith. Hands on hips, head bobbing from side to side. "You can sell them when they throw dirt over my cream-colored casket with gold-and-diamond inlays."

Hope scrunched her forehead. "Really, Mama? You gon' be that specific about a casket?"

"I can be specific because I already bought it."

Faith and Hope both sucked in air.

Ruby ignored them. "When my time comes, don't let Pete down at that funeral home cheat me out of what I already paid for."

"You're too much." Faith threw her hands up in the air and then flopped them back to her sides. Giving up, she headed inside. "I can't with you."

"Too much," Hope agreed as she and Nic walked away.

"What? What did I do?" Ruby asked.

"You're not normal," Hope told her.

Leaning against the back gate, Ruby shouted, "Y'all still not selling off my stuff. I'm keeping everything I have left."

Hope heard her mother ranting about not selling her stuff, but she was not entertaining that madness. The money from the sale of those items could pay off that loan and even help fix things around the house. Hope didn't have the money. She couldn't count on having a job since she was in a sense AWOL.

"Your mother is a full-blown mess," Nic said while trying to hold in a laugh.

Hope extended her finger, pointing at him. "Don't laugh. It's not funny. My mother doesn't have good sense."

"I heard that, Hope, and I have more sense than you know. Plenty good sense." Ruby turned and strutted back toward the house.

"She has good ears, that's for sure." Nic couldn't hold it anymore and burst out laughing.

"Stop encouraging her." Hope shook her head as they rounded the corner and were once again in the front yard.

Then Hope saw something else that was no laughing matter. Crystal was in the front yard with Chris. She grabbed her stomach and complained of pain. She prayed the girl hadn't messed up any internal organs. Maybe they needed to finish with the house later and get Crystal to the hospital before she passed out, because she was not looking good.

Chapter 18

By late afternoon, just as Faith was about to put her suitcase in the car and head home, someone had indeed passed out. Ruby had come into the kitchen to put her sweet potatoes in the pot.

Putting the water on to boil, Ruby went into the pantry and took a bag of sweet potatoes off the shelf. She was just about to put the potatoes into the pot when the room shifted on her. "What the devil?"

Ruby stumbled backward as a pain hit so severe that it took her breath away. She tried to grab hold of the kitchen counter, but she missed it as her hand swiped the air. *"Woo-woo-woo."*

She could not right herself. Her hand brushed against one of the chairs. She thought it would stabilize her, but she and the chair both fell to the ground in a loud *plunk.*

As her head hit the ground, she heard Crystal scream, "Oh no, Grammy!" Then her world seemed to fade.

———

When Ruby came to, paramedics were standing over her, and she was lying on a gurney. "W-what's going on?"

"Lay your head back on the pillow, Mama. You passed out."

Ruby turned to the left where Faith was standing. "I passed out?"

"Yes, you did. We're taking you to the hospital, so just lay there and be calm," Hope said.

Ruby's head swiveled to the other side where Hope was standing. "Hospital?" She was so disoriented, she didn't know what was going on. She let her head hit the pillow as the paramedics carried her down the back steps. *So it begins,* Ruby thought as she was lifted into the back of the ambulance. *So it begins.*

Faith and Hope were sitting in the emergency room waiting for the doctor to tell them if their mother was okay. It devastated Faith to see her mother sprawled out on the kitchen floor, incoherent and disoriented.

Ruby was such a force that it never occurred to Faith that her mother was getting older. But she looked old today. Looked like she wasn't invincible after all, and that scared Faith.

One good thing about Chris showing up uninvited was that he stayed at the house with Crystal. Faith was thankful she didn't have to keep an eye on Crystal while worrying about her mother. "What do you think is taking the doctor so long?"

"I don't know." Hope bit her nail, tapped her feet on the floor. "I'm just mad at myself for not paying attention. Did she look sick to you? Maybe she was doing too much around the house. I should have made her sit down and rest more."

"Do you honestly think she would have listened?" Faith shook her head. "She certainly wouldn't listen to me. She thinks I run my mouth too much."

Hope covered her mouth and giggled before saying, "You kind of do though."

"Can I confess something to you?"

Hope nodded, giving Faith her full attention.

"I think I ran my mouth too much to Trinity. I remember saying something about her picking up weight during the summer. I think I was jealous that guys were taking notice, but then she started purging just to lose weight."

"Uh-uh." Hope waved her hands in the air like she was calling for a time-out. "Don't do that. You can't blame yourself for the things Trinity decided to do, and I seriously doubt her purging was just about losing weight. Something else was going on."

Sighing, Faith said, "I blame myself every day—well, the days that I'm not blaming you. That's why it's been so hard to watch Crystal grow up looking like Trinity."

"I can imagine how hard that has been, especially if you've been blaming yourself all these years."

"And you," Faith reminded her.

"How could I forget? You've told me often enough that if I hadn't left, then Trinity would still be with us." Hope sighed. "I have to admit, hearing that year after year hurt."

"That's probably why it was so easy for us to stop talking for so many years." The air was thick with silence as Faith reevaluated everything she thought she knew about the year that changed their lives forever. "I feel awful, especially now that I know the real reason why you left. I have to admit, I'm still in shock."

"If you're in shock, imagine how I felt when I heard that woman on the back patio telling Mama that I was her child. And then Mama acted like those words changed nothing."

"She never told us anything. I never knew the reason you didn't want to be around us anymore." Faith shook her head.

"It wasn't that I didn't want to be around y'all. I was hurting, and Mama wouldn't give me any answers. She claimed that the woman had a baby by Daddy and then gave me to her. But why? I don't get it."

Faith lifted her hands. Eyebrows scrunched. "Who is this woman?"

"I wish I knew. Mama told me that she only knew the woman's first name and that she didn't even know where the woman lived."

"That doesn't make sense. How could they take you from this woman and not know who she is?"

"It doesn't make sense because it can't be true. I've given up trying to get the truth out of Mama." Hope leaned forward. Put a hand on her face. As she sat back up straight in her seat, she told Faith, "I need you to do something for me."

The emergency room doors opened, and a white-haired man in a lab coat came over to them. Faith and Hope stood. The doctor shook their hands.

"Look at the two of you. It seems like just yesterday when you were running around my office, knocking over magazines and coloring on my table."

"Dr. Stein." Faith hugged him. "How have you been?"

"Few aches and pains, but I'm still here," he told her.

When Faith released him, Hope gave him a hug. "Sorry about knocking over all those magazines."

He patted Hope on the shoulder. "You can come to the office anytime."

Faith asked, "How is Mama, Dr. Stein?"

"Your mother is stable for now. She'll be moved to a room in the ICU before her surgery."

Hope looked around as if she thought she was in the wrong place, talking to the wrong doctor. She waved a hand. "Wait . . . wait. ICU? What surgery?"

Dr. Stein turned to Hope. "That's all I can say before you have a chance to speak with your mother. Can the two of you stick around for another hour? We should have Ruby moved into her room and then you'll be able to speak with her."

Faith scratched her head. "Yes, of course, but I don't understand why you can't tell us any more than that."

Dr. Stein sighed, "HIPAA laws prevent me from saying anything further." Then with a wry smile, he added, "And to be honest, your mother has threatened to slice my lips off if I say any more than I already have."

"That sounds like something she would say." Hope shook her head.

"We'll wait here, Doctor." Faith and Hope sat back down. Faith rolled her eyes. "Why does Mama act like this? She should have let Dr. Stein tell us what's going on. We're supposed to sit here and worry without knowing anything?" Faith rubbed her forehead. "She needs surgery for goodness' sake."

"If anybody in this town has a secret, they should tell it to Mama because she'll keep her mouth shut about what she knows until the very end."

Faith felt the pain in the words that flowed out of Hope's mouth. She put a hand on her sister's shoulder. "I really am sorry about what Mama did. I had no idea you weren't her firstborn child."

"Me either. My birth certificate says that Henry and Ruby Reynolds are my parents."

Faith scratched her head again. "How? If Mama isn't your biological mother, then her name shouldn't be on your birth certificate, right?"

"Million-dollar question, sis." Hope put her head in her hands, looking like she was wallowing in self-pity. "It's been eighteen years since I first learned of it, and I still have to put it out of my mind so I can have any kind of relationship with Mama because she hasn't told me anything. Every time I ask for more information, she just shuts me down and says, 'What's done is done.'"

"And you let her get away with that?"

"After I left Hallelujah, I called the county clerk's office and asked if my birth certificate had been doctored, but they said it wasn't. I called Dr. Stein, since he supposedly delivered me, and asked him to explain what happened. But he said that he was involved in my birth and he signed my certificate, so he had no idea what I was talking about." Hope rolled her eyes.

"If Mama wasn't sick, I'd pull Dr. Stein's coattail and demand he tell us the truth."

Hope told her, "I gave up. At the end of the day, I came to realize that Mama raised me, and she loves me. Blood shouldn't matter."

"I wish I was as forgiving as you 'cause you know I probably still wouldn't be speaking to Mama after some mess like that."

"Don't I know it. You have held my leaving town over my head for years."

"I wish you had told me what Mama did back then. I would have been more understanding of why you couldn't stay."

Nodding, Hope confessed, "It was just too raw back then. I didn't know what to think or who to turn to. I was just lost."

"And then Trinity got lost."

Hope added, "And then you and I stopped speaking, so I just kept it to myself." Hope turned to Faith. She put Faith's hand in hers. "Look, sis, I don't want there to be any more secrets between us, so I need to let you know something."

"Okay. Shoot." It had been a long time since she had been this close to her sister. They had let so many years and so many misunderstandings get in the way. Never again. Faith was going to hold on to her sister from now until eternity.

"Since Mama is refusing to take that DNA test to determine if they have found Trinity's remains, Nic asked me to do it, but I'm scared."

Faith didn't understand that, so she asked, "Scared of what?"

"I'm afraid that if we use my DNA, we might not know for sure whether those remains are Trinity's or not."

Faith's eyebrows furrowed. "We might not have the same birth mother, but since we have the same father, then the DNA should show you're related, right?"

"That's what I'm worried about. What if Daddy isn't really my father? I don't think I could deal with finding that out after all these years."

Faith shook her head. "That's crazy, Hope. You look like Daddy."

"That's what I used to think too. But then I saw my birth mother. And I promise you, Faith, I look like that woman."

"You might look like your birth mother, but you also look like Daddy, so stop tripping."

"I might just be tripping, but I'm not prepared to find out that my whole entire life has been a lie."

They both sat there for a minute, neither saying anything. Faith wasn't sure what to tell Hope. She could understand why her sister wouldn't trust anything their mother told her about her paternity. This was too much for Faith to contend with. First they lost Trinity and now Hope might not be her blood sister. It wasn't possible. They might not have the same mother, but they had the same daddy. She was sure of it.

Hope said, "So if we want to know without a doubt whether those are Trinity's remains, then I need you to do the DNA test."

Faith leaned back, put a hand to her chest. "I don't know. Digging all of this up after all this time makes me nervous."

"I know, but if we want to know what happened to Trinity, then I need you to do this."

Faith's mind went back to the last minute she and Trinity were together. Her sister smiled at her and said, 'Don't worry. I'll be right back,' but she hadn't returned. Faith had let her walk out that door because she was tired of arguing with her. She closed her eyes and wrapped her arms around her chest. Faith would give anything to have that moment in time back.

"I wish I could get a do-over. I wish I had snatched Trinity and sat on her until Mama got back home from work."

Hope nodded. "I wish I had been there instead of in Washington nursing my pain and not speaking to anybody."

Sighing, Faith said, "But we can't go back, can we?"

Hope shook her head as she put an arm around Faith's shoulders. "We can't."

"Let me think about this DNA thing, sis. I'm not sure that I'm ready to deal with that, with everything else that's going on."

Chapter 19

HOPE DIDN'T KNOW WHAT SHE WOULD DO IF FAITH DIDN'T take the DNA test. It truly bothered her that they never found Trinity. She wanted to bring her sister home, one way or another. The last thing Hope wanted to do was upset her mother before surgery. She still couldn't believe that her mother needed surgery, and this was the first time they were hearing anything about it. But that was life in the land of Ruby Reynolds.

Tapping her foot, Hope tried to think of something else she could say to convince her sister to take that test.

Faith put a hand on Hope's knee. "Are you nervous about seeing Mom or what? That tapping is distracting me."

"Sorry, boss. Didn't mean to disturb you." Hope used her hand to motion the sectioning off of her space, swiping downward. "I'll just sit right here and stay as quiet as I can."

"Not trying to boss you around." Faith held up her phone. "I was doing some more research to see how I can help Crystal."

Hope turned toward Faith. "Oh yeah? What are you finding?"

Sighing, Faith said, "So far all I'm getting is to be patient and listen. Oh, and this site right here," she pointed toward her phone, "tells me not to force her to eat because she'll just throw it up anyway." Faith put the phone down.

Putting a hand on Faith's shoulder, Hope said, "I know it's frustrating, sis, but you're the only one of us who stayed in church. Keep praying and trust that God will show you a way forward."

Faith nodded. "Thanks for that. I—"

Faith was about to say more, but a nurse came out and gave them the room number where their mother was being moved to. They grabbed their purses and headed for the ICU.

The ICU? That didn't even sound right. Why was her mother in the Intensive Care Unit? Ruby seemed fine and just as cantankerous and full of life as she'd always been that morning. Then in the afternoon, she fell on the floor, and now she and Faith were headed to the ICU. "I can't believe this is happening."

"Me either," Faith said. "I didn't notice anything off-kilter, and now the doctor is talking about surgery." She scrunched her face into a frown. "What's that about?"

The dreaded part for Hope was that they were about to find out, and she didn't know how she would handle any more bad news this week. Her family thought she was so strong, so resilient, but in truth, she was more like the mother who raised her to avoid situations that were unpleasant. Just put on a happy face and pretend everything is all right.

But things weren't all right. Hope only prayed that this awful feeling in her gut wasn't preparing her to lose the only mother she had ever known.

Ruby was lying in the hospital bed with a light-blue hospital gown on. Her mother looked tired and in need of rest. There were two chairs on the left side of the bed. Hope sat in one, and Faith took the other.

Ruby gave them a weak smile. "My girls."

"You gave us a scare, Mama," Faith said while holding on to her purse like it was a pillow.

Hope's purse wasn't a big duffel bag like Faith's, so it wouldn't have given her the same support. She needed something to hold on to

VANESSA MILLER

also, so she gripped the arms of the chair. "What's going on, Mama? Why is Dr. Stein talking about surgery? Did you injure yourself that bad with the fall?"

Ruby winced as she repositioned herself in the bed. "These bones of mine aren't so brittle that a little tumble in the kitchen could break anything."

When Ruby pursed her lips and twisted them to the left side, Hope knew her mother was up to her old stalling tactics. After Daddy died, Ruby waited hours before sitting them all down and telling them. But even then, she made it sound like Daddy's heart attack hadn't killed him, like he was lying in the hospital trying to recover. It wasn't until Hope jumped up and said, *"Let's go see about him,"* that Ruby formed her mouth to say the word *dead.*

"This is no time to beat around the bush, Mama. Tell us what's going on."

Faith chimed in. "We're not putting up with any of your nonsense about what is and isn't our business. Not this time, Mama."

Ruby seemed to shrink into the mattress. She pulled the blanket over her arms. Sighed. "I've got cancer."

"What?" Hope jumped out of her seat. "How long have you known this?" Her mother accused her of keeping secrets the other day, but it was Ruby—she was always the one lying and keeping secrets.

"I was planning to tell you and your sister. Why do you think I asked y'all to come down here?"

Faith put her purse on the floor as she scooted closer to the bed. "You told us we were coming down here to help you get the beach house in order so you could open your bed-and-breakfast and earn money so can keep the house."

Had she really heard the word *cancer?* How long had her mother been holding out on them? "And you told us that some contractor stole your money. Now was that true or just something you made up to get us down here?"

"Sit down, Hope, and I'll tell you and your sister everything. I promise." Ruby lifted her right hand like she was in court about to swear to tell the whole truth and nothing but the truth.

Taking her seat, Hope took a few deep breaths and blew them out like she was in a Lamaze class. "Okay, Mama. You wanted me and Faith here with you. We're here. But we can't truly help if we don't know what's going on."

"I had my annual mammogram about three months ago. That's when I got the bad news," Ruby confessed.

Faith's eyes went wild with confusion as a tear drifted down her face. "You've known for three months, and you're just now telling us that you have something as serious as cancer? How could you keep this from us, Mama? We're not kids anymore. We should have been told."

Ruby nodded in agreement. A look of sorrow swept across her face. "You're right. I should have told you. I just wanted to get the house ready for you girls first."

"What's the big deal about having the house ready?"

"That is our land. It's our due, and I can't leave here without making sure it's passed on proper."

"You should have told us." Hope furrowed her brow, tapping the arm of the chair. Her mother was up to something. Lord knew what this time, but it wasn't going to be good, and Hope knew it.

Faith rubbed her forehead. A tension headache was on the way. "I don't get it either, Mama. This makes no sense."

"Dr. Stein says my tumor is growing fast, so I couldn't go into surgery without taking care of the house. I promised Henry that you girls would always have a place to call home." Ruby turned away from her girls as tears ran down her cheeks. She wiped her face. "I'm sorry. I tried. God knows I tried."

Hope rushed to Ruby's side and rubbed her mother's shoulder. Since she was a child, Hope could never stand to see her mom cry. Ruby had been wrong with how she handled this matter and many others. But Hope couldn't chastise her any further. "Just tell us what the doctor said. What stage are you in?" Silently, Hope prayed, *Please tell the truth.*

Ruby sighed, lip twisted to the left. Put her arms across her chest.

"Tell us, Mama. Please don't shut down on us. Not this time."

Hope thought that Faith's voice sounded like she was pleading for her own life. And maybe she was. Losing a mother was a big deal. As the saying goes, you only get one mother. But in Hope's case, she had two. Only, she had no clue where her birth mother was. Didn't know if the woman was happy, sad, sick, or if she had passed away after all this time.

"The mammogram showed a tumor in my breast," Ruby finally admitted. "I'm in stage three. And you might as well know that Dr. Stein doesn't just want to take the lump out of my breast. The cancer had only been in my left breast, but it has spread to the right one, so he wants to cut them both off."

"But . . ." Hope murmured, knowing that with her mother, there was going to be a *but* in the mix.

Ruby shifted her weight from one side to the other, then covered her face. She spread a couple of fingers to peek out at her daughters.

Hope rarely saw her mother embarrassed. And wondered if she really saw what she thought she saw or if her mom was playing some weird game of peekaboo with them.

But then Ruby said, "What if I get another boyfriend? What if he doesn't like the fact that I don't have"—she motioned toward her breasts—"my girls?"

Faith rolled her eyes heavenward. "Mother! You are a seventy-year-old woman. If you get with some man, and he doesn't like the fact that you chose life over," Faith pointed at her mother's chest, "'your girls,' then you don't need him."

"I second that," Hope said. "If this doctor thinks that doing a double mastectomy will increase your life expectancy, then I think you should consider it."

Ruby waved that thought off. "I'm keeping my girls. He can just remove the tumor, and that's that."

"You're being ridiculous, Mama. I'll call your doctor myself and tell him that you're getting that mastectomy." Faith stood and reached for the call button.

Ruby moved it out of her reach. "You'll do no such thang." Ruby raised her voice, then she pointed toward the chairs. "Now y'all sit down so I can tell y'all what you need to know."

Hope and Faith both took their seats.

"I need y'all to listen because I've got some important things to tell you." Ruby looked from Hope to Faith. "I haven't made up my mind about what I'll allow Dr. Stein to do during this surgery yet, but no matter what I decide, I need y'all to know about what your daddy and I agreed to because it's in my will."

Hope shook her head. "I don't want to hear about your will at this point in time, Mama. Do you think you're going to die or something?"

"With the way things work in this world, none of us know when our last day on this earth will be."

Faith lifted her hands next to her head as she gave Ruby an I'm-confused look. "If you think you might die in surgery, why can't the man cut your girls off? It's not like Jesus is going to be checking for breasts for you to enter heaven's gates."

Pointing a finger at Faith, Ruby said, "I done told you about that sassy mouth of yours. You better let me say my piece and leave me alone."

"Whatever, Mama." Faith waved a hand in the air. "Okay, tell us about this will, since that's the only thing you're willing to talk about."

Narrowing her eyes at Faith, Ruby then formed a fist with her right hand. "You better be glad I'm in this bed."

"Mama, stop. Don't get yourself all worked up." Hope watched the monitors that her mother was hooked up to, and her blood pressure had elevated a bit.

Inhaling and exhaling. Inhaling and exhaling. Ruby appeared

to calm down. "Like I was saying about the will . . . First, y'all need to understand that our property consists of two parts. There's the house and there's the land. The land belongs to me, but Henry built the beach house . . . and he asked that I leave the beach house to Hope in my will."

"What?" Faith was out of her chair again. "Are you saying Daddy played favorites like that?" Faith's chest heaved as her face displayed anger and rage.

Ruby turned to Hope while her thumb jutted in Faith's direction. "Now who needs to calm down?"

Ruby thought she was funny, but Hope didn't feel like laughing. "She's angry, Mama, and I don't blame her. You've just told us something that neither of us knew. How could you have kept this information from us—from me—all these years?"

"What would you have done if you knew the house would one day be yours? Would you have hit me over the head to get rid of me?"

Hope shook her head. "That's not funny, but I should have known."

"You should have told us about this, Mama," Faith said as she sat back down while cutting her eyes at Hope.

"Well, just so you both know, I have willed the land to Faith and Trinity."

"What?" Hope and Faith said at the same time.

"That doesn't make sense, Mama. What am I going to do with the land if Hope owns the house?"

"Makes perfect sense to me." Ruby gave each of them a pointed stare. "Looks like the two of you will have to get along after all, huh?"

"What are you talking about, Mama?" Hope asked.

"I know you, Hope. You loved your daddy." Ruby turned to Faith. "And you were always with your daddy. Following, learning from him. He was an architect, and you became an interior designer. Neither one of you wants your daddy's hard work to go to waste, so you'll simply have to work together to keep the house and the land from the vultures that want to take it from us."

Chapter 20

FAITH WAS FUMING AS SHE AND HOPE LEFT THEIR MOTHER'S hospital room. It didn't make sense that her mother had cancer. It didn't make sense that her mother would be going into surgery tomorrow, and it didn't make sense that her daddy wanted the house left to only one of his children—the one who wasn't even sure she was his.

"I'm going to God's Holy Word Church," Hope told her as they waited on the elevator to go downstairs.

"Going to pray about how you can steal it all—the house and the land?" Faith's eyes narrowed as she challenged her sister.

Hope held up a hand to her. "I can't with you right now. You can be petty if you want. I'm concerned about Mama and her surgery." Hope walked away from her and headed for the stairs.

Faith wanted to go after her sister and apologize, but she was stuck, not understanding what had just happened to her. Faith had loved her father dearly and thought he had loved her just the same, but if he had, how could he give the beach house to Hope when he knew how much she loved every architectural element of that house?

It amazed Faith how quick life could turn. One minute she was doing her thing and growing her company. The next, she discovered she had marital problems, a daughter with an eating disorder, a half sister, a mother with cancer and a father who disinherited her. The weight of it all was enough to take her under.

The elevator door opened. Faith was about to step in, but then she heard, "Faith Reynolds, oh my goodness. I can't believe I'm seeing you in the flesh."

That voice . . . Something about it was familiar. She looked up and found herself staring into the gorgeous face of Colton James. The guy she dreamed about marrying and having kids with, but then Trinity vanished and nothing was ever the same.

Colton had called her a few times after Trinity disappeared, but her mother didn't like the James family, so she demanded he stop calling their house.

Not talking to Colton was fine with her because she didn't want the constant reminder of the day she let her sister walk out of the house. The day she gave up on her sister. So she gave up on her crush and moved on.

"Hey, Colton. It's been a long time. I didn't know you still lived here." He had on a tan pair of slacks, a white shirt, a black jacket and a tan-and-black tie. It looked good on him. But he was missing that I'm-a-big-deal smile he used to have. Life had a way of wiping that kind of youthful I-can-do-anything smile right off your face.

"I moved back a month ago." He shrugged. "I got a divorce, and my parents are getting up in age. They started needing my help more and more, so I moved my practice here."

"Your practice? Are you a doctor?" He wasn't dressed like a doctor, more like an executive.

"Yes. I go by Dr. James these days. But I'm not a family physician. I'm a psychologist."

"Oh wow. I didn't know you were interested in anything like that. I always thought you'd go pro with basketball or at least coach the sport."

"I didn't know myself until I took a psychology class in college. My fate was sealed after that." He pulled a business card out of his jacket pocket and handed it to her. "My practice is small but growing, so if you know of anyone in need of my services, please give them my card."

She took note of the wedding ring on his finger as he gave her the business card. Faith wondered why he wore it even after the divorce. "I'll do that."

As he walked away from her, Faith thought about Crystal and wondered if God was giving her a nudge. Colton needed business, but Faith would rather wait until they were back in Atlanta to find a psychologist for Crystal. She was, however, thankful that she ran into Colton because she hadn't even thought about having her daughter sit and talk to a professional.

Faith left the hospital and drove back to the beach house. To her surprise, Chris had cleaned the back deck and was tightening the screws on it.

Why was he doing all of this? Why was he pretending that his family mattered to him when she knew the truth? Why had she married Chris?

As she sat in her car, Faith wondered just for a moment how life would have been if she had told Colton how she felt about him when they were younger. Would they have gotten married and had a couple of kids? Would they be happy? Faith shook that notion out of her head. She was in no way attracted to Colton anymore.

Getting out of the car, she felt the weight of the hours spent at the hospital. She was tired. Tired of so many things and didn't know which way to turn in order to get some relief.

She began her trek up the stairs but hadn't realized that she was heading up the right side until her foot went through the worn and weathered wood on the fifth step and she fell forward. She screamed, "Oh no!"

Chris put down his tools and ran toward the front of the house. When he reached Faith, he pulled her leg out of the hole it was stuck in. "You all right?"

Faith reached for her ankle, rubbed it. "I think I'm good. I can't believe I forgot about these steps."

"I can. You've got a lot on your mind." Chris helped her down. Then they walked up the stairs on the left side. "How's your mom?"

Sharp intake of breath. Faith's grip tightened on the banister. "She has cancer." Then as if saying those words did something to her very soul, Faith buckled over and released a torrent of tears. "Oh Lord, my mother has cancer."

Chris pulled Faith into his arms. "I'm sorry, babe. I'm so sorry."

She wanted to push him away from her, but she couldn't. She needed the warmth of his body next to hers. Needed to feel compassion. Needed someone else to care that her heart was breaking. "Sh-she's known f-for months. Surgery i-in the morning."

"Come over here. Let's sit down and talk." Chris moved her over to the side of the house and helped her to sit in one of the rocking chairs. He then moved a rocking chair in front of her, sat down and held on to her hands. "God is going to get us through this, honey. You said your mom will have surgery in the morning. Let's pray and believe that the doctor will remove all of the cancer, and she will live many more years."

Where was all his faith when he needed money to start his flipping business? Why couldn't he have just asked God for the money rather than taking that home equity loan out on their home and helping himself to the money in her bank account? She had a thousand questions about that and about his God-walk, but her mother was in the hospital with cancer and was about to undergo surgery. So she held on to Chris' hands and allowed him to pray.

But deep inside, she wondered if God was even listening. Because if He was, why was Trinity still missing? Why was her mother lying in the hospital with cancer, and why did her father give the beach house to Hope?

She had a whole other list of whys that included Crystal having an eating disorder and her husband have a cheating-and-stealing disorder. Why God? Why?

Chris said, "Amen."

Faith removed her hands from his. Her mind was so all over the place that she hadn't heard a word of his prayer.

"I can take Crystal back to Atlanta so the two of you won't be bumping heads while you're dealing with your mom's situation if that will help," he suggested.

Faith shook her head. "We both need to keep an eye on her with this eating disorder. I'm going to look for a psychologist back in Atlanta. I think it might be good for Crystal to see someone there. Once I get her an appointment, you'll probably need to take her home for that."

Chris nodded his agreement. "Then I'll stay here with you a while longer." He shifted his eyes toward the house, then he said, "I saw the estimate you received for work that needs to be done on this house. Why don't I make myself useful and be your contractor?"

Was he trying to be helpful or trying to make a buck off of her mother during her time of need? She stood. "We don't have all the money needed to pay that contractor, and we don't have it for you either."

He stood with her. "That's what I'm trying to tell you. If I do the repairs around here, I should be able to shave anywhere from twenty to thirty thousand off that estimate."

Stunned into silence, Faith stared at him for a minute. Stepping back, she squinted, trying to get a good look at him. Was this man in front of her a clone of her husband or the real thing? "So you're telling me that you'll do this job for just the cost of the materials?"

Nodding, he said, "Your mom is my family too. I want to help in any way I can."

Oh, wait. She knew exactly what was going on. He was probably hoping she'd let him sell the beach house sometime in the future. "Do what you want, Chris. Just know that this beach house belongs to Hope, and I doubt she will let you make a fool of her by selling it and taking the money for yourself."

She walked away from him, leaving him standing there looking like he thought something was wrong with her. That was fine with her because she thought something was wrong with him too. She doubted he'd be so willing to do a bunch of free labor now that he knew the house belonged to Hope.

She wished she didn't immediately think that Chris was up to no good. Wished she could trust that his motives were pure. But she had lost the ability to trust like that a long time ago.

She went inside to let Crystal know what was going on. She wouldn't be like her mother, hiding things and wishing for the best. She couldn't live like that.

Faith knocked once, then put her hand on Crystal's doorknob and opened the door. She peeked her head in. "Hey. You got a minute?"

Crystal was lying in bed reading a book. "Yes. Come in." She sat up, put her book down. "How's Grammy?"

Faith sat on the bed next to Crystal. She pressed her lips together, took a deep breath as she put Crystal's hand in hers. "Grammy is sick."

"Sick?" Crystal raised an eyebrow.

Faith hated the big *C* word. She didn't want to split her lips to say it again, but she couldn't lie to Crystal or sugarcoat things the way her mother used to do to them. Faith needed Crystal to know that she could trust her, so she had to tell the truth, even when it was painful. "She has c-cancer."

"No! No!" Crystal jumped off the bed, her chin quivering. "I don't want Grammy to die."

Before Faith could stop herself, she was crying again. With tears streaming down her face, she pulled Crystal into her arms. "She's not going to die, baby. She's having surgery in the morning."

Crystal wrapped her arms around her mother. They were both crying. "But how do you know she won't die?"

"Just trust me on this." Even as she said the words, Faith knew that she was asking Crystal to do something that Faith hadn't been able to do since Trinity went missing: trust.

They held on to each other a little while longer. Faith's mind traveled back to the hundreds of times Crystal had come to her in need of a hug. Those were some of the best days of Faith's life, before things got complicated. Before Faith started her design business.

"I want to go to the hospital to see Grammy before her surgery," Crystal said as they ended the embrace.

Faith wiped the tears from her daughter's face. Stood up. "Okay. I'll take you with me in the morning."

Faith left Crystal's room. As she closed the door, she felt drained and wanted to lie down, but she looked to the left into the living room, and she saw Chris' cell phone on the arm of the sofa.

Chris had slept on the sofa last night, so his duffel bag was on the floor next to the sofa as well. Faith looked around the living room, then poked her head toward the kitchen, making sure Chris wasn't inside the house yet, then she rushed over to the sofa and picked up his phone.

It killed her that she didn't know who he had been on the phone with last night. She wished she didn't care, but she did. God help her, she did. She typed in the month, day and year they got married, as she had done on a few other occasions when she checked his phone. But this time, it didn't unlock.

"What are you doing?"

Faith swung around, Chris' phone still in her hand. Chris was standing in the doorway. He walked over to her and snatched his phone out of her hands.

"You changed your passcode." Every syllable, every word came out as an accusation. Pursing her lips, she stared at him with her head cocked to the side.

"So?"

"So?" Her head bobbed backward. Hands on hips. "Is that all you have to say? You must be up to no good or you wouldn't have changed your passcode."

He rolled his eyes at that. "Or maybe I'm just tired of you checking my phone like I'm your kid rather than a grown man."

"Okay, grown man." She smirked at him. "Don't grown men have their own money?"

"I've got my own money. I just closed on the house I was working on. I would have told you when I first arrived, but there's been a lot going on."

She wanted to put her hands around his neck and strangle him. "If you closed on that house, then why am I still light twenty thousand? Why do we still owe on that home equity loan?" She was yelling and didn't care. This was too much. He wasn't going to get away with this.

Chris raised his voice as he yelled back at her. "Have you noticed that we haven't received a call from the bank in days?" He jabbed a finger into his chest. "That's because I paid them. We're no longer behind on that equity loan."

"What? When?" Faith scrunched her eyebrows as she tried to make sense of what he was saying. "Did you pay them with the money you took out of my account? Now that's rich." She clasped her hands together. "You rob your wife to pay a debt that I was told I wouldn't have to help with."

He threw his phone on the sofa, lips tight as he said, "You are a cold woman." He shook his head. "Loving you hasn't been easy all these years, but I stuck by you." Chris opened the door, but before he stepped out of the house, he flung back at her, "You might want to check your bank account. Maybe then you'll stop calling me a thief."

What did she need to check her bank account for? She knew how much she had in there. Seven hundred fifty-two dollars and thirteen cents.

Crystal opened her bedroom door. She was crying again. "Y'all can't even stop arguing while my grammy is in the hospital. Get a divorce already, why don't you." Crystal then slammed the door shut.

Chris slammed the front door as he went back outside, and Faith went to her bedroom. She was sorry that she'd caused this disturbance in the house, especially after telling Crystal about her mother's cancer, but it wasn't all her fault. What Chris did to her was wrong, but she somehow always ended up looking like the bad guy.

She closed the door behind her once she was in her bedroom, then pulled her cell phone out of her purse and clicked on the bank app.

When her checking account opened, she saw that she now had twenty thousand seven hundred fifty-two dollars and thirteen cents. Her mouth hung open, completely astonished. "He put the money back?"

Instead of being happy about it, Faith replayed Chris' words in her head. *You are a cold woman.* She sighed. Everything was so hard these days.

Chapter 21

PASTOR O'DELL WAS IN THE SANCTUARY WHEN HOPE WALKED into God's Holy Word Church during Wednesday night Bible study. The pew cushions had been burgundy the last time she had been inside this sanctuary. Now they were a royal blue. The carpet was no longer burgundy either. There was a mix of blue, tan and black in the fibers of the carpet.

Hope fixed her eyes on the pulpit area where she used to sit every fourth Sunday morning as a member of the youth choir. She was an alto and loved to sing praises to the Lord. Her sisters had been sopranos and sat on the opposite side of the choir, but they would smile at each other as they sang.

She missed those days. Missed Pastor O'Dell because he always had a kind word for the youth. Never looked down on any of the youth group members, even when someone messed up. Pastor O'Dell had this been-there, done-that attitude of grace about him. She prayed that the years had been kind to him.

Pastor was into his third closing. Hope laughed and shook her head at the notion that he still used that same old corny line. And that the people were still laughing. She sat down in the fourth pew from the back since it was empty.

Pastor was saying, "God is good to us all the time, even when it doesn't feel good or look good. Even on days when all we can do is throw up our hands and say hallelujah anyhow. He's still good."

Pastor O'Dell's mustache and beard were now full of gray hairs, and he sported a bald head, but he was the same old encourager she had known him to be when she was a teenager. Hallelujah anyhow was quite a concept.

When she had been young, before things completely fell apart, Hope believed everything Pastor O'Dell preached. These days, she wasn't so sure. How did she praise a God who allowed so much pain, allowed people who professed to be Christians to stand in her face and tell her lie after lie? Hope didn't understand it, which was probably the reason she had become a whenever-the-mood-hit-her kind of church-goer for years now.

The mood didn't strike but maybe twice a year, but since she was at Bible study tonight, she was going to congratulate herself for being in the Lord's house three times this year.

Pastor O'Dell gave the benediction. Everyone stood and made their way out of the sanctuary. Pastor stood at the entrance, shaking hands and giving well wishes to his members as they left. Hope let the room clear out before approaching Pastor O'Dell.

There was a gleam in Pastor's eye as he watched her approach. "Are these old eyes deceiving me, or am I looking at one of the most beloved youth church members this church has ever had?"

Hope put her hands over her face. She just knew she was blushing. "Wow! Beloved, huh?"

"You are one of God's beloved, and you were always a joy to this ministry." Pastor O'Dell hugged her. "It's so good to have you back home."

"Thank you, Pastor O'Dell."

When they ended the embrace, Pastor O'Dell said, "I was sorry to hear about Ruby. How bad was the fall?"

Hope almost asked how he knew, but then she remembered that

in a small town, word traveled like a rocket to the moon. "That's why I came to see you. It's more serious than a fall."

"Let's go into my office." He directed her to follow him as they left the sanctuary and went into his office, which was on the left side of the church building.

Hope took the seat in front of Pastor O'Dell's desk just as he sat down.

Pastor said, "Ruby hasn't been an active member of this church for more than fifteen years, but we have kept her on the prayer list and call her name out to the Lord often. And we still mail her our ministry updates."

"I'm thankful for that, Pastor. She truly needs your prayers now, and I was hoping that you would stop by the hospital for a visit."

"Of course, I will." Pastor O'Dell opened his drawer and took out his planner. "I conduct my hospital visits on Fridays." Scanning the calendar and picking up his pencil, he said, "I can fit her in around noon."

He was getting ready to pencil in the date when Hope stopped him. "It can't wait until Friday, Pastor. I know that tomorrow is Thanksgiving, but Mama is supposed to go into surgery in the morning, and she's not thinking clearly. I was hoping that if you visited her tonight or first thing in the morning, she might do the right thing."

Pastor O'Dell threaded his fingers together and leaned back in his seat. "And what is the 'right thing' as you see it?"

Letting out a whoosh of air, Hope told him about Ruby's diagnosis. She then told him, "I'm just worried that she might only allow the doctor to remove the lump and that's it. The doctor thinks a double mastectomy is necessary, but she is talking foolish. We just need someone to talk some sense into her, and you're the only one I know who's ever been able to do that."

Laughing at that notion, Pastor O'Dell said, "Not me. Ruby hasn't paid much mind to anything I've had to say for a long time. But I do know Someone she used to listen to." He put his calendar away and stood. "Let me get my jacket, and I'll head on over to the hospital."

Hope jumped up and hugged him. "Thank you so much, Pastor."

"Don't thank me just yet. Ruby is a hard nut to crack. Let's both pray that the Lord will be able to get through to her tonight."

"I will." Hope and Pastor O'Dell left the church together. He got in his car and headed to the hospital while Hope got in her mom's Jeep and headed for the Ice House, which was only two miles down the road from God's Holy Word Church.

She didn't care that it was November and sixty degrees outside. She was going to get her niece an ice cream cone.

Truthfully, she needed an ice cream fix herself. The Ice House had been one of hers and Nic's favorite hangouts. And not just hers and Nic's, but she, Faith and Trinity made their way to the Ice House after every Sunday service.

Stepping inside the parlor felt like she was going back in time. Nothing had changed from when she was a kid. The same seventies posters of *All in the Family* and *The Jeffersons* were on the walls. The jukebox playing sixties and seventies oldies but goodies. She half expected to see CJ and his younger brother, Colton, standing outside making obnoxious comments as she entered the store.

The icebox was in the same spot as well, directly in the front of the store, next to the cash register. That way you could walk down the line, requesting all the toppings you wanted on your ice cream cone or waffle bowl, which would get filled with all types of ice cream goodness, then you could pay for all of the items while the clerk made your order.

Tonight, she was going to keep it simple. Just strawberry ice cream in a waffle bowl with crumbled graham crackers, whipped cream and a cherry on top. Okay, maybe not so simple but simpler than some of the other creations she had come up with. She ordered the same for Crystal. Faith loved strawberry ice cream when she was a kid. She would see what Crystal thought of it.

As she was taking her money out to pay, she heard, "I got this."

It was Nic. He had just entered the store. She shook her head. "You don't have to. I've got it."

"Now what kind of an ex-fiancé would I be if I didn't buy you an ice cream cone? Especially when you look like you've had a rough day."

Hope patted her hair. "I look that bad, huh?"

Nic handed the cashier the money for the ice cream. "You don't look bad at all, but I know you." He touched her face and let his fingers run across her forehead. "You always get those little lines in your forehead when you're worried about something."

The clerk handed the box that contained the waffle bowls to her. "My mom's in the hospital."

"Oh, that's terrible."

Hope swung around as she heard another voice. It was Scooter Evans, Nic's dad. "Hi, Mr. Evans. How have you been?"

"I'm doing well." Scooter put a hand on her arm. "You make sure to tell your mom that I'll be praying for her."

"That's very kind of you," Hope said as she stepped outside with Nic. Scooter, unlike his wife, had been nice to her back when she and Nic dated, but according to her mother, Scooter was the devil, so even though Hope didn't see what Ruby saw, she kept her distance.

While she was taking a bite out of her ice cream, Nic asked, "Is there anything I can do to help? Gosh, I'm sorry to hear about this."

"Thanks for saying that, Nic. I know my mom gives you a hard time, but she could really use your prayers."

"That goes without saying." Then he asked, "With Ruby in the hospital, who's going to cook Thanksgiving dinner?"

"You know what, I really hadn't even thought about it. We probably won't have a big dinner, especially since Mama's surgery is set for tomorrow morning."

"Aww, wow! She has to have surgery, and on Thanksgiving morning? I'm sorry to hear that. I wish I had some M&M'S to give you."

She laughed at that. "Yeah, me too." She almost told him about the cancer but didn't want to further burden him.

"If there's anything I can do, you'll let me know, right?" Nic put her hand in his. "I'm here for you."

Out of her peripheral vision, Hope saw blond hair and blue eyes. Eyes that were staring at her. Hope slowly turned her head and looked into the black Nissan Maxima that Nic pulled up to her mother's house in the other day. Nic's mother was sitting in the front seat. Melinda Evans' eyes bore into Hope's. But it wasn't a shooting-daggers-because-I-hate-you kind of stare. It was more like she was trying to place Hope—like she thought she knew her but wasn't sure.

The look on Melinda's face unnerved Hope. She turned away from the woman and walked to her car. "Let me get back to the house. Faith and I need to make plans for tomorrow."

Scooter rushed out of the Ice House with two waffle bowls full of ice cream. "It sure is nice seeing the two of you together again. To tell you the truth, Hope, if the two of you had stayed together, my boy might be in banking with me rather than running around chasing after ghosts."

Hope didn't like the image of her sister as a ghost, but that was what Scooter's words brought to mind. She prayed that Faith would take the DNA test since this might be their chance to put Trinity's "ghost" to rest. "I doubt if he would have listened to me. Nic has a mind of his own."

"Yeah, you're right about that. Nic gets it from my daddy. Never a more stubborn man on the face of the earth." Scooter seemed to have another thought. Then said, "Well, except for my dad's business partner. That guy was a real piece of work."

Hope's lips turned up into a smile. "I wonder who gave my mom lessons in stubbornness, because I think she is the number one prize-winner in that department."

"Don't I know it," Scooter said. "That beach house and the land it sits on is now worth about two million dollars, but she won't even consider selling it."

Hope's eyebrows rose. "How do you know how much it's worth?" Why was this man so deep in her family's business like that?

"Because I've tried to buy it from her. I own the property on either side of your beach house. Once I get y'all to sell me that property, I'm going to build the biggest resort hotel this island has ever seen."

"I'll talk to y'all later." Hope got in her car. She put the key in the ignition and set her box in the passenger seat. Just as she was about to start the car, she heard Scooter's words again—*your beach house*. How did he know the beach house belonged to her?

She shook it off, pulled out of the parking lot and headed back home, all the while admonishing herself not to act like her mother, being suspicious of everybody and everything. Her mother did take a loan out from Scooter's bank, putting the house up as collateral. So Scooter had every right to know the value of the home.

Chapter 22

If it wasn't one thing, it was another. Ruby was so tired of dealing with one storm after the next. Seemed like the minute she opened her eyes, something else would hit her. But she had a trick for them tonight. She wasn't going to close her eyes. That way she wouldn't wake up to any more bad news. She'd already be awake and ready for whatever the day was about to throw at her.

The nurse came in and checked her temperature, then another tech came into the room and pricked her finger to check her blood sugar. Why couldn't they just leave her be? Wasn't it enough that she had to endure surgery in the morning? A surgery that she wouldn't even be contemplating if not for her kids.

Despite her protest, her eyes were drooping. Ruby picked up the remote and started channel surfing. *House Hunters*; *Diners, Drive-Ins and Dives*; Discovery Channel. She was just about to click the button to accept an animated movie that was a redo of Michael Jordan's old movie with Bugs Bunny, Elmer Fudd and the crew when there was a knock at her door.

Ruby wanted to throw the remote at the intruder. How many times did these people need to poke and prod? Exactly the reason she didn't like doctors or hospitals. Ruby refused to say, "Come in," choosing rather to wait and see how long the intruder would stand at her door waiting on an invitation.

Within seconds, she watched as the door slowly creaked open and Pastor O'Dell peeked inside. "Are you decent in there?"

"Hahaha. So you done gave up preaching to become a comedian now?"

Pastor O'Dell took his hat off as he stepped into the room. He had a Bible in one hand and his hat in the other. "I never thought of a career as a comedian. You think I need to give it a shot?"

Pursing her lips as she stared at him, Ruby said, "I think you're too old to be changing careers. If you're tired of God, you're in a pickle because I don't think no other profession would have you."

"You might be right about that, Ruby." He sat down in the chair to the left of her bed.

"As right as rain, and you know it."

O'Dell and Henry had been the best of friends growing up. She and Henry started attending his church right after they jumped the broom. O'Dell was a good man and had always held a shine in hers and Henry's eyes. But Ruby had questions about several things that O'Dell couldn't answer, like why God had shut her womb for so long—until her husband had to find another woman to give him a baby. And why God had allowed Henry to die so young, without enjoying the fruits of his labor, and why, oh why God had allowed her baby girl to go out of the house during that awful storm and never return to her.

God giveth and God taketh away was not good enough for her. Three strikes, and she was out. She stopped going to church, figuring she would just wait until God gave her the answers Himself. But the answers never came. So she and God were at a standstill.

Pastor O'Dell opened his Bible and began reading from John 16:33:

"These things I have spoken to you, that in Me you may have peace. In

the world you will have tribulation; but be of good cheer, I have overcome the world."

He then turned to 1 Thessalonians 4 and read from verses 13–14:

"But I do not want you to be ignorant, brethren, concerning those who have fallen asleep, lest you sorrow as others who have no hope. For if we believe that Jesus died and rose again, even so God will bring with Him those who sleep in Jesus."

When he finished reading, Ruby said, "What are you doing? Why did you even come here?"

"To finish the conversation you and I started a long time ago."

Ruby shook her head. "Oh no, you don't. If I haven't set foot in your church in more than fifteen years, what makes you think I want you waltzing in to my hospital room reading scriptures to me?"

Pastor O'Dell sat his Bible down and answered, "Because I know what happened. We've been praying for you for years, Ruby. It's time to get your faith back. You're going to need it for this fight."

Ruby waved that notion away. "What good will faith do for me now?"

"You obviously believe in faith and hope, or you wouldn't have put those names on your daughters."

"Past tense, Pastor. I believed—all up until the bottom fell out."

"I know you've been through a lot, Ruby. You've had more sorrow than any woman should have to carry, but God doesn't want us to carry our sorrows. He wants us to give them to Him."

"Give them to Him? For what? What's God going to do with all the pain that's locked up in this old frail body?"

Pastor O'Dell lifted a finger. "I'm glad you asked. I've got one more scripture and then I want to answer that question for you."

"I doubt it. You never answered any other questions I had."

"I've gotten older and wiser, Ruby Reynolds. You might be surprised." He flipped several pages in the Bible and then landed in the book of Revelation. He started reading from chapter 21, verses 4–5:

"And God will wipe away every tear from their eyes; there shall be no more death, nor sorrow, nor crying. There shall be no more pain, for the former things have passed away.

"Then He who sat on the throne said, 'Behold, I make all things new.'"

He closed the Bible and leaned forward in his seat, making eye contact with Ruby. "I know the things you've been through weren't right, and I will never be able to explain why a good man like Henry left this earth so soon. Nor do I know why it took you so long to birth your first child or why Trinity isn't here with us.

"But I do know that God wants to take all that pain away, and He wants to assure you that what was lost now belongs to Him. Won't you let Him wipe the tears away and make you brand new in Him again?"

His words sounded so sweet, like a song that Ruby had long since forgotten the words to. Her eyes watered as she leaned her head back against her pillow. "I don't know if I can put my trust in God again. It was so painful when things fell apart. How can I experience that kind of pain again and keep on living?"

"I think the better question to ask is, how can you, a woman who has loved and trusted God, keep on living without Him in your life?"

Ruby was fighting with the emotional tug that was trying to pull at her heart. She had shut God out—no sense opening the floodgates now.

Pastor O'Dell wasn't ready to give up yet, it seemed, because he asked, "What if your loved ones are with Jesus or someday will be? Don't you want to see them again?"

That got Ruby to thinking. She had lost a lot, but if she could one day see her loved ones again, what a glorious day that would be.

Pastor O'Dell stood. He approached her hospital bed and then put a hand on her shoulder. "God loves you, Ruby. Receive His love and live the rest of your days confident that God cares about what concerns you."

Ruby could stand no more. Her heart exploded with the strain of all the pain she had been holding inside. And as she cried out to God, she told Him just how sorry she was for not trusting, not believing . . . for giving up on Him.

As she lifted her hands heavenward, reaching, as if trying to grab hold of God . . . trying to receive something from Him, she said, "What a fool I have been to not recognize Your love for me, even in my darkest hour."

Tears streamed down Pastor O'Dell's face. "He's here with us, Ruby. Don't you feel it?"

Ruby started clapping. "I want to believe again. I feel God's love. It's like warm, oozing chocolate moving all through my body."

With a smile, he told her, "We've been praying for you for so long, I would have expected God to move through you like hot coals of fire, so I'm going to keep on praying."

Taking a deep breath, with tears bubbling in her eyes, Ruby said, "Keep praying, Pastor. You've convinced me that God loves the Reynolds family. I feel His love, but I still don't know if I can trust Him all the way like I used to."

Ruby pressed her lips together, then sighed. "I hate admitting this, but after doubting for so long, I'm at a point where I truly need to trust, and I don't know if I can."

"You have surgery in the morning, right?"

She gave a determined nod. "Yes, and after talking with you, I've decided that old doctor can do whatever he needs to in the morning."

"Can I pray with you?" He held out his hands to her.

Years ago, on the fifth day of the search for Trinity, Pastor O'Dell reached out his hands to pray with her; she slapped them away. But now, after so many years of feeling numb and at war with herself, she was finally ready to pray. "If the good Lord spares my life, I'm going to set some things right with my family. It's time." She grabbed hold of Pastor O'Dell's hands, closed her eyes and took in every word he prayed.

In the morning, Hope, Faith, Chris and Crystal stood around her bed. Ruby was so thankful that her family was with her before surgery, so thankful she was able to look at each one of them and kiss their faces.

"Wow. What's gotten into you?" Faith asked after Ruby took her face in her hands and brought her toward her for a kiss on the cheek.

Ruby stretched out her arms. "The love of God has gotten into me, and I don't ever want Him to go away again."

"Amen to that," Chris said, then added, "I have a men's prayer group. I added you to our prayer list a long time ago, so this is music to my ears."

Ruby lifted a hand and touched Chris' face. "You're a good boy, but I need you to work harder at making Faith happy. Can you promise me you'll do that?"

Chris lifted his face and looked directly into Faith's eyes, as she was standing on the opposite side of the bed, next to Hope. "I promise you, Ruby. I will do everything in my power to make your daughter happy."

Ruby patted his face as she glanced at Faith, but she didn't say anything. Life had taught her about words spoken out of turn. Faith would need to make up her own mind.

Ruby turned her attention to Hope. The child looked like she was afraid she was about to lose something. She wanted to reassure her that nothing was ever truly lost with God. "I'm the one who picked your name; you know that, right?"

Hope nodded. "You told me."

"I named you Hope because you were a gift from God to me. You were all my hopes come true, and every time I said your name, I wanted to remember to keep my hope in God. I lost sight of that for a while, but I'm trying to get back to that place, and I need you to always remember how special you are to me and to God."

Hope gave her a weak smile. "I'll try, Mama."

The attendant came in to wheel her to the operating room. Ruby wished she had more time with her family. Needed more time to remind them not to shut God out of their lives the way she had done for so long—the way she was still doing in some areas.

"Come back to us, Grammy." Crystal held on to the rails of the hospital bed.

"I will, baby. I told my surgeon to do whatever he has to do to get rid of this cancer, so Grammy is going to be around to watch you grow into the beautiful woman God made you to be. You hear me?" Ruby wagged a finger in Crystal's direction as if daring her not to become all she was meant to be.

Crystal nodded. "I hear you."

As Ruby was being rolled out of the room, she saw the shocked expressions on her family's faces. She hadn't explained to them about how God moved in her life last night, but she would tell them everything once this surgery was over and done with. "I wish I could fix you all a big ol' Thanksgiving dinner," was the last thing Ruby said before being wheeled out of the room.

Chapter 23

"HEY, WHAT YOU DOING?" COLTON JOGGED UP THE BEACH. HE stopped in front of her.

Faith just knew she looked a complete mess. Tears stained her face, and she hadn't combed her hair before coming outside to look for Trinity, but none of that mattered, not even while she stood in front of Colton, the most handsome guy in town. "My sister didn't come home last night. We think she ran away." Actually, Faith thought she ran away, her mother thought she might have been abducted and is in somebody's basement waiting for someone to come save her.

"Why'd she do that?" Colton asked with a lifted brow.

She's fourteen and pregnant, that's why she ran away. At least, that's the answer Faith wanted to give. With all that throwing up Trinity had been doing lately, she was sure her sister was pregnant, but she hadn't told her mother about her suspicions, thus the reason her mother believed that Trinity had been abducted.

"Teenagers come up with all sorts of reasons to do the things they do." Faith shook her head. "I just hope we find her before nightfall. I don't like the idea of her being off somewhere with no one to protect her." She held up the flyers. "That's why we're passing out these flyers that my mom printed off this morning."

Colton reached out. "Give me some of those."

Faith's head tilted to the side. She noticed Colton didn't have his basketball. Most every time she saw him, whether on the beach or in town, he was either bouncing his basketball or carrying it in his backpack. No backpack today either.

Ruby walked over to Faith, giving her and Colton the eye. "This is serious business, Colton James. We don't need to find these flyers in the trash can a mile down the beach." Ruby tapped Faith's shoulder. "Come on, girl. When we finish on this beach, we need to drive into town and pass out some flyers there too."

Colton was still holding his hand out. "I'm not going to throw the flyers away, Ms. Ruby. I really do want to help."

"Hand him some flyers, and come on here," Ruby told her.

Faith's head popped up. She wiped the corner of her mouth, adjusted herself in her seat.

Hope leaned close to her. "You were snoring."

And dreaming about Colton. What was that about? Faith wanted to tell Hope about seeing Colton in her dream, but they were in the ICU waiting room, and Crystal and Chris were seated directly across from them while their mother was in surgery.

Faith glanced over at her daughter, noting that Crystal was seated next to Chris rather than next to her. It seemed to Faith that Crystal had already made her choice. Once she and Chris were divorced, her daughter would want to stay with her father.

Faith understood why Crystal was so close to Chris. In these last few years, Faith had chosen career over family. But she could now see how that choice had damaged her daughter. She wanted to make things right between them and prayed that she would be able to get Crystal the help she needed.

Chris was writing on a pad and looked like he was in serious thought about something. He put his pen down, then got up and walked over to her. Chris grabbed a chair and sat it in front of Faith and Hope. He then said, "I figured we all needed something to take our minds off the surgery, so I've been working on the plans for the house."

Faith was shocked. She told Chris that the house belonged to Hope. He knew he wasn't going to be able to trick her into selling the property, so she honestly thought he would ride out of Hallelujah and go back to Atlanta to find another project to work on.

"Plans for the house?" Hope's eyebrows furrowed. "Are you working on the house?"

Chris nodded. "I think we can keep this in the family. I can save Ruby twenty to thirty thousand by doing the work and not charging my normal contractor fees."

"Chris, that is so nice of you. Mama will be so happy to hear that." Hope gave her brother-in-law a playful punch to his shoulder.

"Yes, that is nice of you, Chris. I thought you might have changed your mind. That's why I didn't tell Hope about your suggestion." Faith eyed him, trying to give him a way out. It would be so much easier if he left now, rather than starting the job and then leaving because a better offer came along.

Chris shook his head. "I just finished a big job, and I'm waiting on permits to clear before I start my next job, so I can make the repairs to the house while I'm here."

"And how long are you planning to stay here?" Faith asked with tight lips. She was trying not to raise her voice and cause Crystal to feel some kind of way about how her father was being treated, but Faith didn't know how long she could sit there and listen to her husband acting like he deserved the saint of the year award.

"Two weeks, easy," he told Faith. "If the job isn't finished by then, I can come back on weekends and finish up."

Faith harrumphed at that.

Chris rubbed his eyelid with his index finger, then looked over at Faith. Hurt swirled around in his eyes. "You know what, Faith? I promised your mother that I would be good to you, and I'm going to keep that promise, whether you like it or not." He got up, put the chair back where he moved it from and then sat next to Crystal.

Hope looked at her like what's-wrong-with-you? "Why are you giving him such a hard time? Seems to me, he wants to help us get Mama's house in shape."

Faith side-eyed her sister. "Why you keep calling it Mama's house, when you know good and well that it's your house?"

"Not yet, it's not."

Faith rolled her eyes. "Whatever."

Huffing, Hope got out of her seat and wrapped her hand around Faith's arm, pulling her up. "Come on. Let's go to the cafeteria."

"I'm not hungry," Faith protested.

"I don't care. I'm tired of your messy attitude, and you and I are going to have it out today."

Faith tried to pull back from her sister while Hope pulled her forward. "Let go of my arm. We can talk here."

Glancing over at Crystal, Hope shook her head. She then leaned in and whispered in her sister's ear. "I think you've acted out in front of Crystal enough, don't you?"

Faith glanced over at her daughter, who was most definitely watching her with disapproving eyes. She stopped struggling and left the waiting area with Hope. Faith hated that she was mad at her sister over something their father requested, but she was. She even hated that she was mad at her mother for gifting the land to her *and* Trinity, because nobody had seen Trinity in eighteen years. So what was Faith supposed to do with that land if something happened to her mother?

"Now you listen to me," Hope said the moment they took a seat at the back end of the cafeteria, "you're my sister and I love you, but your attitude is so stank you make me want to lay hands on you."

"You did lay hands on me when you pulled me out of my seat."

Sighing, Hope said, "I really don't want to fight with you. I'll be back in California soon. Can't we just be sisters for now?"

"Why do you even want to go back to California when you have a beach house right here?"

Hope closed her eyes. Exhaled. "I don't have a beach house. That house belongs to Mama, so please get that through your thick head."

"Yeah, but when Mama passes . . ." Faith lifted a hand, waving it in the air as if wiping those words away. "And that will not be today. It will be a long, long time from now. But when she does pass, the house is yours."

"And the land is yours. What's the big deal? Like Mama said, you and I will have to get along to figure out what we want to do with the house because we can't do anything without each other's approval."

"You say that now, but how do I know that you won't cut me out?" Faith didn't know why trust was so hard for her. It just was.

Rolling her eyes and nudging her sister, Hope said, "Oh ye of little faith."

"Funny, haha." Despite herself, Faith smiled at the pun on her name. "I'm really not mad at you. I think I'm mad at Daddy and Mama. I mean, come on. I'm the one who used to follow Daddy around, watching as he worked on plans for the house. It's because of his love for buildings that I fell in love with the interior design. I have an eye for what works in different homes."

"Daddy and I used to talk about turning our beach house into a bed-and-breakfast, something cozy and warm that guests would feel right at home in. And now after all these years, Mama is ready to do it. It just seems like Daddy's vision is coming to pass."

"I can see that," Faith said, but then she frowned. "I think I'm mad at myself, too, because I hate that Mama left the land to me and Trinity. It's like giving me a gift and snatching it back."

Hope put a hand on Faith's arm.

"I don't like feeling this way," Faith said, "but the truth is, Trinity may never come back to us, so why is Mama doing this to me?"

"Go take the DNA test, Faith. It's the only way. Because if we know for sure that Trinity is really and truly gone, that will be the only way that we will all be able to let go and move on."

Tears filled Faith's eyes. "I'm not ready to move on." She wiped a few tears from her face. "I'm just being real with you because the thought of that test . . . I just don't know if I can do it."

"I'm not saying that we move on by forgetting. I never want to forget Trinity. I want to remember everything about her—the way she smiled, the way she always wanted to race us home from the beach."

"And how she lost every time." Faith laughed at that memory.

"But it was the effort that counted. Because that girl believed she could beat us each time we raced."

"She thought she was some kind of track star." Faith shook her head. "I guess she wanted to be like you, getting that track scholarship for college and all."

"You wanted to be like me too. That's what little sisters do. I just tried to be a good example for you both."

Faith noticed that Hope had this look on her face, like she wasn't so sure if she had been the kind of example she wanted to be. "I will probably be apologizing to you for the rest of our lives, but I want you to know that I am really sorry for blaming you for Trinity's disappearance. I had no right to lay my guilt at your feet."

"You've already apologized for that. Now I need you to forgive yourself, because I've already put it in my rearview."

"What about the way I treated you after Mama told us you are getting the beach house?"

Hope's lips twisted into a frown. "I'm still working on that one."

"Bet. All right. It's like that." Faith stood. "I think we need to get back. They might be looking for us."

"Okay. Let me grab a turkey sandwich or something first. I mean, it is Thanksgiving."

"You know what, let's take a couple of turkey sandwiches up for Chris and Crystal too."

After getting their food, they headed back to the ICU. On the way there, Hope asked, "Why are you giving Chris such a hard time? I've always thought he was one of the good ones, church boy and all."

"Well, that church boy is a cheat and a thief. He took most of my money out of my account to cover his business expenses and didn't even ask."

"No, not Chris."

"Yes, sis. And not only that, he took out a home equity loan on our house, and we almost lost our home because of it."

"Chris needs his behind whupped."

Faith lifted a finger and begrudgingly admitted, "He did return the money, so I guess I shouldn't actually be calling him a thief anymore, and he did pay the home equity, but I'm still mad."

Hope stopped, cocked her head to the side, and held on to her sister's arm as she looked thoughtful for a second, then said, "Can I tell you something?"

Faith nodded.

"I don't know why this is, but Mama seems to think the worst of people, like how she has always told us that Scooter Evans is basically the devil, but sis, I've got to be honest, Scooter has always been nice to me. I don't see what Mama sees."

Nodding her head, Faith agreed. "He's always been nice to me too."

"Now I'm not saying this to make you angry." Hope put a hand on her sister's shoulder. "But have you noticed that you act like Mama? You also tend to see the worst in people before seeing anything good in them."

Faith squinted at Hope. "I don't act like that."

Pursing her lips, then taking a deep, long-suffering breath, Hope said, "Yeah, sis, you do."

Faith was quiet for a moment. She put a finger to her chin. *Tap, tap, tap.* "So you're saying I need therapy?"

"Sis, we all probably need someone to talk to. Believe me, it's not just you."

Faith held on to her bag full of sandwiches while putting an arm around her sister. "I've missed you."

Hope planted a kiss on Faith's forehead. "Ditto, sis. Ditto."

Chapter 24

THE SURGERY LASTED FIVE HOURS, THEN HOPE AND FAITH had to wait another hour while Ruby was in recovery before they could see her. Hope was tired of the waiting game as far as Trinity was concerned, and Faith couldn't make her mind up, so Hope called Nic to tell him that she would take the DNA test. Somebody had to bring Trinity home, one way or another. She was prepared to do her part.

"I don't want to say that this is great because this isn't a joyous moment for anyone, but I'm happy that one of you will be taking the test."

"Let me ask you something, Nic. You remember that I told you Ruby isn't my birth mother?"

"I doubt I'll ever forget. It was eighteen years ago, but I still remember it like it was yesterday," he told her.

She swallowed. Exhaled. That was the day everything changed for them. But she couldn't think about that now. "So do you think my DNA will tell us anything?"

"Don't worry about that, Hope. You and Trinity have the same father, so if we have her, the test will show relation."

Hope didn't tell him about her doubts of whether or not Henry was her father. She couldn't speak those words again. She gripped the phone. "Do I need to make an appointment, or how is this handled?"

"They're not open tomorrow, but I know people. Let me make a call, and I'll text you the information."

"Okay. Thanks."

"I thought you were calling to tell me how your mom was doing. Is she still in surgery?"

"No. She's in recovery. We're just waiting until they move her back to her room so we can see her."

"But she held up through the surgery? That's good news, right?"

"Yes, of course it's good news. My mind just traveled somewhere else. The doctor said the operation went well. I'm just not sure how she's going to feel about it once she wakes up."

The reason Hope was unsure was because the doctor also told them that it had been necessary to do the double mastectomy to ensure that the cancer wouldn't quickly resurface. Hope was trying to prepare herself for the kicking and screaming her mother would do once she woke up without "her girls." She heard her mother say that the surgeon could do whatever he needed to do as she was being wheeled out of the room, but Hope was skeptical about how far "whatever" went with her mother.

"I did something . . . Not sure if you'll be happy about it or not," Nic said, bringing her back.

She tightened her hand around the phone. "What did you do?"

"I made you a plate, plastic wrapped it and everything."

"Who cooked?"

"I've got mashed potatoes, green bean casserole, fried turkey and corn bread dressing."

"Who cooked it?" she asked again because Hope knew good and well that Nic didn't think she was going to eat one thing that his mama cooked.

"Well, I fried the turkey and made the mashed potatoes. My dad made the green bean casserole and the corn bread dressing."

Putting a hand on her hip, Hope pursed her lips. "You're telling me that your mother didn't make anything . . . on Thanksgiving?"

"My mom hasn't been doing well lately. Dad and I figured we'd cook the meal to cheer her up."

There was something in his voice . . . sadness. She wanted to ask about his mother just as he had asked about hers, but nothing in her wanted to care about the woman who had treated her so poorly just because she was dark-skinned. "Let me get back to the waiting room with the family."

"Wait." He stopped her. "Is it okay for me to bring your plate to the hospital? And do you think Faith might want a plate also?"

She almost told him that her family didn't eat mashed potatoes on Thanksgiving—it was mac and cheese all day long—but she couldn't hurt his feelings like that. "Faith is going back to the house with her family. I'm spending the night at the hospital with Mama tonight. So I'd appreciate a plate. Thank you, Nic."

She ended her call and then went back into the waiting room with her family. Faith was sitting on the opposite side of the room from Chris and Crystal, searching Google on her cell phone. She wondered how long her sister would keep her distance. Didn't she want to make things better with her daughter?

It just seemed to Hope that a mother should keep the lines of communication open so her daughter—her teenage daughter—would feel like she could talk to her about anything. But what did she know? She hadn't found out that her mother wasn't her birth mother until she was twenty-one, so those lines of communication certainly weren't open on her end.

She slipped into a chair next to Faith and nudged her. Hope then tilted her head in Crystal's direction. "Have you talked to her about . . . you know?"

"You probably should whisper if you want to talk in code." Faith glanced over at Crystal.

Now whispering, Hope said, "Do you think she heard me?"

Faith shook her head. "She's got her face in that phone. But to answer you, no, I haven't talked to her yet. But after talking with Colton, I've decided to get her an appointment with a psychologist."

"Colton who?" Hope widened her eyes. She snapped her fingers a few times, then said, "Colton James . . . your ex?"

"I can't call him my ex since Mama wouldn't let me go out with him and forbade him from calling the house."

"But you liked him."

Faith shushed her sister, then said, "I ran into him last night when I was standing at the elevator. Colton is a psychologist. After he told me what he does, it got me to thinking that Crystal might benefit from talking to a professional."

"Good thinking." Hope was about to ask if she was going to go to the counseling sessions with Crystal, but the nurse came out and told them that Ruby was back in her room.

Breathing a sigh of relief, they all stood. Hope was worried about how her mother would react once she knew that her breasts were gone. "What do you think she's going to do to the doctor once she's able to move around?" Hope asked Faith as the four of them walked to Ruby's room.

"I don't know, but it won't be pretty," Faith assured her as they rounded the corner.

They walked past two more doors and then entered the room that Ruby had been in before the surgery. Ruby looked groggy as she lay in the bed with the cover pulled up to her shoulders. A tear pricked at the corner of Hope's eye. Her mother had made it through surgery. She looked to heaven. "Thank You, Lord."

"Hey, Mama. How are you feeling?" Faith asked.

"I'm living," Ruby responded and then broke into a grin that seemed to light up the whole room.

Hope hadn't expected that. "Wow! Mama, you came through like a champ." She stood on the left side of the bed while Faith, Crystal and Chris were on the right side.

"You look happy, Grammy." Crystal smiled back at Ruby.

Ruby lifted a hand and touched Crystal's face. "I'm happy to see you, my sweet, sweet Trinity."

Faith put her hand on Crystal's shoulder. "It's the drugs, hon. She knows who you are."

Hope got ready to tell her mother that she was looking at Crystal, but that's when the snoring started. "Well, she's out. Hopefully, whatever they gave her will wear off by the time she wakes up."

They sat down around Ruby's bed.

Hope watched her mother as if she was afraid she'd fly away if they turned their heads, then Hope's cell rang. The caller ID showed that it was Nic. She answered.

"Hey. I'm at the reception desk in the ICU but they won't let me come back there since I'm not family."

"I'll be right there." She ended her conversation and then told Faith, "Nic brought me a plate. I'm going to go get it."

Chris frowned at that. "I wish someone had brought us a plate. I'm getting hungry."

As Hope stood, she said, "Nic did offer, but I told him that you all were going to the house. Sorry, I should have checked with you all before telling him that."

"I was planning to do that." Faith looked concerned. "But what if she wakes up and we're not here?"

Hope pointed toward the bed where Ruby was snoring so loud the monitor next to her bed was shaking. "I think she'll be out for a while. I'll have the nurse roll a bed in here so I can spend the night."

When Faith still looked hesitant, Hope said, "I promise I'll take good care of her."

Crystal turned to Faith. "Grammy does snore loud. I can hardly think in here."

"Okay," Faith agreed. "You go eat your food and talk to Nic. When you get back, we'll head out."

Hope put her cell back in her purse as she walked out of the room. On her way to the waiting area, her stomach growled. It had been three hours since she had that turkey sandwich, which wasn't very good, so she was grateful that she didn't have to go back to that cafeteria. Nic was a good man, bringing her food and checking up on her like this. Spencer could never compare to Nic. Why she had even bothered was beyond her understanding.

She entered the waiting area, and Nic held out the plate to her. "I tried to keep it warm, but it's more like room temperature now."

"If it's better than this bland cafeteria food, then that's good enough for me." She took the plate from him, but she wasn't looking at the plate. Hope couldn't take her eyes off Nic. That buzz cut was growing on her. He looked distinguished and rugged all at the same time.

The short cut wasn't the only thing that was different about Nic. When they were younger, he had been rail thin. Now his neck was thick with protruding veins, and he had bulging pecs and biceps like he was getting in shape to win a triathlon contest. With her free hand, Hope waved it up and down the length of him. "When did all of this happen?"

Nic glanced down at himself and then back up at Hope. "What?"

Eyebrow lifted, face saying, you know what. "Don't play dumb. You were Nic the stick, and now you're all"—she put her hands on his chest and his arms—"swole."

Nic grinned. He then moved his hand in the direction of a table that had two chairs in the back of the room. "You want to sit over there?"

They sat down. Hope silently prayed over her food, then took the plastic wrap off the plate. Nic had placed a plastic spoon between the turkey and the green bean casserole. She picked it up and began eating.

"Mmmm." She looked at Nic with surprise in her eyes. "Boy, you put your foot in this."

Leaning back in his seat, Nic gave her an easy smile. "I can't take all the credit. My dad did help."

Jutting her spoon in the direction of the mashed potatoes, she asked, "What did you put in the potatoes?"

"Gouda cheese. It's a house secret, so don't tell my mom I spilled the beans."

The mention of his mother almost made Hope want to push the plate away—almost. She was hungry, and this food was good for her soul. She wasn't letting Melinda Evans come between her and this plate of good-good-goodness.

Sitting back up in his seat, Nic looked into her eyes. "If you think that's good, there's a place in town that has the best steak and potatoes I have ever tasted. I'd love to take you there."

Putting her hand to her chest, she imitated her best southern drawl. "Why, officer, are you asking me out on a date?"

With mischief in his eyes, Nic said, "Has it been that long that you don't know when a man is trying to get with you? Because I am, Hope. I want it to be you and me again. We were good together."

Until they weren't. Until his mother basically told her that if her son was going to be with a Black woman, she'd rather it be a light-skinned Black woman. And Hope just didn't have it in her to forgive that insult.

It wasn't Nic's fault, and she didn't want to hold his mother's behavior against him, but ever since those words left Melinda's mouth, Hope had felt less than. How could she be with Nic the way they used to be when she wasn't sure if they were supposed to be together? She didn't know how to respond, so she picked what she thought would be a safer subject. "You're asking me out to dinner, but I still can't believe that you're here. What happened with the FBI?"

Frowning, Nic told her, "I got tired of the politics. The FBI was more concerned with what the White House thought than about actually solving crimes."

"That's deep." Hope took a few spoonfuls of the corn bread dressing. "But that doesn't explain why you came back to Hallelujah. You told me you didn't want to live here. Remember that?"

He nodded. "I remember."

Hope leaned across the table and shoved his arm. "Well . . ."

Looking thoughtful, Nic told her, "In my line of work, I see people in their worst moments all the time. I found myself praying for their redemption story." He hesitated a moment, then continued. "When my mom got sick, I felt ashamed because I hadn't spoken more than a few words to her in over a decade.

"When I finally came back to town to visit, she was in the hospital. It hurt that I had let so many years pass without being here for her. I realized that I had been judging her because of her worst moment."

Hope's mind flashed back to the day Nic stood up to his mother for her. He'd told Melinda that she wouldn't be around their children. But now it sounded like he hadn't seen her all that much either.

"I didn't want to do that anymore," Nic continued. "I realized that I wanted to be around for her redemption story, so when the lead detective position came available, I moved back home."

Nic's words pricked at Hope's heart. She had lost the ability to forgive, especially when the hurt was deep. She wasn't sure what that said about her, but she knew it wasn't right.

She put the plastic wrap back over her plate and stood. "I'd better get back. Faith is waiting for me so they can go home and get something to eat."

Nic stood with her. "Oh, by the way, I'll schedule the appointment tomorrow. Hopefully, you'll be able to get into the DNA diagnostic center by Monday."

"That quick?" Hope jutted her eyebrow upward.

"We're a small town. The wheels may move slow on some things, but we can get a test done."

She stood there a moment, staring at Nic. Wanting to tell him about all the times she'd dreamed of them being back together . . . about all the times she'd whispered his name into the wind. But the longing in her heart wouldn't change the fact that they weren't meant to be together.

So she said goodbye and walked back to her mother's room, carrying her Thanksgiving meal and the ache in her heart.

Chapter 25

IT WAS STILL DAYLIGHT, BUT CLOUDS HUNG IN THE SKY, LOOK-
ing like it might rain again. Faith went back to the beach house
with her family.

The turkey was still sitting in the refrigerator. It was thawed,
but still in the wrapper. It hadn't been seasoned or injected with the
garlic butter sauce they normally injected their turkeys with. And
since it was already four in the afternoon, Faith was not feeling
that turkey.

A pack of chicken with wings, legs and thighs was in the freezer.
Faith took it out, ran some hot water in a roasting pan and submerged
the pack of chicken in the water to cut down on the thawing time.

Her mother was a from-scratch kind of cook, but she kept her
pantry stocked with quick fix items for those I-just-don't-want-to
days. Faith took a box of macaroni out of the pantry along with
two cans of Glory greens and Jiffy corn muffin mix. She set the fire
under a pot of water on the stove and poured about a tablespoon
of salt in the pot.

Chris walked into the kitchen wearing one of her mother's
aprons, which sported hearts and roses across its entire length.
There was also a big pocket in the middle. He looked ridiculous,
and Faith couldn't help but laugh.

"Oh, you laughing now, but you know I can burn in the kitchen." Faith twisted her lips to the left. "Burn what? That's the question." Chris was trying to be nice—Faith could see that—but after the blowup they'd had the other night, and Chris changing his phone passcode, she didn't know if she could trust what she was seeing.

"Don't play me like I can't cook. Who do you think feeds Crystal while you're off being decorator to all those reality wanna-be TV stars?"

She slammed the greens on the kitchen counter. Her hands went to her hips, and her neck rolled. "I know you aren't saying anything about the job that pays the mortgage, because I take my responsibilities seriously. I'm not the one who has all these pie-in-the-sky dreams that don't pan out."

Chris held up a hand. "I was just joking, Faith. I didn't come in here to argue with you. I just wanted to help, but it's obvious you don't need my help."

As Faith and Chris stood on opposite sides of the table glaring at each other, Crystal came storming into the kitchen. She had one arm in her blue, black and white checkered jacket and was putting the other arm in as she said, "I'm going outside."

Faith waved a hand around the kitchen, looking at Crystal like I-know-you're-not. "If you've got time to hang around outside, why don't you help me with dinner?"

"Daddy offered to help you, but all you want to do is argue." Rolling her eyes, Crystal turned to Chris. "I don't have time for this, Daddy. Why can't we just go back home?" Crystal shook her head. She then slammed the screen door as she left the house.

"I know that child did not just disrespect me like that." Faith stepped forward, about to make her way to the back deck to go check a child who must've forgotten which side her bread was buttered on.

Chris got in her way. "She's upset. Just give her some time."

"Easy for you to say." Faith flung her hands in the air. "You are

Daddy Day Camp while I'm the Wicked Witch of the South as far as she's concerned. And you never take up for me. You just let her think I'm so evil to you while you're just a prince of a guy."

"I never said I was a prince. I've made mistakes, and I'm sorry that things have gotten this bad between us, but I'm not the man you've made me out to be."

"Oh really?" The water the chicken was in had turned cold. She drained it and poured more hot water over the chicken while saying, "Then why do I feel so angry when you're around me?"

Chris untied the apron from around his neck. "I wish I had an answer for you, but I don't know why we can't get past these issues that keep popping up in our marriage."

She did the sista-sista neck roll. "Because I don't trust you, that's why. You say one thing but do another. All of y'all do."

"Who is 'y'all'?" He snatched the apron off, threw it in a chair and pointed a finger in her face. "I have never been anything but up-front with you." He opened his mouth to say something else, but then shook his head and walked to the door. Before stepping outside, Chris said, "I told your mother that I would try to make you happy, but I think the best way for me to do that is to step away."

Her voice caught in her throat as she stumbled over the words, "W-what are you saying?"

Chris wiped his eyes. "I can't fight for us anymore, Faith. Send me the divorce papers. I'll sign them."

Of course he was ready to go. He had some money in his pocket now. His ship came in with that house he'd been working on, and now he didn't need her.

"I'm not the man you've made me out to be."

Who was he then? Was she wrong about him? But how could she be? Then she heard Hope say, *"You act like Mama. You also tend to see the worst of people."*

A thousand things ran through Faith's mind. She had been thinking about a divorce for over a year, but Chris had never said those words. He was tired of her? She was tired, too, but she wasn't sure exactly what she was tired of at that moment.

Her chest heaved from pain way down deep as tears formed in her eyes . . . He was leaving her. She went to the back door. She saw Chris sitting on one of the lounge chairs on the deck, but Crystal was standing by the gate talking with Javon. Crystal opened the gate and started walking toward the beach with him.

Something screamed within Faith's soul, *Nooo!* She burst through the screen door and took off running. She had to get Crystal away from Javon . . . away from the beach . . . away from whatever makes girls leave home and never come back. "Crystal," she screamed, "you didn't ask permission to leave this house! Get back here."

Crystal stopped and turned around, her mouth and eyes wide with mortification. "Mom, what are you doing? I'm just taking a walk on the beach."

Faith caught up to Crystal, looking around wildly as she shook a finger in her face. "No, what you were doing was leaving this house with Javon, and God only knows where you were going or if you'd even come back home."

Chris put a hand on Faith's arm. "Calm down, Faith. I told her she could talk to this young man. She said he helped y'all board up the house."

"Did you tell her she could leave the house?" Faith flung her arm wide. "Do you want her to get lost out here and then have to deal with the pain of never seeing her again?"

Chris shook his head. "It's not that deep, Faith. She was just taking a walk."

Faith turned to Javon. "We appreciate your help the other day. You're welcome to come to the house to visit with Crystal as long as an adult is around, but she can't go off on a walk with you or anyone else."

Crystal hadn't moved, like her feet were stuck in the sand, so Faith grabbed her arm and moved her in the direction of the house. "Let's go, little girl. I've got food to cook."

Javon waved at Crystal. "I'll see you later."

Crystal ducked her head, then waved back without looking at him. Chris and Crystal sat down on the back patio instead of coming inside the house with Faith, which was fine with her because she needed to clear her mind. She stepped back into the kitchen and opened the fridge, took out the shredded cheddar and mozzarella cheeses. Her mother also had a block of Colby cheese in the fridge. She took that out and started shredding it so she could place the cheese on top of the mac and cheese before putting it in the oven.

She could hear sounds on the patio. Sounded like Crystal saying, "I hate her, Dad."

Faith glanced out onto the back patio. Crystal leaned her head on Chris' chest and her shoulders shook as Chris put an arm around her. Crystal thought she was Cruella de Vil. But that girl had no idea the things Faith had endured.

She put the knife on the counter and stepped back onto the patio. Faith looked at her daughter. The child that she had been running away from, but now wanted desperately to be closer to. "I'm not trying to ruin your life, Crystal. But being in Hallelujah just brings back all the pain I experienced when my sister went missing. I can't go through that again, so maybe I am a little strict with you, but it's because . . ." Her voice caught. "Even though you hate me, I love you dearly."

Crystal didn't respond to that, just kept crying.

Faith went back into the house and shut the door to drown out the sound of Crystal's tears. But she couldn't focus as she tried to work on her meal. Faith's mind kept drifting back to Crystal sitting on the deck crying as if Faith was making life too hard to bear. She grabbed her phone and went on YouTube to find a gospel mix. She needed something to soothe her soul. The mix included Marvin Sapp, Erica Campbell, and a few others. But the song that spoke to Faith's heart was "I Told the Storm" by Greg O'Quin 'N Joyful Noyze.

There had been too many storms in Faith's life. Too many winds blowing her this way and that. The song was ministering to her because she desperately wanted to tell her storm to go away. She wished she was more like Jesus, able to speak to the winds and waves and make them obey.

It seemed to her that the whole family had endured so many storms that they had lost the ability to trust God. Lost the freedom that comes with going through trials and tribulations, praying about it and then leaving all those problems with God.

As she dropped the macaroni in the boiling water, Faith wondered if they could move past this like Hope was saying earlier. Or was it too late for her family? Had God already passed them by?

Faith seasoned the chicken, floured it and then put it in her mama's cast-iron skillet to fry. She then dumped the Glory greens in a pot, added a few seasonings while she continued listening to the music. She needed the storms to stop raging in her life . . . needed peace . . . needed answers. She hadn't felt much peace since Trinity disappeared.

But what if Trinity never returned to them? Was she supposed to mourn for what she lost the rest of her life? When would the pain stop and her praise return?

She preheated the oven, then put the macaroni in a glass pan. Put butter, eggs, the shredded cheddar, mozzarella and milk in it, then stirred and seasoned to taste. Put aluminum foil over the top of the pan, then put it in the oven.

Faith felt like she was going through the motions as she stirred the greens, flipped the chicken over. Then she turned back to the counter and saw the Jiffy corn muffin mix. She was about to open the box and pour it into the bowl, but she suddenly had an urge to hit something. Hit something so hard that it took her mind off of her sorrows. So she balled her fist and hit the box and then hit it again and again and again until the corn muffin mix splashed out onto the counter.

That's when the tears spilled from a place that had been locked deep inside of her for so long. Tears of regret. Tears of wish-I-could-change-the-past. Her tears could fill a river of regret, but it wouldn't change the fact that her husband thought she was coldhearted and her daughter hated her. Lifting her hands right where she stood, with tears streaming down her face, in a low, deliberate voice, Faith said, "Deliver me, Lord. Please . . . too many storms."

Faith managed to pull herself together long enough to finish the dinner. She called Chris and Crystal in to eat. The three of them filled their plates. Crystal tried to go to her room with her plate, but Faith shook her head. "You can sit down at the table and eat with me and your daddy."

"But I wanted to watch television," Crystal complained.

"It's Thanksgiving, Crystal," Chris said. "We spent most of the day at the hospital, but we're here now, and your mama has cooked us a meal, so let's sit down as a family and eat it."

Crystal dragged her feet as she walked to the kitchen table and sat down with them. Chris blessed the food, and then they started eating.

Faith was quiet because for once she didn't know what to say or who to be angry at. She smacked her lips on her fried chicken leg and then scooped a forkful of mac and cheese into her mouth.

Chris mumbled something that sounded like, "*Mmm*. This is good." He turned his head this way and that, glancing at the stove and the counter. "I thought you were going to make some corn bread?"

Faith had just put some greens in her mouth. She chewed. Swallowed. "I spilled the muffin mix, so I threw the box in the trash."

"Well, this meal is delicious, so we didn't need it." Chris turned to Crystal. "What about you, baby girl. How's your food?"

Crystal had been taking small bites and pushing food around on her plate. "Yes, it's good, but I'm getting full." Glancing at her father she asked, "Do you mind if I go to my room now?"

"I mind," Faith told her and then pointed toward Crystal's plate. "Finish your food and then you can go to your room." What did those people on Google know? Her child needed to eat, and she still had a plate full of food.

"But Daddy . . ." Crystal whined to her father as if Faith's words meant nothing. That type of response from Crystal used to bother her.

Faith didn't know how she was going to make up for the years of neglect, but she knew one thing for sure: she wasn't going to let Crystal get away with doing whatever she wanted just because Faith felt guilty about being an absentee parent.

Chris backed her up. He pointed at Crystal's plate and said, "Eat."

Rolling her eyes, Crystal picked up her chicken wing and ate it. She then finished the mac and cheese but flat-out refused to eat the greens.

After dinner, Chris offered to wash the dishes. Crystal went to her room, and Faith took a seat at the kitchen counter. While he ran the dishwater, she kept her voice low as she asked, "I'm thankful that you gave my money back and paid the home equity payments, but can you tell me why you took the money without asking?"

While putting the cups, plates and silverware in the dishwater, Chris told her, "I wanted to ask, I really did, but lately you've been looking at me like I've done nothing but mess up your life. I was embarrassed to tell you that I was short on funds to finish the house I was working on."

"So you just helped yourself to my hard-earned dollars."

He turned to her. "Remember how Pastor Green is always telling us that if what you have is not enough to meet your need, then it's your seed?"

"Yeah." She shrugged, like what's that got to do with me.

"I knew that the twenty thousand that was in your account—which I had full access to, just like you have full access to my account—wasn't enough to get us over the hump."

His account was always running low, so what difference did it make that she had access?

He continued, "We needed more than what you had in the bank, and I knew that if I finished the job and sold the house, I would be able to take care of our bills, so I went for it."

"Next time, ask first." What was she saying? There wasn't going to be a next time because she was going to take his name off her bank account.

He wiped his hands with the dry towel and walked over to the counter where she was standing. "Can you try to trust me a little more? I'm not the bad guy that you think I am."

Trust. That was a big word for someone like Chris to use. She opened her mouth to tell him just how he had ruined the trust she had for him, but that's when Crystal walked past the kitchen and headed for the bathroom toward the back of the house. Faith nudged Chris and whispered, "She's going for it."

"You sure?" he asked, looking like he still didn't believe that his daughter had an eating disorder.

"I've seen this move before. I know what I'm talking about. Give her a minute, and then we are going to bust in that bathroom on her."

"Why don't we just stop her now?"

"Mmph." Faith shook her head. "She'll keep denying it if we don't catch her in the act."

Faith tiptoed to her mother's bedroom, went into the walk-in closet where the master key that opened all the doors in the house was kept. She took a small white box off the shelf, opened it and took one of the keys out of the box.

She then went back to the kitchen and signaled for Chris to follow her. He got close up on her and whispered in her ear, "Are you going to knock first?"

She whispered back, "I'm going to unlock the door, knock, then bust on in." She side-eyed him. "Are you with me or not?"

When they reached the bathroom, they could hear sounds coming from within that were like someone being strangled or worse. Chris whispered, "I'm with you. Unlock that door."

She did. Knocked once, then opened the door. Crystal's finger was down her throat. Her head swiveled around, and her eyes got big. Then an explosion of mac and cheese and chicken launched across the bathroom floor.

Seeing her daughter with her fingers down her throat, making herself throw up, shook something in Faith. She rushed to Crystal's side, wrapped her arms around her daughter and held on to her. "Baby, baby, baby . . . why?"

"I was too full, Mama."

Chris stood there shaking his head with his hand over his mouth. "Why are you doing this to yourself, hon?"

"I ate too much, Daddy. My stomach was hurting really bad." Crystal started crying.

Faith's heart went out to her. A tear trickled down her face. Her daughter was suffering, and she had to get her some help. She had let her defenses down with Trinity, and they'd lost her. She wasn't going to let history repeat itself. Not this time . . . not with her child. "I'm taking you to the hospital."

Chapter 26

HOPE DESPERATELY NEEDED TO DE-STRESS, SO AS RUBY SLEPT, she took her adult coloring book and colored pencils out of her purse and worked on a mountain scene. When she finished, she went to the cafeteria to get a bottle of water. She had never been in a hospital on Thanksgiving and was surprised to see so many sad faces milling around. This was the day they should be at home eating like there was no tomorrow, playing games and gossiping on family members.

Instead, they were at the hospital, dealing with sickness and sorrow. Hope didn't recognize any of the people she saw, but her heart went out to them just the same. It was a mystery to her how so many people, herself included, could deal with traumatic experiences, such as a sick loved one, without breaking down.

The cafeteria had peach cobbler. It looked a little runny, but Hope had missed out on her mother's peach cobbler, so this would have to do. She purchased a bottled water and peach cobbler and then headed back to her mother's room.

On her way to the elevator, she noticed an ambulance pull up by the double doors in front of the emergency room. She was about to turn up the hall a few feet away to get on the elevator and go back to the fourth floor when Nic and his father rushed into the area.

Nic looked frazzled. His hand went to his mouth, down to his side, then he lifted it again and ran his hand through the fuzz on top of his head. Hope started toward him. "Nic, Nic, what's wrong?"

He turned toward her. Eyes red . . . hand rubbing the back of his head. "Hope! Oh God, I'm so glad to see you." He pulled her into his arms and hugged her like he needed someone to lean on so he wouldn't fall apart.

His father was standing at the door, eyes glazed over, like he'd witnessed some kind of horror and couldn't get it to stop playing inside his head. Then the emergency doors opened again. A bed was being rolled in. It was Nic's mother. She wasn't moving. Hope didn't like Melinda Evans, not one itty-bitty bit, but she felt Nic's pain. It was the same kind of pain she felt when Ruby had been rushed to the hospital. The same kind of pain she felt when she discovered that Ruby wasn't her birth mother.

Nic had been so kind to check on her once she told him that her mother was in the hospital, but she hadn't even asked about his mother, even after he told her that Melinda was sick. How could she have been so thoughtless?

"My mom had another stroke," Nic said.

She heard the trembling in his voice, like he was afraid his whole world was about to change. "I'm sorry, Nic. I'm so sorry."

He pulled away from her. Wiped his eyes. "I've got to go with my dad, but I'm glad I ran into you. I needed that hug."

She wanted to pull him back into her arms, but his father had started walking behind the gurney. She reached out for Nic. "Call me. I want to make sure you're okay."

He reached out, waving as he backed away. "I'm praying for your mother. Please pray for mine."

Her hand dropped. How could he ask her to pray for his mother? He had been there. He heard the awful things his mother said to her: *"Hope is too dark. Do you have any idea what your kids will look like?"*

Did he expect her to forgive and forget? How could he expect that? She turned away from him and headed back to the elevator.

Ruby stirred when she opened the door, but didn't awaken. Hope climbed into the bed that had been brought into the room for her, opened the peach cobbler container and dug in. It wasn't as good as her mother's, but the sugar rush was hitting the spot. She needed something to take her mind off what she had just witnessed and what Nic had asked of her.

She hated how distraught Nic looked and knew he meant what he had said. He had been praying for her mother, even though Ruby had thrown him off her property and called him Nickel Knucklehead. But was she really supposed to pray for a woman who cost her a relationship with her first and only love?

Forgive.

Hope glanced over at her mother. Ruby was snoring, but she distinctly heard the word *forgive*. Was it her subconscious or had God spoken that single word into her spirit, challenging her to come up higher, to be something different than what she had become after all these years of holding unforgiveness in her heart?

Hope tried to shake it off as she lay down and pulled the cover over her shoulders, but her heart wouldn't let it go, and before she could stop herself, she was crying. "I have a right to hate her," Hope mumbled under the covers. She changed positions, trying to get comfortable, before flinging the covers off. She got out of bed and turned on the television.

The news was on. The weatherman was pointing toward a map that showed Hallelujah as he said, "Our system is still picking up Hurricane Lola. It's just sitting in all that warm water in the Caribbean. We're trying to determine which way it will go once it starts moving again, so stay tuned, everyone."

As Hope listened to the weatherman, tears gave way to a severe, wet, and out-of-control downpour.

"What's going on? Why are you crying?" Ruby rubbed the sleep from her eyes, then slowly adjusted her body so she was facing Hope.

Hope pointed toward the television, then wiped the tears from her face. "I'm sorry I woke you."

"I'm not." Ruby glanced at the television, then turned back to Hope, squinting as if she was trying to read her mind. "We know all about storms, so I know that weatherman don't have you all worked up like that. What's wrong?"

Sniffling, Hope wiped her nose again. "Nic's mom is sick."

"And you feel bad for her? Is that why you're crying like that?"

Hope shook her head. "Nic said he was praying for you and then asked me to pray for his mother, but I can't pray for that woman." The tears wouldn't stop coming. She'd carried this hurt for so long. It was too deep. "She was so awful to me, Mama. I don't want to pray for her."

"So why are you crying?"

Punching the mattress with her fist, Hope confessed, "Because I should have forgiven Melinda by now, but I just can't." Hope put her head in her hand as she tried to get hold of herself. What was she doing? Why was forgiving this woman so hard? Why had she let this offense linger so long?

Ruby held on to the side rails and tried to pull herself up, then she signaled for Hope to come over to the bed. Pointing at the bed rail controls, she said, "Lift my head up."

Using the buttons to adjust the bed, Hope lifted her mother's head a few inches. "I'm supposed to be here to provide support for you tonight. I shouldn't have woken you with my drama."

"So I guess you'd rather suffer by yourself." Ruby shook her head. "Sorrow should be shared, and if you can't give it to nobody else, then give it to God. I learned that the hard way."

Hope put her hands on the side rails. "I know you're right, Mama, but when you've held on to something for so long, it's not that easy to let go."

Ruby got a sorrowful look in her eyes. She took one of Hope's hands and held on to it. Sighing deeply, Ruby said, "I need to tell you about something that I've held on to for much too long. I'm worried that you won't be able to forgive me, but I can't keep it from you any longer."

Hope didn't like the look on her mother's face. She wanted to put her hands over her ears and turn away. "I'm scared. Maybe this is a discussion we should have once you're out of the hospital."

Ruby shook her head. "I've kept too much from you, and I had no right. God forgive me, but I've got to tell what I've done." A tear drifted from the corner of Ruby's eye. She wiped it away.

"Let me sit down." Hope got back in the bed, her back against the wall. "I just hope you're not going to make me cry."

Ruby twisted her lips. "I wish I didn't have to make you sad, but I can't hold in this lie any longer. I promised God that I would set some things right with you if I made it out of that surgery alive, and now I'm going to tell you the truth."

The air was thick with silence. Hope didn't respond to her mother's last comment. She just waited. Time seemed to tick . . . tick . . . tick.

Then Ruby said, "I told you I didn't know the woman who gave birth to you. I told you she didn't want you and that she had gone mad, so me and your daddy decided we would raise you. But that wasn't exactly the way it happened."

Closing her eyes, Hope tried to take herself out of the hospital, away from this moment. She wanted to be on the beach, listening to the waves, smelling the saltiness of the water. She wanted to be any-where but here, but here she was, and her mother had just said that she had lied . . . lied again. She opened her eyes and waited. She had begged her mother for the truth so many years ago. Was she ready for it?

"Your daddy and I had been married six years when I started feeling like the good Lord must have decided not to let me bear any children of my own. I was depressed for two years straight, and each one of those years, Donna James' sister, Brenda, came to the island for the summer, flaunting herself in front of your daddy.

"She was a brazen one. Several times while we were on the beach, she asked Henry to help her put lotion on, right in my face. That sister of hers had only been married to Calvin James for three years. He'd brought Donna back from Brooklyn, but that Donna acted like she was born and raised on the island, and she let her sister do whatever she wanted when she came down here."

Hope's eyes got big. "Mama, are you telling me that Donna James is my aunt?"

Ruby lifted a hand. "Just let me finish, okay?"

Hope remembered seeing Donna James at most of her track meets. Donna was there cheering on her son, CJ, but she also cheered for Hope and congratulated her on each win.

"I knew I wouldn't be able to stop Brenda from flirting with my husband," Ruby continued, "so I told him that he could go be with her, but only if he could make a baby with her—my baby. I told him I wanted a baby."

Hope couldn't stay silent on that. "Mama, how could you do that to Daddy? He loved you. He never would have cheated on you."

Ruby nodded. "That's why I had to nudge him. He knew how miserable I was without a child, so he went to Brenda and told her that the only way they could be together was if she gave him a baby. Brenda must have thought that he aimed to stay with her once she had the baby because I don't think she ever intended to lose you in the bargain."

Hope narrowed her eyes on Ruby. "What are you saying?"

"I'm trying to tell my truth and ask for forgiveness, but you got to just sit there and listen, okay?" Ruby stared at her, eyes begging her to understand.

But Hope didn't understand. What had her mother done?

"When Brenda got pregnant, she came prancing up the front steps of our little house, like Henry was going to throw me out and give the place to her." Ruby leaned her head back, looked like she was remembering some distant memory. "Told me she was pregnant and that she and Henry were going to be together.

"'That's news to me,' I said to her. Then I called Henry into the living room with us. I told him to tell that wanna-be homewrecker that she was carrying my baby. When Henry told her that he had already talked to her parents and they agreed that he and I should take the baby, Brenda didn't take that well. She went running and screaming out of our house.

"We gave Brenda's parents seventeen thousand dollars, and they convinced Brenda to sign the papers. They reminded her that she was only twenty and had the whole world in front of her. When she went into labor, they called Henry. He went to New York, picked you up and then brought you home to me. I was happy. For the first time in our marriage, I felt whole, like we were a true family, but that old Donna wouldn't let me enjoy being a mother. She came to the house and told us that her sister had been hospitalized because she couldn't snap out of the depression."

Hope stood, heart beating fast, anger boiling inside. "So she went 'mad'"—she did air quotes—"as you said, but it wasn't until after you and Daddy took me away from her?"

Ruby nodded again. "Brenda came to the house when you were a few months old. Said she'd made a mistake, and she wanted you back. But she had taken the money and signed the papers. I told her she wasn't getting you back."

"How could you do that? And how could you lie to me all these years?"

Ruby lifted her hands and then let them drop back onto the bed. "All I can say is, sometimes right and wrong look like twins."

"Are you kidding me?" Hope's voice elevated. "That's all you have to say for yourself? You completely destroyed another person's life, but that doesn't matter, does it?"

When Ruby didn't respond, Hope asked, "What about my birth certificate? How come it has your name on it, and why is it registered here instead of New York? And why didn't my real mother . . ."

Ruby narrowed her eyes on Hope, daring her to finish that sentence. "I'm your real mother. I took care of you, didn't I? And for your info, I even found a way to get a birth certificate that says I'm your mother." Ruby snapped her fingers two times for emphasis on her breaking news. "I've got the papers to prove that you are my daughter, and you best believe they didn't come cheap."

Blowing out hot air, a look of exasperation on her face, Hope said, "Why didn't you tell me this years ago?"

"I never wanted you to know that I had to get a falsified birth certificate so that you would be legally mine, but I'm telling you the truth of it now."

Hope thought on all her mother told her for a moment. Her mind traveled back to the words her mother spoke about all the money they paid to have her. Growing up in the Reynolds household, money was tight. They had enough to cover their needs, but they didn't do vacations or buy extravagant gifts for each other. She turned back to Ruby. "Where did you get the money to pay off Brenda?"

Ruby turned from Hope. "That's a secret I'll take to the grave."

"No," Hope screamed. "You don't get to keep any more secrets."

The door opened. A nurse peeked her head in. Finger to her lips. "You're too loud in here. Our patients need rest." She then walked over to Ruby's monitor and checked it.

When the nurse closed the door, Hope lowered her voice but said, "I've got some truth for you, Mother." The word *mother* had scorn attached to it. "I'm going to take that DNA test on Monday to see if those are Trinity's remains that were found months ago, and I don't care if you like it or not."

"Hope," Ruby's voice sounded weak as she called out to her daughter.

The tears came again as Hope said, "The real truth is you or Faith need to take that DNA test, because I might not be a match for Trinity because nobody knows if Brenda was seeing someone else besides Daddy. But I'm so tired of not knowing if I truly am a Reynolds, and I'm so tired of not knowing what happened to Trinity that I'm willing to do what I have to do. It looks like I'm the only one in this family who knows how to do that." She stared at her mother, releasing all of the scorn she felt. "So maybe I'm not a Reynolds. Maybe I'm just part of that not-worth-a-quarter-put-together James clan. Isn't that what you said about the people that you now tell me I'm related to?"

Ruby covered her forehead with her hands and closed her eyes. "I didn't mean it like that. I just didn't want Faith or Trinity getting involved with those James boys because I was afraid that Brenda might pop back up and then all my lies would be uncovered."

Good God, how could this be happening? Was she supposed to forgive this too? Stepping away from her mother's bed, Hope darted her head this way and that, looking for a way of escape. The door was right there. All she had to do was go through it, then go to the beach house and pack her clothes. She'd left this town vowing never to return once before. She could do it again.

Chapter 27

Faith and Chris took Crystal to the emergency room. Faith was concerned about the stomach pain Crystal had been complaining about. She worried that her daughter might have harmed herself with all that throwing up.

Crystal confessed she hadn't had a period in the last two months. Faith informed the doctor about that, then the doctor told them that Crystal's blood pressure was low, and she was dehydrated.

But the worst part of it all was when they hooked her baby up to an IV so they could pump fluids into her veins. Crystal had this I-just-wanna-go-home look on her face with her lips scrunched together and her eyes moist from tears.

Faith turned from her child and let out a small yelp as her throat constricted. The ground felt like it moved. Faith stumbled.

Chris came up behind her and put an arm around her waist. "She's going to be okay, Faith. We have to trust that we got her here in time."

His words were meant to reassure, to bring comfort, but Faith felt anything and everything but comfort. *Trust* was too big of a word for her. She held on to Chris' arm as tears streaked down her face. "What kind of mother am I? How did I not know any of this?"

"Shh," Chris whispered against her ear. "I missed it too. We've both been busy. What Crystal is going through is a reminder to us to take time for what matters most."

Faith's phone vibrated in her pocket. She pulled it out and read the message from Hope. Her eyes widened as she told Chris, "Hope says she's leaving, but she's supposed to stay with Mama all night." Faith shook her head and texted her sister.

> I'm in the emergency with Crystal, so I can't come to Mama's room right now.

Faith put the phone back in her pocket and silently prayed Hope would get it together. She needed her sister back in her life, but if she was going to be the same old Hope, disappearing at the drop of a dime, then maybe she didn't need her.

"Daddy, my arm hurts," Crystal said while tugging at the IV.

Chris rushed over to the bed. "Don't touch that, hon. You need fluids in your body."

Faith moved to the other side of the bed. She rubbed Crystal's free arm. "We'll have the nurse come back in and take a look at your arm."

Crystal turned to Faith with tears in her eyes. "It hurts, Mommy. I'm not lying."

"I don't think you're lying, honey." Faith hit the call button for the nurse's desk, then she leaned down and hugged her daughter.

The intercom came on. "Can I help you?"

"My daughter is complaining of discomfort. Can someone check the IV for her?" Faith ran her hand down the side of Crystal's face. "It's going to be okay. Your daddy and I are here for you. We won't let you down this time. I promise you."

Crystal stopped squirming and leaned her head into Faith's hand as if that little bit of reassurance meant the world to her. Faith was no magician, but if she could turn back the hands of time, there were two things she'd go back and get right: the day she let Trinity walk out of the house, and the day she walked away from her responsibilities as a mother, choosing to go hard for her career.

The nurse entered the room to check Crystal's arm. Before the door could close, Hope came barreling into the room, looking as frantic as she had when she came into the beach house after Trinity had been missing for days.

"How's she doing?" Hope tried to catch her breath as she looked from Crystal to Faith to Chris and then at the nurse who was adjusting Crystal's IV.

"She's dehydrated. They're trying to get some fluids into her." Faith walked over to her sister and wrapped her arms around her. "I don't know how to thank you for paying attention to what was going on with her when I was so clueless."

"What did the doctor say?" Hope wanted to know.

Faith had her back to Crystal. She crossed her arms in front of her chest, rubbing them as if there was a chill in the air. She spoke in a low tone as she told Hope, "He says she can recover from this, but only if she stops purging."

The nurse said a few words to Chris and then walked toward the door.

Faith stopped her. "Is she okay?"

The nurse nodded. "I adjusted the IV. It should be fine now."

Hope walked over to the bed as the nurse left the room. She looked Crystal in the eye. "You don't want to harm yourself, do you?"

Crystal shook her head. "I don't want to hurt myself anymore, Auntie Hope, but my stomach just feels so full, and I have to get rid of the food."

Chris took his daughter's hand in his. "We're going to get you some help, honey, so don't worry about anything. Just do what the doctor tells you."

She looked up at Chris with repentant eyes. "I'll try, Daddy. I didn't know I was making myself sick." Crystal's eyes started to droop.

She yawned. "I'm getting tired. I don't have to stay here all night, do I?"

"The doctor will let us know if you need to spend the night once they get more fluids in you. Just try to get some rest," Faith told her.

"I can't rest with everybody looking at me and being all worried."

Chris sat in the chair next to Crystal's bed. "Who's looking at you?" He took his phone out of his pocket and started scrolling. "Not me."

Faith couldn't help herself. Chris made her smile. He loved his daughter, and for now that was enough. She tugged Hope on the shoulder and then pointed to the door. She then told Crystal, "I'll go sit in the waiting area with your aunt."

Crystal reached out for her. Eyes frantic. "Don't leave me, Mommy."

Chris said, "I'm here, hon. Just try to rest."

Faith's heart was both delighted and breaking into pieces at the same time. It had been a long while since Crystal had wanted to be anywhere near her for more than five minutes. But the fear she heard in her daughter's voice did not bring her comfort. Hopefully, this experience had scared her enough to make her stop, drop that finger and back away from the toilet. "I'm not leaving, baby. I'll just be right out there." She pointed toward the waiting area. "I need to talk to your aunt for a few minutes, and we don't want to disturb you."

Faith and Hope walked out of Crystal's room to grab seats in the waiting area, but as they came upon the room next to Crystal's, Scooter Evans stepped out, and Faith and Hope glanced into the room. Faith leaned close to Hope and asked, "Is that Melinda?"

"Yes, she came in earlier," Hope said as they passed the room.

"Oh, hey, Scooter. Is everything okay?" Faith asked as they ran into him in the hallway.

"Much better. Things are much better now." Scooter kept walking down the hall.

Faith and Hope went to sit in the back of the waiting area. Faith said, "If you want to go check on Nic and his mom, you don't have to sit here with me."

Hope shook her head, put her feet up in her seat.

Faith stared at Hope a moment. "Okay, so can you tell me why you are leaving the hospital tonight when you are supposed to be spending the night with Mama?"

Hope sighed and put her hand to her face. After a long moment, she asked, "You know what Mama thinks about the James family?"

"Yeah. She said they're all not worth a quarter put together, and that's why she refused to let me go out with Colton . . . who I might remind you is now a psychologist."

"He's also my first cousin," Hope said as her eyes filled with tears.

"What?" Faith leaned back in her seat. Faith narrowed her eyes as she gave Hope a what-you-talkin'-'bout stare. "Colton is definitely not my cousin."

"Listen to me, Faith. Colton is not your cousin. He's mine because I'm part of the James family."

Faith looked at her like she was trying to make sense of what she heard but wasn't quite putting it together.

"Remember when I came home to look for Trinity?"

"I remember."

"I would have never come back here if Trinity hadn't gone missing. I didn't want to be around Mama, and she knew it."

Faith put her hand on Hope's shoulder trying to calm her.

"I asked Mama to tell me the truth about my biological mom, but she told me she didn't know who my mother was. Told me that Daddy cheated on her with some random woman from Brooklyn and that the woman had been in and out of mental institutions, so she gave me to Daddy.

"But the woman who gave birth to me was Donna's sister, and Mama told Daddy to hook up with Brenda. I don't think her last name is James, since that's Donna's married name," Hope clarified, then said, "Anyway, after Brenda gave birth to me, Mama and Daddy took me from her."

Faith's hand went to her heart. "They stole you from your mother?"

"Who knows?" Hope said while shaking her head. "Mama says that Brenda was young, and her parents made her give me to Daddy, but who knows what the real story is? And who knows if Daddy was the only man Brenda was with back then."

"Are you still on that kick?" Faith wrapped a hand around Hope's arm and shook her. "Now you listen to me: Henry Reynolds is your father. I see him in you, so stop with this already. You are my sister."

"Well, Daddy's not here to take a DNA test, but I'm going to the diagnostic center on Monday and take that DNA test to see if I'm a match for those remains. It's time for us to bring Trinity home, don't you think?"

Trinity had been gone a long time, and yes, Faith would like to have some answers, but her mother had just been diagnosed with breast cancer and her daughter had an eating disorder. On top of all of that, Faith didn't know if she could deal with knowing that it was over—that Trinity would never walk back into the beach house again. She just didn't know.

For years, Faith had accused Hope of being a runner, but it was at this very moment, as she saw the resolve in her sister's eyes, that she realized Hope was the strongest of them all. Always had been.

Chapter 28

GROWING UP ON THE BEACH, HOPE HAD ALWAYS ENJOYED the Thanksgiving season. The weather changed from unbearably hot and sticky to cool and breezy. Her daddy normally took time off work to relax with the family—the family that she thought she had.

Her sister didn't seem to get why she was so upset, but Faith's identity had never been in question. Faith had Ruby's light complexion and her eyes, but Faith also had their dad's high cheekbones and his small nose.

Since she could remember, everyone told her that she looked like her daddy, but that was only because they both had dark complexions. Hope had seen the woman who gave birth to her, and Hope's complexion was more in line with Brenda's than Henry's midnight-Black complexion.

She was so confused and just wanted out, but she had to take care of a few things before she could leave this town and never look back again. The first thing she needed to do was talk to Nic and let him know how she truly felt, but she couldn't do it tonight, not while his mother was in the hospital looking like she was at death's door.

Faith had gone to the fourth floor to sit with Ruby while Crystal was receiving fluids. Hope stayed downstairs with Chris and Crystal. When Crystal was released from the hospital after receiving enough fluids, Hope texted Faith. Once Faith came back to Crystal's room, they gathered their belongings and Hope caught a ride back to the beach house with them. In the morning, she showered, ate a bagel and some eggs, then hopped in Ruby's SUV and drove over to Donna James' house.

It was foggy and gloomy out this morning, like the weather was mimicking how she felt. Because she was absolutely done in. Hope thought she wanted to know all the secrets surrounding her birth. For years, she had thought that her birth mother hadn't wanted the responsibility of raising a child, but the knowledge of the circumstances helped her to see that things may not have been so cut-and-dried for Brenda. And that made her heart hurt.

Donna's house was inland. She lived on a street with rows of houses just like any other suburban street in America. The only difference was her house was just two miles away from the beach, and she could walk there whenever she chose.

The fog still hung in the air as Hope got out of the SUV. She breathed in the sea air and focused on the ranch-style house that was so different from the beach house her father built for them. There were no stilts because it wasn't directly on the water. The house was a sage green with a reddish-brown front door. The nicest part of the exterior was the small screened-in porch that allowed enough space for a small table and two rocking chairs.

The flower bed just below the steps was spectacular with brilliant, bright colors. Hope walked up three wooden steps and, opening the screen door, she stepped onto the porch and knocked on the front door.

Hope's heart felt as if it was going to beat out of her chest. Taking a deep breath, she was trying to calm herself when the door opened and Donna stood there looking at her with eyes that looked like hers.

"Hi, Donna. I was told that you are my aunt, so I wanted to talk to you for a minute if that's okay."

Donna opened the door wide and stepped out of the way, allowing Hope to enter. "Well, now," Donna said as she closed her front door, "I never thought I would live to see this day."

"This is as much a surprise to me as it is to you," Hope assured her.

"Well, follow me." Donna started walking toward the kitchen, and Hope followed. "I was in here fixing my husband some breakfast. He hasn't been doing well these last few months." A look of sadness crossed Donna's eyes as she picked up the coffeepot. "Don't guess either one of us has been doing so well, but at least I'm still on my feet."

"I'm sorry to hear that. I didn't know that you and Mr. Calvin weren't doing well." Hope stood next to the kitchen counter. Donna was in front of her on the other side of the counter.

As Donna poured the coffee in the mug, she gave Hope a raised eyebrow.

It seemed to Hope that Donna didn't believe her, but Hope didn't know much of anything that had gone on in this town since this was her first time returning in eighteen years. And it wasn't like Ruby kept her updated on anything that had to do with the James family. "My mother and I don't talk a lot about Hallelujah, so if you've been sick for a while, she didn't tell me."

"Doesn't surprise me. Ruby's been living in her own world since before you were born." Donna pointed to a seat next to the kitchen island. "Have a seat. I'll be right back." She walked out of the kitchen carrying a plate of food in one hand and a cup of coffee in the other.

Hope sat, placed her hands in her lap. As she waited, her foot *tap-tap-tapped* the floor. What was she doing here? Was it really necessary to dredge all of this up?

The living room in Donna's house was open to the kitchen, so Hope noticed several photos in varying sizes in a cross-like pattern on the wall. She walked over to the photos. Pictures of CJ and Colton when they were younger and playing basketball and running track were on the wall. Seeing that picture of CJ at their high school track meet reminded Hope of how CJ claimed he was the fastest man alive and was going to make it to the Olympics and win the gold.

There were photos of the James family—her family. How had she known these people all of her life but never knew that they were *her* people? Another photo caught her eye. It was a younger version of the woman who claimed that she was her mother. She had on a white sundress and was barefoot, kicking at the water on the beach. The woman was smiling. Her eyes lit with joy.

"Brenda was eighteen when I took that photo. She loved being on the beach and walking on the edge of the water just to get her feet wet," Donna told her, walking back into the room.

"How old was she when she gave birth to me?" Hope's eyes were transfixed. This woman—her mother—had a teenie weenie Afro. She reminded Hope of herself when she first started wearing her hair natural and sporting a TWA.

"Twenty. That's why my daddy still had so much say in what she did. In my daddy's house, a twenty-year-old wasn't considered grown if she couldn't pay her own bills, and the fact that she didn't have anywhere else to go swayed her as well because my husband was dead set against letting her live with us after what she had done.

"Daddy threatened to put her out. Told her that an unwed mother was a burden on her family. A burden and an embarrassment that he couldn't abide with."

Turning away from the photo, Hope said, "That's what I was to her, a burden and an embarrassment?"

Donna waved her hands in front of her face. "No, child. No."

"Then why did she give me away?"

Donna turned back toward the kitchen counter. "Would you like some crumb cake?"

Hope shook her head.

"Coffee?"

"No, thank you."

Donna went to the refrigerator and took out a pitcher of iced tea, took two glasses out of the cabinet, poured the tea in the glasses, then handed one to Hope. "Let's sit out on the front porch."

Hope took the iced tea knowing that it was going to be too sweet for her. Southern iced tea was made with a half a bag of sugar. These days Hope only added lemon to her tea. But it would be rude to not accept the tea. She put her glass on the table next to the rocking chair that she sat in. She waited for Donna to sit in the chair on the opposite side of the table, then said, "I remember how you used to cheer for me at all those track meets. Why didn't you ever tell me that you were my aunt?"

Donna leaned into the rocking motion of the chair. "I saw how much Ruby loved you and how she didn't mistreat you or act different toward you when the Lord blessed her with her own kids, so I figured I needed to stay out of it. And to be honest, things were complicated back then."

"Do me a favor, Donna." Hope leaned in closer to the woman. "Uncomplicate all of this for me because I really need to know why the woman who gave birth to me gave me to Henry Reynolds."

Donna took a sip of her tea. "What did your mama tell you?"

"She said that your sister had the hots for my dad and that she was institutionalized."

Donna nodded. "Brenda did indeed have an eye for Henry. She wouldn't listen to me when I told her that the man was not just married but in love with his wife. She said it wasn't so because Henry took her out for a bite to eat. The next thing I knew she was pregnant and planning to move into that little house Henry and your mama had before he built that beautiful beach house."

"So she did want to take my mother's place?" Sounds like Ruby had actually told the truth about something.

"I'm not going to sugarcoat it because my sister paid a high price for what she did." Donna took another sip of her tea, then set the glass down. "Brenda was young, beautiful and naive. She thought she saw trouble in paradise because, at that time, Ruby was depressed, and everybody knew it. People thought she was unhappy with Henry, but she was just dying inside because she wanted a baby so bad."

Hope begrudgingly gave another point to her mother. She had told the truth about her depression.

"Brenda thought she was going to keep the man and the baby, but Ruby must've forgiven Henry for stepping out on her because the next thing we knew, Henry was talking to our daddy about bringing you here to live with him and his wife. Brenda didn't agree at first, but my daddy was a force back then. She couldn't fight him, so she signed the papers and gave you to Henry."

Donna's eyes filled with tears as she stared out into the front yard. She looked like she was seeing something distant and from the past, then she said, "I never understood how losing a child could cause a woman's mind to snap the way Brenda's mind did . . . until I lost CJ."

Hope's head snapped backward, then swiveled in Donna's direction as her eyes widened.

"Your mama didn't tell you what happened to my boy?"

Hope shook her head.

"No, I guess she didn't. Ruby wouldn't even speak to me if we were walking down the same street. It's a shame, too, because when I first arrived in town, I wanted to be friends with her."

Hope searched her memory. The last thing she remembered about CJ was that his daddy had bought him a souped-up Mustang the summer she graduated from college and CJ graduated from high school. He had received a partial track scholarship, but she didn't remember to what college, and her mother hadn't told her anything. "I'm sorry, what happened to CJ?"

Sighing and shaking her head, Donna's shoulders slackened. "CJ has been missing for about eighteen years. The last time I heard from him was right before Christmas that same year Trinity went missing."

Hope's last summer in Hallelujah. Her mind was taking her back as she tried to remember little moments and details. Was it CJ who tried to talk to Trinity, or was it Colton? No, Colton was interested in Faith. She was sure of that.

"2004 was a horrible year for this town. First that hurricane tore down so many homes. Trinity went missing during that storm and then a month later my CJ went missing on his way home for Christmas." Donna let out another deep, sorrowful sigh. "They pulled his car out of the ocean about thirty miles from here three months ago. My baby stayed in that water with no one to help him for all those years." Donna's body shook as if a cold wind had blown in.

"You would think finding him would have brought us some peace, but my husband bought CJ that Mustang, and it broke him when they pulled it out of the ocean with CJ in it." Looking back like she was trying to make sure her husband wasn't in earshot, she then turned back to Hope and whispered, "Calvin had a heart attack and still hasn't gotten back on his feet."

Putting a hand over her mouth, Hope blinked several times. A tear fell down her cheek. "I am so sorry to hear this. I liked CJ, and now that I know he was my cousin, I would have enjoyed spending time with him."

This news gave her another reason to be upset with her mother. Yes, she lived in California now and was more than twenty-five hundred miles away, but really, she had only been a phone call away. Her mother could have and should have told her about Calvin Jr.

Then another thought struck. Nic had told her that a car was pulled out of the ocean a few months back. They had identified the driver but they were still trying to identify the passenger. Nic thought the passenger was Trinity, but how could that be?

"Ummm, are you sure that CJ's car went in the water at Christmastime that year?"

Donna nodded. "I remember everything about those days. CJ

didn't come home for Thanksgiving because he went skiing with some friends, but he and I traded text messages for the next month. I even missed a few calls from him. He also texted and told me he was coming home for Christmas . . . then nothing. Never heard another word from him."

The air seemed to shift. The sun was rising, but it wasn't bringing warmth. The sadness in Donna's eyes clouded their space and turned everything colorless. Hope no longer saw the brightness of the multicolored flowers; darkness had descended on this house. Just like the darkness that descended on the beach house after Trinity went missing.

Hope didn't have children, but she realized in that moment that no parent wants to lose hope for the return of the child they lost. Looking into Donna's haunted eyes gave her more understanding for why her mother refused to take that DNA test. She didn't want confirmation of Trinity's death.

Hope stood, then leaned down and hugged Donna. "I'm sorry for your loss, Donna. If I can do anything to help, you just let me know." Hope gave Donna her number before she stepped away from the somberness.

When she got in the car and headed back to the beach house, she called Nic. When he picked up, she took a deep breath and made herself ask, "How is your mother doing this morning?"

She heard him let out a *whoosh* of air, before he said, "It was touch and go last night, but she's stable this morning. She'll probably have to go to a nursing home for rehab because her speech was affected this time." He blew out another breath, then said, "Thanks for asking, Hope. That means a lot to me."

"I know it does, and I'm sorry I couldn't be there for you last night."

"Hey, your mother is in the hospital as well. No need to apologize for that."

Hope wished she could tell him about her mommy issues, but this wasn't the time to burden him, so she got to the reason for her call. "I don't want to hold you, but I just came from Donna James' house. I had no idea that CJ has been missing all these years. My family isn't big on sharing information." And that was all she was going to say about that. "But since you told me that the remains you have are from a girl who was pulled out of a car that was in the ocean, I'm thinking that girl must have been in the car with CJ, right?"

He hesitated, but only for a moment. "Right."

Hope pulled up to a red light. As she sat there with her foot on the brake, she said, "Then I don't get it. Donna said that CJ didn't go missing until a month after Trinity went missing. Do you think he had her with him for a month?"

"That doesn't seem likely. As close as you girls were, I wouldn't think Trinity could be gone a month and not call if she was with CJ."

"Right. So the remains that you have might not belong to Trinity." Hope didn't know how she felt about that. If that girl wasn't Trinity, she wouldn't have to see that haunting look in her mother's eyes that she'd just seen in Donna's, but then their family would still be left without answers.

"But you're going to take the test on Monday, so you'll know for sure then."

Hope was sure that Nic thought his words were encouraging, but she wasn't positive that her test would tell them much of anything. She hung up with Nic as she pulled up to the beach house. Before she could get out of the car, her cell rang. It was her boss. She refused to think of him as her boyfriend or even her ex, since he was a cheat. She picked her phone back up, accepted the call.

Spencer said, "Thank you for finally taking my call."

It was time to get this over with. If he was going to fire her, then . . .

"Look, I want to explain about Erica—"

She cut him off. "Not necessary. I'm good."

"I must admit, I was very upset when you left during our busy season, but I guess I can understand why you were so upset."

"Let's not make this about you, Spencer. My mother needed me, so I had to come home, and I have plenty of vacation time."

"You do have vacation time, but we have a board meeting next week, and I need you here so we can put together our presentation."

Why don't you get Erica to work on that presentation? she wanted to tell him, but then she realized that she hadn't thought much about them since she'd been back home. Whatever they had going on didn't concern her anymore.

When she didn't respond, he said, "My assistant has checked flights, and we can get you back here on Saturday, if that works for you."

Hope opened her car door. "Thing is, my mother is in the hospital, and I have something I have to do on Monday morning."

"Oh wow. That's too bad about your mother," Spencer said. "I was hoping that you could be in the office on Monday. We need to convince the board that even with the loss we had last year, this hotel is well positioned for next year."

He didn't care about what she had going on—it was all about the business. For a while, all she had cared about was climbing that ladder of success, but that wasn't as important anymore. "I can teleconference with you on Monday afternoon, but you'll need to book my flight for Monday evening."

"I don't know, Hope. The board meeting is Wednesday morning. If we don't get this presentation right, some heads are going to roll."

It was strange to Hope how something that had mattered to her so much a few weeks ago now paled in comparison to everything else in her life. "It's the best I can do, Spencer." She ended the call, determined not to let anything stop her from doing what needed to be done for Trinity. The fog was clearing as she looked up to heaven. "Dear God, You don't make it easy, do You?"

Chapter 29

FIRST THING FRIDAY MORNING, FAITH TOOK THE CARD Colton gave her out of her purse and called to make Crystal an appointment. She figured that since they were still in Hallelujah, it would be best for Crystal to start seeing a psychologist now.

Colton was available at eleven o'clock. Faith arrived at the hospital at nine so she and Crystal could spend time with Ruby. After Crystal's scare with dehydration last night, she wasn't as flippant this morning. She was quiet as she sat next to her grandmother's bed, holding her hand.

"Are you feeling better this morning, Mama?" Faith asked.

"I don't have a choice but to feel better because these people are throwing me out of this hospital first thing Sunday morning."

"Uh-uh." Faith shook her head. "That's foul. They can't just send you home if you're not ready to go."

Ruby pointed to her pillow with her free hand. The other hand was still holding on to Crystal like they needed to cling to each other. "Fix my pillow for me."

Faith got out of her chair and did as her mother asked. "I'm going to have a talk with your doctor about them releasing you so soon."

Ruby said, "I know you're used to bossing everybody around, but you can't tell Medicare what to do, Faith."

"I don't boss people around, Mama. I wish you would stop saying that."

Crystal side-eyed her.

Faith put her hands on her hips. "I'm your mother, so I have a birth certificate that qualifies me to boss you around."

"You hear that, Grammy? I bet you don't boss my mom and Aunt Hope around like she bosses me."

Ruby patted Crystal's hand and gave her a lopsided grin. "I must admit that I've done my share of what I thought was best for my children and then told them to like it or lump it." Ruby laughed at her joke, but it wasn't a hearty, this-is-funny kind of laugh, more like life-will-sure-teach-you-some-things kind of laugh. "So I guess I'm bossy too."

"I'm glad you finally admitted that because, baby, let me tell you." Faith laughed to herself, crossed her legs and leaned back in her seat.

She and Crystal sat with Ruby until the chime on her phone went off, reminding her of the appointment Crystal had with Colton this morning. She looked at Crystal, nudged her head toward the door. "We have to get to your appointment."

Crystal stood, leaned across the bed rail and hugged her grandmother. "See you later."

"Have you eaten anything?" Ruby asked her.

"I ate some fruit this morning."

Faith exchanged glances with her mother as she put a hand on Crystal's shoulder, walking toward the door. "I'll be back to sit with you later," she told her.

"Did your sister leave town?" Ruby asked.

Faith looked back over her shoulder. Her mother was biting on her lip. Faith hated that she was in distress over Hope, but really, she had brought it on herself. "She's still in town."

"Please ask her to stay until I'm released. I need to talk to her and help her to understand some things."

"Okay, Mama. I'll try." Faith left the room so she and Crystal wouldn't be late for her appointment. They got on the elevator. Colton's office was on the second floor.

Faith then turned to Crystal and said, "I'm proud of you for taking this step."

Crystal bit at the corner of her lip. "It's not like I have a choice."

Her daughter didn't seem happy. She put a hand to Crystal's face. "Parents don't always get it right, Crystal. I'm sorry about making you eat all that food at dinner last night. I don't know what to do to help you, but I promise that I won't stop trying. Can you try too?"

The elevator door opened. They stepped out, and Crystal nodded. "I'll try."

The best thing Faith could have done was to bring Crystal to the hospital last night because it seemed that being hooked up to that IV and being told she was destroying her body had scared her enough that she wanted to change. Faith put an arm around her daughter as they walked to Colton's office. "Like I said, I'm proud of you."

Colton was waiting for them as they entered his office suite. He took Crystal into his office, and Faith sat down in the waiting area. The news was on the television, which was on the wall in front of her. They were showing a looming hurricane that was growing in strength as it sat in the Caribbean Sea. The last thing Faith wanted to hear about was some hurricane in the Caribbean.

She pulled her cell out of her purse and started scrolling. Faith was friends with a few other interior designers who were on Facebook. She enjoyed seeing the pictures they posted of their designs. But as she was scrolling down her home page, instead of seeing home designs, she saw a post that took her breath away and demanded her attention. It read:

I pray that you have eyes that see the best in others,
A heart that forgives the worst,
A mind that forgets the bad,
And that you never lose faith in God.

For a moment, Faith could do nothing but stare at those words on her phone screen. Hope said that she saw the worst in people before considering anything good in them. Why was she like that when she truly wanted to be a person who could see the best in people and trust God with the rest?

Then one word seemed to illuminate on the page: *pray.* If she wanted to become the type of person this post spoke of, she needed to pray. Yes, God knew her struggles, but from this day forward, she was going to confess her faults in prayer and ask God to help her. Starting now.

She lowered her head and prayed, *Lord, please help me to be the kind of mother Crystal needs. I'm doing this all wrong. Help me to be the kind of woman who sees the best in others.*

Her cell phone rang. It was Hope. "Hey," Faith said when she answered. "I hope you didn't get on a plane this morning because I told Mama that you're still in town."

"I'm here until Monday. I told you I'm going to take that DNA test for Trinity before I leave town."

Faith didn't know what to say to that, so she asked, "Where'd you go this morning?"

"That's what I'm calling you about. I just left Donna James' house."

"No kidding. I'm sitting in the waiting room at Colton's office. He's talking with Crystal now."

"Donna said something that floored me. Did you know that CJ went missing the same year as Trinity?"

Faith nodded as if Hope could see her. "Yeah. I remember that. Colton helped us look for Trinity. He passed out flyers and everything. Then a month later his family was looking for CJ."

"Did anybody tell you that CJ's car was pulled out of the ocean about thirty miles from here?"

"Noooo!" Faith's eyes bulged. "What? When?"

"A few months ago." A beat of silence, then Hope said, "So Mama didn't tell you either?"

"She didn't say a word, but she didn't like talking about the James family, and I guess we know why now."

"Yeah, we do." A pause on the line and then Hope said, "There was a girl in CJ's car when it went into the ocean. Nic thinks the girl was Trinity."

Faith jumped out of her seat. "That can't be. CJ was always driving that car fast and racing up and down the street. He probably swerved off the road into that ocean on his way home from college that year. Trinity wouldn't have been with him though."

"I know, it doesn't make sense to me either. I'm just hoping we get some answers after I do this DNA test."

When they hung up the phone, Faith was in a daze. She was so confused and wondering why no one told them about CJ. But then again, she and Hope hadn't stayed in touch with anyone in this town except their mother, and she wasn't big on providing information, especially if she didn't want to talk about the situation at hand.

Faith wondered why Colton hadn't mentioned anything about this when she ran into him the other day. She still remembered how torn up he had been when his brother didn't come home for Christmas. He'd told her that his mother filed a missing person's report all those years ago, so why didn't he tell her that CJ had been found?

The door to Colton's office opened, and Crystal entered the waiting area. Colton walked behind Crystal. Faith got out of her chair.

"Thanks for allowing me to speak with your wonderful daughter. She and I had a good conversation."

Faith glanced over at Crystal. Her daughter wasn't saying anything but she didn't seem stressed or unnerved. She prayed that Crystal got something from the session. "Thank you for seeing her so soon."

He gave a small laugh. "I told you, I haven't been back home long, so I don't have a lot of patients yet."

"Why did you say you moved back home again?"

"After my divorce, I was ready for a change. And Chicago is too cold anyway."

"Hope just came from visiting your mom. Donna told her that CJ's remains were discovered a few months ago."

Colton's head went back as if he'd received a jolt. He adjusted his wire-rimmed glasses so they sat straight on his nose. "Ah yes, yes, CJ was found. The whole thing was hard on my parents, so I came back home to help them."

"And the remains of the girl that was in the car with him . . . Do you know who that was?" Faith held her breath. Dear God, was she ready for this answer?

Colton shook his head. "The police never said."

Faith was transfixed—she couldn't move, but couldn't open her mouth to ask the next question. She just couldn't say, *Do you think it might be Trinity?*

Crystal nudged her. "Mom, are you ready?"

Coming out of her trance, she scheduled another appointment for the following week, and then they left. Faith decided to take Crystal to the beach house before going back to sit with her mother.

Faith was thankful the fog had lifted, but it still felt gloomy out, like the sun was hiding from them. She turned to Crystal as they drove to the beach house. "What did you think of the session with Dr. James?"

"It was okay."

"Do you think it helped to talk with him? You've been kind of quiet. I don't want to overwhelm you."

"I'm not overwhelmed. I was just thinking."

"Oh yeah? About what?" Faith pulled into the driveway in front of the beach house. She turned off the car and then adjusted herself in the seat so that she was looking at Crystal.

"Well, Dr. James said that I shouldn't keep stuff bottled inside and that I should talk about things that bother me."

Yes. Yes. Yes. Faith was so glad she gave that man her insurance card, even though her insurance company was just going to turn around and send her most of the bill and tell her that she hadn't reached her yearly deductible yet.

"Mom?"

That one simple word sounded so sweet coming out of her daughter's mouth. It wasn't an "Oh, Mom, you're getting on my nerves" or a "Leave me alone, Mom." It sounded like, "I need you, Mom."

"You're ready to talk now?" Faith asked.

She nodded. "I'm not blaming you for what I've been doing, and I know I act like I don't care, but I've really missed having you around."

Faith remembered watching an old movie called *Cooley High* with her mother. They played a song, "It's So Hard to Say Goodbye to Yesterday." That's how Faith was feeling now as tears formed in her eyes. Yesterday had stolen the right here and now from her.

She pulled Crystal into her arms. "I'm sorry, baby. It was never about you." When they came out of the embrace, Crystal and Faith were wiping tears from their eyes. Faith touched Crystal's hair and then looped her hand around the rubber band that held up her ponytail.

Faith removed the rubber band and let Crystal's hair fall down. Stare. Swallow. Sigh. "You are growing up on me and looking more and more like Trinity every day. When I first noticed the resemblance, I thought it was a bad thing, but you know what I think now?"

Crystal shook her head.

"I think you are a gift from God. The one perfect thing I managed to do with my life. I'm so sorry that I pulled away from you, but I'm here now, and I love you."

"I love you too, Mom."

They got out of the car, and as they headed up the stairs on the left side of the house, Faith saw Chris pounding away with a hammer and nails on the right side. This was the third day she'd seen him working on the house. Was he truly willing to help, even though there was nothing in it for him? As her mind tried to think negative thoughts, she refused to allow it. Instead she chose to be grateful. She had fallen through those steps the other day and now Chris was fixing them.

"Hey," Faith waved and smiled at him. Chris was doing a good thing for the family.

"Hi, Daddy." Crystal took the stairs on the left two at a time and walked over to the other side. "You need some help?"

Chris looked up from his spot on the fourth step. "You want to help your daddy, baby girl?"

"If I help, you might be able to get it done quicker."

He lifted the hammer and pointed to the other staircase. "Go back down and come to this side. I don't want you falling through any of the loose boards like your mama did the other day."

Crystal followed his directions and then began handing her father things out of the toolbox as requested.

Faith went inside the house, opened the fridge and started taking out yesterday's dinner. She then went into the pantry and found another box of Jiffy mix. This time she would not beat the box to death. She turned on the oven, then pulled the muffin pan from the cabinet.

Hope walked into the kitchen, grabbed an apple out of the fridge and took a bite as she leaned against the counter. "You 'bout to fix dinner?"

"I'm going to bake some muffins to go along with the dinner I cooked yesterday."

"Good. I'm starving."

"Still don't cook, huh?" Faith laughed at her as she stirred the muffin mix in the bowl with eggs, milk and melted butter. The butter wasn't needed, but Faith added it to the mix because everything tastes better with butter.

"It's just me. Easier to just order out or grab a sandwich."

Faith wondered why her sister was still single after all these years. Since she had refused to talk to Hope for years on end, she didn't feel like she had a right to get in her business like that, so she said, "Mama wants to see you."

Hope shook her head. "Uh-uh. Not ready for that."

Faith greased the muffin pan, then filled it with the mix. "Well, you better get ready. They're trying to release her on Sunday morning, so unless you plan to go to a hotel, you and Mama will be in the house together soon."

"My job called earlier today. They want me back on Monday," Hope told her.

Faith put the muffins in the oven, then turned to Hope. "But I thought you were taking that DNA test."

"I am. I told them I can't come back until Monday evening." Hope took another bite out of her apple. "We have an important meeting, but I can't be in two places at one time, and nothing is going to stop me from taking that test."

Faith looked at her sister with newfound respect. "You're serious about this, aren't you?"

Hope nodded. "It's time to bring Trinity home, one way or another."

Faith warmed the chicken, mac and cheese and greens and then set the table, all the while rewinding Hope's words in her head: *It's time to bring Trinity home.*

Faith called Chris and Crystal in to eat. They all sat down at the table. Chris said grace and then asked Crystal, "Do you think you can eat some food for us?"

Crystal looked at the food as if it was going to jump up and bite her.

Hope said, "Just eat a little. You don't have to eat it all."

Crystal looked to Faith for confirmation.

Faith put a hand over Crystal's. "Just eat what you can. Matter of fact, there's some applesauce in the refrigerator. If you'd rather eat that and a muffin . . ." Faith's words trailed off. She didn't want to pressure Crystal. This wasn't going to be an overnight fix, but they were going to get on the other side of this disease.

"I just don't want to feel so full that I feel like I need to make myself throw up."

Faith appreciated that Crystal wasn't hiding her thoughts from them. She tried to lighten the moment by saying, "Well, I'm about to go in on this chicken and mac, so I'm gon' eat enough for the both of us."

Crystal laughed. "Your mac and cheese is really good, so I guess I can eat some of that."

Crystal brought a forkful of macaroni to her mouth, chewed, and swallowed. And then everyone around the table let out a collective sigh of relief.

After dinner, Faith went back to the hospital, hoping for an uneventful evening with her mother, but she should have known better. Nothing was ever uneventful with Ruby Reynolds.

Chapter 30

Saturday night Hope called the Hallelujah Inn and booked a room for Sunday. Faith had spent the night at the hospital, and Hope did not want to be on the premises when her sister drove back to the beach house with their mother. When she got up that Sunday, she packed her clothes and put them in her mother's SUV. She would bring the SUV back on Monday and see if she could get Faith or Chris to drive her to the airport.

When she got on that plane tomorrow, Hope didn't know if she would ever return to her hometown, so she couldn't leave without attending God's Holy Word Church and hearing Pastor O'Dell preach the Word one more time.

God's Holy Word Church had meant so much to her during her formative years. She would never forget her youth group or all the words of wisdom and the kindness Pastor O'Dell bestowed on her. She headed back inside the house to get dressed for church. Chris was in the kitchen scrambling eggs.

She smiled at him. "You build houses and cook too? My sister is a blessed woman."

Chris shrugged. "I don't think she sees it that way. I think she would prefer that I had chosen another line of work."

Hope laughed at that. "I don't think you realize just how right you are for my sister." Leaning against the kitchen counter, Hope asked, "Has Faith ever told you about the hours we spent sitting on the beach while we watched our father build this house?"

Chris slid his eggs from the skillet to his plate. "She told me that your father was an architect and that he built this house but not much else."

Pointing to the kitchen table, Hope said, "Sit down. Eat your eggs while I tell you a story."

Chris walked over to the table and sat down. "I'm all ears." He had his plate in front of him, said grace, then started eating.

Hope joined him at the table. She waited a bit, allowing Chris a few moments to chew his food. "Our father graduated at the top of his class, and he was indeed an architect, but he couldn't get anyone to hire him for that position. Daddy struggled for a long time with this job and that job, just so he could feed his family."

Chris pointed his fork in Hope's direction. "Sounds like some of my struggles, but things are on the up for us now. I'm building and flipping houses. I'm bringing in money. I don't know what else Faith wants me to do."

"Daddy became a builder as well. He built many of the houses in this town, and he made enough money to buy the supplies needed to build this beach house. And my mother loved him for it. She loved Henry Reynolds for every sacrifice he made for his family."

"I love my wife, Hope. I truly do, but I can't seem to convince her of that."

"Let me ask you something, Chris." Hope lifted a hand. "I don't want the answer to this question. I want you to dwell on it. Are you willing to sacrifice everything just to ensure that your wife and child are happy?"

Her daddy had loved Ruby dearly, so it must have been a great sacrifice to go along with her Sarah-and-Abraham scheme to get a baby. Then he gave the ultimate sacrifice when he began patching up the house after a storm and died of a heart attack. But the thing about it is, even if her father knew that would be his last day on earth, he still would have done the work needed to keep his family safe from the storm. That was the kind of man Henry Reynolds was.

Looking across the table at her brother-in-law, Hope saw so much of her daddy in him. She believed that he was the type of man who would make the ultimate sacrifice for his family. She just didn't know if he believed it. Hope stood. "I'm going to church this morning. Do you and Crystal want to join me?"

Chris rose, scraped out his plate. "Let me wake Crystal. I'd love to attend church with you."

⌒

Praise and worship was wonderful. Then Pastor O'Dell lit the match and set the place on fire when reading from Psalm 139:

"You have searched me, LORD, and you know me. You know when I sit and when I rise; you perceive my thoughts from afar. You discern my going out and my lying down; you are familiar with all my ways . . .

"If I say, 'Surely the darkness will hide me and the light become night around me,' even the darkness will not be dark to you; the night will shine like the day, for darkness is as light to you. For you created my inmost being; you knit me together in my mother's womb. I praise you because I am fearfully and wonderfully made; your works are wonderful, I know that full well. My frame was not hidden from you when I was made in the secret place, when I was woven together in the depths of the earth. Your eyes saw my unformed body; all the days ordained for me were written in your book before one of them came to be."

⌒

Those words spoke volumes to Hope. She felt them in her innermost being. For so long now, she had doubted her identity. Felt like an outcast because her complexion didn't match the rest of her family. But these scriptures were telling her that she was fearfully and wonderfully made, and even though she was conceived in secret, this thing was not hidden from God. She was no mistake or accident. She wasn't even someone's scheme to get a child. She was God's creation.

Crystal leaned over to her. "Auntie Hope, you're crying."

Hope touched her face, then nodded. "I am." She wiped her face, then hugged Crystal. "Did you hear those scriptures? They were just as much for you as they were for me. Because God made you just the way you are, and I don't ever want you thinking that anything is wrong with that."

Crystal twisted her lips. "I'm not perfect, Auntie Hope."

"No one is, hon. The most beautiful person you've ever seen has some kind of issue. That's just the way God made us." Hope put her hands on both sides of Crystal's face as she looked deep into her eyes. "And we are glorious in His sight."

Hope didn't think the service could get any better, but when the altar call was made, Chris stood and went down to the altar for prayer. *Fix it, Jesus,* Hope silently prayed. She was rooting for her brother-in-law. The way she saw it, he was a good man who had made some mistakes. But everybody deserved a second chance.

It was drizzling when they left church. Chris and Crystal headed back to the beach house. Hope drove toward the inn with the wipers on low to catch the bits of rain hitting her windshield.

Hope figured it was best that she wasn't at the house when her mother arrived. Ruby needed to recuperate from her surgery. Hope didn't want to bring on more stress—and the two of them together would cause stress.

She was just a couple of blocks from the inn when her cell rang. It was Faith. "Hey. What's up? You and Mama on your way to the house?"

"Mama's not coming home."

Hope didn't like the way Faith sounded. "Why? What's happened?"

"She has a fever. The doctors are in the room with her now." Faith paused for a second. "I think you should come to the hospital."

"Come to the hospital? But I thought she was doing good. You told me they were going to release her today."

"They were . . . Look, I don't know what happened. We were laughing and joking through the night, then this morning she complained of a headache. When the nurses came in to check on her they said she had a fever. And now . . ." Faith's voice broke. "Just get here as fast as you can."

Hope was about to ask something else, but the line went dead. The Hallelujah Inn was on her left. She had booked a room there to get away from her mother. Running . . . running was what Hope knew. Not only had she been a star track athlete, but it seemed to Hope that she had been running from her past and the truth of who she was for far too long.

But even as she ran, the past had caught up with her. She hadn't realized it until she looked at that picture of Brenda on Donna's wall. She wore her hair natural, and the reason Hope went natural was so that she could recognize who she was when she looked in the mirror. But looking more like Brenda had not snuffed out the love she had for Ruby.

Her earliest memory was of her mother's hugs, kisses . . . her love. And the mother that she remembered, the one whose love she felt deep in her heart, was now lying in a hospital bed, and she wasn't doing well. How could she run away from that? She swerved in the middle of the street, made a U-turn and headed to the hospital where she belonged.

It was a ten-minute drive to the hospital, and Hope used every one of those minutes to pray that God would allow her mother to live. She didn't know what happened to cause Ruby's fever.

"Lord, take it away."

But even as she prayed, Hope was reminded of all the other prayers that had gone unanswered through the years. She had believed in God so thoroughly when she was younger. But one hit after the other had left her wondering if she could trust God with the things that concerned her. "Please, Lord. Help us."

She parked in the visitor lot, got out of the car, ran to the elevator, hit the Up button, then started tapping her foot. She looked around for the stairs but didn't see a sign. The elevator inched downward, sixth floor, fifth floor, fourth floor.

"Oh my goodness, come on already."

"These things take forever when you're in a hurry," a male voice said from behind her.

She swiveled around to see who was talking to her and was greeted with Colton James' smiling face. She smiled back at him. She'd always thought he was a cute kid and had a great personality. Girls were definitely interested because he had been on the basketball team too. Things had always been easy between them—a quick "Hi, Colton" and "Hi, Hope"—and then they went about their business. But now she knew that he was her cousin.

She wanted to reach out to him and give him a hug, especially after learning that CJ had been found in the ocean, but she didn't want things to be awkward between them, and how could they not be, if she suddenly blurted out that she was his cousin.

"Mom told me you stopped by the house the other day," he said.

"I did." The elevator chimed, and the door opened. They got in the elevator together.

"I have to admit," Colton began, "I was kind of upset to discover that all these years my mother kept the fact that you are my cousin from me, especially since I had the biggest crush on you when I was in grade school."

Hope laughed at that. "You did not."

"Sure did. You were always being talked about because you kept breaking records when you ran track. I thought about fighting Nic so you could be my girlfriend."

"And then quickly forgot about me when you became Mr. Basketball and all the girls in town were after you, including Faith." They both laughed.

The elevator opened on the second floor. Colton held the door. The smile lines in his face eased. "But seriously, I'm glad to know that I have more family in this town. After what happened to CJ . . ." He shrugged, stepped out of the elevator. "Let's go to dinner, hang out or something."

She didn't know how to tell him that she wouldn't be in town much longer, especially since he looked like he needed a friend. Just before the doors closed, she yelled, "I'll get your number from Faith."

The elevator closed and climbed two more floors, then opened again. Hope got out of the elevator and rushed around the corner and down the long hall to her mother's room. In the distance, she could see Faith in the hallway.

One moment, Faith was leaned against the wall next to her mother's room. The next, she put her hand to her face and slid down the wall as her body shook. Everything seemed to go slow from that moment on. It felt like the faster Hope ran down that hall, the more it seemed like a force field of despair was keeping her from getting to the finish line.

As she got closer, she heard Faith moaning, "No! No! No!"

Hope bumped into one of the monitors that was in the hallway. She pushed it out of her way. "Faith! Oh God, no! Please don't tell me she's gone."

Hope searched her mind, trying to remember the last words she'd said to her mother. Their last discussion had not been good, and Hope had expressed serious displeasure over her mother's inability to tell her the whole truth about how she was conceived. But it seemed that Ruby had told the truth this time. Hope just wanted the opportunity to tell her mom that she believed her and that she loved her.

Please, God, just tell me it's not too late.

Faith wrapped her arms around Hope. Tears streamed down her sister's face as she said, "She won't wake up."

"What do you mean she won't wake up?" Hope let go of Faith. She turned to the left, looking down the hall, then turned back the other way while putting her hand to her head. "She was awake this morning. Weren't they going to release her this morning?"

"I don't know what happened, sis." With hands steepled and pressed to her chin, Faith leaned to the left. "She was fine." Leaned to the right. "And then she wasn't."

"Oh, my good Lord!" Hope flapped her hand in the air. "I'm going in there. Why are you standing out here?"

Faith grabbed her arm, pulling her back. "They are working on her. We can't go in yet."

Hope's eyes were wild. "How long have they been in there?"

"Two minutes, tops. They told me to step out so they could work on her."

Hope stared at the door, willing it to open so she could go in that room and tell her mother how much she loved her, how much she appreciated everything that she and her father did for her. Blood or not, they had sacrificed for her like parents do for their children. And they held that place in her heart, and that was all that mattered. She just needed the chance to tell her mother . . . *Please, God, give me that chance.*

Hope remembered praying for years that Trinity would come back to them, but that never happened.

The door opened, and technicians rushed out, taking their equipment with them. Then several nurses filed out of the room. One stopped in front of Faith, placing a hand on her shoulder. "The doctor will see you now."

Wringing her hands, Faith said, "Thank you. Thank you for everything."

Hope rushed into the room. The doctor was standing by her mother's bed. Ruby had all sorts of tubes in her nose and mouth helping her to breathe. Putting her hand to her head, Hope glared at the doctor. "What did y'all do to her? She was fine when I left the other day."

Faith came in behind her. She looked at Ruby and gasped. "Where'd all these tubes come from?"

The doctor said, "Your mother has an infection. We are giving her medicine to clear it up and Tylenol to reduce her fever." He pointed toward the tubes. "I know all of this looks scary, but if we can get the fever down and take care of the infection, we'll be able to remove the tubes and wake her up first thing in the morning."

"Why won't she wake up now?" Faith whined.

Calmly, the doctor explained, "Her fever is too high."

"This looks like life-support equipment," Hope said as fear stomped all over her heart.

"We feel it best to aid her breathing until morning." The doctor's voice trailed off as he added, "Then we'll see."

Hope wanted to know what they were looking for. What were they going to "see" in the morning? "Are you waiting to see if she can breathe on her own?"

Eyes downcast, the doctor nodded. "We can meet first thing in the morning after we monitor her through the night. I should be able to tell you more once we run a few tests." He walked out of the room.

What if she couldn't wake up? What then? Hope stepped over to the bed. Hands on the bed rail, she said, "I'm here, Mama. You told Faith you wanted to talk to me, so you need to wake up and tell us what's on your mind."

Tears dripped from Hope's face onto Ruby's bed cover. "Did you hear me, Mama? You need to wake up and talk to me."

Chapter 31

WATCHING HER MOTHER BREATHE WITH THE HELP OF A VEN-
tilator was one of hardest things Faith ever had to do, and if it
wasn't for Hope encouraging her to think positive, Faith would
have asked the nurse for a sedative to calm her nerves.

Hope sat next to the bed, rubbing her hand up and down their
mother's arm. "I'm here, Mama. I can't wait to talk to you. I'm
going to sit right here next to your bed and wait for you to tell me
everything you want me to know."

"What if she doesn't wake up?" Faith whispered.

"Don't even think like that, Faith. Mama is not done. You see
how feisty she is." Hope pointed at Ruby. "This woman right here
has got a lot of life left to live. We have to find a way to believe that.
Okay, sis?"

Faith. She was always being asked to have faith in something or
someone. The ironic thing was that her mother named her the very
thing that she struggled with. "I've been struggling with my faith
since Trinity disappeared, so you'll have to dig up enough faith for
the both of us."

Hope shook her head. "No. What you've been struggling with
is guilt. You blame yourself for what Trinity decided to do."

"I was her big sister. Trinity was just being a stupid little kid wanting to play out in the rain, but it wasn't just rain. It was a storm that had so much force that it knocked down trees and destroyed twenty-something homes." Looking off into the distance, wishing she could catch yesterday and put it in a bottle just as they used to do when they caught lightning bugs, she said, "I should have stopped her."

Hope left her mom's bedside and came to sit next to Faith on the opposite side of the room. She took her finger and lifted Faith's chin. "I need you to think back to when we were younger. I need you to remember the way things were, not just the way you imagine they were. Then tell me, do you really think you could have stopped Trinity from leaving the house that day?"

Faith closed her eyes. For years, she used to dream that she had run after Trinity and dragged her back into the house—boarded the place up from the inside out and then dared her to leave again.

But that wasn't reality. Faith opened her eyes. Hope was still right there next to her. There was so much compassion in her sister's eyes.

Faith had missed those eyes—missed being around her sister. Hated that she held a grudge for so long. She leaned over and hugged Hope. "I'm so thankful that you are my sister."

They both started crying. Hope wiped the tears from her face. "I'm thankful for you too. I'm so sorry for all the years we let go by being angry over something neither one of us could have changed."

"We have been acting silly, haven't we?" Faith wiped the tears from her eyes as her cell phone rang. It was Chris. She pointed to her phone and told Hope, "I'm going to take this."

Faith answered the phone, then left the room. As she walked toward the waiting area, she said, "I'm sorry. I know I was supposed to be there to help with Crystal by now, but Mama isn't doing well."

"I'm not calling to get on you about anything. I figured you were still at the hospital." Chris sounded concerned.

She sat in the waiting room, rubbing her forehead, trying to relieve some of the stress of the day. "Thanks for calling. I was freaking out after Mama slipped into a coma, but Hope calmed me down."

"I'm sorry to hear that, Faith, but I want you to know that I'm praying for Mama Ruby. She's coming out of that hospital. I believe that."

That voice. When they were dating and Chris would call her, she would actually shiver at the sound of his low and slow southern drawl. How long had it been since she shivered at his voice? How long had it been since they spoke sweet nothings to each other over the phone?

Chris cleared his throat. "Anyway, I called to see if you've been watching the news."

"To be honest, I don't even know if the television is on in Mama's room. I haven't been able to focus." Her voice broke as she said the last few words.

"I can hear your pain, but I need you to believe that she is going to wake up. Trust God."

It sounded so simple: just trust God, and everything would be the way it should be. But Faith had learned a long time ago that things don't always work like that. "Let me get back to Mama's room. Give Crystal a kiss for me, and tell her I'll see her in the morning."

"Wait, before you go, I called because we have a problem. A hurricane is headed this way."

"No! We only have a few more days in November. Hurricane season is done—it should be done." Then she remembered seeing the news when she was sitting in Colton's office yesterday. Hurricane Lola had been sitting in the warm waters of the Caribbean gaining strength. "Please tell me it's not the one that's been over by the Bahamas."

"That's the one, Hurricane Lola. It's predicted to hit us in the next seventy-two hours, so I'm going to board the house up, and then we need to get on the road."

The right thing to do would be to leave first thing tomorrow. Faith ran her hand through her hair. "I can't leave my mother. Not like this."

"We don't want to leave without you. I'd never forgive myself if something happened to you and I wasn't able to get back in town."

"I appreciate that, Chris, but I don't want anything to happen to Crystal." She didn't want anything to happen to him either but couldn't bring herself to tell that truth.

"Let's just play it by ear. I'll board up the house, and then we'll see when Ruby is going to be released from the hospital."

Released? Her mother was on a ventilator. She couldn't think about when Ruby would be released, when all she wanted was for her mother to wake up. It seemed to Faith that she was always dealing with one storm after another. Just barely able to come up for air before the currents of the next storm swept her back under. "Let me get back to the room."

"What should I tell Crystal about Ruby?"

Standing back up, Faith said, "I don't know. I don't want to lie to her, but I don't want her to know that Mama is on a ventilator either."

"How about I just tell her that Ruby had a few complications, and we are praying and believing for her recovery."

Faith started walking back to the room. "Sounds good."

"I fixed soup for dinner. Something light. Crystal said it didn't make her feel too full."

Please, Lord, please let my mother be awake when I go back into her room.

"Did you hear me?" Chris asked.

"Sorry. I was praying. I'm glad the soup didn't give her that full feeling." Faith took a few more steps, and then she reached her mother's door. "And, Chris?"

"Yeah?"

"I know things haven't been good between us, but I'm glad you stayed. This would have been even worse for Crystal if she didn't have you here."

They hung up, and she entered the room.

No change. Hope was sitting next to the bed holding Mama's hand and talking to her like she expected Mama to answer back. Faith started to question Hope about what she was doing, but then she remembered a book she read about coma patients possibly being able to hear conversations and changed her mind. "Hey, my turn. Let me sit there and hold her hand."

Hope pointed to the other side of the bed. "She has two hands."

"You know what, sis, you're right." Faith moved her chair over to the opposite side of the bed and took her mother's right hand in hers. "It's me, Mama. Hope and I are going to stay here until you wake up so you can boss us around." Faith's head fell backward as she laughed. "That's right, Mama. You're the bossy one, not me."

Hope shook her head. "I would have to say that both of you are bossy. Like mother, like daughter."

"Like mother, like daughter, huh? Okay, well, who do you act like?"

Eyes downcast, Hope's lips twisted. "I–I don't know."

"Stop it, Hope." Faith pointed toward Hope's leather purse. "I bet you have a coloring book in that purse."

Hope nodded.

"I remember how you used to watch Mama paint, wishing you could paint like her. I also remember how pretty all of the pages in your coloring books turned out because you were always so precise with them."

Hope's eyes sparkled. She smiled. "I couldn't get that paintbrush to work for me, but I work those colored pencils like nobody's business."

Faith glanced over at the television. It was off. She pushed the button to turn it on. "We need to watch the news. Chris said that a hurricane is headed our way."

Hope shook her head. "How can we be dealing with an impending hurricane while Mama is stuck in this hospital? This can't be happening."

"This is life on a beach, which is why I moved to Atlanta." Faith rubbed her temples. "What are we supposed to do now?"

Hope's mouth gaped open as the weatherman predicted that a category 4 hurricane would hit the island within the next three days. "I can't deal with this right now. I'm going to the cafeteria before they close. Do you want me to bring you anything?"

"I'll take some chocolate chip cookies. I need chocolate to calm my nerves . . . Oh, and a Sprite. Yes, bring me a Sprite." Before Hope stepped out of the room, Faith asked, "Did he just say category 4?"

Hope looked over at the nonresponsive form of her mother and sighed. News like they just received would have normally sent her packing and rushing to the airport for the first flight out of here, but she couldn't leave Ruby, and she couldn't leave without finding out what happened to Trinity. "Yeah, he did."

"You leaving?"

"I want to, but I can't," Hope told her sister, then slipped through the door.

Hope took the elevator down to the first floor and made her way down the long hall toward the cafeteria. It was almost nine at night. The cafeteria was about to close, so there wasn't much food out. She did find a grilled cheese sandwich and a bag of Cheetos for herself and a pack of cookies for Faith. Hope opened the refrigerator and pulled out two Sprites, then paid for her goods and walked back to the elevator.

Waiting for the elevator to arrive, Hope saw Nic walking in her direction, but he wasn't by himself. An attendant was pushing the bed that held Melinda Evans.

Hope froze. She wanted to speak to Nic and ask how he was doing, but his mother was with him. Hope looked around, trying to determine which way she could go to be anywhere but there.

Nic saw her before she could turn and run. He waved and rushed over to her, wrapped his arms around her. "I've been thinking about you all day. How are you?"

She stepped out of his embrace because his mother was watching. It made Hope feel uncomfortable. "I'm holding on. H-how are you doing?"

Nic moved to the side, thrusting his arm toward his mother. "She's doing better today, so I'm happy."

"Did you hear about the storm?"

Nic nodded. "We have a few days to prepare. Just need for my mom to be released so we can take precautions."

Melinda grunted and then grunted again.

The elevator opened. "I'll talk to you later, Nic." Hope tried to walk around Melinda's bed.

Melinda grunted again and then reached for Hope.

Nic grabbed Hope's arm and gently pulled her back. "I think she wants you."

Hope stared at Nic, wanting to tell him that she couldn't be anywhere near his mother, but Melinda put her hand in Hope's and squeezed it. That didn't feel like the action of someone who hated her.

Hope side-eyed the woman at first, but then she thought she saw tears on Melinda's face, so she turned toward the woman and moved closer to the bed. She was right. Melinda was crying.

Nic held the elevator door open as Melinda motioned for Hope to come closer.

Everything in Hope wanted to run the other way, but Nic was smiling, and his mother was motioning for her. She couldn't turn away. She leaned in.

Melinda's voice was garbled as she said, "I-I'm s-sorry."

The attendant then pushed Melinda's bed into the elevator. Nic's eyes brightened as he looked at his mother as if she had redeemed herself in his eyes. He motioned for Hope to join them inside, but she shook her head.

Hope needed a moment to process what just happened because there was a hurricane on the way, and Melinda Evans had just apologized to her.

It felt like she could breathe again. Like life made sense. Like being in love with Nic wasn't wrong. Just as her being darker than her sisters wasn't wrong, and she wasn't some mistake. She was who God made her to be, and that was good enough.

She hit the Up button for the elevator after it closed. When she got back to Ruby's room, she handed Faith her cookies and drink, then sat down and ate her sandwich. Her movements were normal, but nothing felt normal to her right now.

Melinda's cruel words had played in her head day after day for years after she left Hallelujah. Hope had struggled with thoughts of unworthiness and admittedly had a chip on her shoulder about her complexion.

She had two thoughts simultaneously as she ate her sandwich: Melinda said "I'm sorry," and God said to forgive. Hope felt her heart constrict. She closed her eyes and silently told God, *I want to forgive her, Lord. I need to be free. Help me to forgive.*

She wasn't there yet, but her heart was pulling her ever closer to the place of forgiveness. Hope ate her sandwich, all the while wondering if she would be thinking about forgiving Melinda if she hadn't apologized. *Help me, Lord*, she prayed again. *I need to learn how to forgive.*

The news was still on, bringing doom and gloom. Faith bit her nails as she said, "Mama has got to wake up so we can get her out of this hospital."

Hope sat next to Faith. "Can I tell you something, sis?"

"I'm listening."

"I've been struggling with my faith, too, but I used to believe that God could do anything. I want to believe that again." Hope held out her hands to Faith. "I think we should be praying for Mama."

Faith nodded her agreement. "Let's pray."

Hope and her sister spent the next hour calling on Jesus for their mother's healing. After praying, Hope and Faith took turns staying awake to watch Ruby. A nurse kept coming into the room to check on her as well, so no one but Ruby was getting any rest tonight. At two o'clock in the morning, the nurse came in and checked Ruby's fever. She told them the fever had broken.

"Yay! You hear that, Mama? Your fever is gone," Hope said.

Faith dance around the room, shouting, "Hallelujah! Prayer works."

The nurse put her finger to her lips.

"Oh, sorry," Faith said and then sat back down.

At three o'clock in the morning, Ruby started squirming. And then at exactly a quarter to four, she opened her eyes and tried to remove the tube connecting her to the ventilator. Hope hopped out of her chair and grabbed Ruby's hands. "No, Mama. You can't remove it."

Faith jumped out of her seat. "Is she awake? Oh my goodness, her eyes are open."

Hope rubbed the sleep from her eyes, then looked at her mother, realizing the miracle that had taken place. "Oh my dear Lord." She put a hand to her chest. "Mom, you came back to us." She then hit the button for the nurse.

A nurse came on the line immediately. "Can I help you?"

"Yes!" Hope was yelling and didn't care. *Just let them try to shush me now*, she thought. "My mother is awake."

Faith jumped around the room. "Somebody needs to remove this tube from her throat so she can boss us around again."

Hope laughed at that. Ruby still looked weak as she lay in the bed, eyes filled with confusion. Her fever was gone. Hope was sure her mother would indeed be back to her old tricks of bossing them around and doing what she thought was best, no matter what anyone else had to say. And as long as Ruby Reynolds kept on living, that was all right with her.

Chapter 32

It HAD BEEN AN ABSOLUTELY EXHAUSTING DAY AND NIGHT AS they sat in that hospital room praying that their mother would wake up. And now that she was awake and the technician had taken her off the ventilator, all Faith wanted to do was to catch a few hours of sleep.

Faith laid down on the cot. The minute her head hit the pillow, she drifted back in time . . .

Faith and her mother walked the beach, passing out flyers. "Have you seen this girl? Her name is Trinity. Please help me find my sister."

Faith repeated those words over and over every time she handed out a flyer. Trinity had been gone for three days now. Someone had to have seen her. She couldn't be lost to them forever.

"I'm over here, Faith. Come get me."

Faith whirled around. At first, she thought she'd heard Trinity's voice behind her, closer to where the beach house sat, but no one was standing by the house. Faith shook it off and continued passing out her flyers.

"My sister's missing," she said as she tried to hand the flyer to a man who didn't seem the least bit interested. "Please, sir, just look at her picture. Maybe you've seen her."

He glanced at the flyer, shook his head and then continued on his way.

"Don't leave me here, Faith. Come find me."

That was Trinity's voice. Faith was sure of it. But as she looked around, she couldn't see her anywhere. Then she looked toward the sea. The water had been calm, but now it seemed to come alive. The waves were growing bigger and bigger, and then Faith heard Trinity say, "Come find me" again.

Faith dropped to her knees. As the sand ground into them, she stared out into the sea. Was her sister calling her from out there? Tears sprung to her eyes. "I'm sorry, Trinity. I shouldn't have let you go."

The waves jumped, and the wind blew.

"I'm sorry, Trinity. I'm sorry. So sorry, Trinity."

"Faith! Faith! Wake up."

Someone was shaking her. Faith's eyes popped open and she jumped. It was Hope. Faith sat up. "Thanks for waking me up. I was having this awful dream."

Hope grabbed her purse. "You can tell me about it later. I have an appointment to get to this morning."

Yawning, stretching, then Faith clapped a couple of times. "The DNA test?"

Hope glanced toward Ruby, who was watching them but not saying anything. "Yes." Hope kissed Ruby on the cheek. "I'll be back to see you before my flight today."

Ruby reached out to her. "Don't leave. This is where you belong. I want you to stay with us."

Hope smiled at her mother, but the smile didn't quite reach her eyes. Clutching her purse, Hope headed toward the door.

In her nightmarish dream, Trinity asked Faith to come find her. Trinity didn't want to be left wherever she was. Faith could not and would not ignore her sister's plea for help. She threw off the blanket. "Wait, Hope. I'm coming with you."

Hope's eyes lit up. Faith was going to do the DNA test. When they stepped outside of their mother's hospital room, Hope pulled Faith to the side. "If you're going to do the DNA test, then I don't have to do it. I can stay here with Mama until it's time for my flight."

Faith shook her head. "Either we both take the test or neither of us will do it."

That irritated Hope. She already had her bags packed and in the trunk of her mother's SUV. She would love to have a few more hours with her mother. "Why do you have to be difficult all the time?"

Faith took hold of Hope's arm and pulled her toward the elevator. "I'm not being difficult. You have to take this test with me because if they have found Trinity's remains and you don't do the DNA test, you'll never truly believe in your heart that you're my blood sister, and I need you to know the truth."

Hope's thumb jutted in the direction of Ruby's room. "But what about Mama? I don't think she wants to be alone right now."

Faith rolled her eyes to that. "Girl, please, you're leaving town today anyway. Just come on so we can take this test and get back here."

"Okay, Ms. Bossy. We'll do it your way." Neither of them wanted to discover that Trinity had drowned in the ocean all those years ago, but if their sister was not alive, they wanted to do whatever they could to finally put her body to rest.

But Faith's comment about her leaving their mother didn't sit well with her. It wasn't like Hope wanted to leave while Ruby was still in the hospital, but a hurricane was on the way, and she had responsibilities to her job. She tried to explain that to Faith as they drove to the diagnostic center to take the DNA test.

"I'm not running away from anything this time, Faith, and believe it or not, I wish I could stay, but my boss is demanding that I return today."

"And he knows your mother is in the hospital?"

Hope nodded.

"See, that's why I run my own business. I'm not working for any-one that has the nerve to tell me I can't sit with my mother during her time of need." Faith scrunched her nose. "Uh-uh, not me."

Hope couldn't defend her boss on this issue because she was start-ing to feel the same way. She wished Spencer could give her more time.

Faith wagged a finger at her. "Oh, and you're not leaving town without saying goodbye to Crystal. She would be devastated if you just up and left, like . . ."

Faith didn't have to finish her sentence because Hope knew her sister had been devastated when she left town that long ago summer. Hope pulled into the diagnostic center and turned off the car. The rain had stopped so they wouldn't need umbrellas.

She turned to Faith, put her hands up to do patty-cake with her, and in her best Nettie from *The Color Purple* voice, she said, "Me and you, us never part."

Faith's head fell back as she laughed hard, but she clapped hands with Hope, doing patty-cake.

They both laughed, then Hope pulled Faith into her arms. "You're my sister, and I won't let any space, distance or your bad attitude come between us again."

"Good," Faith said. "Now let's go get this test over with."

They went into the diagnostic center and had the inside of their cheeks swabbed. When they pulled up to the beach house, Crystal was sitting on the front porch. She ran down the stairs to greet them.

Hope hugged her niece.

"How is Grammy? Is she doing better?"

Faith hugged and kissed her daughter on the cheek. "She's doing better today, sweetheart. I'll take you to see her later."

"Daddy said he would take me to the hospital today after we finish boarding up the windows."

Faith looked toward the house. Most of the windows were cov-ered. Now they just needed to get Ruby out of the hospital and get out of town. "Let me go talk to your daddy." She walked away, leaving Hope and Crystal in the driveway.

Hope told Crystal, "I stopped by to see you because I'm going to be leaving today."

"You're leaving because of the hurricane?"

"Not entirely." Hope hated hurricanes, but if her family had to tough this hurricane out, she really wanted to be here with them. Hope was praying that Ruby would be released from the hospital so Faith could get her out of Hallelujah. "I have to get back to my job."

Crystal narrowed her eyes with sadness. "I was hoping you would be here a few more weeks."

"I was for that, too, but my boss wants me back in the office."

"Will I ever see you again?" Crystal's eyes watered as her lips tightened.

Hope put a hand on Crystal's shoulder. She pulled her niece closer to her. "I'm going to talk to your mother about letting you visit my 'hood. Would you like to spend a summer in Los Angeles?"

"Are you kidding? I would love it." Crystal jumped into Hope's arms, then ran back up the stairs, yelling, "I'm going to California!"

"Well, I guess that sad train has left the station." Hope smiled as she watched Crystal. But as Hope stared at the house she grew up in, her sad train pulled up and did a *toot-toot*. She hadn't wanted to come back home when her mother called on her. She didn't think she fit in Hallelujah, South Carolina, anymore. But the truth was, she had never gotten this place out of her system.

Her phone rang. It was Spencer. She let the call go to voice mail and walked to the back of the house. At this moment, she couldn't care less about a board meeting or about the promotion she had worked so hard to attain. She no longer had any entanglements in Los Angeles since she and Spencer were no longer together. She didn't want to leave her sister to take care of her mother and the house with a hurricane rolling in.

It felt to Hope like this was her watershed moment. She needed to make a decision about her future before she got on that plane. What did she want, and where did she want to be?

She took off her shoes and left them on the deck, then opened the gate and walked out onto the beach. It was a little windy out, but Hope didn't care. She needed to feel the grittiness of the South Carolina sand under her feet. She walked all the way to the water's edge, rolled up her pant legs and stepped in.

The coolness of the water caressed her feet as it splashed over them, moving onto the shore and back out again. So much of her life had taken place in this town. She had her first kiss right on this beach. Fell in love, had her heart broken . . . She'd gotten baptized right in this very water. She'd made promises to God during youth camp. Some of those promises she'd kept until this very day; others she'd let slip away.

Glancing up at the sky, Hope noticed that the sun had broken through the clouds and was beaming down on the water, giving it a shimmer. It was almost like God was smiling down on her. The water swept over her feet again. Hope sighed. Then the sun disappeared behind the clouds once more.

She kicked at the water, then turned to head back to the house. Faith was standing behind her with her arms folded, looking like she was studying her. "What?" Hope asked with a raised eyebrow.

"I figured out why Daddy left the beach house to you."

Hope waved a hand in the air. "Faith, I didn't scheme to get the house. I didn't know anything about it because Mama never said a word."

"I don't think you're a schemer." Faith unfolded her arms and walked closer to the water. "I think Daddy knew that there would come a day when you questioned where you belonged, so he left you the house so you would know that your home is here—always has been."

Hope turned, looked at the sparkle on the water, breathed in the beach air. Then as the truth of the matter became clear to her, she realized that she hadn't left her heart in California. She'd found it right here in Hallelujah. She repeated Faith's words, "Always has been."

Chapter 33

On Monday night, as Faith and Chris sat in the lounge chairs on the back patio talking over the designs she had in mind for the interior of the house, Chris got up while she was mid-sentence, got on one knee in front of her chair and said, "I want you to know something, Faith."

He caught her off guard with the seriousness of his tone and how his eyes sparkled with affection. Faith laid her sketch pad on the table beside her and sat up. She felt like whatever he had to say needed her undivided attention. "What is it, Chris?"

"I don't think that getting a divorce is God's perfect plan for us. I want to keep our family together, and I want us to keep trying." Tears shone bright in his eyes as he said, "I fell in love with you after our third date when you had mustard and ketchup on the corners of both sides of your mouth but didn't bother to wipe it because, as you said, the burger was too good to worry about looking cute."

"It was." Faith rubbed her stomach. "To this day, I still remember that burger. I can't believe that place closed down."

"What about us, Faith? You're not ready for us to give up and go our separate ways, are you?"

"Chris, can I ask you something?"

"Ask away."

"What is the real deal with you and this woman who sent me the picture of you and her through Facebook?" She grabbed her phone and opened Facebook. Went to her messages, clicked on one, then turned the phone toward Chris so he could see the kissy-face picture the woman sent her. Granted, Chris wasn't actually kissing the woman, but she was standing directly in front of him with her lips pursed like she was longing for a kiss.

He sighed. Turned away from her phone and shook his head. "I have made a lot of mistakes during our marriage, Faith, but I swear, I have never cheated on you."

She wanted to believe him. Throughout their marriage, he'd never given her any reason to suspect he was cheating—until she received that picture. "Then why did she send me that picture?"

Without hesitation, he said, "I'm going to lay it all out for you and hope that you can forgive me."

Here it comes. And he was always talking to her about trust. How could she trust someone who wasn't trustworthy?

"I was partnering with Linda on an upcoming house project. I normally do these deals on my own, but I knew I had to get our debts paid, and I was worried that my last flip wasn't going to come in with enough profit to make good on everything.

"But the housing market went up overnight, and I made over six figures on that last flip, so I told Linda that I would not be working with her on the next project."

Did she have to beat the information out of him or what? "That doesn't answer my question. Why did this Linda send me a kissy-face picture of the two of you?"

"I was not doing kissy faces with her. Linda did a kissy face in front of me and then snapped the picture."

"And why were you anywhere near a woman who would do some mess like that? It's obvious that she wants you, or she wouldn't have sent the picture to me."

"That's the part I need forgiveness for, because you're right. I did know that Linda was interested in me for more than business. I needed to get our bills paid, so I pretended that I didn't see the smiles and winks, but I never imagined that she would take it as far as sending you a photo to make you think something was going on between us, because it's not."

Faith didn't know what to believe—didn't know if she could trust him.

"I love you, Faith. Things haven't been good with us for a while now, but I haven't stopped loving you."

"You said I was coldhearted." His words had hurt her, and she really needed to know if he still felt that way.

Chris nodded. "The last few years, you have been distant and cold toward me, but I'm man enough to accept responsibility for the part I played." He took her hand in his. "I know you haven't felt financially secure with me while I've been building my business."

"I could have been more understanding," she admitted.

"And I could have communicated with you more." Looking into her eyes, he said, "What do you say, bae? Don't we deserve a second chance?"

Chris had been here for her at the time she needed him most. They hadn't been arguing so much lately, but they had other issues. "I don't know if we can go back to the way things used to be."

"Thank God for that," Chris said as he got off his knees. He sat on the lounger with Faith and rubbed his knee. "I don't like the way things were between us, so I'm looking forward to a change."

She agreed with him and could accept her own responsibility for how wrong things had been between them. "But just like we have Crystal in counseling for her issues, I also think you and I need to see a marriage counselor. Are you willing to do that?"

Holding on to her hand, Chris said, "When Crystal and I went to church with Hope yesterday, I went down to that altar and prayed for our marriage. I told God I would do whatever it takes to keep us together, so if you want counseling, then yes, I will do it. And I promise, if I ever run into financial difficulties again, I will discuss it with you."

At this point, her family needed a lot of prayer and counseling, but Faith was okay with that as long as they kept making forward progress. She hugged Chris, then he turned her face toward his, and they kissed. But it wasn't a baby-I'm-back kind of kiss. More like I'm-getting-to-know-you-again kiss. And she was. Faith felt as if the blinders had been removed from her eyes, and she was beginning to see Chris in a different light.

She wanted to explore where this was going, but right now they had a hurricane to deal with. When they pulled apart, she told him, "I need you to get Crystal out of here."

"Coming to see if I finally kicked the bucket?" Ruby asked Scooter Evans as he opened the door to her hospital room and stepped in.

"You know I don't wish ill toward you. How could I when we once were such good friends?"

John Evans, Scooter's daddy, had been business partners with Ruby's daddy. Her daddy had been a well-known businessman with a family and a mistress. Her mother had loved a man who wouldn't even acknowledge that he had a child by her.

That had been the first secret Ruby had ever had to hold. The first secret she had to keep and never ever tell a soul. Her high-and-mighty, important daddy was not to be exposed. She couldn't even speak to him outside of her mother's house.

Her reward for keeping that secret had been the land Henry built their beach house on. Her father had left the land to her in his will. But she'd had the last laugh because she never uttered her father's name or let anyone know that she had received the land from that man.

Scooter unbuttoned his jacket and sat down next to her bed. "I was worried about you. I had to come by to check on you."

"I'd sooner believe that you came in here looking for Hope to see if she would sell you the house, than believe you care anything about me." Ruby turned away from him.

"I had a right to be upset with you, Ruby. You went back on your word."

Looking at the wall, Ruby put her arms around her frail body. "Do you know how much it hurts to know who your daddy is and not be able to speak to him in public? . . . To know you have a father but not be able to tell anyone? He owed me that land, and I wasn't giving it away."

"But you and I had a deal," Scooter reminded her.

She wanted to call him a bald-face liar, but he wasn't lying. Ruby would have done anything to become Hope's mother, including making a deal with Scooter Evans. If she was being honest with herself, Scooter wasn't such a bad guy. The two of them had built mud castles on the beach together when they were kids.

As they grew up, Scooter never denied knowing her. He always spoke to her whenever they saw each other. But Scooter and his daddy had their eyes on the beach land that Ruby's daddy owned. They made plans to buy it from her father, then discovered that he had given the land to Ruby while acknowledging her as his daughter in his will.

When Ruby needed help with the scheme she had cooked up to become Hope's mother, she called on her childhood friend. She knew Scooter wanted her land, so she promised it to him if he would help her.

Scooter had sent a midwife from Dr. Stein's office to Brooklyn so Brenda could have the baby at home, then Dr. Stein, who was also Scooter's doctor, checked Ruby into the hospital and gave her a birth certificate with Henry and Ruby Reynolds' names on it. Hope's birth certificate was filed with the county clerk's office and then Ruby finally had her a baby.

She appreciated his help, but when it was time to pay up, Ruby just couldn't do it. Scooter pestered her relentlessly about her promise. Years later, when Henry had enough money to build on that land, Scooter came to her, ranting and raving, threatening to tell the police what he knew about Hope's birth certificate.

Ruby dared him to do it and reminded him about a little thing called aiding and abetting. After that, she and Scooter didn't say two words to each other. Then Hope started dating Nic.

"Don't you think it's time for us to bury the hatchet? Nic and Hope love each other. They'll probably get married."

"She does seem to glow when that knucklehead son of yours comes around." Ruby adjusted herself in the bed as she turned to offer Scooter an olive branch. "I like Nic. You raised him well."

"He's a good son. He has softened some of my edges, that's for sure."

They sat in silence for a little while, then Ruby said, "I'm sorry I ruined your plans for building a resort on the beach."

He leaned back in his seat, crossed his legs and waved off her apology. "Maybe our little beach town should stay just the way it is."

Chapter 34

EARLY TUESDAY MORNING, CHRIS PACKED THE TRUCK FOR the drive back to Atlanta. Faith was sad to see them go, but she couldn't bear the thought of Crystal being in harm's way. There was no rain this morning, but the wind and the choppy ocean water told her everything she needed to know. A storm was coming.

Crystal was standing in front of the full-length mirror eyeing herself from different angles.

Faith walked up to her. "Hey, beautiful."

Smiling as she turned to face her mother, Crystal asked, "Do you really think I'm beautiful?"

Faith gave her a *duh* expression. "How could I not? Everything about you is beautiful to me. Those pretty brown eyes." Faith touched her nose. "That cute little nose of yours."

Crystal cocked her head to the side. "Can I ask you something?"

Faith nodded. "Shoot."

"Do you think I'm thick?"

"Thick?" Faith scrunched her eyebrows. She'd thought her daughter was about to ask some profound question, but no. It was about being thick. "Where did you get something like that?"

"Kenneth said I was getting thick."

Faith wished she had known Kenneth was saying stuff like

that to her daughter when she caught him in their house. She would have sent him home to his mama with a knot on his head. "Girl, you weigh a hundred and five pounds. That is not thick by any means."

Crystal shook her head. "Not now. He said it back in the summer."

Faith closed her eyes. Inhaled, then exhaled. While her absence in her daughter's life had undoubtedly caused Crystal pain and confusion, her daughter also had to deal with people saying things to her that shouldn't be said. "Crystal, I took you for your annual physical right before summer break. You only weighed a hundred and seventeen pounds then."

Turning back to the mirror, Crystal said, "But when I look in the mirror, to me I look fat."

"What mirrors are you looking at? They must be some serious fun house mirrors because there isn't an ounce of fat on you." Silently Faith was praying for the Lord to give her the right words to say to her daughter.

Faith took her daughter's hand, moved her away from the mirror and sat in the living room with her. A thought struck. "Remember when you were younger and we watched *American Idol* together and how we would laugh our heads off about all those contestants who thought they could sing but they actually sounded terrible?"

Giggling at the memory, Crystal said, "They thought they could blow."

"Correct. And I want you to remember that, because they wouldn't have come on national television just to embarrass themselves like that. Something must have been wrong with their ears because they told them they could sing."

"Something was really wrong with their ears," Crystal agreed.

"So remember that the next time you look in the mirror and think you're fat. Move away from the mirror and then tell yourself that you aren't going to fall for the *American Idol* syndrome, and then go on about your day."

WHAT WE FOUND IN HALLELUJAH

Crystal smiled at that. "I'll try that. Thanks, Mom."

Faith held up a finger. "And if you do gain weight as you get older, you need to understand that having a few extra pounds does not make you any less beautiful or wonderful."

Chris opened the front door, clasped his hands together. "Time to get on the road."

Faith walked down to the driveway with them. Tears were threatening to explode all over her face, but she didn't want to cry because she didn't want them to know how sad she was to see them go.

"I want to stay here with you, Mommy." Crystal hugged her.

"I know, baby. I wish you could stay, too, but I want you and your daddy to be safe."

"But you're not safe. Come with us." Crystal pulled Faith toward the car.

Just as Crystal didn't want to leave her mother behind, neither did Faith. She couldn't leave town until she could get her mother out of here. "I'll be right behind you and your daddy. Don't worry. I'm bringing Grammy to our house. Maybe she'll spend Christmas with us."

Chris opened the passenger door. "Get in, Crystal. We have to get going."

Crystal did as she was told.

Chris wrapped his arms around Faith. "Be safe, honey. Please come home to us," he whispered in her ear.

She loved the sound of his voice against her ear. It was a sweet melody that she wanted to set on replay. Stepping out of his embrace, she wiped her eyes. "Be safe. Get our child out of here."

Faith rushed back into the house to grab her keys. She needed to get to the hospital to check on her mother. Her cell phone rang once she was in the car and pulling out of the driveway. She answered. It was Gladys.

"Hey, Faith, I was just confirming our dates for the kitchen project. My husband is so gung ho that he wants you to start the day after Christmas. Will that work for you?"

Another time in her life, Faith wouldn't have thought twice about starting the project during the Christmas season. "I'm sorry, Gladys, but my daughter will still be on winter break. The earliest I could start the project would be around January fourth after she goes back to school."

Hanging up the phone, Faith wasn't the least concerned if refusing to start the project early might cost her business. Family comes first and that's the way she was going to play this thing from here on out.

By the time Faith made it to the hospital, Hope was pulling at her hair and biting her lip. Hope had decided to stay with them instead of going back to California. Their plan was to wait on Ruby's release and then ride out of town together.

"What's wrong?" Faith looked from Hope to Ruby, and then at the doctor who was in the room looking like he had rocks in his jaw.

"Ask her." Hope pointed toward Ruby.

Ruby directed Faith's attention to the television. "Lola is on the way, and I'm not going to be laid up in the hospital when I need to be at home."

"We've already boarded up the house, Mama, so you don't have to worry about that," Faith told her.

The doctor stepped forward. "We are well aware of the hurricane, but you had a setback after your operation, so you need to stay in the hospital at least a couple more nights."

Faith didn't like what she was hearing. "I was hoping you'd release her tomorrow so we could get out of town."

"You talking crazy," Ruby tried to sit up in the bed, fell back against her pillow but kept right on protesting. "I'm not staying here another night. I know my rights. You can't keep me here against my will. I'm ready to go home, so you just go out there and get my discharge papers together."

"Mama!" Hope stood, shaking her head. "Why won't you listen to the doctor?"

"Because I need to get home." Ruby wagged a finger at Hope and Faith. "And y'all need to take me home. As long as I have breath in my body, I'm going to protect my house and my land."

Faith closed her eyes. Inhaling and exhaling. When she opened her eyes again, she spoke slowly. "You can't do this. You need to stay here at least one more night."

"Who says I can't?" Ruby demanded to know.

"Listen to your children, Ms. Ruby. You'll be safer in the hospital," the doctor said.

"And you listen to me." She wagged her finger again. "My surgery was five days ago. Medicare wanted me out of here on Sunday." Ruby narrowed her eyes at the doctor. "I'm going to get out of this bed with or without anyone's help, and I'm going to my house—the house that my husband built—and I'm going to weather this storm right there."

The doctor threw up his hands. "I'll have the nurse bring in the against medical advice form for you to sign before we can release you."

When he left the room, Ruby turned to Faith and said, "Help me put my clothes on."

"Are you serious, Mama? The doctor wants you to stay." Faith didn't move.

Ruby turned to Hope and asked her to get the clothes. When Hope didn't move, she said, "Listen to me, and hear me clearly." Her voice broke as she said, "I can't take no more losses. That house is the only thing Henry had to give me, and I will protect it with everything I've got until the Lord calls me home."

Putting her head in her hand, Hope blew out a puff of air. "What do you want us to do, Mama? This hurricane is projected to hit as a category 4. Faith and I should have already left town, but we stayed for you."

"That's right." Ruby was beaming as she said, "We're together, and we're going to stay together." She reached for them. Faith came and stood on the left side of the bed, and Hope stood on the right. Ruby put her arms around their waists. "I'm tired of losing. I just want to go home, okay?"

Ruby won the battle at the hospital. She signed the release form and the against medical advice form, and then Faith drove them toward home.

But they faced a whole new set of problems. Each gas station they tried to stop at had mile-long lines. They wouldn't be getting any gas, and there was only a quarter of a tank in the SUV.

"What are we going to do?" Faith asked, worry lines etching across her forehead.

Hope shook her head. "I have no idea."

When they made it to the beach house, Ruby was too weak to climb the stairs by herself, so Faith and Hope helped her. Once they were at the top of the stairs, a police car pulled into the driveway.

"Oh goodness, here it comes. They want us to leave." Ruby sat down in the rocking chair while Hope looked in her purse for the key to unlock the door.

Faith bent and whispered in Ruby's ear, "What did you expect, Mama? They can't just leave you here."

"They can, and they will," Ruby declared as the officer got out of the car. She waved at him.

"Hey, Ms. Ruby." He stood at the bottom of the stairs. "I'm making my rounds. This storm is going to be pretty bad, and we have a mandatory evacuation in place."

"Thanks for letting me know," she said, staying seated as Hope and Faith gave her wide-eyed glances.

The officer said, "I'm serious, Ms. Ruby. There won't be anyone here to help you if you don't pack up and get going this afternoon."

Ruby lifted her arms for her girls to help her out of the chair. They pulled her up, and she leaned against the banister. "Here's the thing, officer. I just got out of the hospital. I need to make sure my house is secure and then get my bags packed." She turned and grabbed hold of Hope's and Faith's arms and then walked inside her house.

The officer yelled up, "God help you if you don't get out of here soon because none of the city workers will be here until this storm blows over."

Faith closed the door and began rubbing her forehead. "Okay, Mama. We brought you home. We're going to get everything set the way you want it, then we're getting on the road."

Ruby saw fear in Faith's eyes. She turned to Hope and saw the same fear. She hadn't raised her girls to be afraid of anything—life had taught them to fear. "Okay, girls. Listen to me. I'm tired. I need to lie down in my bed and rest, but if the storm hasn't turned or if Lola is still forecasted as a category 4 by morning, then I'll leave, and I won't put up a fuss."

"Do you promise, Mama?" Hope asked.

"I do, but I think this storm is going to turn, so fix your faces."

Chapter 35

I'M SORRY ABOUT YOU NOT BEING ABLE TO MAKE THAT MEET-
ing, but I'm not going to lie, I'm happy that you will be home for a
while longer," Ruby said.

Hope's snake of an ex-boyfriend/boss took care of all her
problems about her job. Even though she'd told him several times
that she still needed his numbers from the last two events he held
at Hillsboro Hotel, he didn't include them in the report and then
blamed the inaccuracies on her.

Thanks to Spencer's lies, Human Resources called to inform
her that she no longer had a job. Apparently, they thought she was
lounging around the beach instead of doing her job. In truth, she
actually felt relieved that she didn't have the tug of her job on her
mind anymore. She would go back to California to collect her
things and cancel her apartment lease. After that, she would come
back home to work on dreams that had been deferred.

Ruby adjusted herself in bed, pulled the covers up. "*Whew!*
Feels so good to be back in my own bed."

"I'm glad you're home, too, Mama, but just remember, if that
storm doesn't turn, we'll have to get on the road." It was a terrible
thing to do to a woman who had just had surgery and then complications from it. All Ruby wanted to do was rest in her own bed,
but Hope couldn't make that promise.

"Storms like these always turn. We'll be all right."

Hope looked out the window next to her mother's bed. Clouds filled the sky, looking as if they were ready to burst. "Please hold until tomorrow. Just give us one more day, Lord." Her mother needed a good night's rest before getting on that highway and sitting in traffic for hours on end.

Hope helped her mother get settled, made sure she had everything she needed nearby. The remote and a glass of water were on the nightstand next to her bed. Hope had placed a peanut butter and jelly sandwich on the table as well because her mother loved that stuff. "Don't get up. Use your cell phone to call one of us if you need anything."

"You're enjoying bossing me around, aren't you?" Ruby smiled, but it was lackluster.

"Mama, you're still so weak from everything you went through at the hospital. I just don't want you overdoing it."

Ruby waved her out of the room. "You go on and get some rest yourself. I promise you, that storm is going to fizzle out."

She pointed at Ruby as she walked toward the door. "Don't move."

Hope went out back with Faith. She rubbed her arms as a wind blew that chilled the air.

Faith pointed out to the ocean. "The water is getting choppy. We probably should get this stuff off the patio now."

"Do you think we're making a mistake by waiting until the morning to leave town?"

Faith glanced out at the ocean. She turned back to her sister. "I hope not, but Mama is not well enough to travel. I doubt if she'll be ready tomorrow, but that's the best we can do."

They started taking things like the potted plants off the patio. Hope prayed that the storm would turn, but the clouds, which were getting bigger, were taking all her hope away.

They spent the next thirty or so minutes tying things down on the patio and removing the items that couldn't be tied down. Hope stepped to the edge of the patio, looked out at the ocean, then breathed in the air. Fear clenched her heart as she looked at the darkening clouds. She turned back to Faith and said, "We can't stay here tonight. This hurricane is not going to turn."

Faith pointed toward the house. "But Mama—"

"I know." Hope bit on her bottom lip. "I hate to do this to her, but at this point, we have to figure out where she would be safer. In the car several miles up the road or in this house with a category 4 hurricane barreling down on us."

Faith massaged her neck with her hand, then rolled her neck to get the kink out of it. "I'll go pack her bag. You go break the news to Mama."

Faith ran into the house as if they were playing a game of tag and Hope was "it."

"Chicken." Hope laughed as she walked back into the house and went to Ruby's room. Her mom was asleep. They had two bad choices, and Hope hated that she had to make the choice her mother wasn't going to like.

She sat down on the bed next to her mom, put a hand on Ruby's shoulder to gently wake her.

Ruby's eyes slowly opened, but she didn't lift from the bed. She leaned into her pillow. "Don't tell me it's morning already."

"No, Mom, it's not morning, but this storm isn't going to turn, so we need to get out of here tonight. Faith and I have secured everything around the house, so you don't need to worry about anything here."

Ruby's eyes flashed concern. "What if we leave and we can't get back to take care of any repairs that might be needed? This is the only legacy I have to give you and your sisters."

This house was special to all of them. This was the place they called home, but it wasn't all they had. Hope shook her head. "This house isn't the only thing you have to give. The most important thing you've ever given me is love." Hope teared up, sniffed. "The thing I remember most about you is how hard you love. I want to be like that, Mama—to love someone so much that I refuse to let go."

Ruby reached up and wiped the tear from Hope's cheek. "We've held on to each other."

Nodding, Hope agreed. "I love you, Mama, and that's why I can't let you stay here and ride out this storm. We've got to go."

"Okay," Ruby said. "I won't give you a hard time. Just help me get dressed."

"Yay!" Faith entered the room with a suitcase in her hand.

Hope's back was to the door. She turned to her sister. "Ear hustling at the door, I see."

"I had to. We don't have time for you to mess this up. We still need to get to a gas station and fill up before we hit the highway." Faith opened the suitcase and started throwing clothing in it.

Hope helped Ruby get dressed, and then she and Faith helped Ruby walk to the front door. "We're going to carry you downstairs, so sit right here until we get our bags in the car."

Hope helped Ruby into the recliner in the living room.

Faith opened the front door, getting ready to head down to the car with the bags, but was stopped dead in her tracks. Crystal was standing on the front porch, hand lifted like she was getting ready to knock on the door.

⌒

Faith's eyes widened. Was she seeing things? Her child was not in front of her. Crystal was on the highway heading home. Faith shook her head, closed her eyes. But when she opened them again, Crystal was still there. "Why are you here? You're supposed to be home."

Chris ran up the steps. No! This wasn't happening. They were supposed to leave her here and go home—to safety. Crystal went inside the house while Faith stepped on the porch with Chris.

"What happened? You were supposed to get Crystal out of here."

"I tried. We waited in line at one gas station for two hours. By the time we got to the pump, they were sold out. We then went to another gas station, and the same thing happened."

Faith rubbed the palms of her hands against her forehead. "Don't tell me you're stuck here with us."

Chris nodded. "It looks that way. The highway is backed up for miles. It's a madhouse out there. I didn't want to chance being stuck on the highway with this storm rolling in."

Faith sighed as she headed inside with Chris. "Well, at least we're all together. That's what matters most."

Chapter 36

FAITH TOOK A PILLOW AND THE BLANKET FROM RUBY'S BED and brought them to the living room. She laid the blanket over her mother while Hope extended the recliner to put Ruby in the lounging position. "How do you feel?" Faith asked.

Ruby situated the pillow behind her head. "I'm okay. Just praying that we all stay safe through the night."

"Me too, Mama." Faith silently prayed for peace of mind because her nerves were getting the best of her. Storms. She hated storms.

Within an hour of Chris returning to the house, the rain started. It first came in as drizzles, but by nightfall, the rain was beating down on them like God Himself was crying over all the sins in the world.

Then the wind kicked up. Faith shivered as she looked out at the raging sea. Chris placed the heavy sandbags against the doors. A hurricane was barreling down on them. They were stuck here. It was time to get the generator out.

Thunder roared, and the house shook.

"Oh my good Lord!" Faith just about jumped out of her skin.

Chris came up behind her and held on to her arm to steady her. "You okay?"

Faith straightened. She put her hand to her head and walked over to the window. "These storms didn't used to bother me so much. We always came through them okay, so I never thought they were a big deal when I was a kid, then . . ." Faith inhaled, opened the curtain and looked through a crack between the pieces of the plywood that were against the window. It was really coming down out there.

"I wish y'all had left me in the hospital and hightailed it out of town. I think I was wrong about this storm. I shouldn't have been so stubborn." Ruby started biting on her finger as sweat beaded down her forehead.

Faith was nervous about the viciousness of this storm as well, but there was no turning back now. They had all made the decision to stay with Ruby. She lifted her eyes heavenward. *Get us through this, Lord.* Faith stepped away from the window, stood by her mother's recliner and patted her arm. "We're all together, and that's what counts."

Chris went to the window, trying to see out of the cracks in between the plywood. "You might as well step away from that window," Ruby told him.

Chris pointed toward the beach. "I can hear the waves. Sounds like they're trying to swallow this house whole."

"Don't say stuff like that." Faith nudged him in the stomach with her elbow, then went to her room and got a blanket, came back to the living room, found a spot on the floor, sat down and wrapped the blanket around her body.

Situating her pillow under her head, Ruby told them, "We're on the left side of the hurricane right now, so we're getting all the rain. Heaven help us when this thing turns and we're on the right side of it."

Crystal was sitting on the floor with a book in her hand. She raised her eyes from the book and gave her grandmother a questioning glance. "What happens on the right side of a hurricane, Grammy?"

Faith never wanted to be anywhere near the right side of a hurricane again. It was the strongest side, with winds so treacherous they could blow a house down. "Don't scare her, Mama."

"I'm not trying to scare the child, but the truth is the truth. We're in for a long night with this storm."

Hope came back into the living room. She had her adult coloring book in her hand with a canister full of colored pencils. "Who wants to color with me?"

Crystal jumped up. "I do."

Hope tore a page out of her coloring book and handed it to Crystal along with some colored pencils.

"You got enough for me?" Ruby asked.

Thunder roared, and lightning flashed in the sky.

"Whoa," Crystal said as she sat back down on the floor.

Hope's whole body shook—looked like she wanted to leap out of her skin—but she took a deep breath, then tore another page and handed it to Ruby. "Let's see who can finish their page first."

"I guess this is your attempt to keep us calm." Faith held out her hand. "I can't just sit here with nothing but this storm on my mind, so I'll color with you."

Chris sat on the sofa. "I'm not good at coloring, but if we make a contest out of this, I can judge whose drawing is the best."

Faith was shaking like a scared rabbit during hunting season when her mother mentioned the right side of the storm, because she had experienced a storm with strong winds twice in her life. The aftermath of the first one caused her daddy's heart attack and the second one left them without Trinity. She was thankful that Hope brought her coloring book out. It would take their mind off how hard the rain was beating against the house.

"Well, since I'm your wife, I'm sure you'll pick my page." Faith winked at Chris, like they were in this together.

But Crystal objected, "Hey. I'm his daughter. He should pick mine."

Ruby laughed at them. "Why don't we color first, then the two of you can plot on how you're going to cheat me and Hope out of the victory."

Crystal laughed, then Faith joined in with the merriment. "Okay, Mama. We'll be good." But she winked at Chris again.

Even as the wind and the rain descended on the house, Faith realized that there was no place she'd rather be than with her family. She glanced up and saw Chris watching her as she colored.

Her husband had given her a tsunami of reasons to want to leave, but life with her hadn't been easy either, yet he was still here. She hadn't recognized it in a long time, but Chris was the kind of man her dad would have wanted for her.

"I need a green colored pencil."

Crystal's words brought Faith back to the moment. She tossed her daughter a light-green pencil. Crystal thanked her. The house shook again, the lights went out, and then a loud angry roar of thunder burst forth.

Someone screamed. Then another person, then Faith screamed as well.

"I can't see anything," Crystal yelled.

Faith stretched out her arm in Crystal's direction. "Reach out your hand. I'm crawling over to you."

Ruby had spent her whole life on this island, so it took a lot for storms to get to her. Right now, she was thinking about the child she'd lost in a storm and was praying to God that she wouldn't lose any more. *Not tonight, Lord. Cover us and protect us.*

Ruby hadn't prayed for God's protection in such a long time. It felt good to do so again. Was she truly ready to lean and depend on God as she once had so long ago?

As her girls screamed in fear because of the lights going out, a scripture she used to recite in Sunday school came to mind: *"The Lord is my light and my salvation; whom then shall I fear: The Lord is the strength of my life; of whom then shall I be afraid?"*

"Amen to that," Chris said as he stood. "Can anyone tell me where the candles are?"

Ruby pointed toward the kitchen. "Bottom drawer, next to the microwave."

Hope turned on the flashlight on her cell phone. "Why hasn't the generator kicked on yet?"

"Be patient, Hope." Ruby pointed to the sofa. "Sit back down, and give it a moment."

Chris took his cell phone out of his back pocket, turned on his flashlight and headed toward the kitchen. He returned within a minute with two lit candles. He set them on the sofa table.

Hope sat down, then turned her flashlight off. "I need to save the battery on my phone. Thanks for thinking about candles, brother-in-law."

Glancing around the room, Ruby saw that Faith and Crystal sat on the floor with their backs against the wall and Faith's arm wrapped around Crystal. That made Ruby smile. Faith had seemed distant with Crystal when they first arrived, but if she was clinging to her daughter, the wind of change might just be blowing their way.

Lightning flashed, and then they heard something banging against the house. Faith screamed, then Crystal screamed.

"Faith, you are no help to Crystal if you're going to be screaming and carrying on like that," Ruby told her.

"Sorry," Faith said. "I just can't deal with these storms anymore."

"When's it going to be over, Grammy?" Crystal was shaking.

"Soon, baby. Soon." Ruby heard the fear in her granddaughter's voice and knew she needed to do something to take their minds off the raging winds and the pummeling rain, so she said, "What's the first thing you're going to do when this storm is over?"

"Oh, Mama, not that whatcha-gonna-do game again," Faith complained.

When they were younger and a bad storm hit, Ruby and Henry would sit in the living room with the kids and play the whatcha-gonna-do game. Henry had made up the game, and the kids had enjoyed it. "You don't have to go first, Faith. Let me ask Chris."

"Me?"

"Yes, Chris, you. What's the first thing you want to do when this storm passes?"

Chris took a moment to answer, but then he said, "If I were at home and we had a bad storm, I'd go outside and check around the house and then fix any damage from the storm. Since I'm here, I think I'll do the same for you."

Her son-in-law was a good man. She hoped that he and Faith could get past whatever issues they had. She prayed her daughter would learn that, just like houses, marriages don't fix themselves. It takes work.

"Well, we are glad to have you here because it sounds like there will be a lot to fix once this storm passes."

"Happy to do it for you, Ruby."

Ruby then turned in Hope's direction. "So what do you want to do once this storm passes?"

Hope thought for a minute, then said, "The first thing that I should do is exchange my plane ticket and go pack up my apartment, but I don't think I'm ready to leave you yet."

Those words sprung up joy from way down deep. Ruby said, "Okay, so what *are* you going to do?"

"I don't know for sure if I'm going to do this, but I'd like to go check on Melinda. Nic said they might be moving her to a rehabilitation facility."

"That would be nice of you." Ruby then turned her attention to Crystal. "Now what does my grandbaby want to do when this storm is over?"

"I'm not a baby anymore, Grammy."

"I'm sorry. I keep forgetting. Yes, you are growing up so fast. Okay, what do you want to do?"

"Well, I know I don't want to go to my science class tomorrow, so if the power lines are down, I'll be okay with that. Then Auntie Hope can take me to get some more of that ice cream she brought me the other day."

Before Ruby could say anything else, the generator kicked in, and the lights came back on. Ruby was thankful that her family wouldn't have to sit in the dark and freeze for a week while waiting on the energy company to restore their power.

Everyone jumped up and started shouting, "Yay! Yes!"

Ruby tried to lift from her seat, but a pain hit her. She plopped back down. She'd gotten so worked up with this storm that she'd forgotten that she'd just had surgery.

Faith blew out the candles and was about to head into the kitchen, but Ruby stopped her. "Wait one second, Ms. Lady. You don't get off that easy. Everyone else has said what they want to do after the storm. Now it's your turn."

Faith shifted her eyes upward. She scratched her forehead with her index finger. "It's not so much that I want to go anywhere, but you know how you said earlier that you were tired of taking losses? I guess that's where I'm at. I just don't want to take any more losses once this storm rolls out of here. If we're all safe, then I'll be okay."

The room got quiet. Ruby figured that her girls were thinking about all that they had lost in these Carolina storms through the years. Seemed like the storms kept winning, and the Reynoldses kept showing up on the losing end. Kind of like trying to box the wind. Nobody was going to win that fight—just gonna be left with tired arms from the swinging.

Ruby didn't want to take any more losses either. She prayed that God was listening to her this time. Don't think about it; just believe. Ruby rocked in her chair like she didn't have a care in the world. "Shouldn't be much longer now. This storm is about to pass." She nodded her head, leaned back in her chair. "Yes indeed, all storms pass over sooner or later." To herself she mumbled, "It can't keep raining in our lives."

Chapter 37

HER MOTHER'S PREDICTION ABOUT THE STORM PASSING OVER soon turned out to be real, real wrong. They were having a Freddy-Krueger-come-to-town kind of night—just all bad. Several times during the storm, Hope wished she had gotten on the plane and headed to California where hurricanes don't roll in. She should have purchased a ticket for her mother as well. Then Faith could have gone home with Chris and Crystal.

All the woulda, coulda, shouldas of this world weren't going to change the fact that they just might die tonight. The wind wouldn't stop howling and attacking the house like it was trying to get inside.

Her phone beeped. She had a text message from Nic.

Are you okay? Hope, please tell me that you're okay.
We're okay for now.

She wished she could have sent a more positive message, but she wasn't feeling real positive right now. Not even her adult coloring book could relieve the stress she was under.

How is your mother?

As Hope texted those words she wondered if she would have asked about Melinda if Melinda hadn't apologized to her. She had let Melinda's hateful words change the trajectory of her life. Hope was now questioning herself about everything. Had Melinda messed things up for her, or had she been so heartbroken after uncovering her mother's big lie that she simply couldn't handle rejection of any kind?

The text message failed to send, and Hope's phone shut down. Had the strong winds knocked a cell phone tower down? Hope got up and went into the kitchen. Maybe if she was munching on some chips or something, she would stop thinking about how bad the house was shaking. Daddy always told her that the house had been built to withstand hurricane winds, but it seemed like this wind was calling his bluff.

She took a bag of salt-and-vinegar chips out of the pantry and was headed out of the kitchen when there was a shaking so bad that Hope thought the house was being split in two. She held on to the counter as she yelled, "Is everybody okay?"

Ruby yelled back, "We're okay. Come back in here with us."

"I'm coming." Hope let go of the counter, took two steps toward the living room. The roof lifted as shingles ripped off. Hope's eyes got big as she saw the swell in the ceiling until a piece of it caved in.

Hope fell to the ground as pieces of the ceiling flew her way, then water gushed into the kitchen like it was the Niagara Falls. "Help! Help! Oh my dear Lord, don't let us drown in here."

Chris and Faith ran into the kitchen. Stark terror filled Faith's eyes as she looked at the water gushing through the hole in the roof.

Chris asked Ruby, "Do you have any duct tape?"

"It's in the second drawer next to the sink. Oh my Lord. Help us, Jesus!"

Hope got off the floor, started looking through the drawers for the duct tape.

Chris rushed into the pantry and came out with a flat piece of board and several black trash bags. He climbed onto the counter. But it was slick from the rain, and the wind was so strong that he fell backward. *"Whoa, whoa, whoooa."* His arms flailed in the air. The trash bags flew across the room. But he was still holding onto the board.

"No!" Faith screamed as she put her hands out, holding on to the back of his pants. "Don't break your neck up there."

Hope held on to Chris' legs to steady him. "You need us to come up there with you?"

Chris got down on his knees. "The counter is too wet."

"I'll get some towels," Faith told him as she ran toward the hallway closet. When she came back into the kitchen, she and Hope placed towels on the counter.

The rain was beating down so hard that a river was flowing in the kitchen. Something would have to be done or they were all doomed. Hope prayed that this was not how things would end for all of them.

"Hand me those trash bags," Chris said, pointing to the direction where the trash bags had fallen.

"Be careful in there," Ruby yelled from the living room.

"We're trying, Mama, but we've got to close this hole in the ceiling or we'll all be swimming in here," Faith told her.

"Oh my good Lord," Ruby yelled back.

"Mama, I need you to pray like you used to when we were kids. When you told us the God of Abraham, Isaac and Jacob could do anything." Hope handed the duct tape and scissors to Faith and then picked up the trash bags.

"You better believe I'm in here praying. Fix it, Jesus! Fix it!" Ruby called out. "I believe, Lord. I'm depending on You to get me and my family through. Lord, please, we need You to show up for us this time."

Chris stumbled as he tried to stand. He tried to get back up, but the wind was winning and kept pushing him backward.

Hope saw fear in Faith's eyes again, but it wasn't fear for herself. Her sister leaped onto the counter. "I am not going to let you kill yourself."

"Get down, Faith. It's not safe up here."

"No! No!" Faith yelled at him. "I told y'all, we are not taking any more losses. You and I are doing this together."

"She's right, Chris. You need our help." Hope climbed onto the counter. Then the three of them stood, with Faith and Hope on either side of Chris. The wind was fierce. Hope was thankful that Ruby was praying. She could still hear her calling on the Lord to deliver them. Right now they needed all the help they could get.

Crystal stood by the entryway into the kitchen. She looked as if she was watching a horror movie as she witnessed the conditions they were dealing with. "Don't fall," she yelled at them.

Chris' cheeks flapped in the wind as he said, "Hand. Me. A. Strip. Of. Tape." Chris then folded the trash bags in half, put them behind the sturdy little piece of board and then lifted them to the ceiling.

Hope's and Faith's drenched hair swiped across their faces and then swayed in the wind like a blow dryer on the highest setting was pointed at them. Hope held out her hand. "Hurry, Faith. Cut the tape." Hope could hear Ruby still praying; it sounded like she had put all her trust in God. It sounded like back in the day.

"Jesus! Jesus! Jesus!" Ruby kept calling His name.

Faith rolled out a long strip, cut it and handed it to Hope.

Hope helped Chris stick the tape and the trash bag to the ceiling. She then grabbed another strip from Faith and handed it to Chris. They kept working until they had every side of those trash bags covered with duct tape. And the trash bags were pressed firmly against the board. Chris then put a few extra strips of tape across the bags to strengthen the hold. "We did it." They were all soaking wet, but they had closed the hole in the ceiling.

Hope climbed down from the counter and was about to go in

search of more towels and blankets to mop up some of this water when Faith slipped.

"Help," Faith yelled as she lost her footing.

"Mommy, no!" Crystal ran over to the counter, wading through the puddle of water on the floor, hands outstretched.

Chris was able to grab Faith before she fell to the floor. As Hope looked back, she saw her sister with her husband's and child's arms wrapped around her like she was the most important thing in this whole world. Hope's heart leaped. Her sister was going to be all right. If they survived the raging storm outside, Hope was confident that Faith would also survive the storm she had been running from for so long because she had love by her side.

As Hope walked around the house searching for more towels and blankets, she found herself wishing for the kind of love that would ride out a storm with her and wondering if she was truly ready to do what it would take to keep such a love.

⌒

Faith, Crystal and Chris made a pallet on the floor and wrapped up in blankets. Hope slept on the sofa, and Ruby snored loudly in her recliner. And, thank God, it was morning and the wind and waves decided to behave.

Faith was the first to rise. She went into the kitchen to see if their patch job was holding. It was leaking. Faith found two buckets and put them on the floor to catch the *drip-drip-drip* from the ceiling. Chris got up and moved the sandbags from the doors, and they went outside to begin the clean-up process. Pieces of the siding had been whisked away, and pieces of the roof were lying on the front lawn.

Faith had a notepad and pen in hand, jotting down the damage she saw as she walked around the house. She took out her cell phone and snapped pictures of the damage as well.

Hope yelled to her sister, "Hey, we're all picking up this debris, and you're walking around like a boss, taking notes and snapping pictures. Get over here and help us."

"I'm working," Faith protested. "These notes and pictures are going to the insurance company so we can get that roof fixed and the siding put back on the house without Mama taking another hit to the budget."

"Okay. I'll give you a pass because we're going to need that insurance money." Hope dumped some of the debris in the trash can, then went back to the yard and continued the cleanup process.

Faith finished her inventory. With all the shingles on the ground and the damage that had been done to the kitchen, she was positive they'd be able to take the roof and a few other items off of their list because the insurance company would be paying.

Chris put a tarp on the roof, then they searched the front and back of the house for missing siding. They brought it back to the house, and Faith helped Chris put the siding that wasn't broken in bits and pieces back on the house.

A couple of neighbors down the way were picking their siding up from the beach and hauling it back to their homes as well. But Faith took note of the empty space just three homes away from their house. The house had crumbled. Plywood and pieces of the roof lay on top of each other. She looked to heaven and thanked the Lord that they had survived. But her heart ached for the homeowners who would come back to discover that they now had to rebuild their home.

Shaking his head, Chris told her, "I don't know how you lived through stuff like this while growing up in this town. I couldn't do it."

"This is the worst storm I have ever experienced," she told Chris. "The storm wasn't this bad the year Trinity went missing." Faith turned and looked out at the sea. For a moment, she was captivated by its calmness. There were no crashing waves, no angry, rushing winds.

The beach was once again a beautiful, picturesque sight, but Faith wondered if it had swallowed the life out of anyone last night. She was thankful that she and Hope had taken that DNA test because they would soon know if that had been Trinity's fate.

Chris put his nail gun down. He walked over to her and put her hand in his. "Don't do that."

"Huh? Don't do what?"

"The look on your face. I can tell that you're thinking about Trinity, but I don't want you to let thoughts of your sister make you sad anymore." He positioned himself directly in front of her, hands on her arms. "Let your mind settle on the good times that you and your sisters had in this town."

Faith looked in her husband's eyes and saw so clearly the love he had for her. This man was in this thing with her. How had she allowed herself to become so completely and utterly blind to that fact? Faith exhaled. "Honestly, I think I'll enjoy being here if we can just discover what happened to Trinity. Also, there's something I need to tell you."

"Yeah, what?"

"I told you that the house belonged to Hope, but I didn't tell you that the land belongs to me. The way my mom sees it, Hope and I will have to work together to decide what we will do with the property."

He looked confused for a moment, then asked, "Your mom's will gives the property to both you and Hope?"

"Basically, yes. She also gives ownership of the land to Trinity." She lifted a hand, "But I don't want to talk about that. I just wanted to be truthful with you about the property."

He nodded. "Thanks for telling me, but I would help your family with this house anyway because I know it means a lot to you."

Faith's eyes filled. She was overcome with emotion. "I've been such a fool, Chris. I don't know how you put up with me."

"We put up with each other." He laughed at his own joke while wiping tears from her face.

Faith was tired of just putting up with things in her marriage. She wanted to enjoy being with this man and appreciate him for every-thing he brought to the table. She wanted to see the good in him without focusing on anything else.

Pastor O'Dell stopped by to bring water and a bunch of pea-nut butter crackers. Faith should have known he would have stayed behind. Since she was a child, Faith had watched Pastor O'Dell quietly help out in the community.

They kept cleaning around the house for a few more hours, but then exhaustion weighed Faith down. She was weary from the storm, and her shoulders ached so bad that all she wanted to do was lie down with her husband. "I'm ready for bed." She reached for his hand. "Are you coming?"

His eyes brightened. "You think your mom will allow me to sleep in your room?"

"You got jokes." She headed for the front door. "Let's go to bed."

After they showered, changed into their pajamas and then got in bed, Chris leaned over to kiss her. Faith's eyes drooped. She was too exhausted to do anything but sleep. Chris held her in his arms as she drifted off.

As tired as she was, Faith expected a peaceful sleep, but instead she found herself right back on the beach searching for Trinity and dreaming about Colton again.

Faith handed Colton some of the flyers that she and her mother were passing out on the beach. "Thanks for helping, and if you see Trinity, please tell her to come home and stop playing."

"I will." Colton walked away from them and started passing out the papers to everyone he came in contact with. The look on his face was stoic as he told each person, "We really need your help. If you've seen the girl in this photo, please call the number on the flyer."

"Come on, girl. Stop staring at that boy. He and his whole family ain't worth a quarter put together." Ruby rolled her eyes heavenward and then headed in the opposite direction from Colton.

Her mother was wrong. Colton was one of the good ones. She'd been crushing on him for two years now and had been writing her first name with his last name for the last few months. He was helping them pass out flyers for her missing sister, so no one was going tell her that Colton James wasn't all of that and some more.

She handed a flyer to a young girl and asked her, "Have you seen my sister?"

The girl shook her head.

What in the world was Trinity thinking? She was only fourteen. Why would she run off like this? Faith looked heavenward, praying for answers to her musings. "God, please, just show us where Trinity is. We just want to bring her back home."

After that quick prayer, Faith went back to passing out the flyers. As she walked down the beach with Colton several steps ahead of her, she saw him pull a cell phone out of his pocket. He flipped it open and started pecking at the buttons on the phone.

Her mother refused to get her a cell phone until she graduated from high school. She thought Colton's mom had told him the same thing. She ran over to him. "I'm jealous. How'd you get your mother to buy you a cell phone?"

Colton jumped, swung around. He dropped the flyers and the phone in the sand.

Faith bent down and picked up the flyers. He picked up the phone and put it in his back pocket. "I'm just holding it for a friend," he told her as she gave him the flyers he had dropped.

Their eyes locked. She saw a flicker of sadness in his. Life was golden for Colton. He was a star basketball player, had several colleges recruiting him for a full ride. His eyes always seemed to sparkle with the promise of this great future coaches had been telling him he would have, but not today.

"Where's your basketball?" Colton without a basketball in his hand seemed odd. At about the age of eleven or twelve, it seemed like Colton

had glued a basketball to his hand. He was rarely without that trademark got-the-world-in-my-hands smile or his basketball. Today he had neither.

"Just felt like running on the beach today."

Ruby came up behind Faith, grabbed her arm and turned her toward their house. "Come on, girl. We got to pass some of these flyers out on the other side of town."

"I'm sorry, Mama, I didn't mean to hold you up." Her mother wouldn't be out here passing out all these flyers if Faith had just stopped Trinity from leaving the house.

"Don't leave, Trinity. Don't leave!"

"Faith! Wake up, honey. You're having a bad dream."

Faith's eyes fluttered. She opened her eyes and looked around. She wasn't on the beach. She was in bed with her husband but had dreamed about Colton again. She didn't understand why. She wasn't infatuated with Colton anymore. As she sat up, flashes of things that were important but hadn't seemed important at the time swirled around Faith's mind.

Why had Colton been so eager to help that day? Why had he been sad? And whose cell phone did he have that day? Was God trying to show her something? If so, she needed to follow where this thing was leading.

Chapter 38

THAT NIGHT, AFTER THE GIRLS AND CHRIS HAD FINISHED the cleanup, Ruby lay in her bed thanking God for how He had kept them safe in the midst of the storm. Her hands were steepled as she said, "You are a good God."

Ruby felt tears swell in her eyes, but they weren't sad tears. It felt like joy was bubbling up in her heart—the kind of joy she hadn't known since Henry died. She was feeling it now because last night, in the midst of the storm, when it seemed like everything was going wrong, Ruby decided to trust God with her family's lives. And God came through for them.

There was a knock on the door. "Come in."

Hope opened the door with a plate in her hand. "Are you hungry? I brought you a sandwich."

Ruby held out her hand. "Thank you, daughter. I was getting a little hungry."

Hope pointed toward the cup that was on Ruby's nightstand. "Do you need more to drink?"

Ruby shook her head. "I don't want any more lemonade, but you can bring me a bottle of water."

Hope turned to leave the room, but Ruby stopped her. "Hey. I don't think I ever thanked you for asking Pastor O'Dell to come see me at the hospital."

Hope swung back around. She was smiling at her mother. "The way you were praying last night, Pastor O'Dell must have given you a portion of the anointing he has."

"He gave me a lot to think about. Helped me to see that God loves us, even though things haven't always been easy. I needed that reminder." Ruby pointed to her dresser. "Would you mind opening that top drawer and getting my Bible out for me?"

"Sure, Mom." Hope opened the dresser. Searched around, moved clothes to one side until she found the Bible at the bottom of the drawer. She handed it to her mother.

Ruby held the Bible close to her heart. She wiped away tears of joy. "Thank you," she said as Hope left the room.

The next morning, Crystal had an appointment with Dr. Colton James. Chris came with them. Chris and Faith sat in the waiting area. This time they were seated next to each other with Chris' arm around her shoulders.

When the door opened and Crystal's session was over, Faith asked Chris if he would take Crystal to get something to eat, then she turned to Colton and said, "Do you have a minute to speak with me?"

Colton laughed as they walked into his office. "You need a therapist too?"

"Actually, my husband and I were just discussing that." She sat down behind Colton's desk and pointed him toward the couch his patients sat on. "But I'm here to be your therapist today."

With a raised eyebrow, Colton played along and sat on his couch. "My therapist?"

She nodded, then asked, "What happened to your basketball career?"

Laughing, Colton shook his head as if he didn't believe the way this was going. "You want to know about how I failed at my goal of going to the NBA?"

"No." She put her elbows on his desk, index finger under her chin, and leaned forward. "I want to know why you stopped trying."

The laughter died down. Colton twisted his lips.

"When we were kids, you had that basketball with you everywhere you went. You were big-time around here, and everyone had you pegged for going in the draft. You even had your pick of college scholarships to choose from. So what happened?" Faith was positive that God had showed her some things in her dream that she had missed when they were taking place all those years ago. Colton had some answering to do, and she wasn't leaving until he told her everything.

With a heavy sigh, he said, "I just lost my love for the game. By my sophomore year in college, I didn't want to do it anymore."

"You didn't have your basketball on the beach that day when you helped me pass out flyers for Trinity."

Colton's eyes glazed over, like he was trying to take his mind back to that day. "I didn't?"

"No, you didn't, and that was the first time I'd seen you anywhere without that basketball. But the game wasn't on your mind that day, was it?" She felt like a detective, pulling bits and pieces from a suspect.

Colton shook his head. "No, it wasn't."

"The cell phone you had that day didn't belong to a friend, did it?"

He scrunched his nose. "What cell phone?"

She wasn't going to let him pretend anymore. She couldn't, not when he held the key to unlock the mystery that had torn her family apart. "Remember, you and I didn't own cell phones because our parents refused to get us ones until we went off to college, but Hope and CJ had cell phones because they were already in college.

"Your mother thought CJ hadn't gone missing until around Christmastime, but that wasn't true, was it?" Her eyes bore into his, daring him to turn away, daring him to play make-believe. "You had

CJ's cell phone, and you were the one texting your mother, weren't you?"

She waited a beat as the memories flowed like a river. "For some reason you stopped texting her right before Christmas. What happened? Why'd you stop?"

Colton had been holding a straight face. She couldn't make out any emotion. Faith was sure he'd learned to do that with his patients so he didn't seem shocked by anything they said, but as she finished with her last question, his face broke, and tears spilled out.

Colton stretched out on the couch and cried. Faith didn't say anything. She just let him cry it out.

Then he said, "I couldn't keep the lie up any longer. My mother was complaining about missing CJ's calls and about only being able to reach him through text. Christmas was coming up, and she expected him to be home."

Faith lifted her head heavenward. God had indeed been showing her something in that dream. She exhaled as she turned her attention back to Colton. The next part was not going to be pleasant for her, but she had to know. "Hope and I took DNA tests to see if the other remains they found in CJ's car belong to Trinity. We will know soon enough, but do you care to tell me now?"

His lips tightened like he was about to clam up.

Then she reminded him. "Remember when you approached me on the beach that day, you said you wanted to help? So help me now, Colton. Tell me what happened to my sister."

"Faith, I'm so sorry." Colton's grief exploded as the dam broke. His body shook as the floodgate opened up. "I'm so, so sorry for what I did."

Tears were streaming down Faith's face. Her sister was gone. She would never see her again, and that knowledge hurt so bad that she wanted to take Colton's place on that couch and cry a river of tears, but after all these years, she couldn't fall apart because she desperately needed to know the truth. "I need you to calm down, Colton. Please, my family deserves to know what happened to Trinity."

He nodded and nodded again, pulled some tissue out of the box, wiped his face and then blew his nose. "You're right. You deserve the truth. I've held it in for so long that thinking about it is overwhelming me." He blew his nose again, then began.

"CJ drove into town to surprise my mom, but he wanted to hang out before he went to the house. I called Trinity to see if she wanted to hang out."

Faith scrunched her nose. "Why would you call Trinity?"

"She and I had been talking on the phone for a few weeks."

Her eyes bulged. "You were messing around with my sister behind my back?" That was a revelation that Faith didn't need. Okay, yeah, she only had a crush on Colton, and they hadn't dated or anything, but Faith had always thought that they hadn't dated because her mother didn't like the James family, not because Colton wasn't that into her.

Shaking her head, trying to get the visual of Trinity and Colton out of there, Faith finally told herself, *It is what it is* and allowed Colton to finish his story.

"Sorry, Faith. We were young and dumb back then."

Lifting her hands in front of her face, she said, "No apologies necessary. It was many years ago."

"Okay, anyway, I called Trinity, and CJ called another girl, but his girl refused to come out because her mother had warned her about the impending storm. When Trinity and I got in CJ's car, he and I got into an argument—I still don't remember what we argued about. He had his phone sitting on the dashboard, so I took it and called one of my friends and asked if he wanted to shoot some hoops.

"I got out of the car and told Trinity to come with me, but she complained that she didn't want to stand out in the rain and watch me shoot hoops." He put his hands over his face. "God help me, but I got mad at her too.

"I told CJ to take her home since she didn't want to watch me play basketball." Colton's chest heaved as the tears kept coming. "I played a pick-up game, then went home as the rain started to come down hard.

"Later that night, when CJ didn't come to the house, I got worried, but I couldn't call him because I had his cell phone. I ran down to the beach the next day because I was worried that something might have happened to them. I was going to knock on your door and ask to speak to Trinity, just to see if she had made it home safely, then I saw you and your mom passing out flyers, and I knew . . ."

Faith slumped back in her seat.

"I should have never asked CJ to take her home. I knew how he liked to speed up and down the strip and how he drove too close to the beach waters. God only knows what happened, but I suspect he lost control of the car and then it drifted into the ocean."

Tears dripped from the corners of Faith's eyes. "I warned her not to leave the house that day. I wish I had done more to stop her."

"You can't blame yourself for this, Faith. We were just a bunch of stupid kids. You did what you could, and you have to believe that and live your life."

Rubbing her chin, Faith thought about the words that had been on Trinity's screensaver that year—*Live until the living is done.* That's what Trinity had been about. She was vibrant, fearless, adventurous, and she was troubled and left the world way too soon.

Faith stood. "I'll take your advice, but I'm going to give you some as well." She moved from behind Colton's desk. "You lost that sparkle in your eyes when CJ and Trinity went into the ocean. I think you're dealing with survivor's guilt, just as I have been. You need to realize that your brother's actions weren't your fault. It's been a long time, Colton. Take ownership for your part, and then forgive yourself and live your life before the living is done."

Chapter 39

HER SISTER DROPPED MIND-BOGGLING INFORMATION ON HER about Trinity's last hours, and Hope felt dizzy and had to lie down and rest with the knowledge that her baby sister was gone from them forever. She further understood the haunted look in her aunt Donna's eyes. It was one thing to think that she'd never see her loved one again, but a whole different matter when those thoughts were confirmed.

When she was finally ready to get out of bed, she looked out her window and saw Faith on the front porch. Hope went into the kitchen, poured two glasses of lemonade and joined her sister. Faith was sitting in one of the rocking chairs, staring out at the front yard as she rocked back and forth. Hope handed her one of the glasses of lemonade and then sat down in the rocking chair next to her. "Are you feeling any better?"

Faith shook her head. "Not really. I just keep looking out at the front yard and remembering how we all used to run around playing tag down there." Faith bit her lip. Her voice broke as she said, "I just miss her."

"I think we're going to miss her every day for the rest of our lives. When she left, she took a piece of our hearts with her, and we'll probably never get that back. But"—Hope emphasized the *but*—"we have a lot of good memories with her."

They were quiet for a long moment, then Faith told Hope, "We'll be leaving to go back home this weekend. We need to find Crystal a psychologist since Colton is taking a leave of absence."

"Colton probably needs a break. He's been running from his guilt a long time."

"Yep." Then Faith added, "We'll be back in two weeks though. Chris ordered all the supplies needed to do repairs around the house, but they won't be in for a couple of weeks."

"Did Mama give him her bank card? Do you know how much she has left in that account in case I need to order some things? I really want to work on rearranging those rooms so we can get this bed-and-breakfast opened."

Faith waved a hand. Shook her head. "We didn't want to put all of that on Mama while she's still recuperating. Chris had some extra money from a house he just sold, so he ordered the supplies with that. We'll get the money from her when we come back to town, and she can move around enough to go to the bank."

"That was good of Chris. My brother-in-law is all right with me." She nudged Faith. "You need to get with the program."

"We're working on it. I just hope he'll be patient with me because I'm running on empty right now."

"Tell me about it." They rocked in silence, mourning what they had lost even as they remembered the good times. "When do you think we should tell Mama?" Hope wanted to know.

Faith stopped rocking, planted her feet on the floorboards and looked at her sister. "I don't think she's going to take our word for it, so we probably should wait until the DNA test results come back. What do you think?"

Knowing Ruby the way they did, she would probably yell at them and throw them out of her room. Their mother wasn't up to her normal speed, so it would be terrible to see her in such pain, when they would only have to bring the same bad news to her once they received the DNA results. The moment she opened her mouth to say, "Let's wait," Nic pulled up.

As he got out of the car, Faith turned to her and said, "Now that is one fine white boy. Why'd you let that man get away? I just don't understand."

"Girl, mind your business." Hope got out of her seat and stood at the top of the stairs. Watching as Nic made his way up, she sighed as she noted his detective badge clipped to the top of his pants and two manila envelopes in his hand. This was an official visit.

Instantly fear clinched her heart. She put her hand on the railing to steady herself. She wanted to tell Nic to go away just as her mother had told him when he came around asking for Ruby's DNA. Colton had already confirmed that Trinity had been in the car with CJ, but if Nic had the DNA test back, he could confirm whether or not Henry Reynolds was her biological father. Could she deal with the answer to something she had questioned for years?

Her eyes shifted upward toward the great blue sky. "Oh Lord, I need You. Help me to deal with these results."

"Hey, Hope," Nic said as he climbed the final step and then put his hand over hers.

"Is your mom doing better today?" she asked, wanting to discuss anything but the reason he was here with his detective badge and two manila envelopes in his hand.

"She's getting there. The doctor said as long as her blood pressure is stable, they will move her to the rehabilitation center so she can get help regaining her speech."

"That's good, Nic. I'm happy for you, and I'm happy that your mother is doing better." Hope said those words, and she meant them. She didn't wish tragedy on anyone, not even Melinda Evans. The apology Melinda gave her had been like a balm to Hope's soul, allowing her to finally release the person who had torn her down simply because of the darkness of her skin.

Nic looked toward Faith and waved. "Hey, Faith."

Faith waved back.

Hope closed her eyes, took a deep breath. "So are you here to bring us news about Trinity?"

He nodded. There was a somber look on his face as he asked, "Would you like to discuss this with your mom present or just you and Faith?"

Hope motioned for Faith to come over to them. "I don't think my mother would ever forgive us if we received this information about Trinity without her."

Putting a hand on Hope's shoulder, Faith said, "I think you're right. Let's go in the house and get Mama ready before we discuss this any further."

Hope opened the front door. "Have a seat in the living room, Nic. Let us talk to Mama first."

Nic sat down on the sofa as Hope and Faith walked toward the back of the house. Ruby was lying comfortably in bed watching a *Golden Girls* rerun. Faith picked up the remote and turned the television off.

"Hey, I like that show," Ruby said, giving Faith the eye that said, I can't wait until I get my strength back.

"We need to talk to you, Mama," Faith told her.

Then Hope said, "Nic is in the living room. He has brought the results of Faith's and my DNA tests."

Ruby looked from Faith to Hope and then back again. "Y'all went behind my back and took that test, so just tell me what it says."

"I didn't go behind your back," Hope said. "I told you I was going to take it."

Pointing at Faith, Ruby said, "She didn't tell me nothing, and the last time I checked, I'm still y'all's mama, and I'm Trinity's mama, so I need to know about anything that concerns my children."

"That's why we didn't ask Nic for the results, Mama. We came to get you so we can all hear it at the same time." Faith looked heaven-ward like she was praying for patience. "Do you think you can go in the living room, or should we bring Nic back here?"

Ruby was silent for a long moment. She exhaled. "Bring him in here."

Hope went to the living room to get Nic. They were back in Ruby's bedroom within a minute. Hope didn't want her mother accusing her of putting words in Nic's mouth.

Nic stood in front of Ruby's bed. There was no hint of a smile on his face as he said, "I'm glad to see you are home from the hospital and rested from the awful storm, Ms. Ruby."

"I'm glad I'm still among the living too."

Hope and Faith leaned against the wall. Faith was biting her nails while Hope stared at the envelopes in Nic's hand.

Nic shuffled his feet, looked hesitant, like he knew he was about to break their hearts and just wanted another minute before the world turned upside down. "Ummm, Ms. Ruby, as you know, a car was pulled out of the ocean a few months back. The owner of that car was Calvin James Jr., and we were able to determine by DNA sampling that his remains were inside."

He cleared his throat. "We were also able to determine the other person who was in the car by DNA sampling, and I am so sorry to inform you, but Trinity Reynolds' remains were discovered in that car as well."

⌣

In all her days, through all the things that she had endured, nothing had ever hurt as bad as hearing that her baby girl was dead . . . dead. Drowned in the very ocean she loved so much.

Ruby let out a long guttural sound.

She was supposed to find Trinity. Her child was supposed to come back home. "Oh God!" she yelled as she squirmed in the bed, reaching for her chest. Her breasts were gone . . . her baby was gone. "Dear God, not my baby."

Hope and Faith rushed to the bed. They put their arms around their mother. Ruby cried as she held on to all she had left in this world. Her girls cried with her.

"I'm so sorry, Mama," Faith said through tears of regret.

"I wish it wasn't true," Hope said as tears dripped from her face. "I miss her so much."

Ruby calmed herself, then patted Faith's and Hope's arms, trying to comfort them. "It's okay, girls. It's okay. I'm just thankful y'all came when I called. I wouldn't have wanted to go through any of this alone."

"I'm glad you brought us back home, and now I just want to bring Trinity home," Hope told her mother. They all started crying again.

Nic was still standing at the foot of the bed. He asked, "Should I step out?"

"No!" Faith practically screamed. "Don't leave without giving us those DNA results."

Nic pointed toward the door. "I'll go sit in the living room."

Sorrow etched across Ruby's face. "I was watching the news the day they pulled that boy's car out of the ocean. I remembered what it looked like because he was always hot rodding it around town." Ruby shook her head. "Trinity should have known better than to get in that car."

Pain. The pain Ruby felt now was worse than anything she dealt with when the cancer attacked her body. This was something deeper—something no human could bear without the help of the Lord.

Ruby wiped the tears from her eyes. She looked from Hope to Faith. "I thought I needed you both here with me so that I could endure the storms that were to come, but now I realize that if I had not opened my heart to my Lord and Savior, this would have been too much for me."

She lifted her eyes heavenward, steepled her fingers. "Thank You, Lord Jesus, for the time I had with Henry and Trinity. I didn't always appreciate that time because I didn't know it would be so short." She closed her eyes. More tears.

When she continued praying, she added, "But I don't only want to thank You for what I lost but also for the things I found—like love and faith. I trust You again, Lord. I'm thankful for that. You brought my girls home again, Lord. I'm thankful for that. You kept us safe during this last storm, Lord, and I'm so thankful for that."

Not a dry eye or an unthankful heart in the room. Praise was becoming the new melody the Reynolds women were finally ready to lean into. Hallelujah!

Chapter 40

HOPE AND FAITH SAT IN THE LIVING ROOM HOLDING THE envelopes that had their DNA test results. Faith opened hers and said, "It says there is a seventy percent probability that Trinity and I are related. That's odd, I would have thought it would be something like 99.9 percent like you hear on those judge shows."

Nic was able to explain. "Sibling DNA is different than parent DNA. Usually siblings with the same mother and father share anywhere between fifty percent to one hundred percent DNA, but you normally only get one hundred percent with identical twins."

Hope opened her envelope. Her eyes widened as she stared at the thirty-two percent. Her head lowered as tears sprang to her eyes.

"What does it say?" Faith stood and came over to Hope. "It's no big deal, Hope. Stop tripping. We're sisters no matter what the DNA says."

Hope handed her sister the paper. "See for yourself."

Faith took the paper and looked at it. "Oh my goodness, thirty-two percent is a lot." Faith turned to Nic for confirmation. "That's a lot, right?"

Nic nodded confirmation, then explained, "When you get a DNA result that is below fifty percent, that usually indicates that the two individuals are half siblings."

At Nic's words, Hope and Faith giggled and then did their patty-cake, me-and-you-never-part routine. Hope wrapped her arms around her sister and clung to her like peanut butter clings to jelly. "You're stuck with me now."

Faith wiped her eyes as they moved apart. "I wouldn't have it any other way."

Hope then walked Nic out to his car. "You headed back to work?" she asked.

"I've got a minute if you want to talk."

Nic opened the passenger side door, and Hope got in. When he got in on the driver's side, she reached for him, and he pulled her into his arms. "I'm so sorry I had to bring you this news today. I wish Trinity was still alive. I wish you didn't have to go through this pain."

Tears drifted down Hope's cheeks as she moved out of Nic's embrace. She wiped the tears. "I hate knowing that Trinity will never walk down the beach again or be in the house with us, but it's been hard all these years not knowing what happened to her. I'll take the pain for now. Like my mom was just saying, instead of thinking on the things we lost, I'm thankful for what we've found."

"Oh, babe." He took her hand in his.

She liked hearing him call her babe. Sitting here with him, hand in hand, felt right. She had let the world and all the disapproving people in it dictate who she could love and who she couldn't. She was just a dark-chocolate girl who fell in love with a sun-kissed white boy. Years of separation hadn't changed that. And now she was ready to lean in and be with the one she loved. "Thank you for being patient with me."

"What else can I do? I've been praying that you would come to realize that we are perfect for each other and that we always have been. The only disagreement we ever had was that I wanted to leave this town, and you wanted to stay here forever."

"And now you're back home." Hope squeezed his hand.

"And now you're back home, but I just don't know how long you plan on staying." Nic adjusted his position in his seat so he was looking Hope in the eyes. "I'm willing to go wherever you go."

She closed her eyes, wanting to savor this moment. She and Nic belonged together. He was hers, and she was his. No distance, no location, no colorism could keep them apart. As she opened her eyes, she told him, "I just lost my job so I'm not going anywhere for a while."

An I-got-you-now grin did a two-step across Nic's face before he pulled her back into his arms and kissed her with the sweet abandon of two people who were old enough and wise enough to know who and what they wanted to do with the rest of their lives.

When they came out of the embrace, Hope told him, "I let you down years ago when I found out about my mother and then your mother disrespected me. I should have trusted your love, but I now realize that my faith in everything had been shattered. I think that's why I had such a hard time forgiving Melinda.

"But I've started praying again. My faith is growing stronger, and I'm pressing forward, believing that God will be with us. Can you believe with me?"

"Baby, I never stopped believing."

Later that night, Hope and Faith were in their mother's room just hanging out with her when Ruby said, "I have a confession to make, and since I rededicated my life to my Lord and Savior, I'm through with schemes and lies."

Faith looked nervous. "Oh no, what did you do this time?"

"Remember when I told y'all that Slick Rick stole half the money I borrowed from Scooter's bank?"

"Yeah." Hope stepped back. "You told me that Scooter was about to take the house from you—said if we didn't get down here to help turn the beach house into a bed-and-breakfast, you wouldn't be able to make the money back that was stolen."

Ruby bit down on her top lip, took a sip of her water, then turned back to her girls. "The truth is, no one robbed me because I didn't take a loan from Scooter."

"Mama, why do you lie so much?" Hope let out an exasperated sigh.

"Correction." Ruby lifted a finger. "I used to lie so much. I'm a new person since being in the hospital. I promise you girls that."

Shaking her head, Faith asked, "Why did you lie to us in the first place?"

"I already told you why. With CJ's car being pulled out of the ocean and my doctor telling me about the cancer, I thought I needed y'all here in order to deal with what was to come."

"Why didn't you just tell us the truth, Mama? Did you really think we would ignore the fact that you were sick?"

Ruby put a hand on Hope's arm. "I haven't been able to get you to come home in almost eighteen years."

"I should have come home more, Mama. That was on me. But you still should have trusted that we would be here for you."

Faith folded her arms. "Chris paid for all the supplies needed for repairs around this house because we thought you had thirty thousand in your account. What am I supposed to tell him? How is he going to get his money back?"

Ruby widened her eyes in surprise. "He did that for me? I love my son-in-law."

"Well, your son-in-law is not going to be happy when he finds out he is out thousands of dollars because of your fairy tales."

Without hesitation, Ruby said, "We can put those paintings and all those collectible dolls up for sale. That should bring in enough to pay him back."

Putting a hand to her mouth, then letting the hand drop, Hope asked, "Mama, are you serious? You're finally ready to get rid of that stuff?"

Ruby nodded as more tears fell from her eyes. "It's time."

Hope put her hand over her mother's. "If you truly are finished with secrets and lies, then I can forgive you."

"Well . . ." Ruby looked sheepish. "Just one more thing."

"Oh my goodness." Faith threw her hands up. "I can't deal with this."

"Calm down, Faith. This isn't my secret. It's my mother's secret, and I'm finally going to tell you and your sister what I've had to live with all of my life."

Hope knew all about mothers with secrets. She leaned forward in her seat.

Ruby finally realized the weight of the first secret her own mother forced her to carry. She wouldn't hold it anymore. So she opened her mouth and said, "My father was John Evans' business partner. He never wanted anything to do with me. But he left me this land when he died. That's why this land is so important to me. It was the only thing that man ever gave me."

"Wow, Mama. I didn't know," Faith said. She added, "When I was younger I remember you told us that your father died before you were born."

"That was another lie," Ruby admitted. "But the truth of how that man pretended that I didn't exist was too painful to talk about."

"I understand," Hope patted her hand.

Ruby leaned her head against her pillow and pulled up the covers. "I'm not sad anymore. This land is my birthright, and I will leave it to you girls so that the two of you can stand tall in this town, knowing that you'll always have a place to call home."

Life on the beach was good. Hope's relationship with Nic was good. She had leaned into the relationship with the only mother she had ever known because life was too short to hold grudges. At least that's the way she was looking at it now. With the knowledge of how her sister's life was cut short, Hope no longer wanted to waste time wondering what-if.

Hope spent two weeks cataloging all the items that they would be selling to make back the money that had been spent on supplies for the house repairs. Her mother felt good enough to get out of bed by the week after the hurricane, so Hope and Ruby spent quality time together while Faith went back to Atlanta with her family.

Hope stood in front of one of the dolls that they had placed a number on and snapped a picture. "I just don't know how you kept everything in such pristine condition."

"You take care of the things you care about, right?" Ruby winked at her.

"Right." Hope had been sending all of the pictures to Faith. Her sister had partnered with the Auction House, an online auction site. As Hope sent the photos to her, Faith uploaded them to the site.

"Let's take a break," Ruby said as she went into the kitchen and took out a pitcher of iced tea. She handed the pitcher to Hope. "Take that to the back patio, and I'll bring the glasses."

"But Mama, we still need to get everything out of the attic so Chris can work on building the stairs." Hope planned to make two extra bedrooms in the attic. To make that happen, they needed to rework the stairs. She was excited because they would be opening their bed-and-breakfast next year.

"We have time for a break."

Hope went out on the deck, kicked her feet up on a lounge chair and waited for her mother to join her. Ruby came out of the house with three glasses in her hand. "It's only the two of us. Faith won't be back until tomorrow, Mama."

Ruby set the glasses on the table as she looked at the cloudy sky above. "Hopefully, it won't rain too much today."

"It feels good out here." It was the tenth of December and about fifty-five degrees, so they had on sweaters as they lounged on the patio enjoying the calmness of the sea. The warm-weather season was over, so there weren't many people on the beach. It was quiet out back today.

Ruby took a sip of her tea. "It does feel good, but I think we should be having hot tea out here instead of this iced tea. I'm shivering." Ruby stood. "Matter of fact, I think I'll go inside and get a blanket."

"I can get it for you, Mama." Hope placed her glass on the table and moved to get up.

Ruby put a hand on her shoulder and gently pushed her back in her seat. "You stay here. I'll be back."

As Ruby went into the house, Hope saw something out of the side of her eye. She turned her head to the right. There was a woman walking down the beach. The woman's hair was braided in cornrows that went all the way down her back. She was older now, but she looked like the woman who had been on the back patio many years ago, arguing with Ruby.

Hope stood. She walked down to the end of the yard where the gate was. Looking to the left, she smiled, seeing Trinity's tombstone. They had kept their promise and brought Trinity home where she belonged.

The woman approached the gate, and Hope realized that she was indeed looking at that same woman she had run into on the beach the day of her college graduation celebration.

The woman stuck out her hand to Hope. She said, "I hope you don't mind that I stopped by. I wanted to formally introduce myself to you. I'm Brenda St. Amon, your mother—well, your birth mother anyway."

Hope turned her head and looked back up to the house. Her mother was standing in the doorway. She motioned to Hope and then hollered down, "I raised you with better manners than that. Open the gate and let her come up here to sit with us."

Hope shook Brenda's hand and then opened the gate. "H-Hi. I'm Hope."

Brenda said, "I know," and they both laughed as they walked up the steps to sit on the back patio.

Ruby poured Brenda a glass of iced tea. Hope looked at her mother. "I thought we agreed that there would be no more secrets."

"This wasn't a secret," Ruby told her. "It was a surprise."

Hope sat down on one of the lounge chairs. Her birth mom was on her right side, and the mother who raised her like she was her very own was on her left side. It was a bit awkward being with the two of them like this, but life wasn't perfect. It sometimes threw things at people they wanted to throw right back.

But from this day forward, Hope determined to say "Hallelujah anyhow" to the good and the bad and then trust God with the rest. Hope was no longer looking for or wondering if people were judging her unworthy for one reason or another. Finding Trinity had taught her to listen for that sweet, sweet melody in life and to enjoy it, while there was still living to be done.

She looked to heaven and silently prayed, "Thank You, God, for all of it."

A Note from the Author

EVEN THOUGH *WHAT WE FOUND IN HALLELUJAH* DEALS WITH loss, I loved writing this book because it is also about getting your praise back.

In all the books I have written, I have never created my own town. But you will not find Hallelujah, South Carolina, on a map—you'll only find it in your heart. So, when *praise God* bubbles up in your heart, I hope you think of Hallelujah, South Carolina.

I wrote this book because I know firsthand that sometimes life is hard. We lose the people we love, and we are left to go on with a broken heart. But I pray that you noticed *What We Found in Hallelujah* is about rediscovering your praise and your faith in God. And finding hope in the things that have been left behind. My prayer is that you never lose your faith in God, but if at any point you do, remember how Ruby managed to find her way back to God and how she found hope, even in the midst of her pain.

So now I challenge you to pray for each of your book club members or your family and friends. Ask God to overtake them with His love and bring joy into their lives. You never know what the person sitting next to you is dealing with, so let's all extend grace to one another. And above all, PRAISE Him! For He is worthy of our praise.

Blessings to you,
Vanessa

Discussion Questions

1. The Reynolds women have suffered so many storms that they lost the ability to trust God. How would you minister to someone whose heart has been broken by a series of tragedies?

2. Ruby Reynolds, the matriarch of the family lies A LOT. She was taught to lie from an early age when her mother told her to lie about who her father was. Have you dealt with people in your life who always seem to stretch the truth? Do you think there is a reason behind all the lies?

3. Do you think Ruby was truly delivered from lying? Do you believe that God can deliver us from that sin that easily besets us? If you are dealing with something that you need deliverance from, take this moment to pray and ask God for deliverance. You don't have to tell others what you are praying about; you can pray silently. Go ahead, give it a try.

4. Ruby had a problem letting go of things. She was tired of losing and wanted to keep everything she had left. Have you ever held on to something long past the time you should have let it go?

5. Hope and Faith had complicated relationships with their mother. Why do you think mother/daughter relationships are so hard at times?

6. Hope was a runner. For years, she stayed away from her hometown because she didn't want to deal with the issues with her parentage nor did she want to deal with Nic's mother, who didn't think she was good enough for her son. But was Hope really running from her own sense of self-worth? Has something or someone ever made you doubt your worth? Do you know that you are God's creation and everything God does, He does well? Think on that the next time you doubt yourself.

7. For someone named Faith, she sure didn't seem to have much faith. As a matter of fact, Faith didn't trust anything that she couldn't see and touch for herself. Faith was a challenge to write because I wanted to show what the trauma of survivor's guilt could do to a person, even someone who attends church and loves God. What did you think of Faith? Did she frustrate you or did you understand her? Do you think she can ever truly recover from the trauma she experienced being the last person to see Trinity before she went missing?

8. Faith and Chris' marriage was on death's door because Faith couldn't trust him and there was very little communication in their marriage. But Chris didn't want to give up on his marriage. Slowly things began to turn around for them. What do you think caused Faith to see her husband in a new light and allowed them to reconcile?

9. Crystal's eating disorder took the family by surprise even though Trinity had also suffered from this eating disorder at about the same age. Do you think we sometimes ignore issues within our family even though clues pop up here and there? Are we just too busy to pay attention to what others

might be dealing with, or is there another reason why we sometimes miss signals?

10. *Hallelujah* means "God be praised." When I lost my mother in 2010, the last thing I wanted to do was praise God. I was hurt and dealing with so much pain. But when I got my praise back, I discovered joy and hope again. So even though this book deals with loss, the title is *What We FOUND in Hallelujah*, because if we begin to praise God even when it hurts, there you will find hope. Name two or three things you do when you're feeling down. And just for fun, what is your favorite praise song?

About the Author

Photo by David Pierce

VANESSA MILLER IS A BESTSELLING AUTHOR, WITH SEVERAL books appearing on *Essence* magazine's Bestseller List. She has also been a Black Expressions Book Club alternate pick and #1 on BCNN/BCBC Bestseller List. Most of Vanessa's published novels depict characters who are lost and in need of redemption. The books have received countless favorable reviews: "Heartwarming, drama-packed and tender in just the right places" (*Romantic Times* book review) and "Recommended for readers of redemption stories" (*Library Journal*).

Visit her online at vanessamiller.com
Twitter: @Vanessamiller01
Instagram: @authorvanessamiller
Facebook: @Vanessamiller01